Golden Blood

A Novel

By

Donald Bozeman

Golden Blood is a work of fiction. All characters, dialogue and events are products of the author's imagination and bear no resemblance to actual persons or events.

This book is dedicated to my wife Sydney who has endured all the problems inherent in living with a writer. Bless her.

Golden Blood is also dedicated to all the men and women of medical science who struggle daily to alleviate human pain and suffering through their dedicated research.

Golden Blood

Needle-like barbs stung the face of Rupert von Hesse as he raced down the steep, alpine ski run above Zermatt, Switzerland. The lacerating ice crystals felt especially sharp in the frigid early morning air. Across the valley swirling snow formed a rainbow as the rising sun painted the eastern slope of the Matterhorn. As Rupert barreled down the Blauherd to Petrullarve run the view was mesmerizing. He had to wrench his eyes away to watch the trail in front of him. His cheeks were a fiery red despite the goggles covering most of his face. Franck Albrecht roared past on his right at a speed approaching 50 km/h. The incline at the half-way point steepened to nearly 45 degrees.

Rupert and Franck had been the only two passengers on the first car up to Blauherd that morning. The exhilaration Rupert felt as he stepped off the car was unlike any he had ever experienced. This would be, by far, the steepest and most dangerous slope he had ever attempted. Dietrich von Hesse, Rupert's father, had forbidden him to ski on any run with a difficulty greater than the blues even though his skills were the equal of Dietrich's. Rupert had never disobeyed his father—until now.

Rupert von Hesse was turning seventeen. The surprise birthday gift from his father Dietrich was a weeklong skiing vacation at the family's chalet in Zermatt, Switzerland. Rupert and his sister Elise were permitted to invite one guest each. Rupert chose his best friend Franck Albrecht and Elise chose hers, Helga Sturm. The Albrechts own the third largest grocery chain in Europe. The Sturm family has trafficked in international arms for centuries. All four teens attend the prestigious Zurich International School on Moosstrasse in downtown Zurich where the annual tuition of 61,000 Swiss Francs attests to the immense wealth of the three families.

"Come on, Rupert," Franck Albrecht pleaded as the two rolled out of bed at six a.m., "let's catch the fresh snow at Blauherd this morning, before it gets so rutted."

Franck Albrecht was a rangy redhead whose acne scarred face had not caught up to his maturing body. His close set, green eyes spanned a Teutonic nose that overpowered his thin mouth and prominent Adam's apple. All his family's wealth couldn't overcome Franck's insecurities. When slighted he often lashed out, becoming aggressive and spiteful.

"My dad won't let me ski the blacks."

"Why? You're as good a skier as I am, and I've skied dozens of them."

"I know Franck, but when I ask him why, he just shrugs his shoulders and says he doesn't want me to get hurt."

"That doesn't make any sense. Come on, we can be back before he knows we're gone. If he asks, we'll just say we ran the blues below Furi."

"I don't know. I've never disobeyed him before."

"Well, I'm going," Franck said curtly, "you can do as you wish."

4

Rupert bristled at the challenge, weighing Franck's dare against his sense of duty to his father. Then he decided that, at the age of 17, he was old enough to make his own decisions.

Anyone seeing a portrait of the Dietrich von Hesse family would instantly recognize that the son, Rupert Johann von Hesse, was a product of his mother's genes. Therese von Hesse was dark, trim and slight. She bore a striking resemblance to her famous ancestor, Queen Victoria—and like her mother and grandmother before her; had unknowingly inherited Victoria's and Albert's mutant genes. Rupert von Hesse, at five feet seven inches, was thin and dark with hair like charcoal. His eyes were hazel, flecked with small islets of black, and his roundish face, small nose, cleft chin and full lips were reminiscent of a Michelangelo cherub.

The edges of Rupert's Rossignol skis bit into the icy surface as the two made their last turn into Petrullarve. The small hillock of snow that had accumulated overnight in the lee of the overhanging trees was nearly invisible. The groomers had yet to make their first pass of the day. Rupert raised his eyes once more to the sun-dappled Matterhorn. His left ski found the small mound. It was just enough to throw him off balance.

The persistent buzz of the Apple I-Phone on the lamp stand jarred Dietrich von Hesse awake. He looked at his watch. It was nine am. On a normal work day in Zurich he would have been up and at his desk before seven. However, both he and his wife Therese were exhausted from a grueling round of late night parties. Zurich was celebrating the anniversary of the founding of Sagarin Pharmaceuticals. That investment by his grandfather had provided a vital boost to the local economy at a time when economic peril threatened all of Europe. Eighty years later the city fathers sought to recognize that contribution and show their appreciation to the von Hesse family. Directly, or through extended commercial connections, Sagarin supported one of every ten jobs in the entire Zurich canton.

"Hello."
"Mr. von Hesse?"
"Yes."
"This is Dr. Bernhard Weissman at the Zermatt emergency clinic."
Dietrich, now wide awake, flung the covers back so that he could sit up. The commotion jostled Therese awake.
"Dietrich, what is it? What's wrong?"
"Shhh! It's the hospital."
"Dr. Weissman, what has happened?"
"Is Rupert von Hesse your son?'
"Yes, why do you ask?"
"He was just brought in to the clinic with severe injuries suffered in a skiing accident."

"That's impossible! He's asleep downstairs!"

"I suggest you check then. His friend Franck Albrecht is here with him."

"I don't understand. Rupert never goes on the slopes alone. It is forbidden. Hang on while I check."

Dietrich vaulted down the stairs to Rupert's room, phone in hand. The door stood open. His son was nowhere in sight. He ran next door to Franck's room. He too was gone. His worst fears were realized. That injured patient at Zermatt Hospital *was* his son Rupert.

"Doctor, you must be right, both boys are gone. Tell me what happened!"

"Young Mr. Albrecht says they were on the Black Piste from Blauherd to Petrullarve. Evidently, your son failed to negotiate the sharp turn just before the Trockner Steg. He ran off the embankment and crashed into a tree."

"My God! How is he?"

"At the moment, he is unconscious. He has a broken leg and deep bruises to his right shoulder and back and there may be some brain trauma. We're setting the leg now, but we are more worried about the shoulder. We're having difficulty controlling the sub-cutaneous bleeding. The coagulant compound we normally have on hand was exhausted by another patient yesterday. We've placed an emergency order to Geneva, but they can't get it up here until tomorrow."

"Dr. Weismann, I have a helicopter at the Zermatt air terminal. Call them with your information and I will authorize a flight to pick it up."

"Thank you, Herr von Hesse that will be a great help. I'll have the hematologist call them right now."

"We're flying in blood for him," Weissman said as he came back on the phone. "Were you aware of Rupert's rare blood type?"

"Yes, I had him tested when he entered school. My wife's grandmother had told me that hemophilia runs in the family and that some of our ancestors died of it."

"This goes far beyond the normal blood factor VIII problems that characterize hemophilia. Your son is missing the entire Rh blood group. He is the first patient I have ever seen with this condition."

"I didn't realize his blood type was *that* rare! Perhaps the tests they run for school entrance purposes didn't check for that."

"It's possible, but I don't know how any reputable hematology lab could miss this. They may have thought there was a testing error since it was so far outside the 5 Sigma norm. Whatever the case, it vastly complicates the blood transfusion process. People with your son's type, called Rh-null, can donate to anyone, however, they can only receive blood from another Rh-null. It's so rare that the Red Cross has established unique protocols for identifying, collecting, storing and transporting Rh-null blood. Once the blood is unfrozen it has a 48-hour shelf life, so finding and transporting Rh-null blood is fraught with extreme difficulty. We have asked the repository in Paris to express two pints to us.

Dietrich von Hesse looked the polar opposite of his wife. His broad shoulders, strong face and blond hair bespoke his Prussian ancestry. His intimidating eyes were icy blue and so piercing they looked right through you. At six feet three he towered over most of his contemporaries. His strict diet and fanatical exercise regimen—running, swimming, weightlifting— were an urgent attempt to dispel the demons prowling his veins. Now those demons had manifested themselves, not in Dietrich's own body, but in his beloved son's.

"Therese, get your clothes on," Dietrich shouted as he ran back upstairs. "Rupert's been in a ski accident. He's at the Zermatt Clinic with a broken leg and severe contusions—and he's unconscious."

Shock and disbelief registered on the couple's faces as they pulled their clothes on and raced down to the subterranean garage of Schloss Hesse.

"You'd better wake Elise and Helga," Dietrich said as they passed the girl's bedrooms, "and tell them where we're going. I'll back the car out and meet you out front."

Ten minutes later, Dietrich's black s600 Mercedes coupe slid to a halt under the portico of the Steinfeld Clinic. Dietrich grabbed Therese's arm and sprinted for the door.

"Where's the emergency room?" he shouted at the reception desk attendant out front.

"To your left, through the double doors, and down a flight of stairs."

He took the stairs two at a time with Therese struggling to keep up. Ahead he saw Franck Albrecht sitting outside a door marked '**no admittance**' in bold red letters.

"Franck, what the hell is going on here?"

"I'm sorry Herr von Hesse. Last night I told Rupert that I'd like to try the black run from Blauherd down to Petrullarve. He told me you had forbidden him to ski the blacks. I asked him why—he's such a good skier—and he said, 'I don't know, Father just said I couldn't.' We woke up about six-thirty and he said, 'Let's do it.' 'Do what?' I said. 'Let's do Blauherd.' 'Are you sure?' I said, and he said, 'Yes.'"

"That was a very stupid decision, Franck," a furious Dietrich fired back; "I hope you know that now."

"Yes sir, I do."

"Have you seen him?" Therese asked.

'No ma'am. They wouldn't let me in."

Dietrich walked over to the door and pushed it open. There were two draped cubicles along each wall. A flurry of activity in the first cubicle on the left caught his attention. He walked toward it.

"Sir, you can't come in here!" a blue clad orderly exclaimed as he stepped in front of Dietrich.

9

"But that's my son back there! I must see him!"

"Sir, go back outside and take a seat. I'll have someone come out to update you on your son's condition as soon as possible."

Reluctantly, Dietrich relented. He was not used to being ordered around by anyone, especially a lowly hospital functionary, but Walter Kruger R.N., was six-feet five and weighed at least 110 kilos. Discretion replaced valor.

As long as the son was in peril, the father could not sit. Pacing up and down the corridor, Dietrich nervously rubbed his arms and cracked his knuckles. He stopped in front of his wife and Franck.

"Franck, take this money and see if you can find us some coffee. Black for me, cream and sugar for my wife. Get whatever you want for yourself."

Franck was more than happy to escape the intimidating glare of Dietrich von Hesse. He scampered up the stairs and through the swinging doors, looking for a cafeteria. Ten interminable minutes passed before Dr. Weissman came out of the ER.

"Well, the leg is set, and we've stemmed most of the bleeding. As I told you on the phone Rupert has a very rare blood type. It's one I've not seen before it's so rare. We're waiting on the two pints of Rh-null from Paris. That should do the trick if we can control his bleeding in the meantime. I just hope we don't need any more than that. Paris had only the two pints. He's still in a coma. We'll need to keep him in the intensive care unit for a while before we can move him to a private room."

"Can we see him in ICU?"

"Once he's settled in and all the drips are hooked up I'll call you in."

"Were you able to get my instructions to Air Zermatt?"

"Yes sir. They said the copter would be airborne within fifteen minutes after I called and should be back from Geneva within an hour and a half."

10

"Good! And Doctor, if there's anything you need for my son; get it, no matter the cost. I'll cover it."

"Thank you, Herr von Hesse. I think we have everything we need for now."

Dietrich settled down on the sofa next to Therese to await the call to the ICU. He took a deep swig from his Styrofoam cup. The coffee was cold and bitter, but he could finally breathe again. He put his arm around his wife's shoulders and gave her a squeeze of reassurance. A feeling he did not currently share.

The Eurocopter EC-155, painted in the Sagarin Pharmaceutical's distinctive yellow and blue colors, had touched down at the Air Zermatt terminal before noon on Saturday. The run from Zurich in the sleek Airbus helicopter took less than an hour. Sagarin Pharmaceuticals, headquartered in Zurich and established by Dietrich von Hesse's grandfather Johann, controlled several blockbuster drugs for treating cancer, heart disease and diabetes. Annual sales by Sagarin and all its subsidiaries topped 35 billion Swiss francs per year.

Johann von Hesse, Dietrich's grandfather, had held no illusions about Germany's future following President von Hindenburg's capitulation to the National Socialists and the elevation of Adolph Hitler to Chancellor in 1933. As a descendant of the Hohenzollerns, Johann knew his days in Germany were numbered. The purges had begun shortly after former Chancellor Kurt von Schleicher's failed attempt to stop the Hitler juggernaut. Von Schleicher had tried to rally centrist German politicians to help re-establish the Hohenzollern monarchy, first begun by Frederick the Great. For his efforts, Von Schleicher was assassinated by the Nazis. If he didn't know it before, that was Johann's definitive signal to get out of Germany. He had begun converting his holdings several years earlier and transferring the proceeds to the family owned Banque von Hesse in Zurich. He was gambling on the Swiss maintaining their neutrality when war broke out—an eventuality all but guaranteed by Hitler's rise to power. In 1936, Johann von Hesse spirited his family, staff and servants across the Swiss border to Zurich, abandoning their ancestral estate in the Swabian Alps.

Once Johann had established his family in Zurich, he cast about for places to safely invest his money. He convened a gathering of the managers at Banque von Hesse to solicit their recommendations.

"Herr von Hesse," Jurgen Proust said, "there is a small company here in Zurich that I believe holds great promise. It came to my attention a few months back when their managing director came to see me. He was looking for an expansion loan. They have outgrown the small building they lease in Winkel, just north of the airport."

"What is their line of business, Jurgen?"

"They manufacture ethical drugs. The firm has several patents for the treatment of blood disorders of the liver."

"Who owns the company?"

"There are four partners. They issued stock on the Zurich exchange last year, ten million shares. The principals control 80% of them."

"What are their sales," Johann asked.

"Last year they were nearly $12 million."

"Are they profitable?"

"35% pre-tax margin."

"Whewww, that's impressive."

"Debt?"

"Only the $3 million they borrowed from us to build a new laboratory."

Von Hesse leaned back in his chair, steepling his fingers under his chin.

"Who's in charge?"

"Hermann Weinstein?"

"Jewish?"

"Yes, all four principals are. They came from Munich three years ago. Like you they saw the handwriting on the wall— especially for Jews. They read Mein Kampf too."

13

"Set up a meeting for me at their place for Friday. I'd like you to come along with me since you know them."

Six weeks later Hermann Weinstein and his partners sat across the conference table from Johann von Hesse and his lawyers. In front of them were the documents that would cede control of Sagarin Pharmaceuticals to von Hesse Holdings, Ltd. Each partner would leave with a check for two million francs, and for ten years afterwards, as long as they remained employees of Sagarin, each would receive five percent of the after tax profits of the company.

Three months after that, young Friederich von Hesse was welcomed into the family, joining two older sisters and a brother in the expanding von Hesse household on Abendzwig Strasse.

Meanwhile, Johann continued to seek out other investment opportunities. He delved into the inner workings of Sagarin Pharmaceuticals and what he discovered intrigued him. The company's rapidly expanding research into blood disorders such as sepsis and leukemia rekindled memories of stories he heard from his grandfather whose uncle and a cousin had died of the Royal Disease, hemophilia, or its twin killer, porphyria. Johann's greatest fear was of he and his wife passing the deadly mutation on to their children. They had no definitive method to diagnose the blood malady.

Alexandra, Johann's mother, was the daughter of Louis IV, Grand Duke of two German royal houses; Hesse and By Rhein. Louis, in turn, was the son of Princess Alice, daughter of Queen Victoria. Both Alice and her sister Irene inherited the mutant gene that can cause a very rare form of hemophilia. Queen Victoria's son Leopold died from it. The gene appears to have been a spontaneous mutation between Victoria and Albert since no history exists of the disease appearing in earlier generations of either family. The gene is recessive, and it may lie dormant before reappearing in later generations. Ironically, Alice died at 37 of diphtheria, without ever knowing she was exposing her descendants to what became known as the "blueblood disease."

14

The gene was rampant in many royal family descendants throughout Europe, all of the Victoria lineage—including Therese von Hesse.

-4-

It was past noon when a nurse came through the swinging doors to the ICU to address the fearful parents. Dietrich was just returning from his third visit to the men's room. Four cups of coffee will do that. The caffeine high only added to his anxiety. Therese was not in much better shape. She took a Xanax and offered one to her husband. He declined. Franck was sent back to Schloss Hesse to check on Elise and Helga and to fill them in on Rupert's status. He was elated to escape the scrutiny of Herr von Hesse.

"Your son has regained consciousness though he is still groggy and somewhat incoherent. His vital signs have stabilized and there is no more bleeding from his visible wounds. The doctors ran a brain scan and discovered some inter-cranial bleeding, but they have that under control. We're going to keep him in ICU for a few more hours to be sure he is stable. You can see him now but only for a few minutes. Too much excitement might trigger more bleeding."

"Oh, thank God!" Therese said. "I thought we might lose him."

"He was critical for the first hour, but we have some of the best emergency room medics in the area. This wasn't their first

15

horrific ski accident, but it was their first major confrontation with hemophilia."

"Hemophilia?" Therese exclaimed. She looked at her husband. "Did you know Dietrich?

"It's something I've worried about. That's why I didn't want him to play hockey or ski the big runs. My grandfather told me that it ran in the family and several relatives in earlier generations have died from it. Knowing that, I had Rupert's blood screened for it when he went in for his school exams. He tested positive for hemophilia in his DNA. It has skipped the past two generations in my family, so I thought it wasn't a threat any longer. Obviously, I was wrong."

"What does this mean? Will he bleed like that every time he gets a wound now?"

"I can't really say," the nurse said. "Talk to Dr. Weissman when you see him. He's much more knowledgeable about this than I am."

They followed the nurse as she re-entered the ICU. Rupert was in a small cubicle down the right wall. A male nurse was adjusting his covers. Two bags of IV solution slowly dripped their life-sustaining liquids into Rupert's arm. A series of intermittent tones beeped from the computer-like box by his bed. The blood pressure cuff on his right bicep regularly tightened and released. The clamp on his finger transmitted his oxygen levels to the same monitor.

"Herr von Hesse, Frau von Hesse," the nurse said, "he is resting now. He weaves in and out. The sedation has not completely worn off yet. That is typical with the *etomidate* used by Dr. Weissman. It is the anesthesia of choice when the patient is hemo-dynamically unstable or has possible brain trauma, as Rupert did."

Dietrich blanched. He remembered a report he had recently read from Sagarin's genetic studies subsidiary, SciGen, in Los Altos, California It warned of the potential for *etomidate* to trigger hemophilia in patients with certain dormant gene

16

mutations. Could this manifestation of the disease, after a childhood basically free of any symptoms, be a result of the anesthesia? He made a mental note to re-read the report and to contact the researcher who produced it.

"When will he be able to talk to us?" Therese asked.

"I would guess another hour or so. By then he should be ready to transfer to a regular room. I suggest you get something to eat and then check with the information desk to see if he has been moved. I'll ask the doctor to call you if anything happens. I believe he has your cellphone number."

"Yes," Dietrich said, "thank you, I think we'll take you up on that. We didn't have any breakfast and any more coffee will probably send me over the edge."

Dietrich and Therese walked back to the clinic lobby where they found a small café off the main reception area. Over orange juice, waffles and bacon they resumed their earlier conversation about the von Hesse hereditary traits.

"Dietrich, why didn't you tell me about this before?" Therese asked angrily.

"I didn't want to worry you unnecessarily. There hasn't been a recurrence in either of our families for years. I thought maybe we had outgrown it."

"You should have told me. I could have seen that Rupert was not exposed to situations where he could be hurt."

"Like I said, I thought he was safe and I didn't want to worry you."

Therese stabbed at her waffle then she paused, the golden bite stranded in mid-air, syrup dripping. She reached down for her purse to retrieve a tissue and wipe the tears from her eyes.

"What about Dieter, and Elise, do they have the gene also?"

"Yes. Apparently, the genes are passed on by the women in the family but usually they are only manifested in the males.

17

Having been triggered in Rupert, there's a good likelihood it will happen to Dieter as well at some point."

"I'm glad he stayed behind in Zurich with Maxim. All we need is two boys injured in ski accidents at the same time. Dieter is more reckless than Rupert. He would have been the first one out the door this morning."

Dietrich chuckled, he knew she was right. Rupert had always been the more reserved of their two boys. Dieter was the hellion. If there was a challenge about, he was always the first in line.

"I'm sorry I didn't tell you Therese. It was a bad decision on my part. You are stronger than anyone I know, and you could have handled the knowledge as well as I."

"What's done is done." She said resignedly, "The question is what do we do now? We can't keep them in a glass bubble for the rest of their lives."

"You're right. We just have to try to protect them to the degree possible and limit their exposure to injury. In the meantime, I'll amp up the programs I initiated to study the problem. I'll expand our work in analyzing what's going on in other medical laboratories around the world that might hold out hope for a cure. Some of our guys at SciGen in Los Altos are working on some promising research in the area of genetic blood diseases. Our researchers at Sagarin have seeded them with data that's been collected over the years here. I'm going to fly over there soon, and I'll take a look at what they've found so far. I'll take Dr. David Weiss with me. He did most of the work that produced that data."

The phone in von Hesse's coat pocket buzzed.

"Yes? This is von Hesse."

"This is Dr. Weissman. Your son has been moved to the second floor—room 277 in the Critical Care Unit. Everything is stable, but I want him monitored around the clock just in case he begins bleeding internally. I didn't see any bleeding lesions on his brain scan, but one never knows if there is latent damage. If

18

nothing appears in the next 24 hours, I think we'll be out of the woods.

"What then?"

"We'll keep him here for a couple of days as insurance. If there are no further complications, you can take him home."

"Thank you Dr. Weissman…for saving my son's life."

"That's my job Herr von Hesse. That's what we do here. I'm glad it all worked out for Rupert. He seems like a fine young man. When did you first become aware of Rupert's rare blood?"

"I had him tested when he was eight and I knew it was rare. I just didn't know how rare. I was concerned because I know several ancestors died of hemophilia; none in the last fifty or so years, but I understand if one carries the recessive gene that it can be triggered by certain events, including the anesthetic *etomidate,* which I understand was administered to Rupert.

"Yes, it was the best choice for his condition. That was before we got his results back from the lab and discovered that he is an Rh-null. He needed two pints of blood. Thank goodness we had some Rh-negative sera that he was able to tolerate until the Rh-null blood gets here from Paris. Rh-null types can only transfuse Rh-null blood, so you can appreciate the dilemma."

"Yes, I do Doctor, I know how critical his situation was and that he received the best of care. I'm deeply indebted to you and your team. We'll be up shortly to see him."

Dietrich von Hesse made a note to check with the hospital management to see if there were any unfulfilled needs Dr. Weissman might have in his ER.

"What did he say, Dietrich?"

"They've moved him to critical care, room 277. He said we could come up in a few minutes."

"Is he conscious?"

'No, they're going to keep him under until they're sure he has no internal bleeding in the brain."

"Can we see him now?"

19

"He said to give the staff a few more minutes to get him hooked up to the IVs and the monitors."

Dietrich paid the bill and the couple caught the elevator to the second-floor critical care unit. Room 277 was at the far end of the corridor. Two white clad figures brushed past them and ran into Rupert's room.

"Come on Therese," Dietrich urged, "something's wrong."

Dr. Weissman stepped out of the room and stopped them before they could enter.

"Come with me," he said as he led them to a small waiting room across the hall.

"What's wrong Dr. Weissman?" Dietrich asked urgently.

Therese began to cry again.

"We're not entirely sure. Dr. Isaacs was hooking up the monitors when your son went into cardiac arrest. Thank goodness Isaacs was in the room. He defibrillated him immediately and got his heart back into rhythm; however, whatever anomaly this is has affected Rupert's breathing. He's being intubated now."

"What does that mean?" Therese asked anxiously.

"It means he's being put on a ventilator, isn't that right Doctor?" Dietrich answered.

"Yes, we're afraid that the effort to breathe on his own will aggravate his injuries and cause more bleeding, and place more strain on his heart."

"What should we do?"

"Herr von Hesse, we're in uncharted waters here. None of us have ever encountered this situation before. I think we need to call in a specialist for this."

"Who?"

"Well, the world's foremost authority on cardio/hemophilia research is Dr. Sterling Askew."

"And, where is he?"

At noon, traffic was light on I-280 between Los Altos and Palo Alto. He risked a speeding ticket, but it was important to Dietrich that he get to the hospital as fast as possible. Not that there was anything he could do to help his son, but he wanted to be there by his side, along with Therese. He exited the freeway at Alpine and sped past the Stanford Accelerator on Sand Hill Road. He made a mental note to call on Benny Alexander while he was there. Benny was senior partner at Argos Venture Capital, one of the countless VC firms located on Sand Hill. Dietrich was their largest investor.

Stanford University occupies the immense sand hills above Palo Alto. The elite private school was established in 1885 by Leland Stanford, one of the big-four railroad tycoons of the Robber Baron era. Over the years, the initial small campus metastasized into an 8,000-acre sprawl with tentacles extending into every segment of life on the peninsula. Its presence dominates the area and its alumni reign over the mammoth technology companies that dot the Silicon Valley landscape—think Google, Netflix and Facebook.

The Stanford Medical Center occupies a central position on the main campus. Founded by Mr. Stanford in the city, the medical school moved south to the Palo Alto campus in 1959 where it has emerged as the preeminent medical research

30

institution on the West Coast. Over the years SMC has attracted the crème-de-la-crème of medical research scientists; among them one Dr. Sterling Askew.

Therese von Hesse's phone vibrated in her coat pocket. She checked the screen. It was Dietrich. She took the phone into the private bedroom attached to Rupert's suite.

"Hello."

"Hi sweetheart, I'm on the highway. I'll be at the hospital in a few minutes. What room are you in?"

"We're in the Packard children's wing, room 422."

"How's Rupert?"

"Not much changed since your earlier call."

"Has Dr. Askew seen him?"

"Yes, he came by shortly after we arrived at the hospital. He spent about half an hour with him. He ordered some further diagnostics. He also asked that you come by his office when you get here."

"Is it in the same building?"

"He's in the cardiovascular building next door, second floor, room 227."

"Okay, I'll go there as soon as I see you and Rupert."

Dietrich maneuvered the Mercedes though a parking lot cluttered with building materials. A green crane, resembling nothing so much as a giant praying mantis, lifted I-beams to the fourth-floor addition from a fenced in area. Construction seemed to be a permanent condition, and an ever-present hazard, throughout the campus.

An armed security guard gave Dietrich the once over as he passed through the magnetometer. Bells clanged. The officer wanded him and asked him to empty his pockets. He placed the car keys and coins in a tray and then removed the Sturm pistol from its under-arm holster.

"Firearms are not allowed on this campus," the guard said sternly. "Do you have a permit?"

"Yes, I am CEO of a major corporation. There have been several kidnapping threats. I carry the gun for protection."

"May I see your permit?"

Dietrich removed the laminated card from his wallet and gave it to the officer.

"I see this was issued in Switzerland. I don't know if it's valid here."

"I assure you I had my attorneys check its validity with the US authorities. There is reciprocity between our countries."

"Very well, but you will have to check it here. You can retrieve it when you leave."

Dietrich handed over the gun and holster, took the receipt and headed for the elevator.

Room 422 in the children's wing was at the end of a long corridor. From this vantage point he could see a display of colorful umbrellas dotting the outdoor café in the courtyard below. Other windows looked out toward Sand Hill Road. The only sounds emanating from the room were the beeps from the monitors and the ominous wheezing of the ventilator.

"Thank God you are here," Therese said, rushing into Dietrich's arms. "I'm so scared. He doesn't look any better even though the nurses say all his vital signs are good."

"He is in the best hands possible. I'm certain they will nurse him back to health."

The words, meant to reassure his wife, did little to dispel his own fears. Forces at work in Rupert's body defied known science. It was up to Dietrich to marshal the men and machines required to save his son—if there was time.

32

-8-

Dr. Maria Elizondo stood inside the dreary private aviation terminal at the Biarritz airport. She shielded her eyes as she watched the blue and yellow jet glide to a stop and taxi into position. It was wedged in between an Air France A320 and an Alitalia 737. The sun was ferociously bright coming off the Bay of Biscay in late afternoon. Personally, she always flew out of the modern new air terminal in her native Bilbao, and was unfamiliar with the Biarritz airport, but for the money she was getting for this assignment she would have driven to Paris to meet her benefactor.

Maria Elizondo was one of those women who automatically belonged on the stage at La Scala, dressed in a flouncy flamenco costume with a rose clenched between her teeth. Her generous bosom under the chic bolero top tapered into a waist that women half her age coveted. Shoulder length, raven tresses in tight ringlets framed a countenance that evoked Maria Callas. Impeccably turned out in a black and white pants suit over Gioseppo stilettos she was the epitome of class. Her thriving hematology research clinic, Clìnica Hematologìa Basque SA, boasted clients from the most prestigious research institutions, hospitals and universities in the world. She was at the apex of her profession and she played the part well.

Dietrich chose Biarritz since the Dassault Falcon was no stranger to its runways and wouldn't encourage the curious. The Aquitania subsidiary of Sagarin is located in nearby Bayonne.

"Marcel," he said to the pilot, "take Dr. Weiss back to Zurich and wait for my call. I don't know how long I'll be here. Probably two or three days".

"Very well Herr von Hesse, I'll see that your luggage is transported to your hotel. Have a nice stay in Bayonne."

Dietrich saw no need to tell anyone else his purpose for landing in Biarritz. His mission could best be carried out with a minimum of publicity. As far as Marcel and David were concerned he was here visiting Aquitania on company business. He walked across the tarmac apron and up the stairs to the non-descript Mateo-France private aviation offices. Maria Elizondo was there, awaiting him.

"You...must be Maria," he said, a note of surprise in his tone.

"Yes, and you must be Señor von Hesse?"

"I am," he said after shaking her hand and taking a step back to appraise her. "It's a real pleasure to meet you."

He answered her in perfect Castilian Spanish.

"I'm impressed," Maria said. "I had no idea you were fluent in Español."

"In my world, it's imperative to be acquainted with many languages. I interface a diversity of clients and own companies all over the world. It's a facility that also comes in very handy when I want to listen in surreptitiously on conversations."

"I'll remember that when we have potential candidates for you to interview," she said with a trace of a smile.

"How is that coming by the way?"

"Kind of slow but we have identified a few. I was waiting for you before initiating contact with them."

"Good, when can that begin?"

"I wasn't sure how you wanted to proceed."

"You are aware of the reason for this search and its critical nature?"

"Yes sir. Rob Simpson and I had a long conversation before I agreed to take the assignment. For someone with my background in hematology this was a challenge I couldn't pass up. Besides, with what you're paying me, I could hardly refuse."

Dietrich lowered his head and turned away. He cleared his throat before responding.

"If your work, together with that of my researchers, produces a cure for my son...well there's no amount of money I wouldn't pay.

"I've booked us into the Hotel du Palais," he said. "That's where I stay when I'm here on business. I've asked our local plant manager to join us for dinner. I want everyone to think this is purely a local business trip. Aquitania is in the blood analysis, research, preservation and transport business, so having a hematologist along won't seem strange. If he asks, tell him you're consulting on something for another Sagarin subsidiary.

"I'm familiar with Aquitania's work. I've actually used their services before. We had a very critical transfer we needed to make from Lyon to Bilbao and they were able to facilitate it."

"Good to hear. That'll make the evening seem even more plausible. I've asked him to pick me up here so as not to raise any questions. So, if you'll drive over to the hotel, I'll meet you there. Dinner reservations are at nine in the Villa Eugenie. They serve fantastic Basque dishes, especially their *Langoustines Roties aux Saveurs Basque*. It's to die for. You'll feel right at home."

"I look forward to it. Thank you. I'll see you there."

"Sergei Romanoff, manager of the Aquitania operation, was from an expatriate Russian family that fled the country during the Bolshevik revolution. The life expectancy then of anyone whose last name was Romanoff was measured in days not years. Like Dietrich's forebears, Vasiliy Romanoff was prescient enough to see what was coming in 1916 and began moving the family fortunes to France.

Sergei attended the Ecole Militaire and when he finished his military obligation he returned to Paris and matriculated at the

41

Sorbonne where he received a doctorate in organic chemistry. He came to Sagarin as part of the 1995 acquisition of Aquitania. He has been offered positions on von Hesse's staff in Zurich but always declines. His roots are in Nouvelle-Aquitaine and there he is going to stay.

Romanoff's black Peugeot arrived punctually. Dietrich was just exiting the terminal. He opened the passenger door, leaned in, and shook Sergei's hand.

"Sergei, great to see you. I haven't been here in...let me see...over a year. How 's it going?"

Von Hesse knew exactly how it was going. Aquitania's monthly report was one of dozens Dietrich read assiduously. And, it was always one of the most thorough and complete. In the last year two other division managers had been sacked for underperforming and then shading the truth in their reports. Truth was as important as performance to him—no, even more important. A miss on the bottom line may be forgivable. A lie was not.

"Very well I believe. The new cryovac shipping containers seem to be working out very well. We've test shipped over a hundred samples to all corners of the world and only one container had any damage and even that one protected the contents from spoilage. We're also working on a larger version that can be used to transport humans."

"Why?"

"Many diseases now require the patient's blood temperature be lowered dramatically for surgery. The container we're developing will allow for transportation in that condition."

The Peugeot maneuvered through the late afternoon traffic, taking Avenue de la Marine west off the main traffic circle in downtown Biarritz and arrived at the Hotel du Palais in fifteen minutes. Dietrich caught a glimpse of Maria entering the hotel as

Sergei handed his keys to the valet. They caught up with her at the registration desk.

"Sergei Romanoff, allow me to introduce you to our dinner companion for the evening, Dr. Maria Elizondo. Maria is from Bilbao. She is a pre-eminent hematologist. I've asked her to do some work for Sagarin on a new blood diagnostic protocol. She was kind enough to drive up here for our meeting."

"I remember Srta. Elizondo. I believe we helped you with a critical blood transfer."

"That's right Dr. Romanoff. It's was about three years ago. Thanks for remembering."

"If you two will indulge me," Dietrich said, "I'm going up to my room, take a shower, and then a short nap. That flight in from the states always wipes me out. I'll see you at nine. If I'm a few minutes late, Felix the maître d' will seat you at my favorite table overlooking the Bay. He knows my favorite Bordeaux, so feel free to have a glass."

On his way to the room Dietrich punched in the code for his private channel to Therese's cell phone. It rang four times. He began to worry.

"Hello." A drowsy voice came on the line.

"It's me Sweet Heart. I was worried when you didn't answer right away. Is Rupert okay?"

"He's holding his own. We had a fright when he developed a brief episode of arrhythmia. Dr. Askew came up to check him out and said it was a delayed reaction to his seizure in Zermatt. He didn't seem too worried. I was so tired I went into the bedroom for a quick nap. I slept longer than I intended. It was your call that woke me."

"I'm sorry. I know how trying this has been for you. I'll try to get back as soon as I can. I'll be here in Bayonne for a couple of days then I should be able to fly back. Does Askew still think Rupert can come off the ventilator soon?"

43

"He said that if he has no more episodes he'll take him off in two days and then bring him out of the coma 24 hours later."

'Wonderful," Dietrich said. "Did the private nurses we hired arrive?"

"Yes, and they're wonderful. Thank you. They take a great load off my mind."

"That's good news. Have you spoken to Dieter and Elise?"

"Yes, I talked to them this afternoon. They are upset and very worried about Rupert but otherwise seem all right. Maxim said they both went to class today. He said he's trying to arrange activities for them that will take their minds off things. Thank goodness he's there. I don't think either of our parents are up to babysitting two teenagers."

"Have you talked to them?"

"Yes, I brought them all up to date yesterday after you left. They want to come to Stanford, but I suggested they wait until we know more about Rupert's long-term prognosis. They reluctantly agreed."

"Thanks Therese, I'm sorry I dumped all this on you and ran off to Europe, but I can assure you that what I am doing here will be more constructive and beneficial in the long run than sitting by Rupert's bedside wringing my hands. I'll fill you in on my activities here when I get back. Give Rupert a kiss for me and tell him I love him. I know he won't hear you, but it'll make me feel better. I'm going to get some rest before I go down to meet my dinner companions. I love you."

Dietrich sat on the bed and pored over the sheaf of papers in his hand. The SciGen report was on his secure laptop when he opened it. The room attendant had a hard copy run off for him while he called Therese. He didn't understand all the nuances of what Simpson and Askew were asking for, but he was cognizant of the main elements they required. He was certain that Dr. Maria Elizondo would have no trouble deciphering the message. He placed the report in his brief case and locked it before settling

44

into the tub for a long soak. It wasn't until the water began to cool that he grudgingly exited the tub. The hot water had done its job. He was sufficiently relaxed to drop off for a few minutes. He set his wrist alarm for 8:30 and crawled into bed.

There was sufficient wine left in the bottle for one more glass when Dietrich took his seat at the table.

"Señor von Hesse," Maria said as Dietrich took his seat, "I've sampled many fine Spanish Tempranillos but nothing that approaches this Bordeaux," Maria said. "I shudder to think how much it costs."

"Not to worry, Maria. The hotel always keeps a case in reserve for me. I think they get it wholesale," he said with a wink. He signaled to the sommelier to bring over another bottle as Felix approached from the kitchen.

"Monsieur von Hesse, how wonderful to have you dining with us again. Mr. Romanoff was kind enough to introduce me to your lovely dinner companion. Welcome back sir. I'll give you a few minutes to enjoy the '96 Rothschild. Bernard is decanting another for you. I might mention that as an appetizer the Brittany *moules mariniers* are outstanding tonight. I'll leave these menus for you. Basil will be serving you tonight. Bon appétit."

"Thank you, Felix," Dietrich said as the maître d' walked away.

"I never tire of the dining experience here, overlooking the Bay of Biscay. Superb service, excellent food, and an unparalleled ambience. Sergei, I should schedule more visits to Aquitania."

Sergei winced.

"Just kidding. I wish all our divisions ran as smoothly as yours."

"Thank you, Herr von Hesse. I really appreciate the help we get from Zurich. It makes things run a lot smoother."

"Maria," Sergei continued, "what's happening with your consulting business in Bilbao? Still hopping all over the world?"

45

"It certainly keeps me busy. Our staff has grown to 40 doctors, scientists and computer specialists. We're adding an engineer and an architect soon. That might seem strange, but on so many of our assignments we discover that where and how the research is done, the physical layout and the laboratory arrangements, play a major role in the firm's success."

"I certainly agree with that," Sergei responded, "our new cold storage facility has been redesigned to allow sorting and packaging to be done mechanically within its confines. That way the product never experiences a change in temperature and the manual interface is reduced to a minimum; fewer errors, faster production and less chance for contamination."

"I remember approving that project last year," Dietrich interjected. "I saw in your last report that the projected ROI period has been reduced from five years to three. Great work,"

"Thank you, sir."

The business banter continued into the evening, long after the dishes had been cleared and the Armagnac had been poured. As midnight approached, Sergei asked to be excused.

"If you'll excuse me I have an early morning meeting with a prospective customer. It's been a delightful evening."

"Fine Sergei," Dietrich said. "That will give Maria and me time to discuss the project she is running for us. We'll be going over the plans at her office in Bilbao for a couple of days. I'll try to run by Aquitania before I leave. I remember we have some awards and commendations to make to the cryovac project team."

"Yes sir, just give me a day's notice and I can have the ceremony arranged. Maria, it was great to see you again. Good luck on the Sagarin project."

"Thank you, Monsieur. I hope to see you again soon. Good luck with your prospect tomorrow."

"Thanks," Sergei said.

He lifted his Baccarat snifter and drained the last dram of Armagnac. As he walked away he reached into his coat pocket for the Padron Maduro cigar he would enjoy on the ride back to Bayonne. Under pressure from his wife Nicole, he had cut back to one per day. Not only was that good for his health, but at 300 euros for a box of 24 it was kinder to the budget.

"Thanks for not divulging the real reason for my visit to Bilbao," von Hesse said to Maria. "It's imperative that the local authorities don't get wind of what we're up to. Not that it's illegal, but if word gets out, it'll make the targets of our search leery of our motives."

"I totally understand. I've only told members of my staff who will be directly involved, and they've been sworn to secrecy."

"Have you had any luck finding an investigator to help you?"

"I have only one good lead. The man lives in Gorliz, a small village located just ten miles north of Bilbao. The strangest thing about him is that while he is Basque, he's not Spanish. He was born in the US, in Montana, but grew up in Boise, Idaho. His grandparents fled Spain in 1937. That was the year that Franco invited the German's to support his revolution by bombing the Basque village Gernika-Lumo. The Basques were stanchly opposed to the Falangist attempt to overthrow the Republican government of Spain. Thanks to Pablo Picasso the world knows Gernika-Luna as *Guernica.*

"When the last *Stuka* pulled out of its bombing run, 1,654 Guernicans lay dead in the smoldering ruins. Mikel Muñoz' grandparents were part of the anti-Franco faction in the Biscay region of northern Spain. They survived the raid by hiding in the cellar of their home on the edge of town, but they knew it was only a matter of time before the fascist police would arrive to arrest the survivors. They loaded the belongings that had survived the fire and explosions onto a horse cart and made their way to Leketio harbor. They were able to gain passage on a boat to Le Havre, France. Two months later they were settled in Bozeman, Montana, in the middle of a colony of Basque sheep herders. Mikel's parents, who were born near there, weren't keen on the life of a sheep herder. They moved to Boise where Mikel was born in1961."

"Wow, that's quite a story," Dietrich said. "It sounds as if your team is good at investigations itself."

"Researchers become very proficient at using the internet and its many tools. Plus, Diego Barinaga, one of my forensic pathologists, fancies himself an amateur detective. He went up to Gorliz and Garnika and nosed around. It's amazing how much information is divulged over tapas and a few *patxarans."*

"What the hell is a *patxaran?" Dietrich asked.*

"It's an anisette drink, sloe flavored. It's native to this region. At 30% alcohol, it can slip up on you in a hurry."

"I'll be sure to remember that," Dietrich said.

"What makes Muñoz a candidate?"

"That's the most interesting part. He was a detective in the Boise Special Victims Unit for 25 years. He became very proficient at chasing down deadbeat dads and sexual predators alike. He and his wife divorced in 2012 and he began to hit the sauce a little too hard. His work suffered, and he was *"retired."* The couple had no children, so he decided to move to Spain and get a fresh start. His pension and savings afford him a comfortable life, but he misses the adrenaline rush of detective work, so he hung out a P.I. shingle in Bilbao two years ago. Work has been kind of patchy, but an anonymous poll of his clients gives his work high marks."

"Sounds like you may`have found your man."

"He looks good, but I want to check out a few more leads before approaching Muñoz."

"Just don't take too long. Finding these candidates is urgent. Nothing can move forward without them."

"I understand that Señor von Hesse, but it's imperative that we get the right man. I have to reassure myself that Muñoz not only is the best candidate for the job but that his addiction is under control."

"I understand, Maria. As a researcher, you must check and double-check your data before reaching a conclusion."

"Here," Dietrich said as he slid a copy of the report from Sterling Askew across the table, "this is a compilation of the unique blood factors that Rob Simpson and Dr. Askew put together yesterday. These are what they want to see in any candidates you identify. I read it over briefly and while I understand some of the esoterica it contains, by no stretch of the imagination do I understand all of it. Read it over tonight and we'll discuss it on the drive to Bilbao tomorrow."

Maria scanned the seven-page document. She stopped on page four and looked over her glasses at Dietrich.

"What is it?" he said.

"This is a twist I hadn't expected," she said.

"What?"

"The requirement that the candidates also have von Willebrand disease and preferably type 2n.

"What is that?"

"Von Willebrand is another blood factor, vWF. It acts as a chaperone to factor VIII, the main blood clotting protein in the blood stream. The von Willebrand factor and factor VIII, are bound together as they travel through the body. When injury occurs, the two factors disengage at the wound site and factor VIII begins the clotting process while vWF proceeds to perform other curative functions.

"vWF disease, or vWD, occurs in less than one percent of the population. 70% to 80% of those affected have vWD type 1, which is the least severe. 15% to 20% have type 2. The remainder, a very small number, has type 3 vWD, which is the most devastating. Doing the math, less than 3,000,000 people in the United States have type 1, Less than 750,000 have type 2, and maybe 100,000 to 200,000 have type 3. So, you can see that the presence of the factor VIII syndrome together with the vWF syndrome is miniscule.

49

"Factor VIII cannot survive long without vWF. Therefore, anyone who lacks the vWF factor and the VIII factor can be in serious danger of bleeding to death. Sometimes the vWF disease is the result of an Autosomal Recessive Pattern or ARP. That's where both parents harbor the mutant gene and pass it on. At other times vWF disease can be acquired through exposure to other diseases or through certain exogenous factors. For instance, there are certain prescription medicines that can trigger vWD.

"Dr. Askew discovered a vWD 2n condition in Rupert's blood. He believes that it was not caused by an ARP but was triggered by one of the antibiotics your son received. He mentioned that traces of *Lornoxicam* were found in Rupert's blood. That's known as one of the anti-inflammatory drugs that can trigger vWD."

"What constitutes the vWD 2n syndrome?"

"vWD 2n occurs when there is sufficient vWF in the blood, but it doesn't transport the factor VIII properly, resulting in insufficient clotting. This condition is now present in Rupert's case and It makes any further injury likely to be fatal.

Dietrich rubbed his temples and closed his eyes.

"Wow! That's a lot for a relative layman like me to try to digest. Bottom line, I guess it means that what you'll be looking for is the proverbial needle in a haystack."

"That's one way to put it," Maria said. "This certainly doesn't make the task any easier, but I can assure you that if that person or those persons exist, we will find them.

"It's imperative that we keep Rupert in the most sterile situation possible and protected from further injury. Even the insertion of needles could prove disastrous with this added susceptibility. And, you're right. This ramps up the need for speed."

9

Towering waves crashed over the Biarritz sea wall as Maria pointed her Alfa-Romeo sports car down Avenue Beau Rivage. Gale force winds and torrential rains had arrived overnight, on the tail-end of an Atlantic storm that was battering both sides of the Channel. The wind-shield wipers labored to keep pace with the heavy downpour. Mercifully, she was soon able to merge onto A63, the French superhighway that hugged the Franco-España border area.

The ten-mile run to the Biriatou customs station, normally a ten-minute lark, bogged down two miles from the crossing. As her car approached, border agents were seen swarming over a Spanish lorry bearing Andalusian license plates. The lorry was stopped in the northbound center lane. Rubberneckers craned to see what possible legal infraction had caused such a logjam. Maria tuned to a local station for details. A reporter on scene was speaking.

"...the tops of several of the olive barrels have been bashed in and agents are scooping out the contents. In several of the barrels, olives constitute only the first nine inches. False bottoms have revealed plastic wrapped bales of cannabis resin. Someone in the crowd says the police estimate the value of the drugs at around 6.5 million Euros. Rumors are that the cargo was

51

bound for Amsterdam. Traffic continues to be snarled for two kilometers in both directions and…"

Half an hour later, the Alfa-Romeo resumed its 120 kilometer/hr. sprint toward Bilbao. Maria picked up AP-8 along the Basque coast and whizzed past the resort city of San Sebastian. She covered the remaining thirty-five miles before noon and pulled into a garage beneath a downtown office building in Bilbao. The sign over the entrance proclaimed, "Clìnica Hematologìa Basque, SA."

"I'm impressed," Dietrich said. "I'd like the name of your architect. I'm planning an addition to our headquarters in Zurich and I like what I see."

"Santiago Calatrava."

"Where have I heard that name before?"

"Next to Frank Gehry, who designed the new Guggenheim Museum, Calatrava is the most famous architect around these parts. He did the sports complex for the Athens' Olympic games, among other major commissions."

"He must be very expensive?" Dietrich said inquisitively.

"He is. The fact that he's married to my mother's cousin helped. Sort of a family favor, so to speak. By the way, he has an office in Zurich. He got his engineering and architecture degrees at the Swiss Federal Institute of Technology there. I bet he would love to do another project in Zurich."

"Another?"

"His firm did the railway stations in Zurich several years ago," Maria added.

"My, you're full of surprises. I'll have my chief architect give him a call. I'm sure they probably already know each other. That's why his name is so familiar! I've seen it on a plaque at the main terminal."

The elevator stopped. It opened onto Maria's fourth floor office suite.

"Come with me," she said.

Maria led Dietrich through the etched glass doors that led to her inner sanctum. She walked around her desk to the glass wall behind. When Dietrich was standing beside her, she pressed a button and the drapes opened to a view of the River Nervión, placidly winding its way through the heart of downtown Bilbao.

"There she is," Maria said with pride as she spread her arms, *The Guggenheim.*

The sprawling, titanium and glass clad structures of the Guggenheim Museum bore a strange resemblance to some imagined, futuristic, dystopian landscape. It hovered over the Bilbao waterfront like so many giant metal cans and boxes, abandoned in a heap by a petulant child-giant. The museum was built on the once crumbling remains of a derelict waterfront and was embraced by the encircling arms of the Nervión River and its Puente de la Salve Bridge.

To the untrained eye, the mass of geometric shapes and non-linear curves seemed random and somewhat unrelated However, to the trained eyes of Gehry's architectural contemporaries, it was viewed as a modern masterpiece—the building of the century—and it quickly became Bilbao's iconic logo and the city's pride and joy.

Dietrich stared at the museum for a few seconds before commenting.

"I had heard of the Bilbao Guggenheim, but I never imagined it like this. The first impression is a shock and then it begins to take shape and form in one's mind. Gehry needed a lot of chutzpah to present that to the city fathers, and they deserve a lot of credit for approving it."

"Everyone forms their own opinion," Maria said. "Most appreciate its audacity. Others think it resembles a heap of scrap iron and is an eyesore. I like it. I am inspired every time I look across the river and behold its splendor. Oddly, I take inspiration from it. The form and structure inherent in our genes and chromosomes is also a testament to some grand design. Whether one believes that design comes from a divine power or

53

from a natural evolution, it is no less astounding. Every time I peer through a microscope and observe that complex blend of elements circulating in our blood, I understand anew why I entered the field of medicine. I welcome the challenge of discovering the occasional flaws in that design and then seeking answers to them."

"That's why you're at the top of your field," Dietrich said. "That's why I sought you out. I was told, by people that I trust, that If anyone can help us save Rupert, it's you."

"Thank you, Señor von Hesse, but this will be the greatest challenge I have ever faced. I pray that we can find the answer in time."

"We will Maria, we will. And, call me Dietrich."

10

The clinic's conference room was located adjacent to Maria's office. Maria stood at one end of the oval table and Dietrich at the other. A tray of pastries and an urn of coffee occupied the center. Four other employees had joined the meeting, two on either side.

"Gentlemen, this is Señor Dietrich von Hesse. He is president of Sagarin Pharmaceuticals. I'm certain you are all familiar with the company and its products as we use many of them here in our laboratories."

"Señor von Hesse this is Diego Baranaga." Maria indicated the man standing to his left, back to the window. "I spoke to you of him yesterday in relation to our search for an investigator."

"How do you do?" Dietrich said as he shook hands.

"Standing next to Diego is Paulo Echeverria. Paulo is our bio-medical engineering guru."

"Hello Paulo."

"To your right is Alantso Zubiri. Alantso is a hematologist."

"Hello Alontso."

"And last but not least, is Paskal Ibarra. Paskal has been with me from the beginning. He taught me much of what I know. He trained in cardiology but knows more about the entire human organism and how its plumbing works than anyone I've ever met."

"Pleased to meet you, Paskal."

"Everyone grab a pastry and some coffee and take a seat," Maria suggested. When the shuffling and stirring ended and everyone was seated, Maria remained standing.

"Diego is the only one of you who has been briefed in any depth about the purpose of Señor von Hesse's visit here, so I will start at the beginning.

"Señor von Hesse has a 17-year-old son named Rupert. A few days ago, Rupert was involved in a major accident while skiing in Zermatt, Switzerland. As a result of the accident and subsequent treatment he developed severe and uncontrollable bleeding. Prior to receiving all the laboratory analyses, the emergency room doctors followed their standard protocols. It was not until later they learned from Señor von Hesse that both Rupert's parents are carriers of the mutant genes that can exhibit as hemophilia. To further complicate matters Rupert has one of the rarest blood types in the entire world.

"It was known by his father that hemophilia was a possibility. He had Rupert tested as a young boy and discovered the mutant condition. What was not discovered, until all the tests were in, was that Rupert is an Rh-null."

That stunning pronouncement reflected itself in the stricken look on the faces of the four specialists.

"Rupert's life was saved by the quick recognition and action of the emergency room doctors. They sourced two pints of Rh-null blood in Paris and flew in high-powered coagulants from Geneva.

"It appeared that he was out of the woods until they moved him from intensive to critical care. Something went wrong. We don't know if it was a result of transfusions or the coagulants or some other combination of factors, but the young man went into convulsions and had a seizure. He had difficulty breathing and was placed on a ventilator.

"The doctors realized at this point that they were dealing with a situation far beyond the small clinic's capabilities. They suggested a specialist be brought in. Señor von Hesse asked

56

who. Everyone agreed that the most respected doctor for this set of circumstances was Dr. Sterling Askew of Stanford University."

A nodding of heads affirmed the choice. Everyone at the clinic was acquainted with much of Askew's work.

"Rather than bring Askew to Switzerland, Rupert was flown to California. Dr. Askew examined him immediately and confirmed the diagnoses from Zermatt. Unfortunately, he uncovered something else. In their haste to treat Rupert, and before all the blood analyses were available, he had been given a drug, or drugs, that triggered von Willebrand type 2n disease. Traces of *Lornoxicam* were found in Rupert's blood analysis. *Lornoxicam* as you know is an anti-inflammatory. It's also on the list of drugs that can trigger von Willebrand's disease. In this case it appears to have triggered vWD 2n in Rupert."

Paskal Ibarra's audible moan expressed the feelings of the other three.

"So, you now understand the severity of this young man's dilemma. He is lying in a bed in Palo Alto, California with a trifecta of blood anomalies: hemophilia, von Willebrand's 2n and Rh-null. Any trauma to his system at this point could result in a bleeding episode or seizure that can't be contained. He is being watched by medical experts 24 hours a day. All medications are being administered epidermally or nasally when possible. Even a needle prick at this time could prove fatal.

"And that brings us to the purpose of Señor von Hesse's visit. He has his researchers in Zurich and at his subsidiary, SciGen, in Los Altos, California, as well as Dr. Sterling Askew, working 24 hours a day to try to solve this crisis. The scientists at SciGen have been using CRISPR to develop synthesized genes that can be spliced into Rupert's chromosomes to replace the mutant ones.

"They have made great progress to date; however, perfecting a synthetic protein that does not disturb the telomeres or other chromosomal gene sequences is proving extremely difficult.

57

"So, what can a bunch of scientists and researchers in far off Bilbao contribute. SciGen, based on scientific research and genealogical searches, believes that there is a large pool of rare AB Rh-negative blood types clustered in the Basque region—twice as many as any other place in the world.

"If anyone living has the hemophilia mutation in their blood, is Rh-null and exhibits the von Willebrand 2n syndrome, the odds are they will be found somewhere within 75 miles of where we sit. It is our assignment to find them."

The four men looked at Dietrich with the utmost compassion. He might as well be Don Quixote tilting at Spanish windmills. The herculean task set before them was very likely impossible.

"In order to find candidates that meet these criteria we are going to need to research every health record in northern Spain. We'll need dispensation from the government to review their private medical records. I believe I can arrange that with the authorities in the guise of some research projects they have requested. Everything we do must remain anonymous and confidential until we can locate candidates and gain their permission to engage in this study. As I told Señor von Hesse this will be the proverbial search for a needle in a haystack, but I believe it can be done. A young man's life depends on it. Señor von Hesse would like to say a few words now."

"Thank you, Maria, and thank all of you for this effort. I don't need to tell you that time is of the essence. Every day that my son stays alive is a blessing from God, but we all know that his is a situation fraught with more than the normal peril. However, I can't stand by idly and watch my son die without doing everything in my power to save him. Any contribution you can make to that effort will be profoundly appreciated.

"Now I know that you all will do everything in your power to help us and that money is not a major consideration, but anything you need to perform your piece is available. As I told Maria, I have spent over fifty-million dollars in pursuit of a cure for these

58

diseases and I'll spend fifty-million more if necessary. That's just by way of saying that no price is too high to pay for my son's life."

Dietrich walked over to the window and looked down at the Guggenhem. He pulled the handkerchief from his coat pocket to dry his eyes. That last fleeting look of Rupert as he left Stanford floated before his eyes. He composed himself and returned to the table.

"Diego, Maria told me about the candidate you have identified as an investigator. He sounds intriguing. Maria, do you think we can bring him in for an interview before I leave? I understand that you want to talk to some others, but if he can fill the bill maybe you should go with him. It sounds like he can hit the ground running and has the skill set necessary to get the job done."

"Diego?" Maria turned to her associate.

"I believe we can. He comes into his Bilbao office on Tuesdays and Thursdays. I can run back up to Gorliz and meet with him. If he's agreeable, I'll arrange a meeting for tomorrow here at the offices."

"That's great, Diego. Do you have any objection Maria?"

"No." Then she hesitated. "I just want to be sure we get this right."

"I understand. If you're not 100% satisfied that Muñoz is your man, then I'll back off and leave you alone."

11

Maria dropped Dietrich in front of the Gran Hotel Domine on the opposite side of the Guggenheim from her offices.

"I'll pick you up at 9. I've made reservations at Neura. It's right across the freeway, near the museum. Actually, it's associated with the Guggenheim. They experiment in *nouvelle cuisine*. It's really quite good. Michelin one-star. My husband will join us if you don't mind. My treat."

"Great, I look forward to meeting him. How much does he know about the purpose of my visit?"

"Very little, actually. He knows of Sagarin but not much more. You're just another customer with whom he can cadge a good meal off my expense account," she laughed.

"What does he do?"

"He runs a boutique financial advisory firm. He's in league with the Goldman-Sachs office in Madrid. They refer clients to him who are looking for local connections."

"Sounds interesting."

"It keeps us both busy. Having dinner with customers is one of the few times we can slow down and talk to each other."

"Children?"

"No. Vitorio decided early on that he didn't want children. He said bringing them into our frenetic lifestyle would be a great disservice to them. I sometimes regret the decision, but I didn't fight him on it. Ultimately, I think it was the right one.

"You?"

"There's Rupert of course. Then there's Dieter who's 14 and Elise who's 12. Dieter has tested positive for hemophilia as well, and Elise carries the gene. Therese's ancestry includes Queen Victoria. That's where all the trouble began—the curse of the *Royal Blue Blood*. Also, my ancestry includes Frederick the Great and all the genetic aberrations that entails. So, you can see that being descended from royalty isn't all it's cracked up to be."

"How interesting! I had no idea. Well, I'll see you at nine."

"Thanks."

Dietrich registered and headed straight for his room. He threw his briefcase on the bed and pulled out his Apple. After punching in the requisite 14 digits he waited as the signals pinged off several satellites on their way to California. The phone in Room 477 rang.

"Hello."

"Who is this?" he didn't recognize the voice.

"This is nurse Robbins."

"Oh, hi. This is Rupert's father. Is my wife there?"

"No sir, she stepped out for a bite of lunch about half-an-hour ago. Shall I tell her you called?"

"Please, and can you bring me up to date on Rupert's condition?"

"Certainly. He had a rather restful night and Dr. Askew said he would take him off the ventilator tomorrow, barring any unforeseen problems. We're still being very careful that Rupert doesn't suffer any cuts or bruises. He had a brief episode of nosebleed last night, but we were able to get it under control quickly."

"That's wonderful Miss Robbins. Thank you. Yes, please ask Therese to call me."

"I certainly will sir."

"Good-bye."

Dietrich looked out across the esplanade fronting the museum. He glanced at his phone. Therese had not returned his call. A car drove up and the driver rolled down the window of a BMW sedan. She waved. It was Maria. He pocketed the phone and passed through the hotel's revolving door.

"I'll call when I get back," he thought.

Vitorio Elizondo Vega exuded all the confidence of a "man of the world." His gray, Savile Row, pinstripe suit and his black, Ferragamo wingtips touched all the bases for a successful player in the high-stakes game of international finance. Vitorio exuded self-confidence. His appearance and manner virtually shouted, "Look at Me." Not that Maria was a shrinking violet. Hers was a more reserved confidence, forged in the crucible of her laboratory work and reinforced by the many honors she had collected. She knew who she was and was comfortable in that knowledge. She didn't feel it necessary to engage in self-promotion.

"Señor von Hesse," Vitorio said after they had been seated and all the niceties had been observed, "Maria tells me that Sagarin is a very prominent member of the pharmaceutical world. I took the liberty of looking at your credentials on Dunn and Bradstreet. Very impressive. Your Paydex and commercial credit scores are off the chart. I was considering recommending your stock to my clients and then I saw that you are privately held. I checked with some of my colleagues at Goldman. They said they took a pass at you a couple of years ago but that you turned them down, that you have no interest in taking Sagarin public."

Dietrich was disappointed that this perfect stranger had delved into his company's financials and was speculating about it in a social environment. He glanced at Maria, saw her embarrassment, and picked up his wine.

"Very good Rioja, Maria." He tipped his glass toward her. "I congratulate you. You did find a Tempranillo that approaches the Rothschild."

62

He turned to face her husband.

"You see Vitorio, Maria and I had a little discussion last evening about the relative merits of French and Spanish wines. Since I'm from Switzerland, and presumably neutral, I'll be diplomatic and call it a tie.

"Now, as to your interest in Sagarin, yes, the company is privately held, yes, it is very successful, and no, I'm not interested in taking it public. I have no stomach for answering to a horde of ill-informed stockholders every ninety days or to the *brokerage* houses representing them."

There was a look of distress on Vitorio's face and an expression of near glee on Maria's.

"Sorry old man. I didn't mean to pry. I guess it's sometimes hard for me to leave this business at the office."

Vitorio squirmed in his seat, tasted his wine, and appeared to seek a new tack for the conversation.

"I understand you have engaged Maria's firm to do some work for you. Must be pretty important for the CEO to come personally."

Again, Dietrich couldn't believe the coarseness of the man. Vitorio seemed unable to strike the right balance between social niceties and business polity. He began to wonder how such a polished and successful woman had become entangled with such a boor.

"I don't know how much she has revealed of my purpose here but it's more personal than business. You see my oldest son Rupert has developed a rare blood disorder for which there's no practical cure. My company is struggling to develop such a cure, along with the help of many others. Clinica Hematalogia has some of the foremost experts in the world, including Maria, for dealing with blood diseases. I have asked her to join forces with us to work on the problem."

"I'm sorry. I was not aware. Of course, Maria will do all she can to help. I will pray for his recovery."

63

"Thank you, Vitorio," Dietrich said, responding to the modicum of civility he expressed.

"Well, shall we order," Maria said, thankful for the opportunity to shift the conversation away from her husband. "I understand Neura does an outstanding variation on our traditional paella. I haven't tried it, but Diego said it was wonderful."

"If your forensic pathologist likes it, then who am I to argue?" Dietrich said. "I'll have the paella."

"I'll go with that as well," Maria said. "and you Vitorio?"

"You know me. I'm a red meat man. I'll have the rack of lamb. Looks like an interesting pairing of vegetables."

How appropriate, Dietrich thought to himself. Fits his personality.

Maria continued to steer the conversation away from contentious subjects and managed to get them through the dessert course without any further frostiness. She was relieved when the evening came to an end and they dropped Dietrich off at his hotel.

"Diego was able to arrange the meeting we talked about today," she said through her open window. "He will have Mr. Muñoz in the office at ten. See you then."

"Thanks Maria for a lovely evening and great paella. I trust you enjoyed your lamb Vitorio."

"Yes, it was delicious with the pesto sauce. Good to meet you, old man. See you again soon I hope."

"Same here, Vitorio," Dietrich said through clenched teeth. Not!!!!

He looked at his watch. Midnight in Bilbao. Still only 4pm in Palo Alto. Dietrich hurried up to his room and dialed Therese. This time she answered on the first ring.

"Where were you earlier?" Dietrich asked. "I was worried."

"When I returned from lunch Nurse Simmons told me you had called. Then Rupert started to hemorrhage where his back

64

was injured. By the time all the emergency personnel were able to stop the bleeding you were not available. I knew you would call later."

"What caused the hemorrhaging?"

"Dr. Askew said that Rupert's clotting factors continue to diminish. He says it's a combination of the hemophilia and the von Willebrand problem. They had no choice but to infuse more blood and more coagulant and that caused added problems where the needle was inserted. They flew the blood in from Los Angeles."

"What did Askew say?"

"He looked really worried. I heard him talking to Rob Simpson on the phone. I think they're meeting tonight."

"Did he say where?"

"He mentioned some restaurant near Stanford."

"*La Boheme*?"

"Yes, I believe that's what he said."

"Get the restaurant's number and text it to me. I want to talk to both of them tonight."

"How's it going in France?" Therese asked. Dietrich hadn't yet told her everything.

"Pretty well, I had dinner with Sergei last evening. You remember Sergei Romanoff from Bayonne?"

"Oh, yes, how is he?

"Fine. He sends love and best wishes for Rupert. I think they may be working on something at Aquitania that might help."

A little white lie to spare his wife more pain could be excused.

"Oh, I pray so. Dietrich I'm so scared."

Rob Simpson made the drive up to Palo Alto following several grueling hours in the SciGen lab where his team tested different gene combinations, trying to force the CRISPR splice procedure to work properly. Still no luck. He'd made this drive many times since he joined SciGen. Each time he rolled through the campus he remembered affectionately his days there as an undergraduate biology student and then when he came back for post-graduate work following his Duke Ph.D.

.

His dinners with Askew were always spirited and lively and he always left La Boheme feeling he had learned something new. Now his spirits sagged with the realization that a young boy lying in one of those hospital rooms he just passed was counting on him and his team for his life. His earlier phone conversation with Askew had not leavened his spirit. Every day without an answer was a day closer to death for Rupert von Hesse.

12

Mikel Muñoz didn't fit the mold of most other men in the Basque region. His skin hue was a paler walnut, not quite as dark as the natives. His hazel eyes defied the dark brown color mold of the typical Hispanic. He was clean shaven—most local men wore some form of facial hair; mustache, goatee, or full beard. His once jet-black hair, now liberally sprinkled with salt was parted down the middle and was swept back behind his ears, wavy, luxuriant and neatly trimmed. The physique he had maintained as a policeman in Boise was intact, with maybe an extra pound or two around the mid-section. Mikel Muñoz radiated the charisma and *savoir faire* of a 21st century Cesar Romero, complete with the luminous smile.

Maria Elizondo, Dietrich von Hesse, Diego Baranaga and Mikel Muñoz gathered around the same conference table as the day before. Once again Maria presided.

"Señor Muñoz I'd like you to meet Señor Dietrich von Hesse. He is President of Sagarin Pharmaceuticals."

"Good morning sir, it's good to meet you."

"Mr. Muñoz. How do you do? I'm certain that Diego has filled you in on the purpose of this meeting."

"Yes sir, he has."

"Is this a task you feel qualified to undertake?"

"I believe so. It's not that different from what I've been doing for the last 30 or so years. Diego didn't go into great detail about the underlying reason for this search."

"Mikel, may I call you Mikel?"

"Sure, that's what everyone calls me, or Mike. That's what the guys in Boise called me."

"Before we get into your professional qualifications for this assignment, there are a few issues in your background we need to clear up."

"I thought there might be," he smiled.

"Will you explain to us the circumstances of your departure from Boise?"

Muñoz breathed deeply. He launched into a speech he had delivered countless times before. Clasping his hands in front of him he leaned on the table looking Dietrich directly in the eye.

"I served with distinction in the Boise police department Special Victims Unit for more than twenty years. Not a blemish on my record. I'm sure you know that from your background checks. My wife leaving me for another man was a big blow. She was the love of my life. She ran off with a law professor from the university in Moscow, Idaho when he came down to teach at Boise State for a semester. My wife was in his class for paralegals. She was working as a clerk in a local law firm and seeking to move up. Her leaving nearly destroyed me. I began to drink too much, and the police department finally cut me loose. I couldn't really blame them. I wasn't very effective those last few months.

"Then I took stock of myself and decided that Clarice, my former wife, didn't define me or who I am. I was finally able to move past the he-man macho thing. I cleaned myself up. I was shuffling around, looking for another law enforcement gig, when I got a letter from a cousin in Gorliz. My mother had written and told them what happened. My cousin Felipé invited me to come over for a visit. I fell in love with the area and the people, so I decided there was nothing to keep me in Boise. I went home, packed up my things, and moved. End of story."

"Diego says he found you in a bar in Gorliz."

"I was never an alcoholic. I just dove into the bottle as a way to drown my sorrows. I threw a very, very long pity party.

Once I decided I was okay, and that no one else was coming to my party, I just quit—cold turkey. I still drink socially but not to excess and never when I'm on a case, I'm certain Diego was able to substantiate that."

Diego nodded.

"He was," Maria said, "but we needed to hear it from you. Are there any other skeletons in your closet you need to tell us about?"

"No, I don't think so. My life, both in Idaho and here, is pretty much an open book. Some of the things I did in my official capacity as a detective weren't pretty and I'm not proud of them, but they were all in the line of duty."

"Such as?" Dietrich asked.

"I shot and killed a man once. He had beat his wife to a pulp. He was waving a pistol around when my partner and I arrived. He was obviously drunk and threatening everyone in sight, including two young children. I didn't hesitate. I took him out with a shot between the eyes."

"Anything else?"

"No, that's the worst of it."

"Great. Mike, if Maria decides to hire you and you agree to our terms we're asking you to help us find people whose rare blood type may help to save my son's life. We've determined that the probability of finding these people is greatest here in the Basque region. Maria's team believes they can identify the right candidates through a massive data analysis of government health records. Once they do, we will need to locate them and convince them to participate in this project. If we can find them, and convince them to participate, they'll be brought here to the clinic for study. Specimens of their blood will also be sent to Sagarin's labs in Zurich and California where research teams are already assembled and at work.

"Maria," Dietrich said, "do you or Diego have any further questions?"

Diego shook his head.

"I'd like to spend a few minutes alone with Señor Muñoz," Maria said. "There are a few things I prefer to discuss in private."

"Fair enough. I think I'll invite Diego to go over to that bar across the street and have a *patxaran*. I'm curious. Call us when you're finished."

Muñoz was gone when Dietrich returned to Maria's office. He looked around for the private investigator.

"He had to meet a client at his office at 11," Maria explained. "He said he'd be glad to come back if you have more questions."

"I don't. Are you satisfied?"

"Yes. He can do the job. I asked him to join us for lunch later. I'm having a contract prepared to present to him at that time. Maybe we'll go back across the street. You can have some tapas and another *patxaran.*"

"No thank you. One of those has convinced me of their potency."

"Dietrich," Maria hesitantly began. "I must apologize for Vitorio's behavior at dinner."

"No need," Dietrich said.

"Yes, there is a need! For me! Vitorio has not been himself lately. He's distant and gets easily upset. It's not his normal behavior. I asked him about it when we got home, and he just shrugged it off. 'Business pressures,' he said, 'everything's fine,' he said. It has me worried. I didn't want you to think Vitorio's behavior last evening was his usual conduct."

"I'm sure it's like he said, business pressures. We all have them. I try not to let them intrude on my private life but sometimes the harmful thoughts leak out."

"I trust that's all it is," she said. "I was totally embarrassed."

"Don't worry about it Maria, you didn't do anything wrong, and you're not Vitorio."

"Thank you, Dietrich. That means a lot."

Maria's outside line rang.

"Hello."

"Srta. Elizondo this is Mikel. I've finished with my client. Where do we stand?"

"Meet me across the street at *Redondo*, the tapas cafe. We'll be at the bar. I love their ceviche."

"I'll be there."

At ten past two Mikel strolled in. He took the stool next to Maria.

"What would you like Mikel?" she asked.

"That ceviche looks good, and a plate of olives and onions."

"And to drink?"

She waited expectantly for his response.

"A San Miguel, if you don't mind?"

"Can do, I'm having white wine, Dietrich's having water." He said the one *patxaran* he had with Diego met his minimum daily requirement for hard liquor.

As the tapas dishes came and went Maria explained the contents of the contract she had handed to Mikel. He was to be paid a flat 50 Euros per hour once he was given a name to pursue. If he successfully located the person in question and provided proof, he would receive a bonus of 1,000 Euros. If he brought the person in with a signed agreement, he would receive an additional 4,000 Euros. These terms had been agreed to by Dietrich. The incentives were meant to spur Mikel to maximum effort in finding and producing the people whose names he was given.

"We expect to have your undivided attention," Dietrich said. "Nothing you have ever done in your life is more important to me than this. Maria's team is already crunching the numbers to identify candidates. We hope to have the first name by tomorrow. Will you be ready to go?"

"Yes sir. I've already turned over my current case load to an associate—just routine missing children or cheating spouses. He can handle that."

71

"Okay then," Maria added, "call me first thing tomorrow. I'll update you on our progress. I'm waiting for word back from the Ministry of Health. I've asked for permission to scan all regional health records for the desired blood attributes we're searching for. I expect word back today."

"Okay. Talk to you tomorrow."

Dietrich and Maria were alone in her office. Diego, Paulo, Alantso and Paskal were back in the lab, cleaning and prepping the equipment they would use to perform the intricate analyses necessary to isolate and codify rare blood types.

"What's the population of the subject area?" Dietrich asked out of the blue.

Maria took a moment to digest what he was asking.

"Oh, you mean the Basque region."

"Yes."

"About two and a half million in the defined Basque Autonomous Region. Another million or so in contiguous areas with significant Basque populations."

"So, three to four million in the haystack."

"Yes," she answered, smiling at the pun, "that's about right."

"That means one plus million in the targeted group."

"Give or take."

"And you think most of them will show up in the Health Ministry record system."

I certainly hope so. Most of our work is involved with private institutions; hospitals, clinics, pharmas, etc. We haven't done an awful lot with the government. I couched my request as an incidental adjunct to a study of diseases of the local Basque population which was contracted for by an insurance consortium."

"I'm going back to the hotel," Dietrich said, "There are some phone calls I need to make. Some business, but the most important to my wife to see how Rupert is doing. Call me as soon as you hear from the ministry."

72

system and coding algorithms to your people in Zurich and California so they can incorporate them into their own protocols. I don't trust sending such information on the internet. Last year some of our communications were hacked. We're not certain who the culprit was, but my guys narrowed it down to China or Russia. Needless to say, our patents don't mean anything to those regimes. I was wondering if you could carry them with you?"

"Of course! When can you have everything ready?"

"Tomorrow morning."

"Okay. I'll make arrangements to be picked up in Biarritz around noon. I can be in Zurich by four. I'll leave for California that evening. It'll give me a chance to see my children and our parents and get them up to speed. I can be in California the following morning. By then you should have your answers from the health service, and know what your next moves are."

"I'll be here at eight. Everyone has assured me that the packages will be ready. Some of the guys may have to pull an all-nighter.

"What are your plans for dinner? She asked.

"I don't have any."

"Vitorio is in Madrid. Meet me at Coppola Bilbao at nine. They have great northern Italian cuisine and some Super Tuscans you won't believe. The Sassicaia '06 is formidable."

"Sounds good, I'll be there."

The myDriver limousine picked Dietrich up at 8:45 and deposited him at Coppolla Bilbao at five of nine. The restaurant was wedged in between several cafes, boutiques and auto-repair shops along Barraincua Kale. Three large dumpsters lining the sidewalk across the narrow one-way street in front of the café lent a less than appealing atmosphere for a fine-dining experience.

Once inside, Coppola was another world, totally removed from the disordered scene outside its door. Iñigo Lopez plucked at his acoustic guitar from a stool in the rear of the restaurant. The American folk song he sang was all but drowned out by the din of the crowd. Patrons were scattered around the eclectic interior, most sitting at high tables, munching on oregano scented pizzas while downing rioja or sangria.

Maria was nowhere in sight. Dietrich asked for a table in a far back corner where they might be able to carry on a conversation. The young greeter suggested that the table in the front window may be more suitable for that. He found himself staring across the street at the unsightly garbage bins. The greeter left two menus and a wine list. Judging by the assortment of patrons and the heavily pizza influenced menu, Dietrich found it hard to believe this was the upscale eatery Maria had hinted at. He was almost certain he would not find Super Tuscans on the *Carta de Viño.* However, to his amazement, there was not only a Sassicaia but an Ornellaia, the two wines from the Maremma in Italy that had flaunted the Italian classification system and created a cult following for their deep red blends.

Have you decided on a wine Señor?" the waitress asked.

"Yes, the 2006 Sassicaia."

The listing proclaimed that both Suckling and Parker gave it a near perfect 98 rating.

"Very good sir, that's a great choice."

The smiling young woman headed for the wine cellar with visions of a large gratuity dancing in her eyes as Maria entered the restaurant.

"Over here," Dietrich called. His table was hidden from the entry way.

"Oh, hello," she said, "I'm sorry I'm late. I was on the phone with Vitorio and got tied up."

"No problem, I just ordered one of those Super Tuscans you mentioned."

"Great, I could use a drink about now."

"Work?"

"No, Vitorio."

78

"Is he all right?'

"That depends what you mean by all right. It seems he's healthy enough to have taken a friend with him to Madrid."

"Not business related, I gather."

"No, she's an acquaintance we know socially. Turns out she's more than an acquaintance to Vitorio. One of our doctors returning from London saw them together at the airport. He was reluctant to tell me, but he's never liked Vitorio and he thought I'd want to know."

"I'm sorry Maria. News like this is always difficult."

Maria took her napkin and dabbed at her eyes.

"I've suspected for a while that Vitorio was fooling around. I didn't want to believe it but now there's no denying it."

"What was his response when you confronted him."

"At first denial, then when the evidence began to pile up he became defensive. He said my work had become my lover and he felt like the third leg of a triangle. I know that's not true. It's just a convenient excuse for his philandering."

"Now what?" Dietrich asked.

"I don't know for sure. The wound is too fresh. I'll have to think about it. We have three days until he returns from Madrid. I'll take a stance by then, but I must tell you, it's very distressing—a bolt out of the blue. But, let's not let this spoil our dinner. Have you looked at the menu yet?"

"Yes, it's mostly pizza and southern Italian. Certainly smells good. I asked for this table so we could have a semblance of a conversation. Between the guitar and the raucous conversation, it's almost impossible to hear."

"I'm sorry, I didn't think about the noise. Tell you what, when we're finished, there's a great coffee bar near your hotel. It's quiet and quite good. Then afterwards you'll be able to walk to your hotel."

"Great solution."

"Here you are," the waitress declared with a small flourish as she presented the bottle of wine for Dietrich's inspection.

"Very good," he said, "Sassicaia '06."

She opened the wine and poured a small sample for Dietrich's approval."

"That is really good. Maria, you were right."

"Why thank you. It's good that we can please a man of the world in our little old Bilbao."

The waitress proceeded to pour both glasses, wrapped the bottle in a napkin and placed it in a silver holder.

"Enjoy," she said, "we have a few specials this evening. There is a Bucatini Amatriciana, Canneloni Ragu, Lobster Ravioli and a Mushroom Risotto. All are accompanied by a Caesar salad.

"And what would you recommend?" Dietrich asked.

"I'm partial to the ravioli, but the risotto is heavenly tonight."

"I'll have the ravioli," Maria said

"And I'll have the risotto," Dietrich answered.

"Excellent, enjoy your wine while I place your order."

Dietrich raised his glass.

"Here's to a happy conclusion with Vitorio," he said.

"Thank you and here's to a happy conclusion for Rupert."

"Both of us should be so blessed.

"Did anything happen after I left the office?"

"Miguel's secretary returned my call. She said he would be in touch by nine a.m. tomorrow."

"I hope that turns out well," Dietrich said,

"So do I. Sorting through all those records will be a chore but trying to find the right people without them would be a nightmare."

The waitress returned with their salads.

"This is good," Dietrich said. "A good Caesar like this is a work of art."

For a few minutes the two ate in silence. Maria spoke.

"Do you believe in God?" she asked.

Dietrich was taken aback. He thought for a moment.

80

"I grew up religious, German Lutheran and all, but over the years I've come to have doubts. So many evil things have happened in the world—are happening in the world—that it shakes your faith. I can't imagine a kind and loving God allowing such things to happen. I guess I would classify myself as an agnostic. If someone can show me a kind, loving creator who will stop all the insanity then I'll believe again."

"I grew up Catholic of course," Maria said. "I went through all the requisite church training and rituals. Had the doctrine beaten into me by the nuns and priests. I had to believe. Everyone I knew believed. It was sacrilege not to. That's one of the reasons I wanted to become a doctor, so that I could help people, do God's work. When I look into a microscope and see a vaccine I've helped develop kill a virus, I believe. When I turn on the television and see a madman blow himself up in the midst of a crowd of children, I don't believe."

"Why did you ask?" Dietrich asked.

"I'm not sure. It's hard to explain. I guess it's this thing with Vitorio. You fall in love with someone, you marry them, you each promise to be faithful 'til death do us part and then this happens. It shakes your belief."

"Yeah, it's like that with Rupert. Good kid, never been in trouble, cursed with a blood disorder he didn't even know about, injured in a ski accident, and now we find his life hanging in the balance. Would a fair God do that? I would like to think not, but it surely creates a dilemma. I guess I admire those who can cling to their faith regardless of what happens to them, but you have to wonder if they're saints or naifs. When I look at the history of the world, almost every calamity can trace its roots back to organized religion. Look at the Middle East for the last two-thousand years; look at the Spanish inquisition, the holocaust, the Irish rebellion, Afghanistan—all direct consequences of religious intolerance. I'm not sure how society would have turned out *without* organized religion, but it certainly couldn't have been much worse."

81

"I'm going to see my priest tomorrow," Maria said. "As you know the Catholic church doesn't condone divorce. If I decide to separate from Vitorio the church will still consider us married. So, If I find someone else, do I live in sin with them or do I leave the church?"

"One day at a time, Maria, one day at a time. Don't borrow the future; it'll get here fast enough."

The salad plates were cleared, and the entrees served. The aromas were sinful.

"You're right, Dietrich. One day at a time."

The conversation turned to matters related to the campaign to find a cure for Rupert. They kicked several ideas back and forth and finally concluded that the path they were on had the best chance for success.

The check came.

"I'll get this," Maria said. "I invited you, and besides a therapy session would have been much more expensive."

"I think I'll skip the coffee," Dietrich said. "I'm tired and tomorrow's going to be a very long day. I believe we covered everything we needed to at Coppola."

"Yes, I think so," Maria said.

She dropped Dietrich at his hotel and waved to him as he passed through the revolving doors. Visions of Vitorio with blonde Sophia on his arm drifted through her mind.

"No! Don't borrow the future!"

"Hello, Sergei?"

"Yes."

"This is Dietrich. I won't be able to fit in the awards ceremony we talked about for the cryovac container project. Sorry. I'm flying back to Zurich and then on to California today. There's information I need to get to the researchers. Make my apologies to the team and tell them we'll do it another time."

"You have to do what's best for Rupert," Sergei said. "Don't worry about us. We'll be here when you get back. Give my best to Therese. I pray your son will recover."

"Thanks Sergei. We're doing everything we can. I just hope it isn't too late."

He signed off and caught a taxi over to the clinic.

The myDrive limousine waited outside the clinic while Dietrich picked up the data packages. Maria had not yet arrived. He wondered if it had to do with her news of the night before. Diego was waiting for him in the conference room.

"There are two CDs, a thumb drive, and a hard copy of all the information we have accumulated. Tell your people to call us if they have any questions." Diego said.

"Thank you, Diego, and thanks for finding Mikel. I believe he will be able to help you find the blood types we need."

Dietrich looked around the office.

"I see Maria is not in. Anything wrong?"

"She called and said she had a private errand to run and would be in later."

"Thanks Diego," Dietrich said as he gathered up the documents, "I'll see you in a few days. I hope you'll have good news when I get back."

"So do I, Señor von Hesse, so do I. Have a good and safe trip."

The Sagarin Dassault Falcon 50 crossed the flashing outer markers along the Biarritz sea wall as Dietrich's limo pulled into the private aviation terminal. He paid the driver and took his luggage inside where he sat near the windows as the blue and yellow plane taxied to a stop outside. Marcel and the co-pilot came down the stairs to do their post-flight check of the aircraft. The cabin attendant, Jacques, entered the terminal.

"Good morning, Herr von Hesse. How are you today?"

"Fine Jacques, how was the flight over?"

"A little bumpy over the French Alps but smooth after that. I'm getting some sandwiches and fruit for the flight back. Anything particular you'd like?"

"Yes, I skipped breakfast this morning. Some chocolate croissants and strong coffee would be good."

"Yes sir, I'll be back in a few minutes."

Marcel and Alexander finished their inspection and entered the terminal.

"Good morning Herr von Hesse. We'll be ready to go as soon as Alex files our flight plan and Jacques gets back."

"Good, Marcel. It's going to be a long day. I hope you had plenty of rest."

"Thank you, sir, I did, but since we're going to exceed our mandatory flight hours limit today, we'll need to pick up two relief pilots in Zurich. They typically fly our smaller craft, but both are qualified in the 50."

"Do I know them?"

"Yes sir, they flew you down to Malta in the 10 for that conference last year while the 50 was in for its annual inspection."

"Oh yeah, I remember. Nice guys."

Jacques returned with two boxes from the caterer. Alex returned from flight operations.

"We have a slot out at 10:30 if we hurry," Alex said. "They start to fill up with scheduled flights at 10:45."

"Okay, we'd better hustle," Marcel said as he led the party down the stairs to the tarmac.

Five minutes later, with all three engines roaring, Marcel came on the intercom.

"We've been given a wheels-up in ten minutes. Buckle up and get ready for a mad dash to the runway."

The winds had shifted, and the east-west runway was now active. Dietrich could see the Hotel du Palais below as the sleek craft lifted off. It seemed ages since he had dinner there, just

85

three nights ago. The plane banked to the left taking a southerly leg out of Biarritz to avoid the incoming traffic, as it changed patterns due to the runway shift. They passed over Bilbao at 5,000 feet. Like a giant kaleidoscope the sun flashed off the multiple angles of the jumble of titanium and glass that is the Guggenheim. It really is a beautiful city he thought. He also thought of Maria. What would her priest counsel?

"Fasten your seatbelts," Marcel said. "The Gulfstream that just passed overhead said the turbulence south of Geneva is pretty severe. I tried to change our route, but air traffic control said conditions are bad all along that weather front, so we're stuck with it."

Jacques gathered up the dinnerware and cups then took his seat. The first air pocket over Bern dropped the plane fifty feet. Dietrich had been flying in all manner of weather for years, but he never got accustomed to that powerless feeling in the pit of his stomach.

Twenty minutes later the Falcon 50 was past the front and began its descent into the Zurich airport. Lake Zurich passed below as Marcel banked for a westerly approach into *Flughafen Zurich.*

Dietrich could see the flapping red cross of the Swiss flag atop the Sagarin headquarters tower in Hinkel. He would go there immediately to deliver their data package, before going home. His car was waiting on the airport apron as Dietrich exited the aircraft. He turned to Marcel who was descending the stairs.

"What time should we leave in order to arrive at SFO at nine a.m.?"

"About ten p.m., allowing for a one hour stop in St. John's."

"Okay, have her gassed up and ready to go. I'll be here."

"Yes sir, we'll be ready."

The drive to Hinkel was only ten minutes. David Weiss had gathered his researchers in the conference room,

"Hi David, I see you're ready for me."

"Yes sir. We're anxious to see what you've brought from Bilbao."

"They've put together some pretty impressive programs for blood analysis and matching. I think they may be ahead of what we've done. Here's the package, both hard-copy and software."

" Great. We'll get on it right away. We're anxious to see what it does, together with the algorithms from SciGen."

"Any word from Rob on his CRISPR glitch?"

"His latest communiqué indicates progress but no solution. By the way, he went to see Rupert yesterday. He says they will take him off the ventilator today and see how he does. Dr. Askew is concerned that if he stays on the machine too long it may do permanent damage to his esophagus and airways."

"Yes, I spoke to Therese on the flight over from Biarritz and she said the same. If he can breathe on his own they'll gradually bring him out of his induced coma."

"By the way," David added, "the recombinant DNA work that Baxter Labs was working on was included in their $30B sale to Shire, Plc. Shire is relocating their European headquarters from Ireland to the old Siemens' complex between Zurich and Zug. Their decision was heavily influenced by the fact that Amgen, Biogen, Gilead and several other pharmas have established their continental rDNA operations there. I called a friend of mine from my Oxford days who worked for Baxalta. That was the Baxter name for the division Shire bought. He is making the move from Ireland. I knew they were doing some work on rDNA for factor VIII. He said that project will now be in Zug. He invited me down to look at what they're doing. I have to sign a non-disclosure, but since we're not doing any recombinant work here it should be okay."

"I'm not sure that what Rob is doing at SciGen might not impinge on their work," Dietrich said. "Better check that out with him before you sign anything, and give the lawyers a heads up."

"Right, I didn't think about that. I'll talk to Rob. Maybe you can mention it to him tomorrow when you see him."

"I will, and drop him an email about what they're doing at Shire. I'll discuss it with him. Copy me."

"Will do."

"Anything else?"

"I believe that gets you up to date with everything we've done since you were here last week," David said.

"Good. Go through that data dump right away and be ready to sit in on a conference call with Rob and his guys tomorrow afternoon, California time. I know it'll be late here, but this is important. I want everyone on the same page when I get back to Bilbao."

David looked at the men around the table and nodded.

"Everybody got that?"

"Yes sir, we'll be ready," they echoed in unison.

"Check your supply of amphetamines before you come to work tomorrow," David said jokingly. Several of the crew smiled, having had the same thought.

Dietrich had called his and Therese's parents from the hotel in Bilbao and asked them to meet him at his home in downtown Zurich. Friedrich von Hesse and Dietrich's mother Frieda lived only thirty miles away on a mountain lake. Therese's parents lived in the village of Altdorf at the southernmost tip of Lake Lucerne. Ten years ago, Walter Fostberg retired as a vice-president from Aldi, the large grocery chain headquartered in Essen, Germany. He and Emma moved to Altdorf to be near Therese and their grandchildren.

There were two cars in the driveway when Dietrich arrived home. He recognized the vintage Mercedes touring car that

Friedrich had driven for 35 years. The Audi 6 sedan parked behind it belonged to Walter Fostberg.

Dieter and Elise heard the garage doors opening and rushed to greet their father. The distress of the past few days was etched in their faces.

"Oh, Papa I'm so glad you're home," Elise wailed as her pent-up tears began to flow.

"It's okay my pet, Rupert is going to be all right," he said, more to reassure the terror-stricken girl than to express a confidence he didn't feel.

"Hello Dieter, how are you holding up?"

"I'm okay, I guess. We've been really worried. Mom calls every day to keep us posted. She tries to sound cheerful, but you can tell she's concerned."

"I know. I'm sorry she's had to bear the brunt of this. I'm trying to marshal every force possible to help your brother. I just brought some information to the researchers at Hinkel that may help. I'll be taking the same package to California when I leave tonight."

"I know you're doing everything possible," Dieter said, "but it's still scary being so far away and not being able to do anything for Rupert."

"Just as soon as he's able to have visitors, I'll fly you guys over to see him. Promise. Now where are your grandparents and Maxim."

"They're waiting in the living room. They wanted us to see you first."

"Is everyone all right?"

"They seem to be. Grampa Walter is as grouchy as ever and Gramma Frieda is complaining about her back. Nothing's changed."

"Good," Dietrich smiled, "Let's go join them."

Maxim had already poured brandy and schnapps for the grandparents when the three walked into the room.

"Looks like everyone has made themselves at home," Dietrich laughed. "I'll have one of those Napoleons Maxim. It's been a long day and it's going to get much longer."

"Welcome home sir. You do look a little haggard. Maybe you'll have time for a swim and sauna before you leave."

"That sounds great. I'm putting it on my schedule for before dinner."

Dietrich took the snifter from Maxim and sat down in his easy chair with his head lolled back. He stayed that way for a few seconds before sitting up and surveying the room.

"I don't have to tell you that Rupert's condition is very serious, but you need to know that what we're doing for him is going to pull him through."

He said this with the same bravado he had affected when he reassured Elise, still obscuring the dread of Rupert's situation. He continued by describing all the steps being taken and all the people engaged in the process. When he finished both Frieda and Emma questioned him about Therese and how she was handling all this. Dietrich did his best to dispel their concerns. He explained that she had skilled medical support around the clock and Rupert was getting the best possible medical care. When the questions stopped, he turned to Maxim.

"What's for dinner tonight Maxim?"

"Madeleine told me she was preparing *Tournedos Rossini* with roasted potatoes and asparagus in honor of your return. Everyone on the staff has been on edge, jumping every time the phone rings, At least for today the pressure will be off a little."

"Thanks Maxim. I'll speak to them before I leave." Dietrich leaned back once again, closed his eyes, and savored the tartly smooth liqueur.

He pulled himself out of the pool and toweled off. Twenty laps had him breathing heavily. He entered the sauna and poured water on the glowing coals. The burst of steam and hot air entering his lungs eased the tension in his body. Lying on the

90

teak bench with a folded towel beneath his head, Dietrich drifted off in languorous release. He was awakened by a light tap on the glass door.

"Sir, you've been in there for twenty minutes. I began to worry."

"Thanks Maxim. I'll be right out."

Dietrich emerged from the sauna with the appearance of a boiled lobster.

There was a darkened mood around the dinner table, all thoughts attuned to a hospital bed in faraway California. Dietrich wiped the sauce from his mouth and rose from the table.

"I'm leaving now. Thanks for coming in. I'd appreciate it if you would take turns staying with the kids until this is over. I didn't ask you earlier because I didn't want to burden you. But seeing how happy they are to have you around has changed my mind."

"It's the least we can do," his father said.

"We'll be glad to," Walter Fostberg echoed.

"Good. I'll feel better knowing you're here." Dietrich said as Maxim handed him his brief case.

Maxim Eisner had been with the family for ten years. Therese swore she could not run her household without him.

"Henri is waiting in the garage, sir. He has your luggage. I packed a few extra items since we don't know how long you'll be gone this time."

"Thank you, Maxim."

-15-

Vitorio and Maria Elizondo Vega's casa in the Barrika neighborhood of Elexalde looked down on the meandering Nervión River as it flowed from Bilbao to the Atlantic. On a clear day the cathedral spires of the city were visible among the glass and steel towers. The craggy coastline west of Barrika meandered north around the rocky headlands of San Valentin to the small, private beach below Muriola and on to the Playa de Gorliz.

On her dark days, Maria strolled among the rocks and boulders below Barrika. The roar of the ocean crashing onto the shore had a calming effect that drowned out the troubles of the day.

On her bright days, she hiked down to Muriola and exulted in the bracing waters of the Bay of Biscay. She would lay for hours on the sand embracing the successes and clearing the thousand distractions of the day.

Occasionally she stopped on the way back to kneel and cross herself in the vestibule of the chapel of Iglesia de Santa Maria. The small church's origins dated back to 1052, and it has welcomed the faithful ever since. Maria had often considered moving her membership from St. Francis to Santa Maria, but she couldn't bear the thought of leaving Father Giuseppe. He had officiated at her confirmation, heard her thousand confessions, and had guided her through the many crises of her life.

The filigreed confessional screen at St. Francis slid back with a loud click. The priest, Father Giuseppe, could make out the familiar silhouette of Maria Elizondo.

"Good morning my child, have you come to confess?"

"Bless me Father, for I have sinned. My last confession was three months ago."

"What are your sins, my child?"

"I have neglected my religious duties. I have looked upon another man with carnal thoughts. I have coveted. I am troubled. I am sorry for these and all of my sins."

"For your religious laxness attend Mass without fail for three months. For the carnal thoughts pray to Mary for release. For covetousness give extra to the alms collection. For your troubled mind make an appointment to see your priest."

"God, I am heartily sorry for having offended you, and I detest all of my sins because I dread the loss of Heaven and the pains of hell; but most of all because they offend you, my God, who are all good and deserving of my love. I firmly resolve with the help of your grace to confess my sins, do penance, and to amend my life. Amen."

Maria left the confessional booth and crossed to the church offices beyond the sacristy. She waited outside Father Giuseppe's office for twenty minutes until his last confessor was heard. The stooped figure shuffled down the corridor. He stopped when he saw Maria and placed his hand on her head.

"Come in my child and unburden yourself. I have seldom seen you look this troubled."

Maria followed him into the small cubicle he had occupied for over thirty years. Fr. Giuseppe had been asked many times to accept a higher position in the church. He always refused.

"God wants me to be here among my suffering people as a parochial vicar. He has placed it upon my heart that I must minister to the people of my city; the sick, the bereaved, the hungry, the troubled. This is my place and with the blessing of the church, this is where I wish to serve."

This was the simple response he gave each time, and each time the diocese saw fit to grant his wish. Fr. Giuseppe is the longest serving priest in St. Francis' history.

"What is troubling you so Maria that you come to St. Francis at seven in the morning to give confession."

"I hardly know where to begin. I discovered yesterday that Vitorio is seeing another woman. I didn't know where to turn. I can't speak to my friends about it."

She twisted the handkerchief in her hands and gazed at the crucifix on the wall behind Fr. Giuseppe's desk.

"What does Vitorio say?"

"I've only talked to him on the phone. He's in Madrid on business. One of my employees saw him at the airport yesterday. He was with Sophia Suarez. She's an acquaintance of ours. I've seen her at several parties. I had no idea they were seeing each other behind my back. He complains that I'm married to my work and have been neglecting him."

"Are you, and have you?"

"I don't think so. I've tried to be a good wife. I haven't ever been unfaithful. I've been attentive to him." Maria blushed. "I know that we've not made love as often lately. I assumed it was just the pressures of business. Both his and mine. Obviously, there was more going on."

"Have you noticed any changes in Vitorio?"

"Aside from being less attentive, his mood has changed. I don't know if it's out of guilt or for some other reason."

"What have you noticed?"

"He's quicker to lose his temper and he's been curt with my friends and acquaintances. We were out to dinner two nights ago and he became very rude with the client I was hosting."

"Is he having business problems?"

"None that he has talked about. A few months back he said something about landing a *whale* investor. He was very excited. I asked him what that meant. He said there was a bond

94

trader in London who wanted to make a big investment in Bilbao and he asked Vitorio to help him."

"Did the business deal come through?"

"Yes, just a few weeks ago. This trip to Madrid has something to do with it. Goldman Sachs' Spanish headquarters is in Madrid. Vitorio represents them with a select group of high-wealth clients in Bilbao. I don't understand much of what he does, but he mentioned something about making a big play in "credit default swaps" for several wealthy Bilbao real estate investors. Since then his mood swings have been more pronounced."

"I'm sorry I can't help you there, Maria. My knowledge of high finance is confined to the offering plate," the Father chuckled. "What will you do now?"

"I don't know yet. Vitorio will be home tonight. I guess we'll try to talk it through. I don't think I want a divorce, but if this is just the tip of the iceberg...I don't know."

"Divorce should be your last recourse Maria. Breaking God's covenant of marriage is viewed very seriously by the church. Listen to Vitorio and determine if the marriage can be saved on acceptable terms. If you think it can't, then come back and we'll talk. And ask Vitorio to see me."

The Clinica Hematologia Basque, SA was a beehive of activity when Maria arrived later that morning. Diego Baranaga and Alantso Zubiri were huddled around a computer in the conference room.

"Good morning," she said as she walked in, "what's up?"

"Miguel Ortega's secretary called and said we could search the health records in all seven Basque districts. He will issue a directive to that effect after we supply some key information."

"What information?"

"He wants to know the names of the seven technicians doing the searches. He wants a copy of any record we take from

95

any patient file. He wants a list of what particular blood factors we are looking for."

"None of that should be a problem except maybe the blood factors. He may put two-and-two together and realize we have an ulterior motive. Tell him we are looking for certain blood types that exhibit rare Rh factors that affect blood clotting. If he wants more specificity, I'll go over and talk to him.

"Alantso, has Rubio selected his specialists for the search?"

Rubio Salazar was Maria's head of Internet Technology.

"Yes. He gave me a list of names this morning. I made a copy for you." He handed her a sheet of paper.

The list contained five men and two women. Maria was happy to see Inez Figueroa's name. She had mentored Inez through the University of the Basque Country's engineering program in computer science. She came to the Clinic directly from the school and had excelled in her work. Her promotion to supervisor in the coding group came three months ago.

"Who will make the assignments?"

"I will, together with Rubio," Alantso said.

"Good, have them on my desk this afternoon."

"Yes, ma'am."

Her cell phone rang.

"Hello."

"Maria, it's Dietrich. I'm getting ready to leave for California, I gave the documents and software to Dr. David Weiss at Sagarin, He will call you tomorrow after his team goes over the information. I will give the other package to Rob Simpson when I land. He'll have someone meet me at SFO to pick it up. Then I'm going to see Rupert. Have you heard from your friend on the search?"

"Yes. He has authorized it; however, he wants certain information from us before we can start."

"What kind of information?"

"Mostly innocuous stuff. He does want to know specifically what we are searching for though. I've told my guys to say that it's specific blood types with certain unique clotting factors. If that doesn't satisfy him, I'll go over and talk to him personally."

"Good. It probably doesn't mean anything, and I don't know what he'd do if he knew the full truth. But, it's probably better if he doesn't know we're going to ask these people to cooperate with our study. That might raise a few hackles."

"I'll be as vague as possible," she said. "He has no reason to believe we'd do anything dishonest. We have a very clean record and have cooperated with his agency several times when they needed forensic expertise."

"Okay. Any movement on the Vitorio front?"

Maria's sudden intake of breath gave away her surprise at the question. She walked into her office and stared down at the river before speaking.

"I went to see Father Giuseppe this morning."

"I figured you did when you weren't in the office. What did he say?"

"What I expected. He says we should try to work it out, that the church frowns on divorce, to come back to see him if we can't. He also wants to talk to Vitorio. I don't know if Vitorio will go. He hasn't been inside a church for years. Pretty much given up on religion."

"Well good luck. If you need another shoulder to cry on after you talk to him, give me a call. I don't know how much I can help but I'd be a neutral party you can vent to."

"Thanks Dietrich, I'll remember that. I hope you find Rupert much improved and that SciGen can make heads or tails of our research. Call me when you head back this way."

"I will."

What a mess, she thought; Dietrich may not be quite the neutral party he thinks he is.

16

Miguel Ortega's offices were on the eighth floor, behind the polyhedral, sloping, glass façade of the Basque Health Department headquarters. The building, like the Guggenheim, is a statement to the world that Bilbao has arrived. The Coll-Barreu design rises up and back from the street corner like the slopes of the Matterhorn, hardly an orthogonal surface in sight. The two, seven floor adjunct structures, built earlier, extend back on both streets from the majestic corner glass tower. Heritage zoning restrictions dictated the odd footprint.

Maria entered from Avenida Recaldi. The attendant at the information desk directed her to the eighth floor, accessible only from the rear elevators. The view, rising through the multilayered, wildly angled façade, was dizzying. The architects created an extremely functional interior within a very idiosyncratic building.

"Good morning," the secretary said brightly, "may I help you?"

"Yes, I am Maria Elizondo. I have an appointment with Dr. Ortega."

"Oh, yes. He asked that I show you right in."

Maria followed the stout, matronly woman down a short corridor where she tapped lightly on the door to Miguel's office.

"Come in," Miguel Ortega replied in the deep baritone she remembered.

"Maria, how wonderful to see you. What's it been, two years?"

"I believe so," she said, "it's criminal the way we get so wrapped up in our own worlds that we forget to keep in touch."

"I know. How is Vitorio?"

"He's fine," she lied. No point in starting any rumors. "How's *your* family? I saw where Alicia had another boy. How many's that, four?"

"Yes, they're all doing well. I understand your business is booming. I've signed off on several requests for your services recently."

"Yes, it's doing well, and I truly appreciate your business."

Following a few more social pleasantries, Maria finally got to the nub of her visit. She began to explain her request for access to the Basque Health Service's patient records.

"As you know Miguel, much of our work is for private companies seeking information for their businesses. Most of them are insurance related or pharmaceutical manufacturers. We also get a lot of business from hospitals and universities. Recently we had a client who is doing research on rare blood disorders. Their research pointed to this area of Spain as having the population most likely to manifest such disorders. They asked us if we could help them find patients with those particular blood anomalies."

"I am aware," Miguel observed, "that the Basque community has a population that exhibits a much higher rate of Rh-negative blood types—more than twice that of the rest of the world—so may I assume their interest lies in that direction."

"You may."

She knew Miguel was very bright and intuitive but was surprised that he reached this conclusion so rapidly.

"Your representatives have assured me," he added, "that any data collected will be held anonymously, and in strict confidence, and that anyone contacted will be guaranteed anonymity."

"That is correct. As we responded to your request, all data collected will be made available to your office and the names of any contacts will be sent to you with signed affidavits of consent."

"Will there be a *quid pro quo* for this agency? I have a responsibility to the taxpayers to see that their money is being spent wisely."

"I understand. I assure you that your ministry will receive full credit for your contributions to any advances in hematology that may result from this study. I might add, that as an incentive, the sponsor of the study has committed to underwriting up to five scholarships in medicine at the University in the name of the health ministry."

"How very generous." He smiled before adding, "You wouldn't be inclined to name your sponsor would you."

"They have requested to remain anonymous until all studies are complete and have been published in the appropriate medical journals. They want to establish their intellectual property rights prior to such publication."

"Understandable. I imagine this whole process will be very expensive, and if it only results in an orphan drug, not exceedingly lucrative."

"Yes, Miguel, they are aware. Their stated primary motivation is to save lives in an area of medicine that they feel is underserved. Let's just say the principal considers this venture to be philanthropic in nature— giving back if you will."

"Very well Maria. Having known you and worked with you for many years I know you are possessed of the highest integrity and I know you will not permit anything unethical on your watch. Just keep me informed."

"I certainly will, Miguel and thank you."

"You're welcome. Give me a ring sometime. We're long overdue for a dinner out with our spouses."

"Thanks, I'll put it on my calendar."

She knew full well that was not going to happen under the present circumstances. Maria saw herself out. The brightness of the sun reflecting through the countless glass panels of the façade was startling. She shielded her eyes as she walked out into the street and hailed a cab.

On the ride back to her office she began planning her next moves. Immediately, she needed to assemble the seven computer technicians and give them their marching orders. Accounting would need to be alerted to their travel requests and expense money requirements. Rubio needs to prepare a plan of action for them to follow when they arrive at their health office locations. He also needs to design a reporting algorithm that will filter out non-conforming records. Knowing Rubio's legendary efficiency, she knew he would already have coders at work.

"Anna, call Rubio and the *four horsemen*, she said to her secretary as she brushed by into her office. "Ask them to meet me in the conference room at eleven."

Maria had begun referring to the four doctors on the Sagarin team as the *four horsemen*, as in Revelations. It seemed somewhat appropriate in view of their apocalyptic outlook for the project. After all, they were only attempting to find a cure for a disease that had baffled men of medicine for centuries—and to complete it in a few days.

"Dr. Ortega has consented to our proposal to search the health system's patient records," she said when they had all gathered, "He was adamant that everything we do must remain anonymous and that his agency be copied on any files taken from the system. I assured him we would comply and that we would obtain signed approvals from any patients we contact before interviewing them. She turned to her IT manager.

"Rubio, we'll need a protocol for searching the files and for filtering out the non-conforming patients. We'll also need a standard reporting system for the *seven dwarfs*." She chuckled. "If you guys are the *four horsemen,* then they can be the *seven dwarfs.* We can use a little levity around here to counteract all the serious crap that's going on."

"Yes, Dr., I'm already working on it," he said, thus confirming her previous thoughts.

101

"Diego, Alantso, Paulo, Paskal, do you have anything to report."

"I have been trying to find any instances of hematological events that may have precipitated seizures like the von Hesse boy had," said Paskal. "I have turned up three in the last ten years that correlate with his case. I am studying them to see if there is anything of use to us."

"Great, Paskal, where do you stand?"

"I should have a report for you by tomorrow morning."

"Okay, great progress. What about you Paulo?"

"The conclusions by Dr. Askew that Rupert's hemophiliac bleeding after the Zermatt fall may have been triggered by the anesthetic *etomidate* and the von Willebrand reaction by *Lornoxicam* are intriguing. I'm trying to see if there is some organic chemical connection between the two drugs that would affect the *thalamus* and possibly cause a seizure."

"What have you found?" Maria asked.

"So far nothing concrete, but I've reached out to some old associates who are doing some research for me."

"You didn't tell them why you're looking, did you?"

"Oh no, I told them I'm looking for information for a paper I'm doing. No worry. Besides, these guys are pretty circumspect within the community."

"Good. Diego, anything?"

"Not much I can do until we get some candidates in place. I've followed up with Mikel and he's ready to go. I thought I'd go into the field with him, maybe pick up some pointers on sleuthing in the real world."

"Alantso?"

"I've been researching all kinds of records on both hemophilia and porphyria since they seem to stem from the same mutant genes. I'm trying to get a fix on why certain types of people are susceptible to these diseases, what genetic accidents occur to produce them, even back to Transylvania with its vampire and werewolf legends. Turns out those conditions all

102

derive from the same aberrations in their ancestral genes. There are indications that *heme,* the naturally occurring compound that is released at an injury site, can inhibit FVIII coagulation if produced in excessive quantities. I want to know what causes the excess and its mechanism for clotting inhibition."

"Any conclusions?"

"Not yet, but I've got some of our associates digging through the literature to see if we can come up with answers. I'll put together a report tomorrow."

"Wonderful! It seems everyone is gainfully engaged on the problem at hand. The *seven dwarfs* will hit the streets tomorrow and hopefully we'll have our first candidate shortly thereafter. Okay, back to work everyone. Rubio, please stay."

"Rubio," she said when the others had left. "will you be ready to send the techs out tomorrow?"

"Yes, the algorithms are nearly complete, and the search protocols are ready. Everyone should be in place by the end of the day. I'll conduct a brief training session early in the morning. They should be on their way before noon. They all seem to be very excited even though they're not sure of the purpose of the work. Word is out about Señor von Hesse's visit, so they've guessed it's for Sagarin. Beyond that they're in the dark."

"Thank you. I always know I can count on you. By the way how is your daughter Cassandra doing?"

"She's much better. It turns out the virus wasn't meningitis but some other bug that causes similar symptoms."

"I'm so glad. Give your family my best. I look forward to seeing them again at the company picnic this year."

"Thanks, I'll get back to the computer lab now. Hafta finish up the loose ends for tomorrow."

Maria puttered around her office reading reports and signing papers. Finally, at five o'clock her concentration gave way to thoughts of Vitorio. She turned off her computer, closed the files, placed them on Anna's desk and left the office. She dreaded what was coming but knew she had to go home—and face the possible dissolution of her marriage.

17

For the second time in a week the Falcon 50 lowered its wheels in preparation for landing in San Francisco. The prevailing winds were from the northwest today, putting runway 19R into play. From his seat on the left of the plane Dietrich looked down on the newly completed Levi's stadium at the south end of the bay. Further west he could make out the small triangle of office buildings where SciGen is located. He would go there later today. First, he would see Rupert and Therese and consult with Dr. Sterling Askew.

The same black Mercedes as before met the plane, its driver taking possession of the data package. Its twin was parked nearby for Dietrich. The second driver handed the keys to Dietrich and rode shotgun back to Los Altos.

The morning rush hour traffic had eased by the time Dietrich pulled onto US-101 south. He was at the Oregon Avenue exit to Stanford in 25 minutes. The same *praying mantis* gantry was still shuffling materials to the top of the hospital addition when he pulled into the Stanford University Hospital parking lot. This time he locked his Sturm pistol in the trunk. He wasn't likely to need it in the Stanford environs.

Therese was dozing in the recliner next to Rupert's bed when Dietrich entered room 477. A nurse checked the readings on a monitor and keyed them into her I-pad. She looked up as he entered the room. He put his fingers to his lips. No need to wake Therese. He beckoned to the nurse to follow him into the bedroom.

"Hi, I'm Dietrich von Hesse, Rupert's father. How is he this morning?"

"I'm Henrietta Holmes, Rupert's morning nurse. He had a restful night and hasn't had any more bleeding episodes for 48 hours. Dr. Askew is due at eleven. He said if there were no more episodes he would take your son off the ventilator today and if he does well for 24 hours he'll bring him out of the induced coma."

"That's great news Ms. Holmes. Thank you. How about Therese, has she gotten any rest?"

"Last night was the first time she slept through. Mrs. Kolmes, the nurse I relieved at six, said she seemed more rested than at any time since she got here."

Dietrich looked at his watch. It was a few minutes after ten. He decided to take a chance that Dr. Askew was in his office.

"When Mrs. von Hesse wakes, tell her I was here, and I'll come back with Dr. Askew."

"Yes sir, I will."

Dietrich tip-toed out of the room and crossed over to the cardiovascular building. The door to room 227 was slightly ajar. He could see Askew at his desk. He tapped on the open door.

"Mr. von Hesse, come in. Your wife said you'd be in this morning. That's why I scheduled the patient visit at eleven."

"I got in a little earlier than I expected. The headwinds across Canada were mild last night. I thought we could catch up before we see Rupert and Therese. She was sleeping when I went by the room and I didn't want to disturb her."

"It's good that you did. Rupert is doing okay but he's a long way from being out of the woods. We've started him on choline supplements. They seem to have raised his factor VIII levels a small amount, and believe me, any increase is a help"

"The nurse says you're going to try to take Rupert off the ventilator today."

"Yes, I think the dangers of taking him off are less problematic than the risks of damage to his esophagus and

106

airways due to the intubation apparatus. I'll ease him off and if he can breathe on his own without laboring too much, we'll leave him off for 24 hours. If he's holding his own after that I'll bring him out from under sedation. Then we just need to monitor him closely and be ready to re-introduce the ventilator if needed.

"What is happening on the other fronts," Askew asked, "here, in Zurich and in Bilbao?"

"I assume Rob has been keeping you informed as well as he can. His guys are closer to making a successful CRISPR splice in the chromosome location he thinks controls the factor VIII production. He's not quite there yet. The team in Zurich got their package from Bilbao yesterday and is studying it for application to their work. I delivered the same package to Rob this morning. I'd like to get together with both of you after he's had a look at it. Maria's researchers have done some groundbreaking work in typing, analyzing and manipulating blood genetics, much like what Rob has been doing."

"So, they're into CRISPR work as well?"

"Yes, it seems every little storefront lab in the world has hopped on the gene-splicing bandwagon."

"I guess that's a good thing," Askew said, "as long as the technology isn't used for unethical purposes."

"You're right, but we both know there are people in the world that will always take the path of least resistance to a fast buck."

"Sadly so," the doctor agreed.

Therese was awake when Dietrich arrived with Dr. Askew. She ran to him as he came through the door.

"Oh, Dietrich, I'm so glad you are back. I didn't know how trying it would be to watch our son struggle for his life."

He held her tightly and allowed her pent-up motions to drain out. When she stopped shaking he held her at arm's length.

"I couldn't be any more proud of you. I knew what tough fiber you were made of, but I never knew you were this tough.

107

Both the nurse and Doctor Askew attest to the fact that you are a real trooper."

"I guess a person doesn't know what they are capable of until the chips are down," she said. "Anyway, I'm glad you're here to shoulder part of the burden. I'm looking forward to a dinner away from the hotel."

"Everyone I talk to raves about a restaurant near Fisherman's Wharf called *Gary Danko*. If Rupert is doing well tonight, I'll see if we can get a reservation."

"I've had dinner there once, and I can tell you they are not wrong," Dr. Askew said. "All the waiters dress in tuxedoes."

Two of Dr. Askew's associates entered the room to prep Rupert for the removal of the ventilator. They administered drugs to ease his anxiety and slow his pulse. When they were satisfied with all his vital signs they turned to Askew.

"He's ready."

"Dietrich, you and Mrs. von Hesse might want to leave the room for this," Dr. Askew said. "Sometimes the patient's reactions to breathing on their own may be frightening to the uninitiated. Give us ten minutes or so and we'll call you back in. Maybe you can grab a cup of coffee. We'll call you if there's a need."

"Thank you Dr. Askew. The nurse has my cell number. Have her call us when you are ready."

"I will. Just relax for a few minutes."

The dark circles under Therese's eyes were more pronounced in the fluorescent light of the coffee shop. Dietrich ached for her.

"Tell me the truth, Dietrich, can Rupert survive this?"

He looked deeply into her eyes and summoned all his courage.

"Yes, he can, but it is going to take the combined skills and super-human efforts of many people. At this moment at least forty experts in various medical specialties are working as hard and as fast as humanly possible to find an answer for Rupert. If it can be solved, I'd bet on this team to do it."

That was as far as he felt he could go in reassuring Therese without raising her expectations beyond reality. The teams needed time and they needed luck—two commodities currently in short supply.

Dietrich leaned his elbows on the table and stared down into the untouched latte, awaiting the call. At fifteen minutes his fears overcame his resolve.

"I'm going back to the room. This is taking too long."

"Then I'm coming with you," Therese said.

"No, stay here, I'll come back as soon as I know something."

Dr. Askew leaned over Rupert with his ear near his lips, the ventilator apparatus pushed aside. The two assistants scanned the two monitors attached to Rupert on various parts of his body. Askew saw Dietrich enter and motioned him over.

"He's breathing on his own, but his breaths are rather shallow. We're backing off some of the relaxant drugs and putting him on oxygen."

Nurse Holmes wheeled a portable oxygen generator alongside the bed as one of the doctors inserted a cannula in Rupert's nose.

"Pure oxygen will make it easier for him to breathe. His vitals are holding steady, but I'd like to see his pulse rate a little higher. That'll come with the lowered depressants."

"Is he stable enough for his mother to come back in?" Dietrich asked.

"I think so." Askew said, "Bring her in."

Therese was blankly staring into the distance when he got back to the table. She turned at the sound of his approaching footsteps and wiped away her tears.

"Is he...?"

She couldn't bring herself to finish the sentence.

"He's breathing on his own. Dr. Askew is cautiously optimistic that he can stay off the ventilator for now. Come on, you can see him."

Therese entered the room cautiously, not knowing what to expect and fearful of the worst. It was the first time in a week that her son's face was not obscured by cords and tubes. He looked so pale and helpless—but he was alive—and breathing on his own. She took his hand and caressed it. She thought she felt a slight response. Was there, or was it her wishful thinking?

"Best let him rest for now," Dr. Askew said. "He's been through quite an ordeal. We'll know a lot more about his condition in 24 hours.

"Why don't you two plan on that dinner tonight? He's in good hands."

"Thanks, doctor," Dietrich said. "Therese can use a break. We haven't had any time alone for over a week. I can catch her up on everything that's going on."

The buzz of a cell phone interrupted their conversation. Dr. Askew reached into his inside coat pocket. He looked at the caller ID and motioned for Dietrich to follow him into the hallway.

"It's Rob. I'll put him on speakerphone.

"Hi Rob, Askew here, I have Dietrich with me. I'll put you on speakerphone."

"Rob? Dietrich. Did you get the package?"

"Yes, we've spent the last few hours dissecting it and plugging the software into our system."

"What do you think?"

"They've discovered something that eluded us. I think it may solve our telomere problem."

"That would be a big step forward," Dietrich said, while Askew was nodding agreement.

"If you'd like I can run up there this afternoon and go over it in more detail."

"Good idea. I was going to come to Los Altos but that will save me a trip. They just took Rupert of the ventilator, so I need to hang around for a while. Come on up and the three of us can meet in Dr. Askew's office next door."

He looked at the doctor for approval.

"That will be fine," Dr. Askew said. "I have a brief conference call at 2:30. See if you can make it around four."

He looked at Dietrich.

"That okay?"

Dietrich nodded assent.

"I'll be there," Rob said.

Askew went back to his office and Dietrich re-entered Rupert's room. In the brief time he was away there was a noticeable improvement in the boy's color. Therese was still sitting by the bed holding Rupert's hand.

"He's coming back," Ms. Holmes said. "His color's improved and his breathing is deeper. He's not totally out of the woods but if he continues to improve, with no more bleeding or seizures, I'm pretty sure the doctor will bring him out of the coma tomorrow."

Dietrich walked over, placed his hand on Therese's shoulder and gave it a slight squeeze. She looked up with a wan smile and placed her hand on his.

"I'll be going down to Dr. Askew's office for a meeting with Rob at four. When I get back we'll check in at the Stanford Park across the street. Then we're going to dinner in the city. I'm sure Rupert will be in good hands with Ms. Holmes and the other personnel until we can get back."

"Yes indeed," the nurse said, "it'll do Mrs. von Hesse good to get away for a few hours, and you'll only be a phone call away."

Rob Simpson was coming down the hall when Dietrich stepped off the elevator. They walked together to Askew's office. One of the doctor's interns was leaving as they arrived.

111

"Come in, come in, I was just finishing up. Have a seat, would you like something to drink?"

"I'm fine," Dietrich said.

"So am I," Rob echoed.

"All right then, let's get to it. What is it you've discovered in the Bilbao package?"

"There are spacer DNA elements linking the segmented chromosomes in the Rh-null blood samples we have been using. We've always known they were there but didn't understand their purpose or how they affected the splicing model. These spacers have been contaminated with various viruses that in some way nullify the splicing action. When these viruses are disturbed during the splicing procedure they become active and some migrate to the telomeres. The damage they cause leads to a severely limited life span for those chromosomes."

"I see," Askew said, "so there is no longevity in the treated cells."

"Correct. Within minutes after the splicing process is complete the cells start to die off. Dr. Elizondo's researchers have figured out how to neutralize those viruses and prevent their migration. As soon as we applied their findings to our splicing protocol we were able to replicate the Rh cells with factor VIII intact."

"What does that mean for a hemophiliac?" Dietrich asked.

"In the more common blood types, it means we can generate factor VIII cells within donated hemophiliac Rh-negative blood and then re-introduce it into the patient's blood stream to aid in the normal clotting process?"

"Will that work for Rupert?"

"Not entirely. It will help, but he has the added complication of being Rh-null and having the von Willebrand 2n disease. That's why we need to find the right person on which to test the new protocol and see if we can refine it to work in patients like Rupert."

"This means you've taken a step forward," Dr. Askew said, "but the finish line is still a way off."

"Exactly!"

"What next, Rob?" Dietrich implored.

"We'll keep pressing forward with the new information to see if we can achieve the needed results without the *golden blood*. But we can't count on that breakthrough. We still need to find that *knight in shining armor* out there somewhere—Rh-null, von Willebrand 2n, and a hemophiliac. It's a tall order."

Dietrich looked crestfallen. He had hoped beyond hope that the information from Maria would be enough. It wasn't.

"Well, back to the drawing board Rob," Dietrich said. "Have you sent your results to Zurich and Bilbao?"

"The guys back in Los Altos were putting the information together when I left. It should be in their hands by now."

"Dr. Askew, what else can I do?" Dietrich asked.

"Pray and keep working. I like what Maria's man said about the drug interaction in the *thalamus.* There might be something there we can work with on the seizures; if not for Rupert, maybe for others. I've also got some ideas for dealing with his seizures should they arise again. I've got several of my top associates looking into it."

"Rob have you talked to Zurich since you discovered the splicing fix?" Dietrich asked.

"By the time we discovered the solution it was too late there. We'll talk first thing tomorrow. They'll have out report by then."

The three kicked around a few more ideas before running out of gas.

"Well I'm going to fetch Therese and we're checking in at the Stanford Park Hotel. I'm taking her to dinner at *Gary Danko."*

"Outstanding!" Rob Simpson said. "You'll really enjoy it. I'm staying for dinner with Sterling. There are some other projects we're working on that need some clarification. Call me tomorrow when Rupert regains consciousness. Good luck and enjoy the evening."

The Stanford Park radiates understated elegance. Situated on the tony strip of El Camino Real between Menlo Park and Palo Alto, it has risen quickly to pre-eminence among the upscale hostelries sprinkled along the mid-peninsula. The brick and shingle structure, though relatively new, evokes old New England charm and durability.

Dietrich turned into the courtyard. He handed his keys to a valet as a formally dressed doorman retrieved their luggage and followed them in to registration. Dietrich gave him the room keys and they followed him up to their room. He checked that everything was prepared for their arrival, accepted the gratuity, bowed, and discreetly left.

The immediate focal point upon entering the door of the Stanford Suite was the dramatic four-poster bed, draped in white fabric and accented with gold cord. It dominated the room. The luxurious bath and commodious sitting room definitely played second fiddle to the bed. Therese kicked off her shoes and flopped, spread eagle, onto its plush covers.

"No offense to the hospital and its convenient bedroom in Rupert's suite, but I have so missed my comfortable bed."

"Luxuriate to your heart's content my love, but I'm taking a long soak to see if I can wash off the accumulated grime of the past six days."

The sunken tub and the mineral salts worked wonders for Dietrich's body as well as his psyche. After twenty minutes, he toweled himself dry and donned the plush terry robe before re-entering the bed chamber.

Therese had not moved from her flopped position. She lay in sweet exhaustion, all cares removed for the moment. Dietrich tip-toed to the sitting room, where he sat facing the television. He turned it on and pressed the mute button. He activated the closed-captions and switched the channel to CNN. CNN was the one constant for news in the world of international travel.

"...and the explosion in San Sebastian came out of the blue." intoned the correspondent from Madrid. "It was totally unanticipated since the Basque separatists agreed to a truce and surrendered their weapons in 2011. The ETA has been dormant since then.

"The blast occurred outside a service entrance to the Hotel Anoeta located across the street from the Anoeta Stadium, home to the Real Sociedad football team. Tonight's game with Real Madrid has been cancelled. The visiting team was scheduled to check in to the hotel at three p.m. The explosion occurred at 1:30. It is unclear whether the blast went off prematurely or was only meant as a message to the Madrid authorities. The only casualty was a hotel worker, emptying trash. She received non-life-threatening shrapnel wounds to her back.

"The government is hesitant to ascribe the attack to ETA until their investigations are complete, but local leaders in Bilbao say it has all the earmarks of the separatists and they are at a loss to explain the sudden and violent resumption of hostilities."

Dietrich frowned. I hope to God this doesn't impact our efforts in the Basque territory, he thought. He picked up his cell phone and dialed Maria Elizondo.

-18-

Maria was startled awake by the classic ring of the antique bedside phone. It was a gift from her mother when she and Vitorio moved into the Barrika house. She lifted the heavy ivory handset from its cradle. She glanced at the other side of the bed, suddenly cognizant that Vitorio was gone.

"Hello," she rasped into the phone. Her voice was deep and husky from the previous night's shouting and crying.

"Maria, are you all right?" Dietrich asked, alarmed at the sound of her voice.

"Not really. Vitorio and I had a vicious fight when he got home last night. He stormed out of the house at midnight. I don't know where he went but I can assume he's curled up in bed somewhere with Sophia Suarez."

I'm sorry Maria. Is it over?"

"I don't know for sure but after last night I have to believe it is."

"Anything I can do?"

"You still have that shoulder I can cry on."

"You bet. I'll be bringing it back to Bilbao tomorrow."

"Good, but I'm sure you didn't call to listen to my marital soap opera."

"No. I just saw on the news about the bombing in San Sebastian. What's that all about?"

"No one is quite sure just yet. The ETA has been quiet for several years now. No one is certain what set them off—if it is

116

them. There's speculation that it might be a copycat group that has an axe to grind with Madrid. If so, the *Euskadi Ta Askatasuna* makes a perfect cover. That's the ETA's name in Basque. Loosely translated It means "Basque Homeland and Liberty" in English. It's hard to believe they would break the truce. They extracted nearly every concession from the government, short of total autonomy, and that's not going to happen without all-out war."

"Do you see this having an impact on what your people are doing in the field?"

"I don't think so unless the uprising spreads to other areas in the Basque nation. Naturally, all government offices will be on high alert and there'll be increased security. The health ministry will certainly put on more guards and I imagine the government in Madrid will reinforce the *guardia civil* in the area."

"When do the techs start scanning records?" Dietrich asked.

"Tomorrow morning at nine. Everyone is prepped and ready. We should start getting our first inputs in 24 hours."

"What is your expectation?"

"It's hard to say Dietrich. The specificity required for an exact match is daunting. There may be several, there may be none. What's the latest on your son?"

"He was taken off the ventilator today and is breathing on his own now. The doctors plan to remove the sedation tomorrow, if he continues to do well. I've got my fingers crossed."

"I plan to see Father Giuseppe again tomorrow," Maria said. "I'll ask him to say a special prayer for Rupert and I'll throw in a few more Hail Marys and Our Fathers."

Thanks Maria, I appreciate your concern. On a lighter note, I'm taking Therese to San Francisco for dinner. She's been under so much strain this week. She collapsed on the bed as soon as we checked in and still hasn't awakened. I have my phone in the bathroom, so I won't disturb her.

117

"Oh! I forgot the most important news. Rob Simpson and his men plugged your software into their CRISPR protocol and were able to effect the gene-splicing without damaging the telomeres. That's a major breakthrough. Thanks to you and your guys for that."

"That's wonderful news. How does that affect Rupert's treatment?"

"Rob says it's a giant leap forward, but we still need to find someone with what they've started to call the *Golden Blood.* That's why I almost panicked when I saw the news item about San Sebastian. Anything that sets back our search could be devastating."

"We'll do our best to find it. When will you be back?"

"I'll leave here tomorrow afternoon. That will put me back in Biarritz sometime tomorrow. I'll call you when we are a couple of hours out. I'll be anxious to get an update. I'll rent a car and drive down to Bilbao. I hear Therese stirring in the other room. Talk to you tomorrow, and again thank you."

"You're entirely welcome. Good luck with dinner and tomorrow's events. Good night."

"Good night Maria, and good luck with Father Giuseppe."

It was only six and they were dressed and ready for dinner. Reservations were made for nine.

"Let's go down and have a drink by the pool," Dietrich suggested.

"That sounds lovely," Therese said.

She had just got off the phone with the evening nurse.

"The nurse says Rupert is resting well and continuing to breathe more easily. I so pray that he will be all right when he comes out from under the drugs."

"So far, so good. Just relax and try to enjoy the evening."

"I'll try, but taking my mind off him is not easy."

118

The sun was disappearing behind the cedars lining the streets atop Sand Hill. The evening air began to take on its inevitable chill as the fog rolled over the foothills above Portola Valley. Revelers from the Silicon Valley Science and Technology Association gathered in small knots around the fire pits. This was the last day of their conference on climate change and its effects on coastal regions, especially the lower Bay Area. Three engineers from IBM's facility in San Jose and two invitees from the Manassas, Virginia chip plant, were bemoaning the mammoth reorganization of the company. None were sure what the Gods of Armonk were going to do to their lives. Three rounds of Gentleman Jack, and the future looked less ominous.

The von Hesses settled at the pit farthest from the main building. The young couple they joined was not part of the convention crowd. They were on their honeymoon. They scooted over to give the new arrivals room closer to the fire.

"Hi, I'm Andy Cloud and this is my new bride Miranda."

"I'm Therese von Hesse and this is my husband, Dietrich. Are you on your honeymoon?" Therese asked.

"Yes, we were married last weekend in San Diego," Miranda said. "We had planned to go to Maui, but Andy had to be back for the orals on his PhD dissertation this week. It was scheduled for later in the month, but his advisor must be out of the country during that time. So, we just decided to come back up to Stanford and splurge our Hawaii money here at Stanford Park."

"I take it you're a student at Stanford, Andy," Dietrich said.

"Yes, I'm getting my doctorate in microbial and viral genetics."

"How ironic. My company has a small genetic engineering laboratory in Los Altos; SciGen.

"I've heard of them. They came to one of the job fairs. I was scheduled to interview with them, but my dad got sick that week and I had to go home."

"Have you secured a position yet?"

119

"I have two offers, one is in Boston and one is at NIH in Washington. They're both good opportunities, but we'd like to stay in California, preferably the Bay Area. Miranda is from Santa Rosa."

"Here, take my card. Give SciGen a call and ask for Dr. Rob Simpson. Tell him we met and I asked you to call."

"Gee, thanks. That's mighty nice of you, What's the parent company's name?"

"Sagarin Pharmaceuticals."

Andy looked at the card and title.

"You mean you're the head of Sagarin. That's awesome. They're huge in the medical world."

"Guilty as charged," Dietrich said sheepishly as the waiter brought their champagne.

The awe-struck grad student was speechless, but Miranda was not.

"Mr. von Hesse, that's so kind of you. The thought of staying in the Bay Area, not to mention Silicon Valley, is unbelievable."

"You realize of course that I will not make any decision about SciGen's employment. That will be up to Rob and his team. I'm opening the door; the rest is up to you."

"Still, it's such an amazing gesture on your part. You don't know me from an alley cat and, yet you would introduce me to SciGen's president."

"This is not totally altruistic on my part. You see, Therese and I have a seventeen-year-old son lying in an intensive care bed down the street at Stanford Hospital. He suffers from hemophilia, von Willebrand's disease and to top it off, he is an Rh-null. Everyone at SciGen, Sagarin and Stanford are laboring to help him. I don't want to see any other parents have to go through this ordeal. So, maybe Andy Cloud can help to unlock the secrets that cause such a condition."

"Oh, I'm so sorry Mr. von Hesse. I pray they will find an answer."

120

"Thank you, Miranda. Keep pushing this guy," he pointed at Andy, "to be the finest genetic biologist in the world. We need him."

"I will," she said.

Dietrich and Therese finished their champagne and rose to leave.

"We're letting Therese have a night off from sitting by Rupert's bed. We're having dinner in the city. Good luck on your orals Andy, and good luck in your career. You too, Miranda."

"Thank you again," Andy said, "and I hope everything turns out well for your son. Those are an awful combination of ailments to strike a single individual. I've never run across a case like that in my studies."

"No one else in the world has Andy. As someone said, Rupert hit the trifecta, only in the worst sense of the word. Good night."

Dietrich steered the Mercedes onto US-101 north toward the city until it merged into Van Ness. At North Point it was just three blocks to the iconic restaurant where there was absolutely no parking available. A valet took the car away to some hidden corner of Fisherman's Wharf.

Zagat's gushing review of the restaurant seemed over the top until one stepped inside and experienced the food, the service and the ambience. Just don't look at the tab when you hand the waiter your credit card.

Dietrich had been told that the local Dungeness crab was the dish to order. There was none on the menu. Out of season the waiter said. Oh well, skip to the other coast and have lobster. Therese opted for the scallops. Both were done to perfection. The LeFlave Batard Montrachet was the ideal pairing.

"And for dessert sir?" the waiter inquired.

"Not this evening, thank you, I'm taking my wife down the street to the Buena Vista. I've raved so many times about their Irish coffee that she insisted we go there tonight."

121

"Good choice sir, thank you for dining with us this evening and do come back. I'll be right back with your check."

Dietrich paid, and the couple walked out onto the street.

"Would you like your car sir?'

"Not just yet. We're going down to the Buena Vista for coffee. We'll pick it up later."

"Very good sir. It'll be waiting."

Thanks."

A Hyde Street cable car rumbled past on its way to the carousel at the bottom of the hill. A few casual tourists strolled through the shops and galleries that were still open. The Buena Vista was jammed. The young woman at the reception desk looked around.

"The only seats available are two stools at the end of the bar."

"Perfect," Dietrich said, "I want my wife to experience the real Buena Vista."

Dietrich ordered two Irish Coffees, made with Tullamore Dew Scotch, along with two slices of cherry pie with vanilla ice cream.

Deidre sipped her coffee and spun her seat toward the window.

"What a lovely experience," she said, "let's come back here again when Rupert is well."

"It's a date."

The drive back to Menlo Park was subdued. The brief evening's distraction began to fade. Both their thoughts returned to their son.

"Tomorrow will be a big day," Therese said with a touch of sadness. "I wonder how much Rupert will recall of what happened?"

"The last thing he'll remember is that giant larch looming in his way—assuming he even saw it."

It was near midnight when the black Mercedes pulled into the Stanford Park driveway. A few hardy, alcohol tolerant revelers, refusing to let go of their four-day California idyll, still lounged around the pool area. One young woman, in an obvious moment of over-exuberance—or anger—pushed one of the men into the pool. He came up spluttering and cursing. She took off for her room.

Despite the tension and concern both Therese and Dietrich fell asleep within minutes of their heads hitting the pillow. The frenetic activity of the week had caught up with both of them. Neither awakened until his cell phone jangled at 6:30. He grabbed for it, immediately awake, fearing the worst.

"Hello,"

He could tell the voice on the phone originated from a distance. He relaxed when David Weiss came on.

"Sorry to wake you so early sir, but I wanted to get the news to you as quickly as possible,"

"What news, David?"

"We evaluated the information from Bilbao, and also received the report from Dr. Simpson. With that input we have uncovered a definite connection between the two seizure-triggering drugs *etomidate* and *lornoxicam* and their effect on the *thalamus.* We haven't isolated the exact mechanism that triggers a seizure, but we think we can find it with this added information. CRISPR technology is certainly opening up new approaches to solving old problems."

"That's great news David, any other information in all that data that stands out for you?"

"We haven't had time to totally evaluate everything. We got so excited about the *thalamus* implication we dropped everything else and concentrated on that."

"Rightfully so! Have you assigned other members of your team to follow the other lead?"

"Of course, there's so much information to decode. We've got twelve people working on it."

"Keep at it. Call me if anything else pops up. We'll be at the hospital most of the day. They took Rupert off the ventilator yesterday and they're going to bring him out of his induced coma this morning. Keep your fingers crossed."

"I will sir and good luck today."

The buzzing phone and Dietrich's stifled conversation with David nudged Therese from her deep sleep."

Who was that?"

"It was David from Zurich."

"Why is he calling so early?"

"They believe they have a breakthrough on one element of Rupert's condition."

"What?" she asked, suddenly wide awake.

"Between what Rob found in the Bilbao data and his research, they may have a clue as to what caused Rupert's seizure—and hopefully a way to prevent future episodes."

"That's wonderful, but does that…wait! What Bilbao news. What is Bilbao?"

"I'm sorry; I neglected to tell you about that. That little jaunt I took to Biarritz wasn't about Aquitania."

"What then? You said you had dinner with Sergei."

"I did. What I didn't tell you was that our dinner companion was Dr. Maria Elizondo. She's president of a blood research company in Bilbao. They have been doing groundbreaking work in the typing, analysis and treatment of blood disorders."

"Why would you need to go to that far away corner of the world to find such expertise?"

"Bilbao happens to be ground-zero for the population most likely to produce the person or persons we are looking for."

"I don't understand. Why there?"

"It's a long story, but suffice it to say, a confluence of events over the last 2,000 years resulted in a population in the Basque community that is twice as likely to produce the blood types we are seeking as anywhere else in the world. And, finding a world-class hematologist like Dr. Elizondo, smack-dab in the middle of that, is pure serendipity. As a matter of fact, it was her work, together with Rob's, that allowed David's researchers to discover the *thalamus* trigger connection."

"I gather there's more to the story than what you just told me," she said sardonically. Therese von Hesse is not only beautiful and intelligent, but intuitive.

"Yes. Maria's people, together with some others she's hired, are launching a search, as we speak, to find suitable candidates for our research."

"Does that mean you'll be going back there?"

"Yes. Tomorrow."

"Don't you think you should be here with your son in this crisis?"

"Yes, I do, but I can't do that and also try to find a cure for his condition. There's nothing I can do here that will move the needle forward. There may be nothing there either, but I have to try. I can't sit here and wait for Rupert to die."

The mere mention of her son dying sent Therese into paroxysms. Dietrich held her until the racking sobs slacked off.

"How can you even say that? Our son is *not* going to die!"

"That's exactly why I must go. To make sure he doesn't."

19

Maria arrived home at 5:30. She didn't expect Vitorio until seven or eight. She poured a glass of chilled Albariño. She walked out onto the terrace and settled onto a chaise. She lay back and gazed out towards the sea. The sun was a blazing orange ball resting atop the sea cliff, patiently waiting for God to throw the switch. The light was just beginning to fade. She decided to walk out to the headlands of San Valentin to listen to the waves and clear her head. She finished her wine, slipped on her walking shoes, and exited through the back gate.

Unlike with the Faro de Gorliz across the way, no lighthouse exists to warn unwary sailors of the shoals of San Valentin. Over the centuries, countless seafarers have foundered on those jagged rocks—a tiny archipelago of up-heaved sentinels standing stolidly as isolated defenders of the Basque homeland. It is an isolation that Maria understands deep in her soul and one with which she feels a connection, especially today.

The seclusion of the rocks also appeals to the multitude of sea birds that feed in the breakers. They have few predators to fear because of the natural moat surrounding their citadel. Maria loves to watch as the gulls and terns swoop and dive into the sea, emerging with silvery splinters writhing in their beaks. She was witnessing Darwin's principal in its rawest form. Her thoughts turned to Rupert von Hesse. Was he just a very rich and sheltered pawn who could no more resist the process of natural selection than those silvery fish. Maybe, but those fish don't have a team of scientists fighting to snatch them from the beaks and talons of the sea birds.

The sun was setting across Biscay as Maria arrived back at her casa. She glanced at her watch. Vitorio would be arriving in less than an hour; that is, if he still plans to come at all. She went into the kitchen. She had skipped lunch. She took an empanada from the refrigerator. It was left from last night's take-out. She popped it in the microwave, set the temperature, and poured a glass of sangria. When the timer sounded she went back to the patio, ate the empanada, and waited; for what, she wasn't certain.

She heard the crunch of tires on the crushed gravel driveway. She didn't hear the garage door rising. He doesn't intend to stay. The kitchen door swung open. Vitorio could see Maria on the patio. He walked toward the French door and stepped out into an awkward silence. Who was going to speak first?

"Well, where do you want to start?" Vitorio finally spoke.

"Why not with, 'What the hell were you thinking?'" she said plainly, no rise in pitch.

"Where to begin. I first started seeing Sophia six months ago, right after the Figueroa dinner party. It was a casual get together for lunch one day. It just blossomed from there."

127

"Why, Vitorio?" she wailed, "I've never been unfaithful to you. I thought we had a relatively happy marriage. Sure, we've had a few problems but none that I thought were that serious."

"No!" he shouted. "Do you remember the time I asked you to go away with me to Ibiza for a few days and you were too busy, or the time I asked you to go to London with me and you said you were tied up, or the dozen other times you were otherwise occupied?"

"Yes! I remember!" she exploded, "But do you remember that I was trying to establish myself in a man's world! That's not easy for a woman. Especially in Spain, where a woman's place is still in the home. A woman can't just drop what she's doing and fly off to Xanadu on a whim and hope to succeed in her career. You'll remember that's why you decided not to have any children. We were both too busy. Thank God we didn't."

"They weren't whims to me. I was trying to get us back to the time when we were first married, to recapture the romance. Do you know the last time we had sex? Three months ago. Every time I suggest it, you're too tired or you're waiting on a call. I finally gave up, and then Sophia was there. I'm sorry, but a man has needs."

"I'm sorry too, Vitorio, but that doesn't excuse your infidelity. Why didn't you talk to me?"

"I'm not looking for excuses. Those are just the facts."

"Are you going to continue to see her?"

"I don't know. It depends."

"On what?"

"Jesus! I don't know. She's waiting for a commitment from me before she tells Ronaldo."

"And I'm supposed to wait around until you two decide which way the wind is blowing? Well no thank you! You can pack your bags and get out. When you come to your senses, call me. As of this moment I don't care if I never see you again."

Vitorio turned on his heel and banged the French door open. Sounds of tinkling glass and slamming closet doors were

128

followed by the peppering of gravel against the front windows as he sped away.

20

Dietrich pulled his car into the Stanford Hospital parking lot at nine a.m. It was nearly full of the cars of other visitors, some of whom would leave joyously with newborns in their arms; some with sheepish young children, their arms and legs in casts; and for others, they would leave with the terrible knowledge that their loved one was never coming home again. Dietrich said a silent prayer that he would not be included in that latter group.

The morning nurse was bathing Rupert when they arrived. Therese was alarmed at the paleness of his skin and the protruding ribs that just days ago were sheathed with sinew and muscle. Dietrich's reference to dying came flooding back. She turned and buried her face in her hands. Dietrich stood helplessly, fighting back his own tears.

"How was his night. Mrs. Holmes?" he asked, not knowing what else to say to comfort the grieving mother.

"Mrs. Cassidy said he slept well, only rousing briefly around three. There was a small amount of blood in his urine, but the doctor didn't seem alarmed. He said it is residual blood from his earlier injuries."

"Have you heard from Dr. Askew this morning?"

"His office called to check on Rupert's vitals. They said, based on the readings at six, that they would go ahead with the suspension of the induced coma. We began weaning him off the sedatives an hour ago. He is expected to be responsive to stimuli by ten. Dr. Askew is expected before then. One of his assistants is on his way up."

"Have you participated in this kind of procedure before Mrs. Holmes?" Therese asked.

"Oh yes, many times."

"What should we expect?"

"It varies from patient to patient and from injury to injury. In Rupert's case he'll probably begin responding to stimuli such as a pin prick within a few hours, but don't expect him to open his eyes and say, 'I'm back.' Sometimes it takes two to three days for a patient to be fully aware and fully responsive. The biggest danger is that in a semi-conscious state they may thrash around and try to remove the IV tubes and catheters. We'll restrain his arms initially to guard against that,"

"When do you think he'll recognize us and try to communicate?"

"I wouldn't expect that before tomorrow at the earliest, and since he had some brain trauma it may take longer. The human brain is an amazing organ and we still do not fully comprehend all its workings. But it also has an amazing capacity to heal itself, so in time he should regain full cognition."

"Thank you," Therese said. "That helps. At least we now have some idea of what to expect."

The door swung open and an orderly wheeled in a cart loaded with a sundry collection of medical paraphernalia. He saw the terrified look on Therese's face.

"Don't be alarmed." he said, "this equipment is always brought in when we bring a patient out. The doctors prepare for all sorts of eventualities but, thankfully they're seldom needed."

Seconds later a young resident came in. He greeted the parents and went immediately to Rupert's bedside.

"And how are you today Rupert. Can you hear me? If you can, squeeze my hand."

There was no response.

"We really don't expect any tactile response this early. Sometimes we do begin to get pain response."

131

Dr. Carmody moved to the foot of Rupert's bed and raised the sheets, exposing his bare feet. He took a small probe from his pocket and jabbed it gently into Rupert's left foot. There was a slight retraction.

"That's good. We know he's responding to pain, so we can expect other stimuli to begin to take effect over the next 24 hours. So far, so good, but I caution you not to expect a rapid return to normalcy. This young man has been through a lot of trauma and it'll take a while for his brain and nervous system to re-adapt to the world. Add in the insult to his system by the hemophilia and the von Willebrand disease, and the barriers to recovery are compounded."

"Are there any indications of permanent brain damage?" Dietrich asked.

"We've been running electroencephalograms throughout his stay and we don't detect any abnormal brain function. That doesn't mean that there isn't any, but we're pretty sure he's in the clear on that front."

"That's a relief," Dietrich said. "Hemophilia and broken bones can be managed but repairing a broken brain is a problem of a much higher order."

The doctor looked up at Dietrich.

"Are you a physician?" he asked.

"Oh no," Dietrich said, "I'm tangentially involved with medicine, but no, I'm not a doctor."

"May I ask how?"

"I run a pharmaceutical company and I've become familiar with some of the medical terminology. But, by no means am I an expert."

"What company is that?"

"Sagarin."

The young resident looked at Dietrich with renewed respect.

"That's incredible. We use Sagarin products on a daily basis. Many of our most difficult liver cancer cases will only respond to Nephritone. I'd say you have more than a passing acquaintance with our profession."

"Right now, I'm only concerned with how well acquainted you and Dr. Askew's team are with Rupert's case. I don't know how much Sterling has told you about the research that's going on at this moment to find a solution for Rupert's predicament."

"He has alluded to it, but not in any great detail."

"I truly appreciate what all of you are doing for my son," Dietrich said. "Our problem is that none of the drugs and none of the existing technology are ultimately going to save him. It's going to take an almost miraculous breakthrough to do that. Meanwhile we're depending on you and your colleagues to keep him alive until that miracle happens."

"I assure you Mr. von Hesse that we will do our best to have him ready for that miracle cure."

"Thank you, Dr. Carmody, that's all I can ask."

Dietrich waited for Dr. Askew before leaving. He watched as the doctor read all the records from the night before doing his own survey of Rupert's condition. He removed his stethoscope from his chest.

"Well Dietrich, everything seems as normal as can be expected considering what this young man has been through. His response to pain is a good sign. I expect Dr. Carmody went over with you what you can expect for the next few days."

"Yes, he and Nurse Holmes were very helpful. Should I have any concerns about leaving Rupert for a few days?"

"I don't think so. My team will continue to monitor him closely as he withdraws from the sedation. I don't foresee any major problems. We have to be alert to any bleeding, both external and internal. We are constantly in touch with the blood registry to be sure we have access to Rh-null blood, should we need it. I say that to emphasize how critical it is to develop an alternative supply. The known population of nulls in the world is small and shrinking. There were 49 five years ago. We don't

133

have an accurate census now, and the demand for their blood is outstripping the supply."

"I'm well aware Sterling. Nothing else could pull me away from here but the knowledge that I may be able to help find that new source. Rob is still fine tuning his approach to the promising gene-splicing technique he's working on, and Zurich is focusing on techniques to prevent seizures arising from abnormalities in the *thalamus*. And Maria's team is beginning the search for the man with the *golden blood*. That's where I'm going next. I want to be as near the action as possible in case there's anything I can add. Besides, I can't sit around and twiddle my thumbs. Therese is going to keep our room at the Stanford Park. It's not good for her mental state to be cooped up here with Rupert 24 hours a day."

"I agree. My wife has asked me to invite her over for dinner."

"That's very kind of her. Thank her for me. I'm going to fly my parents over in a couple of days to be with her for a while. I feel so guilty leaving her alone. The kids will be out of school for vacation soon. I promised them I'd bring them over. They've been really bummed out with this whole thing."

"Understandable. Don't worry about things here. We'll continue to ride herd on Rupert and make sure he's prepared for your medical miracle."

Dietrich headed up Sand Hill road when he left the hospital. He had one stop to make before heading south to SciGen.

Benny Alexander was huddled around a table with several of his co-conspirators at Argos Venture Capital. They were examining the scale-model mockup of a new office building. One of their most successful venture investments was planning a new headquarters building on their campus in Cupertino. They were running it by Argos for approval. The $100,000,000 price tag required it.

"Dietrich, good to see you. We're going over plans for Calypso's new office building. Take a look."

"I like the classic lines, not so much steel and glass," he said.

Benny introduced the Calypso team to Dietrich von Hesse. They were all aware of how much their success was due to investments from Banque von Hesse of Switzerland.

"Gentlemen, I'm in a bit of a hurry, so pardon me if I borrow Benny for a few minutes. I promise to have him back to you shortly."

"No problem, Mr. von Hesse. Take all the time you need."

Calypso's president, Tom McAndrew, wasn't about to upset the man who had made it possible for him to be there.

"Benny," Dietrich began as soon as they were in his office. "do you have any connections at Goldman Sachs."

"Sure, what kind of connections?"

"I need some inside information on one of their boutique investment partners in Bilbao, Spain."

"What kind of information?"

"The firm is called *Investimento Basque, Ltd.* It is owned by one Vitorio Elizondo Vega. He handles private clients for Goldman in the Basque region who want to deal with a small local firm but still want the backing of a big firm like Goldman. I want to know how his company is doing. I especially want to know if he is trading in credit default swaps."

"Man, that's pretty esoteric for a small house. What do you know?"

"Only that his whole disposition changed shortly after he went to London recently. He started talking about catching a "whale." His wife is Maria Elizondo. She runs a blood research company in Bilbao that is doing work for me. She confided in me that Vitorio has been cheating on her and that his whole temperament has changed in the past few months. She doesn't know I'm asking you to do this, so keep it *sub-rosa* as much as possible."

135

"Sure thing. The only 'whale' I'm aware of is that guy in the London office that got J.P. Morgan Chase in deep trouble a couple of years ago. He ran up accounts in the billions that crashed when some smart hedge fund guys on Wall Street caught on and bought the other side. When his investments went south, Morgan lost billions and any Ahabs riding that 'whale' went down with him. Dietrich, If this requires an onsite investigation am I covered?"

"Yes, but with the fortune I've made for you, that seems a little cheeky."

Benny turned red and began stuttering.

"I'm s-s-sorry Dietrich, I wasn't thinking. Of c-c-course I'll do it gr-gr-gratis."

Dietrich burst out laughing.

"Just kidding Benny. Do what you need to do."

"Whew!! You got me good that time," Danny said with a relieved smile. "How soon you need this?"

"Yesterday."

"I'm on it. How is Rupert?'

"They took him off sedation this morning so we're waiting to see how he responds. I'm heading to Bilbao tonight. You can reach me on my cell if you need anything."

"Right, and by the way, my guys are looking at two startups in the Valley. They're into Artificial Intelligence—AI. That's the next big thing. Elon Musk has ponied up $50,000,000. If he's smelling smoke, there must be fire. They're looking for 25 large ones from us. I'll include you in if we cut the deal. I still have 250 mil in the bank for you from our last two deals. We should have a prospectus out in a couple of weeks."

"Keep me informed. Don't pull the trigger until I have a chance to review it."

"Wouldn't think of it."

Dietrich rose to leave.

"Good luck on the trip, I hope that Rupert will be okay." Benny said.

"So do I, Benny, so do I."

Rob Simpson was in the lab. He and several associates were huddled around Everett Swenberg, who was staring intently into an electron microscope. Swenburg was Rob's go to guy for the CRISPR technology. At that moment he was introducing a novel Cas9 protein into a blood cell to determine its effects on the collocated factor VIII and vWF. The anticipated outcome would preserve the fVIII and vWF pairing, allowing both factors to coexist in the blood stream until needed at an injury site to provide clotting.

Simpson looked up as the door to the atmospherically controlled room opened. He was ready with a stream of invective for the unauthorized entry but stopped, mouth agape, when he saw Dietrich.

"Sorry Mr. von Hesse. We try to minimize entry to this room. It's a class 3 clean environment. Please put on these booties and a mask and cap."

"I'm sorry Rob. No one was outside; and I saw you through the glass."

"I'm sure it's fine. You'll find this interesting. Everett is attempting for the first time to splice proteins into a hemophiliac AB blood cell. The idea is to add snippets of a certain protein into the DNA chromosome sequences containing the factor VIII and factor von Willebrand to force them to maintain cohesion until they are called on to provide clotting at the injury site. If this works, we hope to resolve the von Willebrand 2n disease syndrome. That will be a major step toward achieving sufficient clotting agents. The next hurdle is goading the production and binding of factor VIII protein in sufficient quantities to stop hemophilia A. It should work for factor IX as well in hemophilia B patients.

Dietrich shook his head.

"You remember when I said I would tell you when I reached overload conditions."

137

'Yes."

"We're there."

"Come on, let's go to my office," Simpson said.

The two men dropped their contaminated clothing into a burn bag on the way to Rob's office.

"How was Danko's last night?"

"Fantastic, although I had to substitute Maine lobster for Dungeness crabs. I was looking forward to them."

"Yeah, too bad. Wrong season."

"The lobster was excellent, and I took Therese to Buena Vista afterwards."

"What did she think?"

"She finally got a good measure of the American scene. Of course she's been to the States before but there's a unique perspective that one can only get in San Francisco."

"I agree, that's why no one has been able to lure me away. How's Rupert?"

"They're taking him off sedation today. So far, so good. The docs say it'll take a few days before we have a firm grasp on his condition."

"You still going back to Spain?"

"Yes, I'm leaving this afternoon. I want to be in Bilbao by noon tomorrow. We should have our first reports from the field by then. I've got my fingers crossed. So much is riding on them."

"I know. I'm encouraged by what we've come up with so far. I feel it in my bones that we're onto something here."

"I hope so. Get this data to Zurich and Bilbao right away. There may be a key to what they are doing buried in there. Meanwhile we'll keep beating the bushes for you. It would be unbelievable if we came up with a treatment for hemophilia, von Willebrand's and thalamus generated seizures all together. Probably too much to ask for. Right now, I'll settle for a few grams of factor VIII protein in Rupert's bloodstream."

138

Dietrich was fastening his seat belt for takeoff from SFO when his cell phone rang.

"Hello."

"Dietrich, its Sterling Askew."

"What's wrong?" Dietrich shouted above the roar of the engines.

"Rupert began bleeding in his esophagus where the tubes had irritated the lining. We got it under control with coagulants without having to do a transfusion. We administered a pint of O-negative sera. There was a mild reaction but that has subsided. We'll have to place a drain tube in his trachea to siphon off the blood until the bleeding completely stops. If blood builds up in the lungs he could contract pneumonia, which might prove fatal in his condition."

"As you can hear we have just taken off. Should I come back?"

"Medically, I don't think it's necessary. I believe he will be fine in 24 hours. Family wise, I don't know. Would you like to speak with your wife?"

"Yes."

Therese came on the line.

"Hello Dietrich."

He could hear the fear in her voice in just those two words.

"I'm so sorry. Bad things seem to happen whenever I leave. Do you want me to turn around?"

He could hear her breathing into the phone and he knew she was struggling with her answer.

"No," she finally said, "I wish you could be here with me, but I know what you are trying to do is more important for Rupert. Just hurry, my darling, please hurry."

The desperation in her cry broke his heart. Now it was his turn to waver. Should he go back for her sake; should he go on for Rupert's?

"If I come back and later find I could have done something to make a difference, neither of us would forgive ourselves. Be

139

strong, my love, for both of us, and for Rupert. I'll call you at your hotel later this evening."

21

Inez Figueroa drove her tiny, red, Fiat 500 into the parking garage at Universitario Donostia in San Sebastian. The car was a gift from her father upon graduation from the University of the Basque Country's Technical Engineering School. She graduated with a degree in Computer Science, with honors, third in her class.

Inez had sowed a few wild oats in her high school years. She rebelled against her family's constraints and was headed for bigger trouble. Iñigo Figueroa knew that Inez idolized his friend, Maria Elizondo. He asked Maria if she would take his obstreperous daughter on as a project. He thought she might listen to Maria—and she did. Maria persuaded the high-strung girl to become serious about her education. She held out the added carrot of a possible position at Clinica if she did well.

Donostia is the largest public hospital in San Sebastian and serves nearly all of the northwest Basque region. The large campus sprawls across a hillside overlooking the Real Nuevo golf course, less than a mile south of Anoeta stadium. It handles most of the area's emergency patients and indigent population. It also houses the Basque Health Ministry's computer records center for the San Sebastian area.

"Good morning," said Juan Battista, the manager of the computer center, "you must be Inez Figueroa."

"Yes, I drove up from Bilbao this morning."

"We received an email from the ministry yesterday saying we should expect you today. Their only instructions to us were to give you access to our patient records and to report back any information you record and take away; also, any names of patients you propose to contact. Can you tell me what this is all about?"

"I work for *Clinica Hematología Basque*. We have a client who wanted to piggy-back on some work we were already conducting for the ministry. They are looking for patients who have particular blood types for use in their research into some unique blood disorders."

"Hmm, that sounds intriguing. Have you done anything like this before?"

"No. I've only worked there a couple of years. I work mostly on blood analysis algorithms and spectroscopy decoding systems."

"That sounds like very interesting work, compared to what we do. We're basically a digital library for medical records. Occasionally we're called on to do some programming but not often. Most of our computerized records systems are off-the-shelf programs. We recently converted to the Abraxas Electronic Medical Records system. It has a module for hospitals and one for clinical practices, so now all ministry doctor's records will be fed automatically into our collection system. Private practice doctors can opt in to the system, and several have. I understand Abraxas is being installed throughout the seven health ministry locations."

"Was that not the case in the past?"

"No, there were a variety of programs being used by the clinics. Some automatically downloaded their records daily. Others that didn't interface electronically to our system would send in their records on CDs or thumb drives once a month. Needless to say, that led to a lot of confusion for anyone trying to find current patient records."

"Does that mean that some records I access in my search may not be completely up to date?"

"I'm afraid so, but if that happens, come see me and I'll help you."

"Thank you, Señor Battista."

"Call me Juan. It sounds like we'll be seeing each other often the next few days."

"Yes, well I'm ready to get to work if you'll show me where to sit."

Juan led Inez to a cubicle in the corner of his office. It was pre-arranged with a terminal to interface the records system."

"I prefer you use this computer, and not your laptop. Come to me with any records or documents that you wish to copy or send back to your office and I will clear it."

"Great, thank you. Am I already logged in?"

"No. I will log you in and out each day. Security and privacy are paramount. Our clients rely on us to protect their records from unwarranted use—not that I think you would misuse it, but safety is the best policy."

"I completely understand."

Juan pulled a small key from his pocket and inserted it into the computer interface and pressed the red button alongside."

"There you go. You're on line. The interface is pretty standard GUI. If you have any problems give me a shout."

Inez looked at the home page that came up. She entered her personal information and the six-digit code Juan gave her. The next screen popped up.

"How may I help you Inez?"

"Wow, that's pretty neat. I think I've got this now."

"Good, call me if you need me," Juan said, and walked back across the room to his desk.

Inez typed in a few instructions and a choice of forms paginated on the screen. She selected the one that asked her to input key words for searching.

'Hemophilia' she typed. Immediately, she was presented with a list of patients that had hemophilia and had used the ministry health service in the past ten years. There were 223 names on the list. She then typed in hemophilia, male. The list of names was pared to 193. She opened her briefcase and took out the folder she had been given by Rubio. She began to type in the other blood indications they were looking for; blood type, Rh type,von Willebrand factor and factor VIII identifiers, plus a host of other markers defined by the SciGen and Zurich researchers. She pressed enter and the list dwindled to 42. Finally, she entered Rh-null and the screen went blank.

Inez knew from her work at Clinica what an Rh-null was. She herself had never encountered any work involving that particular blood type and was not aware of its rarity. She found it strange that there was not a single Rh-null in the San Sebastian database.

She fired up her laptop and logged on to the hospital's Wi-Fi network. She entered Rubio's email address and waited for the electronic handshake.

"Señor Salazar, I have uncovered 53 male names with all the required blood traits except Rh-null. What should I do? Inez Figueroa."

While she waited she decided to go for tea.

"Señor Battista, I thought I would get a cup of tea. Are you free to join me?"

"Juan, remember? It's a little early for my break," he said, looking at his watch, "but why not?"

He led her through a maze of hallways to a cafeteria with outdoor seating. They took their drinks out into the sunlight. There were tiny figures far below swinging at indistinguishable objects in the grass. She knew nothing of the sport of golf. Juan knew even less.

"How's it going?" he asked.

"I'm not sure. I came up with 53 men who have all the desired attributes but one."

"What is that?" he asked.

"Are you familiar with the international blood typing system—A, B, O and Rh."

"Somewhat."

"Well, nearly everyone in the world is identified by a combination of those blood factors. However, there are a very small number who do not have an Rh designator in their blood. They are called Rh-nulls. At the last count there were only 49 known Rh-nulls in the world. The combination of factors we are looking for includes Rh-null. There were not any in your computer data base."

"Considering their obvious rarity, is that surprising?"

"I guess not, except that there are twice as many Rh-negative types in the Basque areas of northern Spain and southern France than anywhere else in the world. We expected that there would be some nulls amongst that population. I'm disappointed that there are not any."

"What now?" he asked

"I've emailed my boss with these results and asked for further instructions. I expect to have a response when we get back."

"Let me know if I can help?"

"Thanks, I will."

The red light on Inez' computer was blinking when she returned.

"Send the 53 names and their records. Rubio"

Inez waited for Juan to hang up his phone before entering his office.

"Señor Battista…"

"Call me Juan, remember?"

"Juan, my boss would like me to send him the list of 53 patients and their records. Is that okay?"

"Let me have a look first."

145

Inez followed Juan to her cubicle where she pulled up the list. He sat down and scrolled through it. Okay, you can send all but this one."

"Why is he excluded?"

"He's the mayor of San Sebastian."

"Oh, I see."

"If it becomes important I can get his permission."

"Thank you. I don't think it will be necessary."

"What now?" Juan asked.

"After I send these records to Bilbao there are a few other parameters I've been asked to look at. Our team created an algorithm that lets me scan all your records for a single blood anomaly. Then I can take those results and scan for a second. I keep going until the program has run through all of them. The remaining names will give me a second approach to finding the target patients."

"You couldn't have done that with the first search?"

"I could have, but we're looking at hundreds of specific antigens spread across the 22 blood groups that cause the most problems in transfusion. All ABO antigens are sugar based; all Rh antigens are protein based. It's the Rh-negative universe that's of most interest. Prior to 1980 newly discovered antigens were classified in a haphazard manner. That's when the international Society of Blood Transfusion stepped in and created a standardized nomenclature for designating new antigens. If we can find the antigen that's causing rejection, we may be able to delete it from donor blood."

Juan looked dazed.

"You've learned all this in two years and your degree is in computer science?"

"You'd be surprised at the similarities in nature and in the digital world. As you know, all computer code is made up of two simple numerals; ones and zeroes. Well, all human organisms are pattern based as well. Discover the patterns and learn to

146

manipulate them and they can be programmed just like a computer."

"I never thought about it like that," Juan mused.

"There are those who believe that, eventually, every human will have his own personal genome record on file. Then, any time they fall ill, the doctors can run tests that detect variations from their base genome and diagnose a treatment. Genetic manipulation will become the scalpel of the future."

Juan wandered back to his office shaking his head.

Inez returned to her search. She knew how important this project was to Maria Elizondo and she was determined to find the patient or patients whose blood held the key to success.

22

Fog shrouded the river bottom in a spectral mist as Maria drove across the bridge into the heart of the city. Father Giuseppe had agreed to meet with her at nine, following the conclusion of morning Mass. She pulled into a parking spot in front of the fish market down the street from the ornate Gothic façade of the Church of Saint Francis of Assisi.

Bells in the church's two soaring campaniles had called the faithful of Bilbao to prayer for centuries. Now the encroaching city with its smothering towers and faltering faithful had diminished the church's presence—both physically and temporally. Many of its former neighborhood parishioners, like Maria, had escaped to the surrounding communities.

She entered, knelt and crossed herself with holy water. She repeated the words of the *signum crucis.*

"In the name of the father, and of the son, and of the holy ghost, Amen."

Maria rose and gazed down the 200-foot-long nave to the chancel of the church. She had walked that long aisle hundreds of times as a young girl to receive communion at the altar. Her heart was heavy now as she walked it once more to begin the process of renouncing her marriage to Vitorio.

Father Giuseppe was back in his office, with the door open.

"Come in my child, and have a seat."

"Thank you, Father."

148

"Tell me what you have decided?"

"Has Vitorio been to see you?" she asked

"No."

"I didn't think he would."

"He came home from Madrid last night and we had a huge fight. He admitted he has been seeing Sophia Suarez for several months. Again, he tried to place the blame on me for failures in our marital relations. I told him I wasn't buying that. I admitted to my own shortcomings but not to his accusations and not to being the cause of his infidelity.

"I asked him if he was going to continue seeing her and he said it depended on Sophia. He said she hadn't told her husband Ronaldo yet. He as much as said that if she goes back to Ronaldo he'll come back to me. I told him I didn't want him back on those terms. He packed his bags and stormed out of the house."

"And what do you plan to do now?"

"I can't continue to live with Vitorio after this betrayal. I feel wounded by him, abused."

"You are aware of the consequences of this decision?"

"Yes, I know the church is strongly opposed to divorce. I also know the Pope's latest encyclical has removed many of the past restrictions on divorce among Catholics and on their relationship with the church."

"Yes," Father Giuseppe said, *Amoris Laetitia* allows divorced and remarried Catholics to receive the Eucharist—under certain conditions. At the same time, it urges them to refrain from sex. We all know that is not likely to happen, so the Holy Father has said the aspiring celebrants must follow their own consciences if they choose to participate. That is, if they feel whole with the Lord and have confessed their sins and done penance, then they are welcome at the altar."

"I have confessed, done penance, and feel absolved of all my sins. I wish to pursue a divorce from Vitorio."

"Very well, Maria, but I must warn you that it is a very tortuous path, and it can be very long and very expensive."

"What do I need to do?"

"There are forms you must submit that support your basis for seeking nullity. The church recognizes four basic defects that allow for nullity. In your case the defect of contract is pertinent. You must show that there were elements of the marriage vow that Vitorio never intended to keep. He will be given a copy of your petition and allowed to respond. Both of you can retain an official of the church as an advocate.

"Once you have presented your case the bishop will appoint a tribunal to review it and execute a trial. The process has been streamlined since the Pope's latest pronouncements and it does not have to be heard by a second tribunal or the Rota in Rome, if the presiding tribunal and the bishop agree. If you make a strong enough case, the tribunal can act rather rapidly."

"Do you have the necessary forms?"

"I do not, but the church secretary does. I will get them for you. You can pick them up this afternoon."

"Thank you, Father. I do not take this step lightly. My heart is breaking, but I cannot live with Vitorio under these conditions."

"I understand. I too grieve when a sacred covenant is broken, but, sometimes we think we have no choice. You must act on your own conviction my child. God bless you and good luck."

"Thank you, Father. Will you act as my advocate?"

"Both you and Vitorio have been members of my flock here for a long time. If he has no objection to my representing you, I will be happy to do it."

"I'll come by after work for the forms," she said as she got up to leave.

"They'll be here in my office on the desk if I am not here."

Maria took that long walk back to the front of St. Francis, relieved to have started the process and saddened that it was necessary.

Rubio Salazar was waiting for Maria outside her office.

"Señora, may I come in?"

"Of course, Rubio. What's up?"

"We've started to receive reports from the field. Four so far. None have identified a null patient. Two have uncovered close fits to our target, Inez in San Sebastian and Henrico Duarte in Vitoria-Gasteiz. They have forwarded a total of 97 patient records that closely resemble our target, but no null. The other two have reported only 27. Three haven't reported in yet."

Maria listened without responding.

Rubio continued.

"Inez and Henrico are now running the secondary sorts on individual antigens in the Rh-negative domain. They may get us closer to the ideal patient, but we still need that null."

"When you have all seven reports, compile them and bring them to me. We'll get together with the *four horsemen* and go from there."

Maria absentmindedly riffled through the sheaf of papers Anna had left on her desk for review. She signed the more pressing documents and then pushed the mundane reports and memos aside. She had no stomach today for the unending minutiae that found its way onto her desk.

She walked to the windows overlooking the city. She never tired of the changing hues of the Guggenheim surfaces as the sun made its way toward the sea. Her eyes lifted beyond the museum to the flashing red beacon atop the Azenága Tower. There, framed against that hideous blemish on the traditional architecture of the city, she could make out the dual campaniles of St. Francis. She had risen far from her church centered childhood. She was now accepted in the upper reaches of Bilbao society, yet her heart yearned for those innocent days where everything was certain, and her parents and her priest protected her from the cruelties of the outside world.

151

"Vitorio, oh Vitorio, what have you done?"

Her phone rang.

"Yes? This is Maria."

"All the techs have reported in. I have compiled the list of potentials."

"Bring them up, I'll call the others."

The five men gathered around her conference table turned to Maria. She looked up from her computer screen.

"Gentlemen, please scan through the 210 names we have and tell me which ones you think we should pursue further."

For the next two hours they were all intent on their screens. There was an occasional remark or observation about some obscure antigen attached to some variant cell. Alantso was last to look up and indicate he was finished.

"What are your conclusions?" Maria asked. "Alantso?"

"I think 12, 42, 79, 127, and 193 deserve further scrutiny.

"Diego?"

"12, 63, 79 121, 181 and 193."

"Paskal?"

10, 79, 84, 169, 193, 204.

"And you Paulo?"

"12, 79, 82, 169, 193. 215."

"12, 79, 169 and 193 appear multiple times. Let's start with them. Alantso, you take 12, Paulo 79, Diego 169 and Paskal, 193. Do a thorough analysis. Repeat the technician's work and add any checks of your own that you deem appropriate. Let's get back together at eight tomorrow."

"Rubio, please stay. There are some other search parameters I'd like you to investigate."

The *four horsemen* filed out and Maria returned to her desk.

"Coffee?" she said.

"No thank you," Rubio said. "I'm so highly caffeinated already that I can't blink."

"I'd like you to look at the 210 names that were sent in. See if you can write a program that will discover any commonality among them; blood type, location, age, physical attributes, etcetera. See if there is any clustering effect around any characteristic you can think of. I have a feeling there may be something hidden in the data that will lead us to the *golden donor.*"

"I'll get right on it," he said. I'll try to have something for you when we meet tomorrow morning."

"Great, Rubio, I can always count on you."

"Thank you," he said as he exited her office.

Maria glanced at her watch; 3:15. She expected Dietrich by now. On cue, her phone rang.

"Hi, it's Dietrich, I just landed at Biarritz. I should be in your office in an hour or so. Anything new to report?"

"Well, we have 210 potentials from the seven regions, but no nulls. We just finished scanning through them and agreed on four for closer scrutiny by the *four horsemen.*

"Who?"

"Oh, I forgot. We've started calling Alontso, Paskal, Diego and Paulo the *four horsemen.* It's easier than calling them all by name, individually. And while I'm at it, the seven techs in the field are the *seven dwarfs.*"

"That certainly covers the gamut – from Revelations to Snow White."

Maria laughed.

"There were four names on the list that had some consensus," Maria added. "Each horseman has one to cover in depth, to see if there is something there we can use. I've also commissioned Rubio to see if he can create a program that will run through the entire list looking for commonalities."

"Good idea, it's disappointing that we haven't turned up a null so far, but we just have to keep digging. See you shortly, my car just drove up."

Dietrich stepped off the elevator across from Maria's suite. He saw Anna in the outer office. She waved for him to go in.

"Dietrich I'm so glad you made it. How's your son?"

"He was doing fine until just before I left. Actually, we had just gone airborne. He had a bleeding episode caused by the ventilator tubes in his throat. They were able to contain it but had to insert a drain tube to keep fluids out of his lungs. They had to reverse the sedation withdrawal but he's still off the ventilator. I talked to Therese before I landed, and she said he's resting comfortably and his breathing is normal."

"That's good."

"Fill me in on what you've found," Dietrich said.

"Come with me into the conference room. We have computers set up with the data from all 210 target patients. We went through them all and the *horsemen* found 18 that looked promising. There were four that appeared on more than one list, so we are focusing on them. I assigned one to each member of the team. They'll be back with more in-depth analysis tomorrow morning. Rubio should also have his new program running by then."

"Good. Now how is it going on the home front?"

"I saw Father Giuseppe this morning. I told him I wanted to proceed with the annulment. He corrected me. The church does not call it an annulment. It is formally a "declaration of nullity." There are four "defects" in a marriage that are valid grounds to seek nullity. I claim that Vitorio did not intend to remain faithful to the marriage from the beginning and therefore it was a fraud. Further, his declaration that he didn't want any children is in contradiction of the church's basic foundation of marriage; procreation. I have asked Father Giuseppe to advocate for me at the trial. I have to go by St, Francis' on the way home to pick up the forms. The sooner I file the sooner this will all be over.

"I could use some company for dinner. Why don't you check in at your hotel and drive up to Burrika. I do a mean Marmitako."

154

"What's that?'

"It's a fish stew or soup. Mainly with tuna. There's a famous seafood shop next door to St. Francis. I'll pop in and get some tuna—right off the boat."

"That's tempting, but only if I bring the wine."

"Deal! See you there about seven. Here's the address. Just plug it into your GPS."

"Maria stopped for the forms and the fish and then picked up the veggies she needed at a nearby market. She was home by six and prepped everything for dinner. She had just turned on the burner under her soup pot when she heard tires on the gravel. She wiped her hands on a kitchen towel and made her way to the front door.

"I see you can be very punctual she said."

"My father said that if I was five minutes early for a meeting then I was late. I've always tried to live by that advice."

"Come in. This way to the kitchen."

She took the bouquet Dietrich had brought.

"Just put the wine in the fridge," she said. "I've already poured two glasses of Sangria. Come out to the patio."

Dietrich followed her through the French doors; he noticed a broken pane in one. She placed the roses on a side table.

"Very nice," he said, "and that's a great view down to the ocean, I love this part of Spain. The coast line is so varied."

"Yes, so do I. This was one of the things Vitorio and I totally agreed on. A house above the sea, I love it here."

"I can see why," Dietrich said. "Why don't you show me around?"

"Certainly." she responded. She topped off their Sangria and said, "Follow me."

She led Dietrich down the rocky path she had trod just before Vitorio's return, toward San Valentin's rocks.

"What a magnificent seascape," Dietrich said as they stood on the headland above Muriola and San Valentin. "I've seen that beach over there many times from my plane and thought what a lovely place it must be."

"The small beach below is Muriola. That's where I go to swim and sun. The larger beach is Gorliz. That's where Mikel Muñoz lives."

"Oh! Then he's not far at all from Bilbao."

"No. Almost as close as I am."

"I can see why you moved out here from the city. Peaceful, clean, airy, all the comforts of home."

They stood for a while gazing at the sea. The sun bouncing off the Atlantic was dazzling. What could be wrong in a world so beautiful as this.

"Better head back," Maria said. "The stew takes about an hour, so I need to get it on the stove."

They paid no attention to the bird watcher with the tele-photo lens. He was intently observing a pair of nesting Scottish osprey's that had been recently re-introduced to the area. Nor did they see him shift his focus in their direction after they passed.

Maria served dinner on the patio, under strings of paper lanterns. It became chilly after dessert.

"Dietrich, will you light the fire pit? It's already stacked with wood. There are matches in the box on the bench."

Dietrich struck the large kitchen match against the emery. It flared as he placed it beneath the kindling. Moments later the dry wood burst into flame, its radiant heat dispelling the night chill as they sat with their wine and talked.

"What will you do when the divorce comes through?" he asked.

"If it comes through," she answered. "There are many twists and turns when it comes to dealing with the Catholic Church. Even though Pope Francis has removed many of the restrictions vis-à-vis marriage and divorce, many in the church are still resisting. I don't know what position the local bishop has taken. If he doesn't want to accept my petition it will be bumped

156

up the ladder to a second court, and if that isn't decisive, on to the Rota in Rome. That's the highest ecclesiastical tribunal in the Catholic Church. It's held at the Vatican. Only the most complicated and contested cases wind up there. If my case goes to the Rota, it's probably dead on arrival."

"Based on what you've told me, it sounds like you have a good case. How long does this process take?"

"It varies, some are resolved in weeks, others drag on forever."

"Well, I hope yours gets resolved in short order. It must be a huge distraction for you."

"I didn't realize how much. I found myself sitting at my desk today, unable to concentrate on the task at hand. Finally, I just got up and stared out the window. I looked down on the city and the neighborhood I grew up in. I saw a carefree young Maria playing in the streets, whose problems were always solved by someone else; parents, priests, girlfriends.

"I know the feeling. For all the success I have had I sometimes long for the time when I didn't have to make the big decisions. Money can buy you many things, but it can't buy happiness, or freedom, or love."

"I certainly agree with the love part. Vitorio and I had a great life; great careers, the admiration of our friends, status in society. But somehow it just wasn't enough for him."

She got up and poked at the fire, turning her back to Dietrich so he wouldn't see her tears. But she couldn't hold back the flood. Her shoulders heaved with racking sobs. Dietrich got up to console her. She turned to him and buried her face in his chest.

"I know it seems that your world will never be the same again. And it won't. But, that doesn't mean it can't be just as fulfilling. It will take a while to come to terms with all that is happening but eventually the sun will come up and it will be tomorrow. It will happen, you just can't rush it.

"There will be someone out there who sees in you what Vitorio never saw. He will appreciate it and love you for it. I know you will grieve for your loss, but don't lose contact with your dreams. They're still out there—waiting for you."

He released her, and she stepped back to dry her tears—and smile.

"Thank you, Dietrich. I needed that."

"I'd better be going," he said. "I hope we have a busy and fruitful day tomorrow."

She walked him to the door and waved as he pulled out of the driveway. The black van parked across the street beneath the trees was nearly invisible.

23

Dietrich had coffee and a croissant in his room. His laptop was open on the table. He scanned through reports from Shanghai, Jakarta, Lagos and Liverpool with one hand while holding the croissant in the other. No major emergencies or *catastrophes du jour* to deal with. He returned to the text from Therese.

"I didn't want to wake you, so I'll fill you in on today's events. Rupert continues to breathe on his own and Dr. Askew said he will remove the drain tube from his throat tomorrow. If all goes well, they'll re-commence the sedative withdrawal. He hopes Rupert will be responsive and cognizant in two to three days.

"Rob Simpson and his wife came by. We had a very nice visit. He said he is encouraged with the progress they've made on the samples you brought from Zurich.

"I'm still concerned about Rupert's color. He always was a little anemic, but this is much worse. Whatever was released into his system when he hit that tree is terrifying. The royal blood coursing through his veins—my veins—is a curse of unimaginable magnitude. I pray that what you are doing—what all your people are doing—can put an end to this cycle of death. I cannot bear the thought of Elise passing this curse on to her children. If you can save Rupert, save Elise and Dieter as well.

I love you,
Keep well,

Therese

Across town, Miguel Ortega was reviewing the list of 210 names that the *seven dwarfs* had uncovered. He swiveled his chair and stared out through his sloping glass cathedral. The multiple layers distorted his view causing the green canopy on the patio of the penthouse across the street to undulate in rhythm with his movements. When he stared too long, the optical illusions aggravated his vertigo. He wheeled back around and focused on a single name on the list—*Alejandro Diaz*.

He thought Alejandro Diaz had been relegated to the musty archives he left behind when he sold his private psychiatry practice. Its location near San Sebastian had been lucrative. Wealthy retirees flocked to the city for its beaches and its affluent life style but they sought out private physicians, who were out of the public eye, especially the aging matrons with too many sun-baked wrinkles and faux anxieties. Others came too, those seeking escape, or seclusion, or privacy. Many discovered that a change of scene didn't necessarily correspond to an escape from whatever drove them here.

Domingo Diaz came to San Sebastian for none of those reasons. He came because Miguel Ortega was there. He bought the villa *on Mount Ulia* overlooking San Sebastian's *Playa de Zurriola,* not the more trendy and popular *Playa de La Concha.* The *Urumea* River and *Monte Urgull* provided a natural barrier to the tourists and *nouveau riche* technocrats from Switzerland who were snapping up *La Concha* beachfront condos as soon as a sign appeared in the window. The river was a barrier not often breached by the *Sebastianos* on *La Concha.*

People in the cars flowing underneath the Diaz compound on *Ulia's* serpentine streets would be hard pressed to know the

160

villa even existed. Above, the forests surrounding *Ulia's* walking trails provided a dense barrier seldom penetrated by hikers. A small segment of the *Compostela de Santiago* passes through the mountain but not many pilgrims stray from its path. A few stop at the upscale *Mirador de Ulia* restaurant that clings to the hillside below the Diaz compound, for its views across to the lighthouse beyond *La Concha.* The *café con leche* is worth the extra two Euros just for that view.

Domingo seldom comes to San Sebastian anymore. His major reason for buying the villa vanished in 2011 after Miguel Ortega sold his private practice in Tolosa and then shuttered his small sanitarium on the hillside facing the sea, near the *Puntas de San Pedro* ship beacon. When the sanitarium gates were closed and padlocked on that wintry morning five years ago, Domingo thought he had closed that chapter in his life, forever.

24

Rubio was first to arrive next morning. He stopped by his favorite *panaderìa* down the street from the office for a selection of *tortas.* He brewed two pots of coffee and was sitting at the conference table munching on a raspberry pastry when Maria came in.

"Good morning, Rubio, you're here bright and early."

"Yeah, I couldn't sleep. I finished the program you requested, and I couldn't wait to run it, so I did it at home."

"What did you find?"

"Look at this."

He turned his laptop so that Maria could see it.

"Notice anything peculiar?"

"Well, most of the names are clustered around Bilbao, San Sebastian and Vitoria as one would expect since they are the three biggest population centers. The others seem to be scattered at random."

"Yes, but do you see these small oases that occur throughout the Basque region where there are no names. There's one south of Bilbao and one south of San Sebastian and two or three others scattered about."

"What do you attribute that to?"

"I don't know but I think it's something we should check out."

"I agree. When the rest of the brain trust gets here we'll see if anyone has an idea."

162

Dietrich was next to arrive.

"It is such a beautiful morning that I decided to walk over. Bilbao was just coming to life. Storefront shutters were banging into place everywhere. I'm amazed at the juxtaposition of restaurants, repair shops and fish markets. I gather the zoning regulations in the city are pretty lax."

"Yeah," Rubio said, "many of those shops have been in the family for generations and were grandfathered in when the new regulations came out. You won't find that hodgepodge in the newer sections. The Old Bilbao natives think the new rules are a farce. 'Live and let live' they say."

"I took the foot bridge across the river." Dietrich said. "That's probably faster than driving and a lot more pleasant.

"Are those for everyone?" he asked, pointing toward the pastries.

"Sure, help yourself, there's fresh coffee."

"I had a croissant at the hotel, but I think I worked most of that off on the walk over."

He poured a coffee and grabbed an apple pastry.

"Dietrich," Maria said, "Rubio's new program has uncovered some anomalies in our patient distribution. Take a look at it."

Rubio cleared the chair next to him, so Dietrich could sit and see the computer screen.

"I ran this sort by location for the 210 names that our techs sent in. The distribution is about what one would expect. Most are clustered around the major population centers. However, there are these small islands where there are practically no patients. I haven't come up with an answer for that yet."

"That's curious," Dietrich said.

"Yeah, maybe the other guys will have an answer."

The *four horsemen* straggled in and were contentedly munching *tortas* by eight-fifteen.

"Rubio," Maria said, "why don't you run your findings by the others and see what they think?"

Rubio completed his third dissertation of the morning for the newly arrived. The response was blank-faced silence.

"Not a clue," Paskal said.

"Me neither," Alantso agreed.

"Have you asked the *seven dwarfs*?" Paulo said.

"No," Rubio said, "Why do you think they may know?"

"They're out there on the front line. Maybe they overheard something that might help."

"Can't hurt to ask," Maria said. "Send an email explaining what you've found and see what kind of response you get."

"I'll do that right now while you get the meeting started."

"Okay, Paulo, what can you tell us about Señor # 79?"

"He's 43. He was born in Santander of Basque parents and moved to Bilbao in1997 to attend university. He has a degree in accounting and works for a branch of Banco Santander here. His father is an officer in the parent bank.

"He presented with hemophilia as a child of eleven. He is an AB negative with von Willebrand 2n. He goes in to an infirmary on a regular basis to receive platelets and occasionally factor VIII clotting compounds. He has partial focal seizures originating in the occipital lobe, not the thalamus. He is treated with Tegretol and Lamotrogine. Otherwise he leads a pretty normal life. I would rule him out as a subject for further study. He's not a null and his seizures do not comport with Rupert's."

"Do the rest of you agree?" Maria asked.

Three heads nodded in the affirmative

"Alantso, what about number # 12?"

"He's 29, born in Bilbao and living in San Sebastian. He's a truck driver. He is blood type AB negative has hemophilia B, von Willebrand 2n, and also has seizures treated the same as #79. His seizures appear to originate in the thalamus. He is AB negative and receives regular transfusions, both platelets and whole blood. He presented with hemophilia at the age of five and had several near-death episodes before his tenth birthday. New

164

drugs and treatments since then have his situation under control. I feel he bears further study."

"Do you agree?" Maria asked.

All three said yes.

"Alantso, get with Mikel and Rubio and work out a plan for # 12."

"Diego, 169?"

"Much as the other two. Sanitation worker in Vitoria. Injured sorting recyclables and treated for hemophilia. Subsequent seizures, also thalamus related. Same drugs. Von Willebrand 2n. He tests negative for Rh D and had a hemolytic reaction to a transfusion containing Rh D. Subsequently his wife delivered two stillborns. He bears further study as well.

"I concur Maria said, if the rest agree?"

"Okay Diego, work with Mikel to see what you can find out about #169."

"Now, Paskal, you get the last shot."

"This won't take long; Alejandro Diaz, priest, Dominican monk, born in Santiago de Compostela, declared insane, confined to an institution near San Sebastian around 2009 or '10. No further entries in his medical history."

That's very odd," Maria said. "Is it a common practice for the church to put its own away for insanity and then for them not to appear again in the national medical system?"

"I don't know," Rubio said, "I've never run into this before. Any of you guys?" he looked around the table.

"I once knew a nun from Santiago de Compostela. She was visiting the Sisters of Mary Reparatrix, a small group that cares for the indigent on the streets of Bilbao, when she went bonkers. She was confined to a convent near Pamplona that cared for mental patients from the clergy."

No one else volunteered any knowledge of the church's practice in relation to insanity among its own ranks.

"Diego, this may be the perfect time to call in Mikel Muñoz," Maria said. "Call him and explain the situation to him. Let's see if he can find out what happened to #193."

"I have an idea." Dietrich said, "Rubio can you run a sort that identifies all the locations of the patients in the ministry population. I'm curious to see if it would expand our understanding of the dispersion patterns we saw. Have we queried the *seven dwarfs* about these patterns? They may have learned something from the personnel in the ministry offices."

"I can, but I'm not sure how the ministry would view that. It's well beyond our original mandate. How would I explain it to them?"

"Tell them that one of our insurance clients is trying to determine the best locations for their service offices," Maria said.

"Will do, I'll get right on it."

Only Dietrich and Maria were left at the table. He poured both another cup of coffee. She added cream and sugar and stirred absentmindedly.

"Did you pick up the forms at St. Francis?" he asked.

"Yes, I went by there on the way in. I glanced at them before I came to the meeting. They're quite extensive and the questions are very intrusive. The priests on that tribunal will know more about my sex life than I do."

"Can you use some legal help? I have a crackerjack lawyer in Zaragoza that can come up if you need him. I'm sure he'd like to get away from his patent applications for a while."

"No thanks, I wouldn't want him to be embarrassed. Father Giuseppe and I have it under control. I'm going to finish the forms this afternoon and get them over to the church. I want to get this over with as fast as possible."

"Okay, suit yourself, but don't forget I offered."

"I won't. What are you going to do with the afternoon?"

"I have several calls to make and a few reports to read. If you don't mind, I'll just do them here."

"Sure, but I have an office you can use."

"Thanks, I'll just finish up here then I think I'll walk over to the Guggenheim. It'd be a shame to be here and not see it. The concierge at the hotel says they have a new exhibit of works by Goya and Velasquez on loan from The Prado."

"Yes," Maria said, "I saw them last month. They're magnificent. I've been encouraging the director to get The Prado to bring *Guernika* to Bilbao but so far, no luck. It's such an iconic part of this area's history."

"Maybe I can help. The Kuntshaus in Zurich has a superb collection of modern art; Pollock, Miro, Munch, Chagall. I imagine they'd be willing to stage an exhibition at The Prado in exchange for *Guernica's* visit to Bilbao."

"You could do that?"

"I'm president of the Kuntshaus board of directors."

"I see. That would be a real coup for the Guggenheim. Maybe when this is all over we can talk."

"Good, now fill out your petition."

Dietrich was finishing his last call when Maria left for St. Francis.

"See you tomorrow," she called.

He looked up and waved.

"Right. Good luck."

"Thanks, I need it."

Dietrich retraced his steps across the footbridge and entered the Guggenheim. The internal layout belied the museums jumbled exterior. He was impressed with the presentation of the Prado collection and the attractiveness of the smaller halls. Thirty minutes in, he had reached his museum saturation point, where one painting begins to blend into the next—he referred to it as his "museum fatigue syndrome."

167

The red light on his room phone was blinking when he walked in. He lifted the handset and retrieved the call.

"Dietrich this is Maria. Please call me when you get this message."

He could hear the distress in her voice. He dialed her cell and she answered immediately.

"Dietrich can you come over to the church; St. Francis. It's only a few blocks away. Something very disturbing has come up and it involves you."

"What!"

"I'll fill you in when you get here. It's about a mile due south of your hotel."

"Okay I'll be right over."

The concierge hailed a taxi for Dietrich. Maria was standing on the steps of the church when he arrived.

"I'm so glad you came," she said, visibly shaken.

Maria led him inside and down the long nave to her priest's office.

"Come in. I'm Father Giuseppe. Have a seat."

"Maria, what's this all about?" Dietrich asked.

"I'll let the father explain."

"First, Vitorio has filed a counter claim to Maria's nullity petition."

"What does that mean?" Dietrich responded.

"It means he's contesting her allegations. He claims that she was unfaithful to him."

"How can that be?"

He looked at Maria.

"What proof does he have?"

The priest picked up an envelope and dumped the contents onto the desk in front of Dietrich. He picked them up.

The first glossy black-and-white showed a couple standing on a cliff overlooking the beach. The second showed the same couple seated on the patio of a house. The third showed the couple embracing.

168

"Is that you with Maria?" Giuseppe asked.

"Why yes, but it's not how it seems."

"Why don't you tell me how it is then, Señor von Hesse?"

"I'm sure Maria has explained this to you."

"She has, but I want to hear your version of the story."

Dietrich took a deep breath. He had to control his urge to scream.

"Father Giuseppe, I came to Bilbao to enlist Maria and her clinic to help me find a cure for my son Rupert. He is lying in a bed in California as we speak fighting for his life. He has a very rare blood disorder that will kill him if we can't help him."

"Why here, why Maria?"

"Our research shows that the most likely place to find a person with the particular blood traits we need for research is here in the Basque region. I won't go into the details. Colleagues recommended Maria as the most experienced hematologist in all of Spain, not just Bilbao, so she became the logical choice.

"The day after Vitorio left, Maria was a wreck. She was crying and despondent. She needed a friend and I stepped in, purely platonically. I am a happily married man. My wife Therese is sitting by my son's bedside as we speak. This is the most unlikely set of circumstances for someone to begin an adulterous affair.

"Maria asked me to come to dinner. She needed a friend and we needed to talk about Rupert, my son. We walked down to the shore to decompress and let Maria vent a little. When we got back to the house we had Maria's wonderful Marmitoko. I asked her for the recipe by the way. After dinner we sat around the fire on the patio and talked some more about life and love and betrayal. She broke down in sobs. I didn't know what to do to console her. I held her as she cried. When she was in control again we finished our wine and I left. I'll bet the scoundrel who took these pictures didn't show you a photo date stamped at 9:00 when I left."

169

"No, he didn't. But your story matches Maria's. I believe you are both telling the truth. Vitorio must be doing this for other reasons."

"What reasons?" Maria asked. "Does he want to block the annulment?"

"I didn't get that impression."

"What then?"

"Money."

"Money? That makes no sense. Vitorio makes as much or more than I do."

"I got the distinct impression that he may have got in over his head with some of his client's investment money and he doesn't have sufficient funds to bail himself out. He needs yours as well."

"Whoa!" Dietrich said, "This is beginning to make sense."

"Father, can we get back together in the morning. I need to do a little research. I think I know what's going on here."

"Certainly, nine o'clock, after morning confessions."

Maria dropped Dietrich at his hotel.

"What's the big secret? You didn't say a word on the way back."

"Oh, I'm sorry. The wheels were turning. I'm trying to figure out what Vitorio is doing and how to counter it. I should know more by morning."

"Okay," she said as he exited her BMW. "I hope you can figure it out. What a mess."

"Benny, this is Dietrich. Where do you stand on the Vitorio Elizondo matter? I need a report by nine p.m., your time. Get back to me."

Dietrich went to bed, his mind a clutter of disparate thoughts—Rupert, Therese, Maria. He fell fitfully to sleep. The cell phone rang. He opened one eye and looked at the radio clock. Midnight. Dietrich fumbled for it. He was climbing up from

170

that dark, watery place he had visited often in the past two weeks.

"Hello?"

"Dietrich, its Benny. You said to call you."

"Yeah, sorry Benny, I'm not quite awake yet. Did you get anything?"

"Yeah. I met with a friend of mine in M & A at Goldman downtown today. He and I worked together there in the naughts. I told him what I was looking for and he went into the bowels of their system and pulled up Elizondo's files at *Investimento Basque*. Turns out he was doing really well up until he started buying up swaps with his client's money. When that went south, he was into the Madrid office for the five million Euros that he needed to make his clients whole. Goldman has him on a short leash and has put a man in his office to monitor trading. He's been given six months to dig out from underneath all this or they'll pull the plug and turn him over to the CNMV for prosecution. That's the Spanish equivalent of our SEC. If that happens he is done for in the investment world and he may face criminal charges. Five million Euros to Goldman could make that all go away."

"Thanks Benny, I owe you one, big time."

"No Dietrich, the debit side of my ledger will never catch up with what I owe you. Good luck. I hope this helps."

"More than you know Benny, more than you know. By the way, what happened with those AI ventures?"

"One withdrew its funding request. I guess he got all he needed from Musk. I'm sending you a prospectus on the other one. Should be in your inbox in a day or two."

"Thanks Benny, I'll check it out. See you soon. I'll be back in Palo Alto in the next few days and I'll check in."

"Good luck. Let me know if there's anything else I can do."

"Okay Benny, thanks, good-bye."

Dietrich turned over and tried to go back to sleep. When he finally dozed off Rupert was lying on a gurney at the bottom of that well calling to him as the water crept higher and higher; 'help me! help me!'

25

Maria met Dietrich for breakfast at the hotel. She looked even more sorrowful than when she dropped him off last night.

"I don't know what to make of Vitorio's behavior," she said as she joined Dietrich at his table.

"Good morning, sunshine," he said, looking up with a smile.

"I'm happy you can smile. I didn't sleep at all. I am so angry with Vitorio. It's almost as if our marriage never existed. His actions have become almost vicious."

"Perk up! I have some news that will make you feel better."

"What?"

"You remember telling me how Vitorio's behavior changed over the last few months, how he'd become sullen and angry. If you recall, I witnessed some of that at dinner with him last week. Now I think I know why."

"Why?"

"It was just a few months ago that Vitorio went to London to talk to some investors. One of them convinced him to put some of his wealthiest clients into something called credit default swaps. Said he could make them a fortune, and one for himself as well. He had to be aware of the previous disaster at Morgan-Chase. They had to write off billions gambled away by one of their traders in London, the so-called "whale." These new guys must have convinced him that things were different this time and that they knew what went wrong at Morgan, and they had a fix for it. These same shysters sent an emissary to Banque von Hesse in Zurich as well. My managers analyzed their prospectus and shot it full of holes right away.

"Obviously, Vitorio fell for their pitch. He came back and bought swaps by the millions for his clients. True to form, the London cabal made millions and left Vitorio and the other suckers holding the bag. His clients in Bilbao demanded restitution and he couldn't come up with the money. Finally, Goldman in Madrid bailed him out and put severe restrictions on his trading. They even put a man in his office to oversee things. He was given six months to straighten the mess out or Madrid would shut him down and turn him over to the CNMV for prosecution. The six months is about up."

Maria was stunned. She tried to speak but just sputtered.

"This is too bizarre for belief. How much does he owe?"

"Five million."

"Five million!" she blurted. "My God he must be crazy. I don't have that kind of money."

"No, but your company does."

"You mean he thinks he can force me to use my company to pay his debts?"

"He must think he has a good chance of convincing the tribunal that you are as guilty of adultery as he is and therefore all the assets, from both of you, should be divided equally."

"Maria dropped her face in her hands and moaned.

"Can he do that?"

"Not on my watch. We'll fight the bastard all the way to Rome if necessary. Look, we need to get back to the problem at hand, finding a cure for Rupert. Don't worry about Vitorio. I'll take care of him."

Maria looked across the table at Dietrich. A fragile smile trembled at the corners of her mouth.

"But can you really? You'll be going up against the Holy Roman Catholic Church and all its powers."

174

"Did you ever hear of a fellow named Martin Luther? Don't worry. I've got this. Finish your breakfast. We have a date with a cherubic little man in a brown robe."

Father Giuseppe crossed his arms on his desk and shook his head.

"This is unbelievable. You're sure?"

"I will produce documentation for you to take before the tribunal. I also have one other piece of evidence that you may want. I had my technical people run a program on my cell phone. It tells you where I have been over the last seven days. It clearly shows my arrival at Maria's house at 6:45 in the evening in question. It shows my movements over the next two and a half hours. At no time did I go anywhere in Maria's house other than the entry way, the hall, the kitchen and the patio. It shows me leaving her house at nine and arriving back at my hotel at 9:30. There's no way we could have betrayed Vitorio that evening as his spy alleged."

"Modern technology!" Giuseppe exclaimed. "I'm glad I don't have to understand it. That's great news. I've already petitioned the bishop for the tribunal. He said he would expedite it. He'll name the three judges today and call for proceedings tomorrow."

"Why is he acting so fast Father?" Maria asked.

"Do you remember a young, wet-behind-the ears priest at St Francis thirty years ago named Father Alvaro?

"Yes, all the teenagers had a crush on him, he was so handsome."

"Father Alvaro is now Bishop Alvaro. I'm just calling in a favor."

It was Maria's turn to be staggered by the news.

"You always said Father that 'God works in mysterious ways his wonders to perform.'"

"Yes, my child, and he still does. I'll call you when the tribunal is assembled. We should meet by nine tomorrow

175

morning. Both you and Vitorio will be required to testify. I'll notify his advocate. I think he's in for a very big surprise."

Maria drove them back to the office, feeling slightly elated that things in her chaotic life were about to take a turn for the better.

"Dietrich, what can I say? I know the decree is not final, but it appears Father Giuseppe is confident it will be. Oh, I so want this to be over. It will be a miracle if the tribunal and the bishop rule on my petition tomorrow. I have never heard of a tribunal moving so fast before."

"I think Father Giuseppe likes you, Maria, in a fatherly sort of way. He recognizes the grievous wrong Vitorio has done you and the sooner he can see it rectified the better. How will the proceeding go tomorrow?"

"The tribunal will call us both in to testify. They'll have both our written petitions. Then we'll both be asked to offer proof of our charges. That's when I submit affidavits that Vitorio and Sophia had carnal relations and that Vitorio never planned to consummate the marriage with children as God commanded.

"Then Vitorio will present the evidence collected by his private investigator, primarily the photos; there's nothing else. Then Father Giuseppe will present our story and the reason you are here in Bilbao, and that we didn't even know each other until a few days ago. Then he'll present additional evidence; the evidence you obtained that Vitorio is not yet privy to. He will have your dossier on Vitorio's dealings with his clients, their loss of money due to his ambition and greed, and the fact that they lost five million Euros due to his misuse of their funds. He may call one or more of the men Vitorio swindled to testify as well. Then the Father will show that Vitorio is under probation from Goldman-Sachs and has to restitute the five million Euros or risk going to jail. Then the tribunal will take all evidence and petitions under advisement and render a verdict. I need two of them in my corner. Cross your fingers."

"With Giuseppe on your side, I don't think you need to worry."

"I pray you are right."

The office was abuzz when Maria and Dietrich stepped off the elevator. Rubio, Diego and Mikel Muñoz were waiting outside Maria's door.

"I assume you have good news or else you wouldn't be here," she joked.

"We do. Where do you want it, office or conference room?"

"Come into my office."

"First," Rubio said, "Inez Figueroa confirmed that many records weren't centrally captured years ago. Furthermore, private clinics didn't have to report their clients at all. Some chose to voluntarily. Many still don't. That leaves a glaring gap in the data."

"That's what I thought!" Dietrich said. "There are a lot more records out there, especially going back ten, fifteen years."

When everyone was seated around her desk Rubio rolled out a three by three sheet of paper depicting the three geographical regions of the Basque Autonomous Community.

"Señor von Hesse, your hunch was right. Look at that."

There were three large and several small pockets that showed few patients from the ministry's files.

"We ran all the directories of physicians through our computer and keyed the chart for them. Reds are ministry physicians, blues are private clinics."

"I'll be damned" Dietrich said. "Almost every area showing few ministry patients surrounds a blue marker. The three larger areas show more than one. Does that signify multiple doctors at those clinics?"

"Yes, as you can see there were five in Tolusa, until five years ago, two in Ammurio, they're still there, and one in Laudio, he's still there but has voluntarily joined the ministry directory recently.

"Mikel, do you think you can find these doctors and get their records for us?"

"It would be highly illegal and unethical," he smirked, "but sure, I can get them. I'll need some help from these two guys for the technical and medical stuff, but yeah, can do."

Okay, let's concentrate first on the three biggest populations and see what we find. How about that crazy priest who went off the grid, number 193, think you can find him?"

"That might be a bit tougher, but I think so. Between his medical records before he went missing and the church records, I should find him."

"Good," Maria said, "what do you need?"

"This guy," indicating Rubio, "some lock-picking tools, alarm bypass electronics, night vision goggles and a portable high-powered computer capable of gigabit downloads at really fast speeds. I have all those things except the computer and someone to work it; like say Rubio here. We need to get in and out of these places in a hurry."

"You realize if you get caught we'll deny any association with you." Maria said. "You'll be on your own but for the money a certain unnamed and anonymous lawyer will provide along with his services. DON'T get caught! Okay get out of here and get busy. Keep the *seven dwarfs* in place for now. We may need them later."

Maria finished her mail and signed the company checks before closing her computer and leaving for the day. Dietrich was still in the conference room, glued to his lap top.

"I'm calling it a day," she said popping her head in.

Dietrich looked at his watch.

"I didn't realize it was already six. Care for a drink?"

"Sure, there's nothing waiting for me at home except maybe a black van with a camera."

"I don't think you'll see any more of him. That game is over. I hope he didn't cost Vitorio too much." he said with

178

sarcasm. "Drop me at my hotel and we can grab a drink on the roof top bar."

"Sounds good, let's go."

He was quiet for the five- minute drive, lost in the text on his cell phone.

"Here we are," she said.

He looked up.

"Already, I forget how close the office is."

"Not bad news I hope."

"No, not bad, but not good either. Askew says Rupert is coming out from under the sedation and is responsive to pain stimuli but still not to tactile. Therese is going stir crazy. I called my parents in Zurich. I asked them to pack up and take the kids over. My secretary told Marcel to get the 50 ready for tomorrow morning. The kids will be out of school for a few days. A good time to go. She needs something positive for a change, before total despondency sets in."

Maria rose early. She had a quick café con leche with a frozen waffle. She needed the extra jolt of sugar for the day ahead. She was going to the office at seven for any updates and then to the Cathedral of St. James, seat of the Bishop of the Bilbao Diocese, and site of the tribunal. The cathedral was less than a mile from St. Francis, nearer the river. She was both apprehensive and elated.

Now that the break with Vitorio was complete she was anxious to discover what the rest of her life held in store. At the same time, there was still an undercurrent of doubt. What if, for some unseen reason, the tribunal refused nullity? Then what? Then in typical Maria Elizondo fashion, head held high, she grabbed her phone and briefcase and headed out the door. Whatever the day held in store for her she would deal with as she always had—eyes wide open, full speed ahead.

26

Mikel and Rubio drove into the small valley town of Tolosa at noon. Tolosa is located on the Orio River, fifteen miles south of San Sebastian. There was no easy, direct route from Bilbao to Tolosa. Motorists were forced to take the tortuous road over the mountains through Zumarraga, deviate north via San Sebastian or south through Vitoria. Mikel opted for the northern route. It was faster and one he was more familiar with. AP-8, a major highway, skirted San Sebastian on its way to France. He could pick up A-1 south near San Sebastian. Many of his clients lived in the beach town. The *Sebastianos* who sought him out wanted privacy and discreetness, and were willing to pay well for it.

Mikel knew he was close to Tolosa when he saw the huge white cross atop the Mount Uzturre massif to the east of A-1. He drove into the center of town and parked two blocks away from their objective—*Clinica Psichiatrica de Tolosa*, located on the *Euskal Heria Plaza*. The plaza is used by the locals for festivals and other community events. *Euskal Heria* is the oldest known term for the Basque region, dating back to the 16th century. It is a name preferred by the old-timers over the more modern term, *Euskadi*.

"There's a café across the plaza from the clinic," Mikel said as they entered the plaza. "Let's grab a coffee and study the area."

180

"The Nest", a tapas bar, was a popular hangout for young couples out for a stroll with their babies. Two families were seated on a public bench drinking coffee and chatting. Another couple sat at a table having a lunch of tapas and sangria as the wife rocked her baby's stroller back and forth, vainly attempting to soothe her fretting infant. Another couple, obviously lovers, and oblivious to their surroundings, sat entwined behind a table in the shadows.

Mikel lolled in his chair while he nonchalantly surveyed the plaza. *The Topic*, a three-floor concert hall was located directly across the plaza from "The Nest." The brochure he had picked up said that the hall was used as a major venue for an international puppet show held annually in Tolosa. The building also houses a major exhibit of ornate and intricate puppets and marionettes from around the world. A small queue had formed outside, waiting for the doors to open for the afternoon.

The psychiatric clinic was to the right of the auditorium. The clinic was four floors with the first floor recessed behind a colonnade of stone pillars. This ground floor colonnade extended around the entire circumference of the plaza, providing a galleria for all the tenants. The first floor of the clinic appeared to be a reception center and waiting room with medical consultations occurring on the three upper floors.

"Let's finish our coffee and join the queue for the puppet show," Mikel said.

"Why do you want to see a puppet show," Rubio wondered, "don't we need to check out the clinic?"

"Bear with me. I need to know what's on both sides, in back, and on top of that building before we even attempt to approach it."

"Okay, you're in charge, just tell me what to do."

"For now, just follow my lead."

Mikel downed the last of his coffee, stood up, and stretched lazily. He appeared to be a man who was in no hurry and had no particular plans for the day.

"Jose, let's go over and see what's going on in that theater?' he said loudly. "Looks interesting."

"Okay, pay the bill and let's go."

Mikel pulled out a ten Euro note for the waiter. He pocketed the return bills and left the spare change. No credit cards; no paper trail.

The line at the ticket booth began moving before they got there; the sign read 'Adults - Five Euros.' Both Mikel and Rubio handed their entrance fee to the clerk, took their tickets, and walked in.

One entire wall was a series of shelves divided into large shadow boxes from floor to ceiling. Each box housed a single unique puppet or marionette, one more elaborate than the next. They stood and admired the incredible collection of puppet art.

"I never knew this was here," Rubio said. "I need to pull my nose away from the grindstone and get out with my family more. My kids would love this."

"Not until we finish this investigation; then I might come back with you," Mikel said.

"Deal," Rubio said.

They proceeded through the entrance to a gallery overlooking the main theater which was to the left and behind the front structure. Most of the exhibits were housed on the three floors of the main building. Mikel was searching for other things as well. He led Rubio up to the top floor, devoted mostly to marionettes. There was a door at the far end of the upper gallery.

"Rubio, I want you to engage that attendant," he said pointing at a girl standing in the doorway. "Keep her facing away until I can get a close look at that door."

"Okay, I think I can do that."

Mikel stood nonchalantly near a garish Pinocchio marionette. As soon as the attendant turned away to answer Rubio's question, Mikel darted to the far end of the room. The door was an emergency exit that only opened from the inside by pushing against a bar. It obviously accessed an emergency fire

182

escape between the theater and the clinic. *Ipso facto,* there must be a similar door on the upper floor of the clinic. Mikel looked back toward Rubio. He caught his eye and twirled his hand in a motion signaling to turn the attendant away. As soon as her back was to him he pushed against the door. It opened, and a blaring claxon horn sounded. He looked across and saw the door's twin leading into the top floor of the clinic. He hurriedly closed the door and apologized profusely as the attendant came running up.

"I'm terribly sorry," Mikel said sheepishly, "I thought that was an exit to a balcony."

She tested the door to make sure it was still locked.

"No harm done," she said dismissively, "just be careful."

"Thank you, I will."

They examined the remaining puppet and marionette displays on their way back to the lobby of the theater.

"That was embarrassing," Rubio said, "didn't you know it would be alarmed?"

"Of course I did. I just needed to confirm that there is an identical door leading into the clinic. There is. Both doors access a fire escape to the back of the building, which abuts the train tracks. It'll be easy to get there without being seen. Now we need to know where the clinic's records are kept and what kind of alarms they have,

"How do you propose to do that?" Rubio asked.

"Watch and learn." he said.

"Señorita," Mikel addressed the young woman at the clinic's front desk, "my uncle was treated here several years ago when the clinic was run by another doctor. He is entering the hospital for surgery and his surgeon would like to have his medical history. He couldn't find it in the ministry records. He's anxious to know if they are still here."

"How long ago was your uncle here?"

"About seven years ago, I think."

183

"That was when the clinic was owned by Dr. Miguel Ortega. He's now the Minister of Health you know.""

"No, I wasn't aware. That's quite a prestigious position."

"We should have your uncle's records. We are required to retain them for at least ten years. We had several cabinets full. They were taking up too much space, so we brought in a company to scan them to discs. What is your uncle's name?"

"José Alvarez Cunha," Mikel said with a straight face.

"Just a minute, Dr. Salazar's records are kept on the old desk top on the top floor. You realize of course that I won't be able to give you his records, for privacy reasons, but he can give the surgeon permission to get them."

The receptionist hurried off to the elevator.

"That's a lucky break," Rubio said. "We can retrieve the old records with the computer as well without having to go through the files."

"What about the records for the new owners?"

"It looks like they are kept here in that computer system behind the receptionist's desk."

"Great, while I'm looking through the old records you'll need to come down and tap into the system and copy the computer records."

"Sure, give me the hard job!"

"As smart as you are, it should be a piece of cake."

"Says a man who can't turn a computer on."

The young woman returned with a blank look.

"I'm sorry, I can't find anyone by that name on any of the discs."

"Well thanks for trying. I guess they got lost in the shuffle."

Mikel and Rubio walked out into the bright plaza.

"Follow me." Mikel said.

He led them down a narrow alley to the back of the museum/theater/clinic. They walked down the edge of the railroad track to the point where the two buildings abutted in back. Just as Mikel thought there was a fire escape dangling off

184

the rear. It was the type where the first ladder hangs several feet above the ground to discourage casual entry to the roof. He looked in both directions.

"Let's go!"

He climbed the retaining wall. Rubio followed.

"Okay, boost me up so I can grab the ladder. I want you to stay here and keep a lookout. If someone comes along, whistle and I'll lay low. Act like you're waiting for a train to pass before you cross over.

Rubio interlaced his fingers and lifted Mikel so he could reach the ladder. The section slid down and a cascade of rust rained down on them. Mikel shook the red dust from his hair and scurried up the fire escape. Rubio sat on the wall and pretended to pare his nails.

Mikel climbed up the escape past the landings on the first three floors of the clinic. He couldn't see anyone through the rear windows. The accumulated grime from the passing trains obscured most visibility from inside. He scaled the last section. It opened onto a six-foot-wide, eight-foot-high channel running from the back to the parapet in front, beyond the emergency doors. The electrical and phone wires were attached to a standoff on the roof adjacent to the landing. The *Telefonos de España* cabinet fed the phone lines into the standoff and an innocuous little brown box co-located with the cabinet bore the logo of a popular alarm company. Mikel noted the make and model for reference. He walked quietly to the front and verified that the emergency door to the clinic's top floor was functional and that it was alarmed. He saw two pairs of wires in the gap between the top of the door and the frame. Satisfied that he would be able to disable the alarm and access the door, he retreated to the fire escape and descended.

"How'd it go?" Rubio asked.

"I think we should be able to get in and out in less than ten minutes, with no alarm going off."

185

"I hope you are right Mikel, I don't relish spending time in a Tolosa jail."

Mikel drove them to a seedy, nondescript hotel in a small village five miles away. He registered with a fake driver's license and paid the 25 Euros in cash.

"What next?" Rubio said.

"I'm going on line to get information on the particular alarm system the clinic uses. I've seen it before, but you can never be too careful. While that's booting up, why don't you show me how to use that device you have for burning disks."

"It's really pretty simple."

Five minutes later, after Mikel had successfully copied several CDs that Rubio brought, he was ready for his task. The signal on his laptop alerted him that the diagrams and schematics for the clinic's alarm system had completed downloading.

Mikel spent the next three hours mentally dissecting the inner workings of the alarm system. He knew precisely which wires inside the little brown box had to be bridged to prevent an alarm from being transmitted to the central monitoring center in Bilbao. He also knew which fuse to pull to neutralize the system once they were inside. The trickiest part was getting into the emergency door without setting off the klaxon. He thought he had that figured too. He was puzzled as to why this small clinic way out here in the boondocks needed such an elaborate alarm system? It obviously had been installed by Dr. Ortega and left in place when he sold it.

The sun was fast disappearing behind the mountains around Zumarraga to the west when he finished. Rubio had fallen asleep watching some insipid novella that his wife liked. The incessant buzz from the TV was as effective as a tranquilizer. Mikel shook him.

"Wake up."

"Wha...whassup?"

"I've got it all doped out. Let's order in a pizza and then get some shut-eye. We're going out at two in the morning."

"Okay?"

"What do you like?"

"Lotsa meat and cheese, and a few chiles."

"You got it."

Mikel picked up the phone and dialed the pizzeria listed on the room circular.

"Dos carnivores con queso y chiles, medio. Dos cervezas ademas. Posada Oria, sala uno, dos, dos. Si. Gracias."

Pizzas and beers dispatched, the two budding burglars turned in for four hours sleep. Mikel set his wrist alarm.

Mikel drove slowly into Tolosa. The streets were virtually empty until they approached the *Euskal Heria Plaza*. The plaza was littered with confetti and streamers from a puppet festival. Several street sweepers were trying to corral the debris in the midst of swirling winds.

Mikel pulled onto the side street closest to the theater and killed the engine.

"Tough luck. Didn't know they were celebrating tonight.'

"What do we do now?

"Hunker down and catch a few more Z's."

"What?"

"That's American for sleep."

"Oh."

Mikel peeked over the steering wheel. The last sweeper was trundling off toward downtown.

"Wake up Rubio. They're gone. It's almost four. We have to hurry."

Mikel led Rubio across the plaza and into the alley to the back. Two minutes later they were on the roof with all their gear. Mikel donned his night vision goggles and opened his tool box. He gingerly removed the alarm box cover. He shielded the box

187

with his body and shined a small pen light on the printed circuit board. He saw the two terminals he needed to bridge. He took a short piece of wire terminated in alligator clips and attached them.

"Okay, now for the tough part."

He walked to the emergency door. He slid a thin sheet of metal between the door facing and the latch. He heard it pop open.

"Okay Rubio, there are four wires running across the inside of the door on top. When I say go, pull the door open. Wait until I have my light ready. Okay, go!"

There was a microsecond of Klaxon before Mikel severed the red and green wires and it stopped.

"Be very still," he said.

He waited a few seconds.

"Okay I don't hear anybody or see any lights. I think we're good."

He propped the door open with his tool box and entered. He could see the outline of a desk with an old computer on top. Next to it were two CD ROM trays.

"Okay Mikel that's your target," Rubio said. "Copy all those disks while I go downstairs."

"Got it. Be careful, Take the stairs."

"Right. I'll whistle if I see anything."

"No, take this two-way radio. If you need me just press the button and speak."

"Man, you think of everything don't you?"

"I've found it's the only way to stay alive in this business."

Mikel sat down and pulled the discs over to him. The night vision lenses produced an eerie glow. Rubio took his computer and a 5-terabit external drive with him down the stairs.

"How's it going Rubio?" Mikel radioed after a few minutes.

"I'm into the system and it's begun downloading. Just a few more minutes."

"Okay, make it fast."

188

Rubio was unplugging his computer when a flashlight beam pierced the darkness through the front window. He froze behind the desk. The light bounced around the room. Whoever was holding it went to the door and shook it. After a few seconds the light trailed away.

"Whew! That was close," Rubio said when he got back to the fourth floor. He was breathing hard from exertion and fright.

"What happened?"

"A night watchman came by and shined a light inside. He almost caught me. He shook the front door like he thought he saw something and then he went away."

"Okay, you got everything?"

"Yeah."

"Let's get out of here."

They sneaked back to Mikel's car, stowed everything in the trunk, and got in. Mikel started the engine and rolled away in the dark before turning on the lights. He didn't see the man in the shadows squinting at his license plate, desperately trying to make out the numbers.

189

27

Maria had been to the Cathedral of St. James twice; once, when she was among a small group of communicants chosen from across the diocese to receive their first communion, to be celebrated by the bishop; the second was to attend the funeral mass for her grandfather, a sexton at St. James for forty years. The first was terrifying for a young girl used to the smaller confines of St. Francis. The second was heartbreaking, saying goodbye to her maternal grandfather who was such a positive force in her life.

Maria was the first to arrive at the clinic that morning. There was a note on her desk to call Miguel Ortega. She thought it curious. She had made sure that the team was scrupulous about reporting their search activities to the ministry. She checked her watch. It was too early to call. Their offices don't open until nine. She would be on the way to St. James by then,

"I'll call him when I get back," she said to herself.

She logged on to her computer and checked incoming emails. There was one from Rubio. She opened it.

"The fishing expedition was successful. I will be in later and bring some of the catch for you to take home. It's on ice."

She had told Rubio and Mikel to be careful and not send any incriminating messages over the internet. His email may have been a little too obscure. Anyway, it was good to know that they had succeeded and, so far, they had not been caught. She would catch up with them when she got back this afternoon.

190

Even though St. James is the seat of the Roman Catholic Church in Basque country, on first appearance it is less imposing than St. Francis. However, unlike St. Francis, St. James is not overshadowed by modern office buildings intruding on its old neighborhood streets. The gothic cathedral's salient feature is its single bell tower soaring above the red neighborhood rooftops surrounding it. The spire rises a full 150 feet and is visible from any location in Bilbao. Its carillon has been calling the faithful to worship since the thirteenth century when Bilbao was just a dusty stop for pilgrims on the way to *Santiago* to venerate St. James, the martyred disciple of Christ. Legend says James had preached in Galicia and was brought back there for burial after his martyrdom in the Holy Land.

Maria crossed the ornately patterned tile square to the neo-classical church annex. She and Father Giuseppe were asked to be available at eleven. The tribunal was to meet at nine-thirty. The old priest was sitting on a bench outside the bishop's offices, head bowed, fingering his well-worn rosary beads. He looked up at the sound of her approaching footsteps.

"Maria, how good to see you. Are you well?"

"Considering everything that's gone on for the last few days I am. And you, Father?"

"Aside from a few pops and creaks every time I get up, I'm fine."

"You're like fine wine Father; you just get better with age."

"You flatter me my child. But like all old fools, I am susceptible to flattery from beautiful young women."

"Have you heard anything yet?"

"They convened at nine-thirty. I got here around ten-thirty and I haven't seen anyone leave the room."

A burst of light flooded the anteroom as the outside door swung open. It was Vitorio and his advocate, Roberto Soares, a local lawyer famous for representing wayward members of the clergy. The two sat on a bench across from Maria.

"How are you Maria?" Vitorio asked.

191

"I've been better. And you?"

"I'm well, but I expect to be better when this is over."

His smirking, imperious attitude rankled Maria. She couldn't resist responding.

"How could you stoop so low as to hire an investigator to spy on me? Especially, since you so blatantly broke your marriage vows."

"Sauce for the goose, or however that old saying goes."

"You know full well I haven't been unfaithful to you."

"Didn't look that way in the photos," he said.

"I think it best you not say any more on that subject," Soares advised.

"Very well, I'll try to keep the conversation light," Vitorio said.

"How's your *work* with Señor von Hesse going?" Again, the smirk after emphasizing the word work.

"It's progressing nicely thank you."

"Did your emissaries to the health ministry turn up anything interesting?"

Maria's face mirrored her shock. She took a moment to recover.

"How do you know about that?"

"I have my ways."

Again, the smirk.

"How's the business doing? I checked Dun and Bradstreet again. They estimate your little company would fetch over ten million Euros on the open market. You should be very proud of yourself."

Maria was dumbfounded by the sheer gall of this man she had called her husband. Dr. Jekyll couldn't turn into Mr. Hyde so fast.

"Do you really think you can do what you did and get away with it?" she said. "I built my company—without you—just as you did yours. You have no right to a claim on any of it."

192

"We'll see what the three priests on the other side of that door have to say. Those pictures are worth a thousand words."

"My son, I would counsel you to be more humble and contrite after what you have done," Father Giuseppe interjected.

"I am only seeking justice, Father. Our vows said we became one when we married. As one, I have a right to our common properties don't I. Obviously we have both committed the same sin of adultery. I would say that puts us on equal footing before the court."

"Vitorio, did you learn nothing in catechism about the cardinal sins. You have trampled on at least three of them in this affair. You are guilty of the sins of pride, greed and adultery. When this is over, I pray that you will go to confession and pray for forgiveness."

Vitorio turned red. He jumped to his feet and crossed the corridor. He stood above the little priest, glaring down at him.

"Enough little man, stop spouting this drivel. You and I both know that religion is a farce perpetrated on the masses to enrich the church."

Giuseppe was struck dumb. He crossed himself and rose to confront Vitorio.

"May God forgive you for such blasphemy Vitorio. Unless you repent and seek God's forgiveness you are doomed to burn in hell for eternity."

The doors to the tribunal opened and a church scribe beckoned them to enter.

"Vitorio," Giuseppe said quietly, "when this is over come to me. God can forgive anything."

Vitorio just stared at the little friar.

"When this is over, I won't need your God."

The three judges were sitting on a raised platform overlooking a row of chairs in front. The scribe sat at a table to one side. They did not introduce themselves. Maria leaned over to Giuseppe.

"Do you know them?"

"No, I think the bishop called them in from another parish. It's not unheard of."

"This is not a court of law," said the center priest. "Our decision in this matter will be a result of prayerful consideration on our part as to the legitimacy of the petitioner's argument. We have reviewed her petition and the response from her husband.

"The decision to nullify a marriage consecrated between two baptized communicants cannot be taken lightly. We will now ask each of you to state your positions personally. Afterwards we may ask questions. You are free to answer your questions or to seek counsel before doing so. We will begin with the petitioner, Maria Elizondo Vegas.

"Señora, do you affirm that all statements made by you in your petitioning documents are true and were not coerced in any way?"

"I do."

"Now, It is our understanding that you were not aware of any infidelities on Vitorio's part until the one alleged with Sophia Suarez. Is that true?"

"Yes, although there have been other occasions in which I believe Vitorio was unfaithful."

"This court cannot entertain any unsubstantiated claims. Now you also claim that Vitorio declared early in your marriage that he did not intend to have children. Is that true?"

Yes."

"And what reason did he give?"

"He said that our lives were too hectic and with our busy travel schedules and late meetings it would be unfair to our children."

"Did you agree with him?"

"No."

"Did you know that part of your commitment to God when you married was to procreate, if possible."

"I did."

"Did you make these facts known to your priest?"

"I did, to Father Giuseppe here."

"Is that true Father Giuseppe?"

"Yes. I counseled the couple that it was God's wish that they have children."

"What was their response?"

"Maria said she would like children. Vitorio said he did not want the responsibility of bringing children into the world."

"Was that the end of it?"

"No, I counseled them on many occasions to change their position."

"So, Maria," the priest continued, "these are the only two charges you have leveled against Vitorio?"

"Formally, yes. There are other things that have come to light since I filed my petition that I believe the court should be made aware of."

"Are you prepared to present them now?"

"Yes, Father Giuseppe will present them."

"Father, are you prepared to intercede?"

"Yes."

"Begin."

"As you are aware from the documents presented by Vitorio, he is counterclaiming that Maria is guilty of adultery, as well as he, and is claiming the right to half of the family assets. His proof of her sin is a series of photographs showing Maria with another man at her house. On first blush the photographs point toward an intimacy between Maria and a Señor von Hesse. Upon further reflection and explanation, it has been shown that there was none. Señor von Hesse was merely comforting a grieving wife.

"A detailed cell phone electronic time-line provided by Señor von Hesse clearly shows there was no intimacy between the couple. We believe the spying and the photographs

195

were merely underhanded attempts by Vitorio to extort money from Maria."

"How so?" asked the judge.

Father Giuseppe approached the dais and placed three envelopes in front of the judges.

"These envelopes contain documents showing that Vitorio Elizondo Vega did conspire to defraud clients of his brokerage firm. Greed and pride drove him to place them in investments that he knew were extremely risky. He thought he would make a fortune through an arcane bond scheme. When it failed his clients were out five million Euros which had to be underwritten by Vitorio's trading partner Goldman Sachs in Madrid. Goldman Sachs remunerated the investors. They placed Vitorio on probation and gave him six months to pay back the money to Goldman. If he does not, they will refer him to the CNMV for prosecution. The end of those six months is fast approaching. I submit that the entire photo expedition was a ruse to force the court to award Vitorio half of Maria's estate so that he could get out from under this cloud.

"On Maria's behalf I urge the court to grant nullity so that she can get on with her life. It is apparent that Vitorio entered into the marriage under false pretenses which have manifested themselves in his subsequent actions. Her company is involved in some of the most valuable work dedicated to the betterment of mankind. It would be a tragedy if she were forced to sell it to satisfy Vitorio's extortion."

"Anything more, Father?"

"No, that concludes our presentation of the facts in support of Maria's petition for nullity."

"Thank you, be seated."

"Senor Vitorio Elizondo Vega, are you prepared to present your rebuttal to your wife's petition?"

The blood had drained from Vitorio's face. He slumped in his seat, unable to rise. He was a beaten man. He grabbed the table edge and rose slowly from his seat.

196

"Everything I have to say is contained in the forms I submitted and the photographs showing Maria consorting with another man. I only ask this court for justice."

He sat back down.

"If neither of you have any more submissions or comments this tribunal will take under advisement your petitions and will render a verdict within the week. Thank you and may God bless you."

The advocates and the petitioners filed out into the hallway. Vitorio turned on Maria with murder in his eyes.

"Where the hell did you get that information?"

"My dearest Vitorio, as you yourself said, 'sauce for the goose', etcetera, etcetera.'"

"This isn't over!" he screamed. "I'll see you dead and in hell before it is!"

He stormed out of the cathedral annex slamming the large oak door so hard that it shuddered on its hinges. Father Giuseppe cringed at the sound.

"Be very careful, Maria. A cornered animal can be extremely dangerous."

28

Rubio Salazar lay crumpled against the passenger door of Mikel Muñoz' aging sedan, sound asleep. Midnight capers were not his forte. He was not only exhausted from sleep deprivation but by the complete draining of his adrenal glands during the burglary. Visions of striped uniforms and iron bars flitted through his subconscious. He came awake when Mikel shook him.

"What? Where are we?" he stammered as he struggled to rejoin the conscious world.

"We're back in Bilbao, outside my office complex."

"Why?"

"I thought it might be best for us to do a trial run through these records before we dump them on your team. I don't know what they would do with the raw data. You're the expert there."

"Okay, what kind of equipment do you have in your office?"

"Come up and take a look."

The Muñoz Servicios de Investigacion were located on the fifth floor of an old warehouse in the Portugatete section of Bilbao. The rear of the building backed up to the Nervión River. A group of ambitious developers had gutted the old structure and converted the spacious interior into loft offices. Muñoz' firm occupied three small rooms in the rear with views across the river.

The renovators had restored and modified the old freight elevator for passenger service. They felt it added novelty and a touch of originality to the building. The hard jolt when it reached the top floor was a bit unnerving to Rubio. He grabbed a handrail fully expecting the ancient pulley mechanism to collapse and crash to the bottom floor.

"You get used to it after a while. It's actually good to have space to bring large items up. Another great feature is, you always know when someone is coming. Follow me."

Mikel led Rubio down a corridor to a vestibule off an abbreviated hallway that opened onto his office and that of two other firms.

"I have an import-export company on one side and a wine negociant on the other. They need the availability of warehouse space nearby."

"So, why is this a good location for a private investigator?"

"It's private, it's inexpensive, nobody just drops in, plus I get some really good wine deals."

Mikel keyed in a four-digit number on the door's keypad. The tumblers fell into place. He stepped inside and entered a code to silence the alarm.

"Come on in."

There was a small reception desk obviously an amenity for future use. The only appliance on the desk was an old, black, land line telephone.

"I hope to hire a receptionist when my business picks up," Mikel added by way of explanation.

Two offices, each four meters square, with windows overlooking the river, were located behind the reception area. Mikel's office on the right was Spartan; desk, filing cabinets, two guest chairs and incongruously, the mounted head of a buffalo.

"What is that?' Rubio asked.

199

"That's to remind me of my humble beginnings in the mountains of Montana."

"What do you mean?"

"No one told you my history?"

"No."

"I was born in the state of Montana in the US. My grandparents fled *Guernika* after Franco. They settled among the mountain region's Basque sheep herders. My parents weren't keen on being shepherds and moved to Boise, Idaho, one state over. I went to college, got a degree in criminology, and joined the police force. I retired a couple of years ago. I came over to Gorliz to visit cousins, liked it, and stayed."

"So, you're an American."

"Yeah, I guess so. Come on. I'll show you my computer room."

Mikel opened the other door. Stacked against the wall adjoining his office were shelves of electronic equipment; printers (2D and 3D), digital recorders, old reel-to-reel recorders, mini-computers, HD monitors and various and sundry other devices used in surveillance work.

"What is this? I thought you knew nothing about computers and such?"

"Never divulge everything. That way you can maintain a few secrets. If people know too much about you there's nothing left to surprise them with. Maintain a little mystery. Keep your adversaries off balance."

"Why show this to me?"

"The one thing you are that I'm not is a coder. I've watched you whip out complex programs with ease. I can't do that. We need that talent to unravel what's going on in Basquerville," he giggled. "Get it, Basqueville."

The blank stare told Mikel that Rubio was not a student of Sherlock Holmes.

Rubio assembled the computer, drives and burner equipment on the workbench in the lab. He ran wires to connect the various machines, preparing to download the data collected in Tolosa.

"Let's start with the old records," he said.

There were 20 CDs containing the records from Miguel Ortega's practice. Rubio systematically loaded them into a high capacity hard drive. He accessed the drive with the high-speed computer he had used to dump the current records from the Tolosa clinic. He then began to scan them using the same software he had developed for the seven ministry offices. Within minutes his monitor screen blossomed with several pages of records from patients displaying the specified blood criteria. He ran a second sort that eliminated children under ten and women. That reduced the list by two-thirds to a much more manageable size.

Since the clinic treated only psychiatric patients, it didn't collect as much detailed blood data as regular medical practices. Rubio began looking for AB types with hemophilia A and von Willebrand 2n symptoms and a history of seizures. The list shrank to less than a page.

"What do you think?" Mikel asked. "Anything pop out at you?"

Rubio stared at the screen, transfixed.

"What? What do you see?" Mikel demanded.

"What was the name of that priest who went nuts, number 193 I believe?"

"Just a sec. I recorded it on my phone. Here it is, Alejandro Diaz. Why?"

Rubio leaned back so that Mikel could see the screen. There, highlighted in yellow, was the name *Alejandro Diaz."*

Mikel let out a whistle.

"Looks like we won't have to search the country for him after all, there he is. Let me see the records that Ortega collected on him."

"I knew it!" Mikel exclaimed after a quick search. "Alejandro was an AB Rh-null withvon Willebrand 2n. He would

201

have been the perfect candidate. We need to find out what happened to him between the time Ortega stopped treating him and the time he died."

"He last saw Ortega in 2009. There are no patient records for him after that, and we know there were none in the public ministry records. Let's see if we can find an obituary for him."

Rubio googled area obituaries for the past ten years. He entered Alejandro Diaz' name. There were 15 responses. None of them fit the profile or location of the mysterious priest.

"Let me try something," Mikel said.

He sat down at the computer and began to key in various codes from a notebook.

"Bingo!"

"What?"

"Check this out."

Father Alejandro Diaz passed away in San Sebastian yesterday following a long confinement. Father Alejandro served the church faithfully in various parishes throughout northern Spain for many years. He will be sorely missed by his fellow laborers in the field, his former parishioners, and his church family. In accordance with his wishes and those of his family Father Alejandro was cremated and his ashes were buried in the churchyard at Sagrada Familia Amara. A memorial mass will be held on Sunday at the chapel of The Sagrada Familia, his last parish assignment.

"Why couldn't you find it in the regular obituaries?" Rubio asked.

"This appeared as a private obituary notice that is confined to the church hierarchy. It is not disseminated to the general public. Most newspapers are aware that it exists but have learned not to publish the obituaries, even if they surface outside the church. The church has made it abundantly clear that anything published from their private communication organs is off limits to non-church authorities. A few breaches of that unspoken

202

agreement have found the offenders either unemployed or banned from any future church communiqués."

"Why should the church care?"

"Most of the items published in this way are directed to a select group within the church. It is a unique way to pass on news to this group without risking regular channels such as the internet or social media networks. Usually, the underlying details, if widely disseminated, could prove embarrassing to the church."

"Such as?"

"For years the church was able to keep a lid on its worldwide pedophilia scandal," Mikel explained. "A nod here, a wink there and the latest embarrassment just went away. It was not until 2003, when some enterprising reporters in Boston refused to be cowed by religious and political authorities that the scandal erupted into public view. Since then scores of priests and high church officials have been either convicted of crimes or banished from the church. Hundreds of millions of dollars in restitution have been paid to victims and their families. The Vatican, under Benedict, made a half-hearted effort to purge its ranks but moving that ossified hierarchy to act has frustrated even Pope Francis."

"Then these internal communications are meant to keep those on the inside abreast of what's going on without arousing public scrutiny or curiosity?"

"Exactly, and some reporters have become very adept at decoding those messages." Mikel added. "For instance, that line in the obituary for Alejandro that says, 'after a long confinement,' means either he was medically incapacitated, or he was psychologically unfit to carry out his duties and potentially dangerous. Dangerous in this sense can carry many connotations.

"You think the latter?"

"He *was* seeing a psychiatrist," Mikel emphasized, "one whose practice was hidden away in a small clinic, in a small town, adjacent to a train station. How convenient. A clinic that had an extraordinary level of electronic security. There has to be a reason for that."

"What are you thinking?" Rubio asked.

"When was the last time you recall a priest being cremated and then memorialized in a small, out-of-the-way chapel?"

"Never. It was my belief that they were never cremated. It has something to do with the promise of the resurrection of the body, when Christ returns to claim the righteous on Judgment Day."

"Exactly. There's something fishy going on here. Someone is trying to hide something. Let's see if we can find out what it is."

29

"Good morning Maria," Dietrich said as he entered her office. "I didn't hear from you after the tribunal yesterday. How did it go?"

"It was very difficult for me emotionally; having to confront Vitorio in front of the three priests. If anything, his behavior has become even more bizarre since we heard about the surveillance and the photos.

"While we were waiting outside the chambers he was snide and extremely rude to me and to Father Giuseppe. He gloated about how the pictures of my infidelity were going to make him rich, that the court would see his side and award him half of our family assets. Then he said something very strange. He said, 'How did it go with the search of the Ministry of Health's files?' How could he have known about that? Someone at Clinica must have told him. I can't imagine who. As far as I know Vitorio was never that close to any of my employees."

"Maybe he got it from someone at one of the seven ministry offices. I don't know how, but it's a possibility."

"That seems farfetched. I'll think I'll ask Mikel Muñoz to check it out."

"What happened after your confrontation with Vitorio?"

We were called into the court chambers where they asked each of us to testify concerning our petition and counter-petition. I presented my case in support of the documents I submitted. They then asked me if I had anything more to add. I told them that new information had come to light concerning Vitorio's actions and motivations. I said Father Giuseppe would present the documents supporting our new charges. The Father presented the papers that you had provided and your timeline information for the night in question, proving there could have been no infidelity on my part.

"The judges then asked Vitorio to present his counterarguments. He was so stunned by this new information as presented by Father Giuseppe that it looked like neither he nor his lawyer was capable of responding. He finally got up and said that all his evidence was contained in his counter charges and he asked the judges to recognize his rights as head of our family and to treat him justly.

"The judges said they would take all the evidence under advisement and would render a decision within a week. Then we were dismissed. When we left their chambers Vitorio became incredibly abusive to me and to the Father. He said he would see me dead and in hell before this was over. I've never seen anyone so enraged."

"I think you should hire some protection until you know what's what. If anything happens to you before a nullity judgment, Vitorio would inherit your estate. I'm assuming you haven't changed your will since this all started."

"No, it never crossed my mind. I'll be fine here at the office, but maybe I'll hire a driver and get a private security service to watch the house. I can't believe all this has happened in such a short time.

"What's happening on your end?" she asked.

"I told you about sending Therese some help. Well, I heard from Rob Simpson and there's been a breakthrough on the work with factor VIII and von Willebrand 2n using CRISPR. He wants David Weiss to come back to Los Altos with some other specifically modified DNA specimens. I said I would send David over and since you have everything under control here, I thought I'd go over with him. Besides, I'm anxious to see how Rupert is

206

doing and I can spell Therese some while the kids are there. She needs some down time from her hospital duty."

"Go! We can handle this end. By the way, Rubio and Mikel were able to get the data we sent them to collect. They'll be in the office this afternoon to see if there's anything we can use."

"Super, I hope there is. I'll only be gone two or three days. Keep me posted by email and I'll let you know what's happening at SciGen."

Rubio finished running the rest of the sorts on the Tolosa records and copied them to two separate thumb drives. Meanwhile, Mikel was next door making phone calls.

"Ready to go?" Rubio asked, poking his head into Mikel's office.

Mikel held up a silencing finger.

"Yes, thank you very much. You've been extremely helpful. Good-bye."

Rubio looked at Mikel inquisitively.

"I'm trying to track down some folks who may be able to shed some light on our mysterious friar."

"Anything to share?"

"I don't have the total story yet, so I'll hold off for now. You got everything wrapped up on your end?"

"Yeah, it's all here," he said, holding up the two thumb drives. "You take one of these for security and backup."

"Good," he said and put the spare drive into a floor mounted safe. "We're outa here."

The Sagarin jet touched down at the Bilbao airport for the second time in less than a week and taxied to the private aviation terminal. The pilots exited the plane. Dietrich's parents and children stayed on board.

"Marcel, good to see you," Dietrich said. "Everything go okay from Zurich?"

"Yes sir. No problems. We will top off our tanks here and be ready to go in a few minutes."

"Dr. Weiss aboard?"

"Yes sir, we had to helicopter him back from Bern, but he made it."

"Good. I'm optimistic that he will be able to make a breakthrough with Rob Simpson's new CRISPR discovery."

"I certainly hope so, for Rupert's sake. Any updates?"

"Still holding his own. He's beginning to respond to Therese's voice. I hope he will be fully awake by the time we get to California."

"I hope so too, sir. We're all praying for him."

"Thank you, Marcel. All prayers gratefully accepted."

Dietrich went aboard to hugs and tears from Elise and Dieter and encouragement from his parents. The strain of the past two weeks showed in Friederich and Frieda von Hesse's faces. He didn't look forward to the rigors of 20 hours on a plane for them but at least their company would be agreeable.

The plane took off and banked over the Bilbao waterfront. Dietrich watched idly as a nondescript old sedan sped down the Nerviòn littoral and crossed to the east side of the river.

Mikel pulled into the clinic's garage and parked in a reserved spot. He was in a hurry and not in the mood to observe corporate niceties. He and Rubio went directly to the fifth floor. They walked right past the secretary and into Maria's office. She looked up from her computer.

"Good work on the fishing expedition," she teased. "Show me what you caught."

"It's even better than we thought. We spent this morning sorting through the files and we came across a very interesting name."

"Whose?"

"Alejandro Diaz."

Maria had a puzzled look, then a light flashed.

"The mad priest!"

"Exactly! He turned up in the old clinic files when Ortega still ran things,"

"Where is he?"

"What's left of him is in an urn buried in the church yard at *Sagrada Familia Amara* chapel in San Sebastian."

"How long ago?"

"2011."

"Do you know how he died?"

"No, but it's very mysterious. There was no obituary published in the regular papers. I found it by digging through some internal church organs. These publications are closely guarded by the powers-that-be in the church. All reporters soon learn that they are off limits. The strange thing is the cremation. Neither of us knows of any Catholic priest, ever, that has been cremated. The question is why this particular priest?"

"Any ideas?"

"Yeah, but nothing I can take to the bank yet," Mikel said.

"Keep digging," she added, "Oh, by the way, while you're here I need a favor."

"Shoot."

"It's no secret that I'm going through a rather nasty divorce from my husband Vitorio. Well, at the nullity tribunal yesterday things got really heated and when we left the building Vitorio threatened me. Now I don't know how serious a threat it was but I'm going to be cautious and treat it seriously. The favor I'm asking is this, do you know someone you would recommend as a security guard at my house until this is over?"

Mikel thought for a moment.

"Actually, I know a couple of guys I could recommend but I have a better idea. I have a vagabond that I rigged up as a surveillance vehicle. Why don't I come out and put together an alarm system for your house? Then, if you want, I can park the vagabond nearby and monitor your house. If an alarm goes off, it'll alert me, and I'll be right there."

"You would do that?"

"Look, I'm single, I live alone in Gorliz, I got nothing better to do."

"I would really appreciate that, Mikel. You're sure it won't inconvenience you."

"Nah, I'm already up to my neck in your business. No problem."

"How much will you charge me?"

"The cost of the equipment. What you're paying me already will cover my time. Maybe, when this is all over, you can take me out to one of those fancy restaurants by the river."

"You've got a deal, Mikel. Thank you."

"Señora Maria," Rubio began, "you've known Dr. Ortega for a long time, haven't you?"

"Yes, we were in medical training together at Cardenal Carrillo University in Valencia. Why do you ask?"

"I believe he was related to Cardinal Ortega's family?"

"Yes, I believe that's true. The Cardinal was a great uncle or something."

"I read that the cardinal was involved in journalism and church politics before he decided to follow his brothers into the priesthood."

"That I didn't know. Miguel and I never discussed it."

"What Mikel and I are wondering is how a little-known psychiatrist with a famous name went from a small practice in Tolosa to the head of the Basque Health Ministry without working his way up the medical, political and ecclesiastical ladder."

"Good question, Rubio. I lost contact with Miguel for several years. I didn't know where he was practicing. I don't think I even knew he went into psychiatry. He was always very bright and studious; something of a loner, so when his name appeared as the new head of the ministry I don't think anyone was surprised."

"Who would have had to pass on his qualifications before he was selected for the job?"

210

"I'm not sure but I'll bet you Mikel can find out."

"I find it very strange," Rubio said. "The whole situation surrounding Ortega; the ministry, the clinic in Tolosa, Alejandro Diaz, Ortega's abrupt elevation to the head of medicine in *Euskal*. Something doesn't add up."

"That you should ask me about Miguel is ironic. I had a message waiting to call him. I didn't have time before the tribunal. I'll call him while you brief the other members of the team. I'll get them up to the conference room."

"Miguel, how are you? Sorry I didn't get right back to you, but I was tied up in some personal matters."

"That's okay Maria. That's part of what my call is about. I'm so sorry to hear about your split with Vitorio. It seems so sudden."

"Thank you, Miguel. It was sudden. I'm pretty sure the sordid details have made it onto the social gossip circuit, so I'll make sure you get the facts straight from the horse's mouth, so to speak.

"A few weeks ago, I found out that Vitorio was having an illicit affair with Sophia Suarez. You remember her. We were with her and her husband Ronaldo at the Figueroa party a few months back. I confronted him. He became infuriated and belligerent, at first denying everything. When it was obvious that I had irrefutable proof, he stormed out of the house. He hired an investigator and cooked up a narrative that I was having an affair as well, which is definitely not true."

That was the other thing I wanted to discuss," Ortega said, "the rumors that you were seeing Señor von Hesse on a personal basis."

Maria was dumbfounded that such information had found its way to Miguel Ortega so quickly. Her head was spinning.

"As you know he is my client. After Vitorio stormed out I didn't want to be all alone in the house. I asked Señor von Hesse to dinner the next night. We discussed the work we are doing for

211

Sagarin and then we began talking about Vitorio and his reaction to my accusations. I became very emotional and Dietrich made an effort to console me. That's when Vitorio's spy took those clandestine photographs of us. On the surface they may look incriminating, but an analysis of Dietrich's cell phone locator app substantiates that there could not have been any improper goings-on between him and me. Father Giuseppe and the tribunal have accepted that evidence."

"*Dietrich*, is it? You're on a first name basis now? This situation could become very embarrassing for me and the ministry if it becomes known that one of your clients was misrepresenting himself to gain access to ministry records."

"I assure you, Miguel, there is not a shred of truth to Vitorio's allegations. My relationship with Señor von Hesse is strictly business."

"I also understand Maria," Miguel said, ignoring her statement and plowing ahead, "that your field technicians gathered data that was not authorized under the original request."

"That's true, but we cleared it with your agency beforehand. No information we gathered has been given to anyone but your own people for approval. Based on the extra data we collected we were able to recommend to an insurance client the most favorable locations for the establishment of their service offices. That should be good for the agency as well as our client's policy holders."

There was a significant pause. Maria could hear Miguel's heavy breathing.

"Have you found anything in the blood data that is beneficial to your client?"

"So far no, but my computer geeks are still running multiple analyses."

"Please keep me informed?'

"I will Miguel, I assure you."

The phone went dead.

Maria walked into the conference room where Mikel and Rubio were finishing up their presentation to the *four horsemen*.

"So, as you can see," Rubio said, "the only major discovery was running across Alejandro Diaz' name in the Tolosa data."

"Do you think there may be more potential candidates buried in all those numbers?" Maria asked.

"It's hard to say," Mikel said. "We certainly hope so. There are a few more angles we can look at. We'll see."

"That's good work on Mikel and Rubio's part. At least we have a lead on one of our four selections, even though he's dead. Mikel is going to try to find out what happened to our crazy Monk and what possible connection he may have to Miguel Ortega, other than as a psychiatric patient.

"How about the other three candidates?"

"We've contacted the ministry for permission to interview them," Rubio said. "So far, no response."

""Keep trying."

"Meantime, Rubio raised a question that I believe warrants further investigation—and I believe that even more strongly now that I just got off the phone with Miguel Ortega. Rubio wonders how and why a little-known psychiatrist operating out of a small clinic in an out-of-the-way village, all of a sudden becomes head of the Basque Health Ministry. I wasn't even aware that Miguel had wound up in Tolosa running a psychiatric clinic.

"I just returned a call to him. He was very interested and inquisitive about what we are doing with our surveys and seemingly upset that we expanded their scope. He's obviously reading everything we report to his people with a high degree of interest. Why?

"Do any of you have any insights on Ortega and how he got his job?" Mikel asked.

"Miguel and I attended Cardinal Carrillo University together," Maria said. "He introduced me to Vitorio. He and Vitorio were friends growing up. Miguel was best man at our

213

wedding. After graduation we moved on to different medical schools and lost touch, until he moved to Bilbao as health minister. Rubio did a little background check and found out that Miguel is a grand nephew of Cardinal Ortega and that the cardinal was heavily involved in journalism and church politics before he entered the priesthood. I don't know if there's anything there or not, but that's a curious nexus. Why was Alejandro Diaz his patient, and why did he disappear at the same time Ortega sold his clinic and later became head of the health ministry? It's certainly worth a closer look. Mikel, add that small item to your growing work list."

30

The long flight was exhausting. Dietrich's car was waiting at the airport. He took his family directly to the Stanford Park while a limo driver took David Weiss to a Los Altos hotel across the street from SciGen.

"Mom, Dad here's your key. I've had your luggage sent up to your room. It's only two in the morning here. Jet lag will hit you as soon as you sit down. Get some sleep. Don't set an alarm. Dieter and Elise are in the room next door to you. Call me when you've had breakfast and I'll come over and pick you up. I'm going over to the hospital now and stay with Therese."

Dietrich slipped quietly into Rupert's room. The night nurse was reading a book by the subdued light of a floor lamp. He could hear Rupert breathing between the intermittent beeps from his monitors. He walked across to the nurse.

"Good morning," she said quietly, "I'm Mrs. Kitchens."

"Good morning, I'm Rupert's dad, how is he doing?"

"He's slept through the night so far. He had a brief spell of anxiety just before I came on duty. He was administered an anti-anxiety medicine and has calmed down. Mrs. Von Hesse retired about ten."

"Do you know when Dr. Askew was last in?"

She checked her i-Pad.

"He was in around three in the afternoon."

"Did he change any of his instructions?"

Again, she scrolled down the tablet.

"No, he checked all of your son's vitals and verified that the medications were properly administered and left at 3:30."

"Thank you."

Dietrich went to Rupert's bedside and gazed down at his son's pallid face. It bore no comparison to the ruddy cheeked teen who skied down that Black Diamond run in Zermatt. He thought about how capricious life could be. One minute a happy family celebrating a special birthday; the next, living every parent's worst nightmare. He touched Rupert's hand and was elated to see him try to pull it back. Dietrich stood by the bed for a few minutes then joined Therese in the bedroom.

She was curled up on one side of the bed, almost in a fetal position. He touched her gently on the shoulder. She swatted at his hand and then realized someone was trying to wake her. She sat up quickly, fear leaping to her eyes until she saw Dietrich standing over her.

"Oh! You frightened me! My first thought was Rupert. I'm so glad you are here. I had planned to go to the hotel for your arrival but after Rupert's flare-up I decided to stay here. Is everything all right?"

"Yes. The kids are asleep by now. So are my parents. I couldn't wait until morning to see you and Rupert. I hope you don't mind a strange bedfellow for a few hours."

"Hardly! Come to bed. You must be exhausted."

"I am tired. It's been a hectic few days."

"Any news?"

"Yes, Rob thinks he may have a breakthrough on a portion of our problem. He asked David Weiss to bring over some DNA specimens to try. David went on down to Los Altos. I'll join him after I bring the kids and my parents over in the morning. You still have that rental car?"

"Yes, it's downstairs."

216

"Good, you can take them back to the hotel after they visit briefly. They probably won't let them all in at once. I asked Dad to call after they have breakfast. I'll pick them up. Now I'm going to get to bed and get some sleep—*maybe*."

Dietrich's phone rang. He checked the bedside clock. 8:30.

"Hi Dad. Yeah. I just woke up. Hang tight for a few minutes. I'll be over in a half-hour."

"I slept longer than I expected," he said to Therese as she exited the bathroom.

"You needed the rest. I checked on Rupert and nothing has changed."

"Okay, I'm going to shower and then pick up the family. Why don't you go down and get some breakfast? I should be back in less than an hour."

"I'll wait until you leave."

"Suit yourself."

Twenty minutes later Dietrich emerged, showered, clean shaven and ready to go.

"Come on, I'll walk you down," Therese said.

"I'm scared Mom," Elise said before she entered Rupert's room.

"It's all right to be scared. Your brother is doing well. We just need to get him past this next hurdle. Your father and the doctors are doing everything they can. We have to trust God that he will see Rupert through this."

Dietrich eased the door open.

"Therese, why don't you take Elise and Dieter in? Mom and Dad and I will wait out here."

Elise bravely walked up to Rupert's bed and took his hand. She felt a slight twitch.

"I think he knows it's me Mom."

"Maybe he does. You know how much he loves you."

217

Elise looked at the pale face of her older brother and began to cry. She backed away from the bed. Dieter stepped in.

"Hi Bro, how ya doin'?" he said with bravado.

Rupert responded to the sound of Dieter's familiar voice. His eyes fluttered open.

"Hey Dee, where am I?" he rasped.

Therese rushed to his side.

"You're in a hospital my darling. All your family is here. You had a skiing accident. Do you remember?"

"Where's Franck? He was here a minute ago."

"He'll be here shortly sweetheart. You just rest. Dieter, Elise, your Dad and I are all here. You're going to be all right."

"Tell Dad I'm sorry…"

He drifted back to sleep. Therese was crying tears of joy.

"He recognized you Dieter. His mind is all right," she rejoiced. She ran to tell Dietrich.

The entire family was now gathered around Rupert's bed as he wakened again and recognized each of them.

"What happened?"

"You ran off the ski slope in Zermatt and hit a tree," Dietrich explained. "You were pretty banged up. The doctors determined you needed some specialized care. You are in the Stanford University hospital in Palo Alto, California."

"What? How long have I been here?"

"About two weeks."

"What's wrong with me?"

"You have a broken leg, you have deep bruises and you have a head injury."

"Why Stanford?"

"The best medical team in the world for your situation is here."

"What do you mean *my situation*?"

218

"Your injuries triggered a latent blood condition that causes uncontrolled bleeding. You also had a seizure which caused your heart to stop briefly."

"Wow! I'm glad I wasn't around to see that."

"I'm glad you still have a sense of humor."

"Hi Gramps, Gramma, when did you come?'

"We all flew in last night," Friederich said. "Your Mom has been here all along and we thought she needed some rest."

"How long did you say I have been here?"

"Almost two weeks."

"Wow! And I've been out all that time?"

"Yes," his mother said, holding tightly to his hand, "the doctors kept you sedated so that you would have complete rest and could heal."

"Dad, I'm sorry I disobeyed you."

"Don't worry about that now son, just get well."

Rupert saw concern on the faces leaning over his bed.

"Is there something you're not telling me?"

"Rupert," Dietrich began slowly, "between the accident and the medications you received your latent hemophilia was activated. You had severe bleeding and it was difficult to stop. You require a special type of blood that is in very short supply. That's why you are here, where the doctors can get the medications and therapies you need."

"Hemophilia! I remember you once saying that some of our ancestors had it, but I thought that was a thing of the past."

"So did I son. Unfortunately, it's not."

"What does that mean for me?"

"It means that I and a bunch of other people are working very hard to find a solution to your unique blood problems."

"How serious is it?"

"I'm not going to sugar coat it. The combination of blood factors you have are so rare no one has ever seen them manifested in a single person. It means we must find a unique solution to a unique set of circumstances. We are making

219

progress. As a matter of fact, that's why I came over with the family. One of our scientists from Zurich also came over to work with the researchers at SciGen in Los Altos. They think they may have a breakthrough. I'm going down there this afternoon. Now I think we should get out of here and let you go back to sleep. I'll see you tonight, after Los Altos."

"Okay...thanks Dad."

Dietrich headed up to I-280 for the short run to SciGen. He thought of Benny as he passed the VC offices on Sand Hill Road. Benny's sleuthing may have made Maria's case against Vitorio. The shenanigans with the "swaps" were clearly out of bounds with Goldman's policies, both in-house and with associate firms.

Dietrich thought about Maria, hoping that she'll get a favorable ruling, quickly. She has an awful lot on her plate and doesn't need that added distraction. It will also mean Vitorio can't threaten her anymore. Once the ruling is handed down he'll have no more leverage.

The SciGen parking lot seemed more crowded than usual; Rob hadn't mentioned any new hires, although he has several open requisitions for the right candidates. Both Rob and David were in the clean room. Dietrich put on scrubs, booties and a cap this time, and joined them.

"Hi Rob," he said over Simpson's shoulder.

"Oh, hi boss. Didn't see you come in."

You and David doing all right?"

"Better than all right. We may be on the verge of solving the CRISPR problem. Together with what Bilbao sent over we've been able to splice the proper cell structure into the chromosome without affecting the telomere. David brought over some fresh DNA samples and we came up with a patch. You won't believe it but we have a new hire who had just done this in a lab experiment. It seems everyone is into CRISPR now. He showed us what they did and with a small tweak it worked here. I'll call him in and introduce you."

"Karen, ask that new kid to come into the lab."

"Yes sir, right away."

"Mr. von Hesse I'd like you to meet the newest member of my staff. This is Andy Cloud," Rob Simpson said, cracking a huge smile.

"Andy! Wow! That was fast work," Dietrich said. "What's it been, a week?"

"About that. I can't thank you enough sir. This is a dream come true for me and Miranda. Mr. Simpson says that the information I gave him from my last lab has been helpful."

"Indeed Andy," Rob said. "You may have found the missing link. We should know by tomorrow when this culture matures. If it does what we expect, one of the three dominoes will fall. If we can force factor VIII and von Willebrand to bind until needed at a wound site, we're a long way toward conquering hemophilia.

"How's it coming on the other front?' Simpson asked.

"I'm sure David told you about the work they've completed on the drug induced thalamic seizures. They think they are close to a remedy for the several known drugs that can combine to induce seizures. So maybe the next domino will fall soon."

'What about the null problem?"

"I don't know if we're any closer on that one. Maria's team has made some headway. They've turned up some near ideal candidates but no null yet. I hope they'll have something by the time I get back."

"We should have an idea here in the next day or two," Simpson said. "The results from the latest splicing exercises are very positive, but if I've learned anything in 25 years of doing this stuff it's to never count your chickens before they hatch."

"Let me pose a hypothetical," Dietrich said. "Suppose you are successful in solving the factor VIII and von Willebrand 2n associative problem and Zurich takes care of the thalamic seizure problem, but we haven't solved the Rh-null dilemma, what do we do?"

"We apply immediately for FDA clinical test approval and prepare for controlled trials. These two breakthroughs alone will set the medical journal world buzzing for months."

"What about Rupert?"

"These two treatments will alleviate much of Rupert's problem, but not all. If the FDA approves them, he will no longer be under the threat of imminent death from bleeding or stroke, but he will still be one of a handful of Rh-nulls in the world dependent on each other for lifesaving transfusions in the event of some medical disaster."

"How long will it take for FDA approval?"

"Dietrich, you've been in this game as long as I have. In the dark ages it took penicillin decades before it was accepted as standard treatment for microbial infections. Today's sclerotic FDA takes a minimum of two years after pristine trials to let a drug go to market."

"That borders on being criminal!" Dietrich exclaimed "What can we do?"

"Most pharmas, including ours, take their trials offshore, where controls are adequate and safe but not punitive. Australia seems to be the *etat du jour* lately. Even there you're looking at several months. Once they are approved in a recognized environment like that, it is easier to get FDA approval."

"What happens in the meantime if Rupert has another life-threatening episode?"

"You either go rogue and administer the drugs without approval, or you seek a venue where the powers that be look the other way—for a price. If you go rogue, at minimum you'll do irreparable damage to Sagarin's reputation; at maximum you'll lose your approval to sell product in the U.S. and any of the other countries that have signed on to the international drug licensing protocols."

"And if we go to a more forgiving location, what?" Dietrich asked.

"Best case, depending on the country, you'll get a slap on the wrist, a wink, a warning, and an upturned palm. Some may even grant compassionate use approval. Worst case, other governments will slap you with sanctions and fines."

"How do we prepare for either eventuality?"

"I would contact reputable medical experts in the most promising countries and contact them. Then have someone begin to get the lay of the land. Four or five, say. Then, after you get their reports and opinions, pick two and build a strategy."

"How would we go about that?"

"Pick the countries and have Sagarin's reps there propose a contact. Our people should have a good feel for the local political climate and the likelihood of cooperation from the medical authorities."

"Okay, I'd like to speak to Dr. Askew this afternoon and get his opinion and recommendations."

"Good idea, he's suffered through a lot of this with Stanford's medical school and the FDA."

Dietrich stayed with Rob Simpson all afternoon going over several of the ongoing SciGen research projects.

"I think I'll head back up to Stanford," he said as he stood and stretched. "It's been a long day; but a good day. Rupert is awake and steady, SciGen is humming, and more importantly, has a potential breakthrough for hemophilia treatment—and Andy Cloud has a job. Well done Rob."

"Keep your fingers crossed Dietrich that it all comes together."

"I will Rob. Let me know how the cultures turn out. I'll probably head back to Spain in a day or two. Let me know if Dr. Weiss is finished and I'll give him a lift back."

"Right, Boss. Good luck with Rupert, and with Maria's work. Let me know what Askew thinks."

Darkness was descending on the Stanford campus when Dietrich turned into the now familiar parking lot. He stopped at the first-floor café and picked up three coffees.

Nurse Holmes was nearing her shift's end and appreciated the coffee. Rupert was sleeping peacefully.

"We have coffee on the floor but it's not nearly as good. Thank you."

"You're quite welcome. Is my wife here?"

"She took your family to the hotel about an hour ago. Rupert was getting a bit tired. She said she would have dinner with them and wait for you to return."

"How is he?"

"A little restless. All the excitement of waking up and seeing his family. Dr. Askew ordered a tranquilizer for him about the time your wife left. He just dropped off. All his vital signs are holding but the doctor is concerned about the buildup of amyloids in his pelvic joints. Typically, these don't occur in young people. These are the same deposits as in the brains of older people that can cause Alzheimer's disease. He is worried that the buildup may lead to spontaneous bleeding in the pelvis."

"What is the treatment if it does?"

"Basically, to drain off the blood and infuse clotting factors. They also use an IV administered antigen that works to dissolve the amyloid, but it's just recently been approved experimentally. It works well on some patients and not others. So far Alzheimer patient's response has been spotty with very little decrease in their plaque deposits. There have been better results with joint bleeding caused by amyloid buildup."

When will he know?"

"It takes several days to see the full effect. He just started the drug yesterday." the nurse said. "By the way, I understand you live in Zurich, Switzerland?"

"Yes, I do, why?"

"I read that one of the discoverers of this effect is Dr. Robert Nitsch of Zurich University. I believe his study is under the auspices of Biogen there and has been given fast track status by the FDA.

"I'll be! Do you know what the drug is called?"

"Let me check my tablet. Oh, here it is. It's an antibody called aducanumab."

"Will you spell that please?"

Dietrich made an entry on his phone.

"I think I'll join my family at the hotel now. Thanks for the input on the adu-whatsits drug. Remembering these names takes an Einstein."

"I know, have a good evening."

Dietrich called Dr. Askew and asked if he could drop by for a few minutes.

"Certainly, I was just finishing up some reports before I go home. Come on down."

"What's on your mind, Dietrich?" Askew asked as Dietrich entered.

"First I want to thank you for all you're doing for Rupert. The joint bleeding caught me off guard. I'm glad there's an experimental treatment for the plaque buildup."

"Yes, we're very fortunate that Biogen began its trials and we were able to enroll Rupert. We'll know soon if it has the desired effects for him. And second?"

"Rob Simpson and I were discussing the next steps if the SciGen and Sagarin developments prove out. He said that it would be almost impossible to get approval from the FDA to use them until clinical trials were complete and that could take years."

"Yes, I've thought about that myself."

"What are the chances of getting compassionate use approval?"

"It's possible but that too will get bogged down in governmental red tape."

"That's what Rob said. He said that we could go rogue and do it anyway but the ramifications to Sagarin and everyone involved would be disastrous,"

225

"He's right about that." Askew agreed. "Did Rob have any other suggestions?"

"He recommended we pick four or five reputable, but friendlier, governments to seek one-time or compassionate approval."

"That's a risky path, but it may be the only one available for Rupert's case. Any ideas?"

"Rob suggested we have our in-country representatives assess the prospects for co-operation in their regions and report back to us. We'll select the most favorable and take it from there."

"Of all the bad choices you have, that may be the most promising."

"Do you have any recommendations?" Dietrich asked.

Askew stood and walked over to a globe he had installed in his office. He spun the globe and stopped it with his finger on a small country in Europe.

"I have one. It may sound off-the-wall."

"I'm open to all ideas."

"There's this doctor that I've co-operated with over the past several years. He's well-placed in the medical community and has a sterling reputation. He's been trying for years to improve his small country's standing in the medical world but has been hampered by their lack of presence and by their unique governance."

"And where is that?" Dietrich asked.

"Andorra."

"Andorra? Aren't they too tiny to carry any clout?"

"My friend, Dr. René Le Clerc, runs a clinic associated with the Meritxell Hospital in Andorra. He Is a world-renowned gerontologist. The average life expectancy in Andorra is 81 for men and 87 for women. He is anxious to spread the word on the research they have undertaken. He readily admits that Andorra isn't the first place people look for cutting edge medical technology, but he believes they have a lot to offer."

226

"Can he help us?"

"Andorra is administered by the President of France and the Archbishop of Urgell in Spain. Le Clerc has great credibility with both. His support would go a long way toward receiving permission to use experimental drugs in Andorra."

"You know him well?"

"We studied together many years ago. He and I confer often on cardiac diseases among the elderly. They're almost non-existent in Andorra. That's why he's so anxious to get his work out to the rest of the world."

"Will you contact him and see if he'll meet with us?"

"Certainly. I'll do it first thing tomorrow, when he's in his lab."

"If he agrees, see if he'll meet us in Bilbao. There are no airfields in Andorra. I tried flying there once. I can get one of our helicopters to pick him up. Should only be an hour or two at most. I'd like you to be there as well. I'll fly Rob and Weiss in. so we can give him the full story."

31

The family was gathered at poolside, both Dieter and Elise in swimsuits.

"What, no swimsuits for you old fogies," he greeted his parents and Therese.

"I think San Francisco is colder than Zurich in the evening," his mother said. "I might try the spa later."

"How was Rupert when you left him?" Therese asked.

"They gave him a tranquilizer and he dropped off to sleep. Say, did Askew talk to you about bleeding in Rupert's pelvis?"

"He mentioned it and said they were beginning a new drug. I really didn't understand it. Do you think it's serious?"

"It could be. If he continues to bleed internally he'll need more blood and as you no Rh-null is in very short supply around the world."

"I understand you're doing work in Spain to find a solution for that, Dietrich," his father said.

"We are, but we're still a long way off. It's a very difficult problem as you know from your time at Sagarin and from our family history as well."

"Yes, I remember."

"Did you guys already eat?" Dietrich asked.

"Yes, we just ate at the hotel restaurant. We didn't feel like going out after the excitement of the day."

"Okay, I'll just order a sandwich here by the pool. Dieter, Elise, do you want something more."

228

"Maybe an ice cream sundae?" Dieter said.

"Me too," Elise parroted.

"I think your mother and I are going to turn in." the elder von Hesse said. "It's well after midnight in Switzerland and I'm beat. It was good to see Rupert responding today. Therese, your courage through all this is amazing. Just remember, one day at a time."

"Thanks Papa V, have a good night's sleep. Maybe you two can take the kids to see some of the sights tomorrow, after we visit Rupert. The hotel can arrange a tour for you."

"Maybe so, I'll see how we feel tomorrow. Good night."

"Good night," she said as the older couple walked away.

Dieter and Elise frolicked in the pool while Dietrich waited for his sandwich and beer. Neither had fully comprehended what Rupert's illness could mean for them. They didn't understand how close their brother had come to dying, nor the perils he still faced.

Dietrich's parents and his children left the hotel at eleven for a grand tour of the city. They saw Rupert briefly, and, assured he was okay, they took off. It was the first visit to the "City by the Bay" for the children and they were excited.

"Good morning, Dietrich," Dr. Askew said as he entered Rupert's room.

Askew checked the charts then listened to Rupert's heart.

"Any new concerns about the plaque problem?" Dietrich asked.

"For now, it's under control and we hope the experimental drug will alleviate any problems. It'll take a few days to know. Meantime we must monitor for internal bleeding and try to keep it in check. My single biggest worry is an episode of uncontrolled bleeding requiring substantial amounts of blood transfusion. We're running up against the limits with the blood registry agencies. We're trying to find AB negative donors who will permit an apheresis donation. While Rupert cannot accept the platelets

229

or cells he can tolerate the plasma. That could be vital to maintaining his system blood level."

"That's where you take extra blood and extract the serum?"

"Yes, it gives us more bang for the buck—three for one—and the good thing is the donor gets most of their fluid back.

"Switching subjects, how did it go with Rob Simpson yesterday?"

"SciGen is making tremendous progress. They employed CRISPR on the DNA that we brought over from Zurich and they're waiting to see the results today. If it works, then one piece of the puzzle may fall into place."

"That's great news. Let me know if I can help." Dr. Askew said.

Dietrich's phone rang. He looked at the caller ID.

"I need to take this Dr. Askew, if you'll excuse me."

"Certainly, I was just leaving. Everything seems under control here."

"Hello Maria. What's up?"

"Mikel and Rubio have uncovered some interesting and puzzling leads from their data-mining exercise. They're out trying to run down some answers now. I think you should come back. We'll need your guidance if they discover anything. There are too many coincidences for this to be accidental. We may need some high-level clout to get answers."

"Okay, I'll leave tomorrow morning."

"How's Rupert?"

"So far, so good. He's developed some joint bleeding in the pelvic area. Amyloid plaque deposits, Dr. Askew says. They're treating it with an experimental drug. The major concern now is Rh-null blood supply. That's why what you're doing is so critical."

"I understand. I have a strange feeling that finding out what happened to our crazy Dominican monk may lead us to an answer."

-32-

Marcel lowered the wheels on the Falcon 50 and let the sleek craft drift to a soft landing at Bilbao's airport in Loiu, a northern suburb. From the air the two wings and the sharp tip at the center of Santiago Calatrava's white concrete and glass structure resembles an abstract dove. Some local wags have christened it *La Paloma*.

Dietrich got off with the pilots who had to re-fuel and re-file for Zurich. Dieter, Elise and David Weiss stayed on board for the short hop across France. School beckoned on Monday for the kids and Dr. Weiss was ferrying vital information from SciGen for his fellow scientists. His parents remained in California with Therese for a few more days.

Dietrich entered the terminal and crossed to the recently completed services building across the way to rent a car. The glass wrapped, sunken building sports an ecologically friendly sod roof with the car park on top. The design was a compromise providing needed ground services without detracting from the aesthetics of the main terminal.

After the eighteen-hour flight it was still early morning Bilbao time. Dietrich drove directly to the clinic. Only a few cars were in the parking garage. He spotted Maria's BMW and took the elevator up to her office.

"Good morning Anna," he said to the secretary as he breezed in, "is your boss available?"

"Yes, Señor von Hesse, go right in. She's expecting you."

232

"Dietrich, you made good time. I didn't expect you so early." Maria said.

"Yes, we had favorable tail winds across the Atlantic. That always helps."

"Have a seat and I'll get us some coffee. Would you like a pastry?"

"Sure, I slept right up to landing and missed breakfast on the plane. A croissant would be great."

"What's the latest with your super-sleuths since we last talked?" he asked as she set the coffee and roll in front of him.

"It seems the Dominican monk, our candidate number 193, was a patient in Miguel Ortega's psychiatric clinic south of San Sebastian, in the small town of Tolosa. According to the records Mikel and Rubio "borrowed" from that clinic, Alejandro Diaz was a patient there until 2009 or '10. Then he disappeared. Shortly thereafter Miguel sold his practice, and a few weeks later he was announced as the new head of Basque Health Services.

"Here's the kicker. Diaz had all the elements we were looking for; hemophilia, von Willebrand and Rh-null. The boys tried to find out what happened to him. He just disappeared. They thought maybe he had died. They checked all the obituary records in northern Spain for the past ten years. No Alejandro Diaz. Then Mikel started scanning through the internal Catholic publications. He explained that many of the internal organs of the church are meant only for the eyes of certain higher-up in the church hierarchy, without using social media and its potential for hacking. If reporters stumble across any juicy tidbits, they have learned not to publish them. It seems the church's influence reaches far into the political and journalistic domain. More than one overzealous reporter has been banished to the nether regions of the newspaper world for transgressing that unwritten code.

"Mikel found an obituary for our missing monk in one of those publications. Diaz died in 2011, not too long after the clinic was sold, according to the obituary. There was no listed cause of

233

death. It only said he died after an extended confinement, with no details. Mikel says that's clerical code for sick or insane. He thinks insane, as we have discovered. The publication also said he was cremated and his ashes buried in the *Sagrada Familia Amara* cemetery in San Sebastian. That had been the site of his last assignment. Mikel finds that extremely suspicious."

"You said on the phone that you had a strange conversation with Dr. Ortega after the tribunal."

"Yes, he was very cold and asked a lot of questions about what we had found. He seemed angry that we had gone beyond the original intent of the search, even though his agency had approved it.

"The strangest part of the conversation was about the nullity trial. He as much as accused you and me of adultery and warned me that anything that reflected negatively on his ministry would incur penalties for me, the clinic and for you personally. Then he hung up. No good-bye, no nothing."

"Very odd behavior," Dietrich agreed.

"Mikel is out there trying to dig up more information. Rubio is poring over the data they collected to see if any other little nuggets pop up.

"Oh, by the way, Mikel has set up his surveillance vagabond near my house. He installed a security system for me that he can monitor from the trailer in case Vitorio's threats were more than just bravado."

"What if Mikel is out of town?"

"He has an associate who will fill in for him."

"Good, you can't be too careful."

Only the sexton was there when Mikel tapped on the office door of *Sagrada Familia Amara.* The morning's few confessions had been heard and the priest was off to visit the sick and shut-ins among his small congregation.

"Good morning," the wizened, elderly caretaker said, "I'm afraid Father Carlos is not here."

234

"Oh, that's okay. I'm up from Gorliz and I have a few questions about a relative of mine who's buried here."

"What's the name? I may be able to help you."

"Alejandro Diaz, he was a priest here before he died. I have been out of the country for several years and unable to pay my respects."

The sexton stiffened and frowned. Mikel perceived that this was a sensitive subject for the old man.

"Did you know him?"

"Yes, he was here for two or three years before he went away," the man said guardedly.

"What do you mean "went away"?"

"Father Alejandro became ill and had to be hospitalized."

"Oh, I wasn't aware, what was wrong with him?"

The sexton hesitated. Mikel saw that he was reluctant to discuss the matter, so he kept his silence and finally the old man began to speak about the priest.

"Father Alejandro was very nervous and suffered from some sort of mental stress. He had a nervous breakdown. He began to see the doctors for a while and seemed to get better. Then the sickness came back."

"Do you know which doctors he saw?"

"At first he saw someone here in San Sebastian. Later he went to someone out of town. I'm not sure where."

"Do you know why he stopped seeing the local psychiatrist?"

"No, but there were rumors."

"What kind of rumors?"

"I don't want to get the church in trouble by talking about this."

"But, if he's dead and buried what will it hurt?" Mikel asked.

"Well, he wasn't actually buried, he was cremated, and his urn was buried."

Mikel feigned surprise.

235

"I thought that was a no-no for a Catholic priest, what with resurrection and everything."

"So did I, but Father Carlos said it was appropriate in this case. It probably had to do with the other rumors."

"And you're not going to tell me what they were?"

"I could get into trouble."

"I promise you no one will know what you tell me. I know this is difficult for you but my aunt, Alejandro's sister, is crazy with worry about the whole situation, the stain on the family. I tell you what. I'll give you fifty Euros to put in the collection plate if that will ease your conscience."

Mikel took out his wallet, pulled out a fifty Euro note and handed it to the sexton.

"If you're sure that no one will know I talked to you?"

I promise. I just want to ease my aunt's mind."

"Well, there were rumors that Father Alejandro had a fondness for young boys, and that's why he was transferred so often. I never saw it here, but I wasn't always around. Anyway, that was the rumor, and then it was said that he had contracted syphilis some time ago when he was in Santiago de Campostela, and that it had affected his brain. That would explain his nervous problems and why he was seeing psychiatrists."

"What happened then?'

"He stopped going to the psychiatrist and a few weeks later he was transferred."

"Do you know where he went?"

"Someone said to a sanitarium, but I don't know where."

"So, you haven't seen or heard anything about him since his ashes were brought here for burial?"

"That's right."

"Will you show me where he was buried?"

Mikel followed the stooped figure into the graveyard behind the chapel down a narrow path between towering archangels and kneeling figures of Christ, to the back of the plot. There he saw an orderly row of five graves with their simple

236

crosses. They were priests who had died while serving the chapel. In the ground nearby, set apart from the other priests, was a small concrete square with a simple brass plaque which read - Fr. Alejandro Diaz.

"Thank you, you've been very helpful," Mikel said to the sexton as he reached the gate, "and you don't have to worry about your secret. It's safe with me. Oh, do you know if Father Alejandro had any relatives here in San Sebastian?"

"I'm not sure but I heard some family members at the funeral mention a home in Santiago de Compostela. I think they had come up from there for the funeral."

"Once again, thank you and God bless you," Mikel said as he headed toward his car. He stopped and turned back toward the sexton. "One more question if you don't mind. Did anyone here see the body of Father Diaz?"

"Not as far as I know. I assume he was sent straight to the crematory from the sanitarium."

"Do you know which crematory took care of him?"

"There's only one in town, Crematorio Polloe. It's located at the edge of the main cemetery."

"Thanks again, you've been very helpful."

Any respectable "private eye" would have to be blind not to see that the black van with darkened windows that followed him from Bilbao was now parked across the street. This guy was either very stupid or very obvious—for a reason. But what?

Mikel drove slowly past the van while staring at his phone as if looking for an address. He was able to snap a photo of the van and its license plate. He meandered through the streets of San Sebastian to see if the van would follow. It did. He made his way to Donostia hospital. He arranged for Inez Figueroa to meet him there at the IT office. He parked across the street and could see the van pull to the curb a few cars back. Inez was waiting for Mikel outside the office of Juan Battista.

"Are you Inez?"

237

"Yes, and you are Mikel Muñoz?"

"That's me. Thanks for seeing me."

"Your welcome. I took the liberty of calling the office to make sure I should talk to you."

"Smart girl. Never know what tricks people may pull. Did you look at the data again?"

"Yes, I told Mr. Battista what I was doing, and he said to go ahead. He said the ministry had sent out an email to the district computer managers warning them not to get too cozy with the *seven dwarfs*. Of course, he didn't call us that. They didn't give him any reason. He looked at what I was doing and said to let him see the results of any searches before giving them to the clinic."

"Did you find anything?"

"I think so. The records show three sanitariums in the area where the mentally ill are sent. I went back ten years to search their records and did not find an Alejandro Diaz. What I did find was a fourth facility that closed in 2011. Several patients were transferred to the other three at that time—but no Alejandro Diaz."

"What was the name of the fourth sanitarium?"

"*Sanitaria de San Pedro*, I think. The records are a bit sketchy."

"Is there a history?"

"I was able to dig out some information on it. It was founded around 2005 or '06 and had a capacity of about twenty patients, depending on their degree of insanity. It appears there were only ten or so just before it closed."

"Did all ten show up at the other facilities?"

"No, that's the strange thing. Only seven did."

"Where did the other three go?"

"No one knows—or no one is telling."

"Very interesting. Thanks Inez. Good work."

"What's next?" she asked.

"I've got one more stop then I'm going back to Bilbao and report what I've found and see where it takes me. You staying here?"

"Yes, for a while. I understand most of the techs are back in Bilbao now. There seems to be more interest in this area."

Juan Battista came outside.

"Inez, who is this gentleman?"

This is Señor Muñoz from our offices in Bilbao. He's following up on some of the leads we turned up."

"You're not seeing them, are you?" he asked Mikel.

"No, not without asking permission. I'm just checking out the areas they live in to see if there's any demographic correlation for the blood anomalies."

"Okay, be sure you tell me before you contact any patients."

"For certain. We appreciate your help and don't want to screw anything up."

"Inez are you ready for lunch?" Juan asked. "I want to show you a new place nearby."

Inez blushed. It seems her relationship with Juan Battista had gone beyond the original scope of her visit.

"So long Inez, any messages for the "head shed"?"

"The what?"

"Oh, that's an Americanism for headquarters."

She laughed.

"No, I report in every day, so they know what I'm doing."

Mikel waved and walked away.

"Why would he use an Americanism?" Juan asked.

"I don't know."

The sole crematory in San Sebastian was conveniently located at the corner of the main cemetery. Not many Catholics in Spain opt for cremation. A solemn, elderly man in a black suit answered his knock on the office door.

"Yes, may I be of service?"

239

"I hope so. I am from Santiago de Compostela. My uncle was cremated here in 2011 and his sister says there remains an unpaid bill for your services. She was not aware until recently that it had not been paid. She feels very bad that it wasn't taken care of by the church. I was hoping you could look it up for me so that I can settle the account for her."

"Why certainly, come in. What was the name of your uncle?"

"Alejandro Diaz. He was a priest at *Sagrada Familia* several years ago."

The attendant stopped and wheeled around to face Mikel.

"I can tell you right now that no man of the cloth has ever been cremated here. First, the church doesn't approve of cremation and second, the owners of this establishment would never cremate a priest."

"You're certain."

"Absolutely! Come, look at the records for 2011 and see for yourself."

He plopped a dusty ledger on his desk and turned to the entries for 2011. He flipped to the page of "Ds," running his finger down the columns.

"See, three Diaz's. None named Alejandro and certainly none a priest. And all buried. No cremations."

"Perhaps it was another crematory then."

"Not if he died in San Sebastian. We are the only one within 30 miles."

"Very puzzling. Thank you for your trouble. I'll check again with the church and see if I have my facts correct."

This was puzzling. Why is there no record of the cremation of Alejandro Diaz in that ledger? Either he was not cremated, or someone doctored the records.

33

The trip back to the clinic was uneventful. Mikel watched as the van moved in and out of the traffic behind him, keeping a respectable distance. When he reached the clinic, Mikel drove into the parking garage and made a U-turn, He sat in the shadows until he saw the black van pass by then he eased out into the street. He kept several cars between his and the van as it crossed the river. He stopped a block away when he saw the van turn into a parking garage across from the Basque Health Ministry building. Seconds later the driver emerged and walked to the glass structure across the street.

The man was about six feet tall with a mustache and salt and pepper hair. He had on dark glasses and a baseball cap. It was hard to get a good look at him. Mikel could see the elevator rise in its glass shaft to the top floor and stop. Whoever had been following him was calling on a very high-level employee of the ministry. Why they were bothering to tail him was confusing since the clinic was reporting everything to the ministry. Someone was very interested in what secondary mission Mikel might be on. He thought back to his trip to Tolosa. Had he been careless? Was he tailed to the clinic there? Did anyone see him and Rubio that night? Was someone sending him a message by being so obvious? Mikel returned to the clinic. He went to the fifth floor and asked Anna to see Maria.

"She's with Señor von Hesse," Anna said.

"Ring her anyway; I think she'll want to see me."

Anna pressed a button and announced him.

"Send him right in," Maria responded.

Mikel was barely in the door when she asked if he had discovered anything new in San Sebastian.

"Indeed. It appears that Alejandro Diaz had, as my informant said, a fondness for boys, if you know what I mean. He was born near *Santiago de Compostela,* served in several capacities there, and was reassigned several times. My guess, he was just a few steps ahead of prosecution. It was also rumored that he contracted syphilis somewhere along the way. He must not have been treated because he developed mental problems in San Sebastian. His last posting was at *Sagrada Familia.* It was there that he began seeing a psychiatrist. That continued for a while until he began to see another one out of town. We now know that was Miguel Ortega. I also stopped by to see Inez Figueroa at Donestia hospital. I'd called and asked her to do some digging for me."

"Yes, she called to vet you. Smart girl."

"Indeed. She was able to find out that there are three mental sanitariums in the area. More surprising she discovered there used to be a fourth that closed around 2011, with ten residual patients."

"What happened to them?" asked Dietrich.

"That's the interesting thing. Seven were transferred to the three remaining sanitariums; the other three seemed to disappear into thin air. Now, we know that Diaz was confined to a psychiatric institution of some sort, and we assume it was in the San Sebastian area. My question is, was he one of the three that didn't emerge from that fourth facility. *Sanataria de San Pedro*

242

was housed in an old lighthouse building east of Mount Ulia. The fortress like building supporting the light was very remote. It was inside a gated compound and all but inaccessible. Did he die there, and if so, under what circumstances? And who were the other two and where did they go? I'm still researching its history.

"I asked the sexton at Sagrada Familia if he or anyone at the chapel saw Alejandro's body. He said no, that it went straight from the sanitarium to the crematory. I thought that strange, so I went to the only crematory within 30 miles of San Sebastian to check the records. Surprise! No record of an Alejandro Diaz as a client of that establishment."

"As Churchill once noted," Dietrich said, "this is rapidly becoming a riddle wrapped in an enigma."

"It gets better. I was followed to the chapel by a black van, presumably, the same one hanging out at your place, Maria. He didn't appear to be concerned that he was so obvious. He followed me back to Bilbao. I turned in to the garage and when he passed I tailed him. Want to guess where he went?"

"Not a clue," Maria said.

"Directly to the top floor of the Basque Health Ministry."

Maria's jaw dropped. She was momentarily speechless.

"My God, why?" she finally got out. "We're already giving them any information we uncover."

"My guess, putting two and two together, is that it has to do with Alejandro Diaz. There's nothing else that ties all this together."

"But why? Diaz is dead. He's been dead for years. We don't know anything about the man except the sordid facts you were able to dig up and that he was a patient of Miguel Ortega at one time."

"I'm not convinced Diaz is dead. If the church will go so far as to doctor records maybe they'll also fake a funeral and publish an obscure obituary. Buried somewhere in there is a reason for all this intrigue. I got the van's license plate and I'll run it down.

Ten bucks it's the same lousy PI that took those pictures. I know most of those guys."

"Thanks Mikel," Maria said, "but, if it's the same man that Vitorio hired, is it just a coincidence that he's also working for Miguel or is there some connection?"

"I don't know. It's one of the things I'm going to find out though."

"What's next?"

"I'm heading to Santiago de Compostela. I think that's where Diaz is from, and where he contracted syphilis and was caught diddling young boys."

"Okay, keep me posted."

"Will do."

"Mikel, would you mind if I tag along to Santiago?" Dietrich asked. "I've never been there and maybe I can offer a second set of eyes. Besides, we can use my rental car instead of that beat-up, old sedan of yours."

"That's a good idea. Mr. Private Eye will not expect to see me in a different car. We can sneak out of town before he misses me. I'll ask Rubio to dress like me and drive my car back to my office. That'll confuse him."

E-70 hugs the rugged northwestern coastline of Spain, skirting the mountainous *Sierra de Ancares* before dipping southwesterly toward *Santiago de Compostela*. The highway is four lanes through twisting mountain passes with hairpin turns and multiple elevation changes. The drive of 350 miles takes six hours if one obeys the speed laws, or five if one fudges a bit.

Dietrich drove into the center of the old town of *Santiago de Compostela*, skirting the cathedral plazas and stopping in front of the *Hostal dos Reis Catolicas,* the oldest continuosly operating hostelry in the world. The hotel faces the great square in front of the *Santiago de Compostela* cathedral. The hostel was built in the late fifteenth century by King Ferdinand and Queen

244

Isabella to provide accommodations for pilgrims completing the "Way of St. James." In more recent years it has morphed into a five-star Parador hotel. Its 127 rooms are arranged around four colonnaded courtyards, ornately decorated with fountains and parterres.

"May I take your car sir?" the liveried valet asked.

"Yes, thank you. How long does it take to retrieve a car if one is in a hurry?"

"About five minutes, less if you call down and request expedited service."

"Thank you, here are the keys."

Dietrich and Mikel watched the BMW 7-class drive away, a smiling young man at the wheel. A second porter snapped up their two bags and escorted them into the extravagantly decorated lobby, adorned with copious silver ornamentation.

"I assume you're picking up the tab for this. My budget doesn't quite stretch this far," Mikel said.

"Don't worry Mikel, I've got it covered. Meet me down here at eight and we'll have dinner in *Libredon.* I understand they have the best seafood in Galicia. It's inside the hotel so we don't have to walk. We can discuss your plans for tomorrow.

The *Libredon* occupied a rectangular room with two long rows of tables, a seemingly odd configuration for a restaurant and obviously a relic of the original structure. The hotel doesn't publicize the fact that in its earliest manifestation the room served as the hostels morgue. Many of the early pilgrims arrived at the end of their journey in bad health. Some didn't recover. Mikel was waiting at the front when Dietrich arrived.

"Sorry I'm a little late. I was on the phone to my wife."

"How is your son?" Mikel asked as they were being seated at the back of the restaurant.

"About the same. He's developed some internal bleeding of the joints because of a buildup of plaque. He's needed more

Rh-null plasma in the last few days. That's becoming a concern because of its scarcity."

"Any progress on that front?"

"Well, two of Rupert's problems are coming into focus. We think we've developed a drug that may prevent the type of seizure he had in Zermatt. And the researchers in California are optimistic about a gene-splicing technique that may eliminate or reduce the mutant cell structures that cause hemophilia. If both those pan out we're two-thirds of the way home. The third leg of the stool is overcoming the lack of Rh antigens in his blood that would help him to fight off diseases. That's what we're looking for here in Spain. That's why we're here in Santiago."

"That certainly puts everything into focus. I pray we'll be successful; for Rupert's sake and thousands of other people."

"Amen to that. Now let's have dinner. I'm starved after that long drive."

Dietrich savored the last few grains of succulent golden rice from his *arroz con bogavante.* The lobster and rice dish had exceeded even the lavish praise of their waiter. The split lobster tails simmered in saffron scented golden rice were simply prepared and wonderfully delicious.

Mikel's heaping plate of *mariscadas* included nearly every variety of shellfish fresh from the day's catch; shrimp, scallops, oysters, clams, mussels…delicacies he could only dream of in land-locked Boise.

They finished off a second bottle of Albariño and Mikel resisted the urge to rub his stomach.

"Señor von Hesse, feel free to join me on any of my trips. I haven't enjoyed a meal like this in years."

"You're welcome Mikel and feel free to call me Dietrich. We're going to be spending a lot of time together and Señor von Hesse is a bit too stuffy. Okay, what's on for tomorrow?"

"I checked on Diaz' posting here in Santiago. He came back here for five years in about 2000 or so. He served at a Dominican convent, *San Domingos de Bonaval,* just outside the

246

old walls of the city. It guarded one of the portals of the *Camino de Santiago,* where pilgrims entered the city in the old days.

"I got all the information I could on the *Sagrada Familia* chapel in San Sebastian. I called Father Alvaro there and told him I had been commissioned to write a history of the modern-day church in San Sebastian and I was researching all the priests who had served there. I told him one was Alejandro Diaz and I understood he had been at *Sagrada Familia.* He said that he had, and I asked him if he could give me some background on him. Turns out Father Alvaro came to *Sagrada* after Diaz died but he said he would call back and tell me what he could find out. He did call back and said Diaz came to San Sebastian around 2006 or '07 from *San Domingos de Bonaval* in Santiago and served for a while before becoming ill and being hospitalized. I asked him where and he said it was unclear, but he thinks at *Sanitaria de San Pedro.* He believes Diaz died there shortly before the sanitarium was closed. It was obvious that Alvaro knew nothing of the scandal."

"What do you expect to find here?"

"I'm going to nose around and see if I can find anyone still here who served with Diaz and then pump them for information. I'll use the same gambit with them and solicit information about Diaz as well."

"Can I do anything to help?"

"Not on this mission, but if you're going to the cathedral you might nose around and see if they have a religious reference library that's available to researchers."

"Okay, consider it done. How long will you be at the convent?"

"Hard to say, but no more than two or three hours."

"Good, I'll meet you back here at the hotel mid-afternoon. Do you need the car?"

"No, it's only a half mile or so. I'll walk."

The *San Dominicos de Bonoval* convent, in its earliest incarnation, was initiated by St. Dominic Guzman in the thirteenth century, following his own *camino*. Over the years it grew in importance as it supported pilgrims coming to venerate the martyred saint. Its style is Gothic/Renaissance. It's most impressive architectural feature is the triple, circular staircase ascending to the bell tower. Mikel located the church offices in an adjunct structure. He knocked on the door. It was answered by a friar in a brown cassock.

"May I help you?" he said.

Mikel introduced himself and explained the mission he was on and asked if there was anyone there who had served with Alejandro Diaz. He got much the same reaction from the friar that he got from the *Sagrada Familia* sexton. Obviously, Alejandro Diaz did not evoke pleasant memories among those with whom he had served.

"I knew Father Alejandro," he said frostily. "I am Father Gerardo."

"Can you tell me about him, a little biography for the book maybe?"

"We were not close. Let me just say that our personalities didn't mesh well."

"I see, was he difficult to get along with?"

"Not that so much but that he had different appetites than I."

The rotund priest seemed to warm to the task.

"What do you mean by that?"

"Alejandro spent too much time with the altar boys in the robing rooms—with the doors locked."

"Do you think he was abusing the young acolytes?"

"Let's put it this way, it wasn't long before he was assigned different duties. A year later he was transferred."

"Father Alvaro at the *Sagrada Familia* chapel in San Sebastian where he last served, said that Father Alejandro became very ill and was hospitalized. Did he seem ill before he left here?"

"He certainly didn't seem all there, mentally I mean. I overheard one of the clinic doctors say that he had a venereal disease. I assumed it was syphilis from the way he was acting. He left shortly thereafter."

"I'm surprised you would tell me this about a fellow priest."

"He was a priest in name only as far as I am concerned. I tell you this in the hope that the church will rid itself of such men. They are a pox on the body of the church and the sooner we rid ourselves of them the sooner the church can heal."

"Were you aware that Father Alejandro is dead?"

"I have heard that rumor, but yours is the first confirmation of the fact. Our leadership doesn't share that kind of news with us."

"Did Father Alejandro have family in Santiago?"

"Once or twice when he was in the clinic a woman came to visit him. I believe she was his sister. I think she lives near Santiago."

"You don't remember her name, do you?"

"No, but it's probably in the clinic records. They recorded all visitors and you know the church, it never throws anything away."

"Do you think you could find it. I'd like to interview her if possible."

"Come with me."

Mikel followed the priest across a courtyard to a two-story annex. It was the convent's library and records archive.

"Wait here," he said, pointing to a bench in the lobby before walking away. He reappeared ten minutes later with a dusty, leather-bound ledger and sat down by Mikel.

"This is the visitors log from the year Alejandro was sick."

The priest unbuckled the clasp and laid the book on his lap. He began turning the pages.

249

"Here it is. August 16, 2008. Lucrezia Diaz, sister, 2227 Rua dos Principes, Villestro. That's a small village about six or seven kilometers west of Santiago."

"You've been a great help Padre. Would you like a copy of the book when it is finished?"

"That would be kind of you. Good luck."

"And to you, Father Gerardo."

Mikel crossed *Obradoiro,* the "stone mason's square," in front of the Cathedral of Saint James as Dietrich was coming down the steps.

"Good timing Mikel," Dietrich said. "How'd it go?"

"A priest there confirmed everything I learned in San Sebastian. He also gave me the address of a sister of Alejandro Diaz. She lives about six clicks from here. I'll call her from the hotel and see if I can visit her tomorrow."

"That's great. I had a bit of luck also. There is a large research library in the cathedral and it's available for qualified researchers. They have documents and icons dating back hundreds of years."

"Depending on what I learn tomorrow, I may want to spend some time there."

Mikel gazed up at the strange mixture of Baroque, Romanesque and Gothic architecture that comprised the cathedral's façade. Two bell towers, each rising more than two-hundred feet into the air, flank a lower but more ornate central tower, dedicated to St. James. It hovers above the *Portico de Gloria,* the main entrance to the majestic cathedral. Over the centuries millions of pilgrims, traveling the thirteen sanctioned routes to Santiago, have crossed its threshold.

"Quite a sight isn't it," he said.

"Yes, especially to devout Catholics."

"If you don't mind," Mikel said, "I'm going to spend the rest of the afternoon being a devout Catholic tourist."

"Go ahead, I'll putter around a bit myself and meet you back at the hotel bar. At six shall we say?"

"Works for me," Mikel said as he bounded up the circular steps to the entrance.

"Well, what did you think of the cathedral?" Dietrich asked as Mikel settled on the stool next to him.

"Mind-boggling. It would take weeks to explore the cathedral and all its annexes. There are more museums around here than in all of Idaho."

"I agree. It rivals anything I've seen in my neck-of-the-woods. Of course, Switzerland is less Catholic-centric than the Mediterranean states. Changing subjects, did you contact Alejandro's sister?"

"Yes, I called her when I exited the church. She was hesitant at first but when I mentioned that Father Gerardo had given me her name, she relented. I'll see her at nine tomorrow. I'll pick up some flowers."

"What do you expect to learn from her?"

"She knows where Alejandro has been throughout his priestly career and maybe she can shed some light on his activities. Did she know about his pedophilia? When and where was he first counseled about it? What punishments did he receive? Most of all I want to know if she saw him in San Sebastian, and if so, where? Did she visit him at a sanitarium? I want to confirm that he was at *Sanitaria de San Pedro* and that's where he died. Does he have other relatives who can shed light on his activities? Did she know any of his victims?"

"Whew, that's a tall order. Do you think she'll cooperate?"

"I got the feeling from the people I've talked to that she loved her brother devotedly but is still carrying a lot of guilt for him. Maybe she'll feel like sharing it."

"What'll you have Mikel?"

"I discovered a Basque drink called a *patxaran* and I think I've become addicted."

251

"Yeah, I remember. I had a couple of those and they knocked me on my can. Pretty potent."

"I limit myself to one and maybe a beer. I don't want to dive into the bottle again."

They finished their drinks and Dietrich excused himself.

"I'm going to my room and call Therese. I'm not very hungry. I may have a sandwich in my room later. Have whatever you want and put it on the room tab."

"Okay," Mikel said, "I'll be down for breakfast about 7:30. I'll leave at 8:30. I should go alone. We don't want to spook her. I'll be back by noon. I'll call when I get back."

"Fine, good luck."

Dietrich walked slowly toward his room, wary of what news awaited him from Palo Alto.

34

Lucrezia Diaz Santos' small house was only a short distance past the cemetery of *Igrexa Santa Maria de Villestro*. It was a modest, white washed structure, simple but well maintained. Mikel parked the BMW and crossed the yard to the front door. He tapped lightly. The door opened immediately.

"Señor Muñoz?" a slight, gray haired woman asked.

"Yes, Señora Diaz Santos? Thank you for seeing me."

"You are welcome. If Father Gerardo sent you to me I am sure it is all right."

Mikel's eyes swept around the room. There were several icons on the wall and pictures of men in clerical garb. He concluded this to be a home that venerated all things Catholic.

"I made some *tortas* this morning. Would you like one?"

"Thank you, yes, that's very kind."

"And *café* as well?"

"Yes, black please."

While she went to the kitchen Mikel took a closer look at the pictures. He saw a strapping young priest standing with his arm around another young man. The priest was obviously Alejandro. The same priest, but older, was in another photo alongside a cardinal. There was a third photo of the same cardinal standing with the pope. It appeared that the family's contacts reached high into the church hierarchy.

"Here you are," Lucrezia said as she sat the pastry on the coffee table. Hers was already there.

"I see you have photos of several men of the cloth framed on your walls. Is that one Alejandro," he asked, pointing at the picture of two young men.

"Yes, that was a few years after he finished seminary. The family was very proud of him. He and Domingo were the youngest. That's Domingo in the picture with Alejandro. They were twins, but not identical."

253

"And the one with the Cardinal?"

"That's Alejandro, taken many years ago when our cousin was elevated to Cardinal. Angel's father was quite a bit older than my mother."

"So, that's your cousin. What's his name?"

"Cardinal Angel Ortega Oria," she said.

Mikel almost dropped his cup, sloshing coffee onto his pants.

"Oh, I'm awfully sorry," he said. "That was clumsy of me."

He wiped the spill from his trousers and the coffee table with his napkin as he recovered from the surprise.

"In my research around San Sebastian I interviewed several people who knew your brother. As I indicated to you, not all the references about him were flattering. Of course, I won't publish anything derogatory about him, but it would help me to understand the priest and the man if you could tell me a bit about that."

Tears welled in Lucrezia Diaz' eyes. What she was about to tell this stranger, she had kept bottled up inside for years.

"First, I want you to know how much I adored Alejandro. He was like a son to me growing up, after our father died. I was so proud when he decided to become a priest. He was a wonderful priest for years and then something happened. Rumors began to trickle out that he was too close to the altar boys and that things went on behind closed doors that were improper. At first, I refused to believe them, but they became so widespread that I had no choice. I went to see him, to get him to deny the vicious rumors. He broke down and cried and begged my forgiveness. He said it was a sickness that he had been fighting for a long time. He said the Monsignor was sending him away to a special monastery where he would receive help for his sickness and when he was well he would be reassigned.

"He was at that monastery for two years before he went to A Coruña. Things were going well for a while, then he had a relapse. He was reassigned to another monastery, one where

254

there were no children around. That was for three years until the archbishop felt comfortable in bringing him home to *Bonoval*. He was here until around 2005 when he became very ill. He never told me what it was. It affected his mind and he was transferred to San Sebastian where he could get special medical help. That's when he discovered that his cousin, Miguel Ortega, the Cardinal's nephew, was practicing nearby and Alejandro began seeing him. He said he was better for a while then he started to lose control of himself and had to be institutionalized. That's when Miguel admitted him to a sanitarium that he ran in San Sebastian."

Again, Mikel betrayed his shock by dropping the torta. He scooped it up from the floor and put it on his plate.

"Again, I most humbly apologize. I must be tired from the long drive down."

Mikel struggled to digest the onrush of information. Pieces of the puzzle were beginning to fall into place.

"Did you ever go to see him in the sanitarium?"

"I once contacted Miguel and he said it would be too dangerous. Then I got the news that Alejandro was dead. I was in shock."

"You went for the funeral?"

"Yes, it wasn't really a funeral. It was more of a memorial service. You see, he was cremated."

"Isn't that unusual, especially for a priest?"

"I thought so, but Miguel and the bishop who was there said it was precautionary because Alejandro had a very contagious disease."

"I'm so sorry Señora Diaz Santos. It sounds as if life was not too kind to your brother."

"No, I guess not, but I often wonder how much of his problem was a sickness and how much was a weakness. I know he suffered on both counts, but I know also that all those young boys suffered too. And that's the part of him that I can't forgive. God rest his soul."

255

"What happened to Domingo?"

"Domingo stood by Alejandro for a long while. When he was sent away for the second time, Domingo washed his hands of his twin brother."

"Where is Domingo now?"

"He was at the funeral but otherwise I haven't been in contact with him for years. He went to university while Alejandro was in seminary. I believe he studied engineering.

"When Angel was ordained a cardinal, he asked Domingo to go to Valencia with him. I understand he helped Domingo join a large company there with ties to the church and that he did very well. Friends who visited Cardinal Ortega said that Domingo has since left that position and re-entered politics. He has risen to a high post in Madrid. I don't know what. I think Domingo still resents that I stood by Alejandro after the revelations of the abuse. He sends me money occasionally, now that I am alone."

"I'm so sorry," Mikel said. "Were you married?"

"No, I entered a convent shortly after my mother died. I wanted to be a nun, but circumstances prevented it, so I came back home."

Lucrezia began to cry. The burdens she had borne for so long came rushing to the surface. She held the napkin to her face and wept. Mikel was deeply touched. When she looked up Mikel saw vast pools of sorrow in her tears. It was obvious that the depth of her sorrow went far beyond a lost brother. He couldn't bring himself to probe any further into the deep wound he had opened.

"You've been very kind and generous with your time and I appreciate it. If there's anything I can do for you in San Sebastian just call me."

The card he gave her said author and historian and gave a different number than the detective agency.

Mikel was almost giddy with anticipation during his drive back to Santiago. He broke his own rule again and dialed Dietrich's number while driving.

"Hello Mikel, what's up?" Dietrich answered.

"Are you sitting down? If not, go to the bar, grab a stool, and order your favorite Scotch. Order a *patxaran* for me. You won't believe your ears. I'll be there in five minutes."

Water was condensing on the bar beneath the sloe-flavored, anisette drink when Mikel strolled into the Dos Reis tavern. He straddled the stool next to Dietrich, lifted the drink, and said, "*Salud.*"

"You look like the proverbial cat that ate the canary. What are you so pumped about?"

"Lucrezia Diaz Santos confirmed that Alejandro Diaz was her brother. She also reluctantly confirmed that he was a pedophile and had been ill. She chronicled all the treatments and reassignments and cover-ups he had gone through. The real bombshells were, one – he was the nephew of Cardinal Angel Ortega Oria, the same Cardinal Ortega who was an uncle to Miguel Ortega. So, Miguel and Alejandro were cousins, and two – he was confined to the *Sanitaria San Pedro* where he died—the same sanitarium controlled by—are you ready—Miguel Ortega."

"You must be kidding!"

"And three," Mikel continued dramatically, "Alejandro had a twin brother, Domingo Diaz Alvarez."

Now it was Dietrich's turn to fall off his stool.

"That's unbelievable! Do you know who Domingo Diaz Alvarez is?"

"No, who?"

"He is a top official in the Ministry of Health in Madrid."

"How do you know this?"

"He had to approve the building of Sagarin's facility in Zaragoza and pass on which pharmaceuticals we could manufacture and distribute."

Dietrich rubbed his forehead and stared into his Scotch, a puzzled look on his face.

"How does that all tie together? What's the common thread?" Dietrich asked. "And will it have a bearing on what we're looking for?"

"Hopefully, I'll be able to shed some light on that tomorrow. I'm going to that library/archive you found and see if I can find the connection."

Mikel and Dietrich entered the records annex to the cathedral library early the next day. A tonsured Dominican in a brown cassock welcomed them. Mikel handed his author card to the priest and explained that he was researching for a book on the church in San Sebastian.

"I spoke with Father Gerardo over at *San Domenicos* yesterday. He said that some of the information I am seeking may be in your archives. My partner and I would like to look through some of the older records."

The priest stared at the card.

"Are you affiliated with the church?"

"No, I have been commissioned by a private benefactor who wishes to remain anonymous. He is funding this at the behest of the bishop in San Sebastian."

"You will not be allowed to remove or photograph any documents. You may take handwritten notes only. Leave your bags and electronics with me until you finish. The records for the San Sebastian area are in room 222 on the second floor."

"Thank you, Father. We will be careful with your documents."

The records pertaining to church property in the San Sebastian diocese were located on the top shelf of a stack of

258

bookcases in the rear of the room. Mikel pulled the files for the past fifty years. He took the massive tomes to a reading desk.

"Here," he said to Dietrich, "you take these three and I'll take the others."

"What am I looking for?"

"Any reference to *Sanitaria de San Pedro* or *Sagrada Familia Amara*. And if you run across the names of Miguel Ortega, Cardinal Ortega or Domingo Diaz alert me."

Two hours later Dietrich opened his second volume. The plume of dust that rose when he dropped it on the table caused him to sneeze.

"I'm glad I'm not into historical research on a regular basis," he said. "This would drive me mad."

"You have to be of a certain personality and passion to do this kind of work," Mikel said.

He was finishing his second volume when he let out a whoop.

"Here it is. The holy grail."

"What is it?" Dietrich asked.

"It's a deed recorded in 2006 for the sale of the old *San Pedro* lighthouse by the local government to the Diocese of San Sebastian for conversion into a sanitarium. The note in the amount of five million Euros is signed by the bishop. A month later another deed was recorded transferring ownership of the lighthouse to Miguel Ortega y Compañia. It doesn't list who is included in "y Compañia.""

"Would Miguel have sufficient money to buy the property?"

"I can't imagine it."

"So where did he get the money?"

"Keep digging."

Two more hours of searching found no more documents about the lighthouse property.

"I have an idea," Mikel said. "Since the property passed out of the hands of the church, any further transactions would be recorded in the San Sebastian property records."

"So, it's back to Bilbao and San Sebastian?" Dietrich said.
"Looks that way."

The pair retrieved their belongings from the priest.

"Thank you, Father," Dietrich said. "Here's a donation for your library. He handed the surprised caretaker a 100 Euro note.

"Bless you my son. May God guide your footsteps."

The trip back to Bilbao seemed faster. Maybe it was the exuberance they felt, having unearthed so much valuable information in Santiago. They arrived at the clinic in mid-afternoon and went straight to the fifth floor.

"Welcome back," Maria said as they burst into her office. "You look ready to explode."

"It's amazing Maria," Dietrich said. "This guy is incredible," pointing at Mikel. "Thank goodness I listened to you."

"So, tell me, what's got you so excited."

Both started to talk at once.

"Go ahead Mikel, you tell her. You deserve all the credit."

"Maria it's unbelievable. Alejandro grew up in Santiago. He had a twin brother, Domingo. Alejandro, was a pedophile and was treated for his "sickness" but never cured. The church sent him to two different monasteries for treatment. Obviously, you can't cure sexual depravity. Then the church kept transferring him around, trying to hide his perversion. When he contracted syphilis, and became erratic they sent him to San Sebastian for treatment and assigned him to a small chapel there. That's where Miguel Ortega began treating him.

"Now comes the interesting part. Alejandro's uncle was Cardinal Angel Ortega Oria. Alejandro's fraternal twin Domingo worked with Ortega before Ortega was elevated to Cardinal and went with him to Valencia. Cardinal Ortega was also Miguel Ortega's uncle. Miguel, Alejandro and Domingo are cousins.

"The old San Pedro lighthouse was purchased by the diocese of San Sebastian and then sold to a group headed by— wait for it—Miguel Ortega. The old crenellated, castle-like building was converted into a twenty-bed mental hospital—

Sanitaria de San Pedro. That's where Alejandro wound up, and that's where we think he died."

"Why did the church buy it?"

"The state wouldn't sell it to private investors. There were those in the Church that wanted the sanitarium built, so they bought it and then sold it to Miguel's group."

Maria was agog at this outpouring of revelations by Mikel.

"Holy Mother of God," she swore, "who was invested with Miguel in the hospital?"

"That's the missing piece of the puzzle. I'll have to go back to San Sebastian to find those records. I plan to go tomorrow."

"That's fantastic Mikel, you and Dietrich make a good team."

"Yeah, we do, especially when he puts me up in five-star hotels. Say Dietrich, you wanna go to San Sebastian with me," he said with a broad grin.

"No Mikel, I'd like to, but I have some things to do here. That should be a relatively easy chore at the local courthouse."

"Should be, assuming the folks at the cathedral haven't intervened."

"What do you mean?"

"It's been known that certain sensitive records can often go missing, if you know what I mean."

"The church actually tampers with official government documents?"

"Maria, our friend here hasn't spent much time around the Catholic social order has he?"

"I think not Mikel."

"Dietrich, never be surprised at what the Catholic hierarchy will do to protect itself."

"Unbelievable, I thought that all went away with the Borgias and Torquemada," Dietrich said.

"Far from it, they were just getting it started."

"Speaking of Catholics and hierarchies Maria, have you heard from the nullity tribunal?

261

"They contacted Father Giuseppe and said they needed a few more days to follow up on some additional information they received. They didn't say what it was."

"I hope it's nothing serious," Dietrich said. "Have you heard from Vitorio?"

"No and that has me worried. Tomas, who's watching my house while Mikel is gone, said he saw that black van cruising through our neighborhood last night."

"Vitorio's probably trying to figure out where I disappeared to," Mikel said. "He's worried about what we're doing. I just have to figure out why. I had an associate run down the license plate for that van and it belongs to a shady PI in Vitoria, Ramon Navarre. Vitorio's leery of using local guys like me for some reason. I'll make myself obvious tomorrow and see if he takes the bait."

35

Ten miles east of Bilbao Mikel ostensibly stopped for coffee. His true reason for stopping was to observe if the van was still following him. It was, and unmistakably. Mikel spotted the black vehicle, brazenly parked at the entrance to the car park. Coffee in hand, he resumed his drive toward San Sebastian as before, however today he chose a different route. After crossing the Orio River inlet, he exited AP-8 at the toll booth and began a climb up to the ridge paralleling the sea. It ran along the ocean cliffs toward the lighthouse at *Monte Igueldo.* The van followed. The rutted, pot-holed two-lane highway was an escalating series of S curves and switchbacks. Mikel increased his speed. The van matched it. Coming out of a particularly sharp curve Mikel veered off onto a small dirt track. The van followed, speeding up to pull alongside. Mikel saw the glint of sun on steel in the driver's window. He jammed on the brakes. A fusillade of bullets riddled his car from bumper to bumper as the van sped past. The driver, distracted by his actions, failed to see the steep embankment where the road ended in a sharp right turn. The van stopped somersaulting when it hit a tree in a farmer's barnyard. The resulting explosion engulfed the tree and the barn behind it in flames as wild-eyed horses fled in panic.

This is getting serious, Mikel thought. He touched his face and felt blood where a shard of glass had penetrated his jaw. He pulled the glass out. Blood spurted. He pressed a rag to his face. It quickly became saturated. He backed his car to the ridge road

263

while keeping pressure on his jaw. He stopped long enough to dial the state police. He reported the accident anonymously and then drove on into San Sebastian.

The emergency doctor at the *Casa Socorro* 24-hour clinic believed Mikel's story that he had run into a plate glass door in his home.

"That's a pretty bad gash you have. There are still some small shards of glass in there. I'll clean out the wound and sew you up. Do you prefer a general or local anesthetic?'

"Local, I have to drive afterwards."

"Be careful, even a local can impair your reflexes for a while."

Fifteen stitches later Mikel headed back to his car, still a bit woozy from the medication and the loss of blood.

The courthouse in San Sebastian is a block from the river, squeezed in between a city park and the Maria Cristina Hotel. Mikel touched his face gingerly as he exited his bullet riddled sedan. The anesthetic was beginning to wear off. He said a silent prayer of thanks for the sturdy steel construction of older cars. He recalled how Dietrich had scoffed at his old clunker.

The tax collector's window was just inside the front door. He asked the clerk for directions to the property records room where a young woman guarded the entrance to the archives. She looked up and winced at Mikel's bandaged face as she asked for identification.

"Cut it on a glass door," he offered by way of explanation. She nodded sympathetically and handed him back his ID.

"My mother did the same thing," she said. "Now we have decals at eye level on all our doors."

"Good idea," Mikel said. "I'll do that when I get home. Where will I find commercial property sale records going back ten years?"

"Aisle five, left side."

"Thanks."

There were three volumes for transactions in 2008. Mikel took them to a reading table in an alcove by the window.

He looked for transactions in the Mount Ulia area. There were none for the address of the old lighthouse in volumes one or two. He opened volume three fully expecting the same result. The page numbers skipped from 200 to 205. Someone had neatly sliced 201-204 from the book.

"Damn, I knew it. The bastards are hiding something, and they are going to great lengths to do it," Mikel said to the wall. "Where do I go next?"

He went back to his car and sat behind the wheel for a long time. He tried to analyze the steps Miguel Ortega went through to acquire the lighthouse/sanitarium. Mikel had made a copy of the original plat of the property when the state sold it to the church. He decided to drive back to *Punta San Pedro.* Maybe there were clues he had overlooked.

The old lock on the chain link gate had begun to rust. He shook it, but it held fast. He noticed that the lower section of the gate had been pried open, probably by curious neighborhood kids. The opening was too small for Mikel to slip through. He dropped down on one knee and tugged at the bottom of the gate. He was able to move it three or four more inches, just enough for him to slide through. The road angled upward sharply toward the lighthouse. It ended in a turnaround. He was surprised to see another fence trailing off toward the river. It was posted with no trespassing signs. There was a weed-grown trail beyond. He could make out the silhouette of a small cottage on a promontory above the river. There had been nothing in the original transfer deeds about a house on the property.

"Can you help me with this?" Mikel asked the girl at the records desk. "Some of the records of this transaction are missing."

He showed her where three pages had been excised.

265

"That's a criminal act!" she said in outrage, "I'll notify the authorities and have him arrested!"

"Who?"

"There was a man in here about a week ago who asked to see this same property. It had to be him."

"What did he look like."

"Six feet, muscular, graying hair, sun glasses, baseball cap."

"Bingo."

"What?"

"I think I know the man. Can I see where he signed in?"

"Here," she said, "it was ten days ago. His name is Pedro Arridonde."

"No, it's Ramon Navarre. He's from Vitoria and he gave you a false name and a false ID."

"Why?"

"Navarre is a private investigator working for the people who bought the old lighthouse from the diocese. Is there any way you can recover those records?"

"Let me see?"

The clerk looked at the records book and scanned the pages before and after the missing transaction."

"This is interesting. There was an out-parcel on the property that was sold after the lighthouse transaction. It was sold to the owner of a shipbuilding company on the river just below the lighthouse."

"Does it list the sellers?"

"Let me see, yes. The sellers were Miguel Ortega and Company."

"Who signed the deed transfer?"

"Miguel Ortega, Domingo Diaz and Vitorio Elizondo."

Mikel held his breath as she read off the names. He exhaled and clapped his hands together.

"Those are the people who hired that PI that sliced the records from your book. They made a huge mistake. They didn't tell Navarre there were *two* transactions involving the property that were made several days apart. Was there a lawyer involved?"

"Yes, a Señor Roberto Soares of Bilbao."

Mikel smiled. He could see the heavy hand of the church reaching into the secular world, seeking to protect its own interests above those of its people. Now the question is, "what interests are they seeking to protect?"

"May I have a copy of that deed transfer? Maybe it will help to find and prosecute Mr. Navarre," he said.

"Certainly, anyone who violates the sacred trust of the public should be prosecuted."

She ran the copy and handed it to Mikel.

"Thank you for finding the missing pages and identifying the man who removed them," the clerk said. "I'll report him to the authorities right away. I'm going to suggest to my supervisor that we install cameras in the reading rooms."

"Good idea, I hope you find him."

He knew she never would, unless she read the obituaries. What she couldn't know was that Ramon Navarre was lying at the bottom of a ravine west of San Sebastian, burned to a crisp.

A small column of smoke still rose from the hillside above AP-8 as Mikel drove back to Bilbao. A fire truck and two police cruisers were positioned around the smoldering funeral pyre. An ambulance circled down the twisting farm road from above. It would have precious little of Ramon Navarre to take back to the coroner.

Maria was still in her office when Mikel called from the road.

"Hello Mikel," she responded to the caller ID.

"Maria, I have a lot of news for you. Is Dietrich still there?"

"No, he went back to his hotel. Why?"

"I'm sure he will be interested in what I have found. You'll probably want Rubio and the *four horsemen* there as well."

"Okay, I'll round everyone up."

"I'm about a half hour away. See you soon."

The usual suspects were gathered around the conference table when Mikel came in. Cokes, Fantas and chips were scattered about.

"Well, here he is," Rubio said, "The prodigal son returns."

"Hello Rubio, you should have been with me. This will blow your mind."

Dietrich sat up straight and put his orange Fanta down.

"What happened to your face?" he asked,

"It's a long story. You know what I said yesterday about baiting our black-van guy?"

"Yeah?"

"Well, he went for it hook, line and sinker. He picked up my trail as soon as I left my office. I let him tail me until I crossed the Orio River where I left the main highway and headed into the sierra, above the ocean. He followed. I jerked my car off the road at a nasty switchback and he tailed me. Next thing I knew, he roared alongside and began unloading an automatic pistol into the side of my car. I jammed on the brakes and he went flying past me. Unfortunately for him the road ended at a steep cliff. The last time I saw him his van had finished cart-wheeling and burst into flames after crashing into a huge oak. Mr. Navarre is toast; in every sense of the word."

"Were you shot?" Maria asked in alarm.

"Shot at, but thanks to the sturdy construction of my old sedan," he smiled knowingly at Dietrich, "the only injury came from flying glass. A large chunk struck me in the jaw. By the way Maria, you'll be getting a bill from *Casa Socorro* in *San Sebastian*."

"What did you do then?" Diego asked.

"I went to the records center to try to find who signed the documents for the lighthouse sale. Guess what, Dietrich? The four pages listing the transaction had been neatly sliced from the record book. Told ya!

"I took a copy of the plat with me and sneaked onto the property. I found an out-parcel with a small house on it that was fenced off from the main property. It didn't show on the original deed. I went back to the records center and told the young lady about the missing pages. I asked if there was any way she could retrieve them. She was incensed that someone had desecrated her records. She remembered Navarre coming in to look at the same records. He registered with a false name and ID, so she was more than happy to help. She thumbed through the book and found another property transaction from a few days later for the out-parcel. The house and acreage had been sold to the owner of a boatyard on the river below the lighthouse, for 150,000 Euros. It seems the conspirators got careless. They didn't tell Navarre about the second transaction. I guess they didn't think it mattered and we wouldn't discover it. Well we did."

"Who signed off on the sale," Maria asked, leaning across the table anxiously.

"Miguel Ortega, Domingo Diaz, and," he drew the last name out slowly......."Vi-to-ri-o El-i-zon-do."

Maria's jaw dropped.

"What...how...when..." she sputtered - and finally she asked... "Why?"

"That's the million-dollar question. That's why I wanted this brain trust together. I haven't figured it out. I thought eight brains might be better than one."

"Let's see," Dietrich began, "what do we know? We know that Alejandro and Domingo are brothers. We know that Ortega is their cousin and that Miguel treated Alejandro and then had him confined to his sanitarium. We think he died there. We know that Domingo is a high official in the Spanish health system and that he approved and helped finance *Sanitaria San Pedro.* We

269

also know that Cardinal Ortega was uncle to all three and influenced Domingo's career, probably arranging his position in the health ministry. But where does Vitorio fit into the puzzle?"

"Miguel and Vitorio grew up together and have been close all their lives," Maria said. "We were in university together in Valencia. That's where I met both of them. Miguel was best man at our wedding. I assumed that was why he was so angry about my dragging Vitorio into the nullity proceedings. But why would Vitorio's name be on the deed transfer."

Paskal spoke up from the far end of the table.

"Stop and think about it. What does Vitorio do? He moves people's money around. If you follow the money, you'll find your answer."

"Good idea," Mikel said. "Five million Euros is a lot, even for Domingo and Ortega. Did they have that kind of money? Plus, it took a lot more to renovate that old building."

"Why did they need to set up a sanitarium in the first place?" Alontso asked. "There were already three in San Sebastian and many others nearby, including some run by the church. So, why did the church buy it then turn around and sell it to these three? What were they hiding in that remote fortress? And, why did they close it so hurriedly after Alejandro died?"

"The state couldn't sell the property to private citizens," Mikel said. "The church bought it then turned around and sold it to the combine."

"We can assume that Domingo pulled the strings that landed Ortega in the Basque Health Ministry position," Dietrich said, "but what I can't figure out is why they were so quick to set up the sanitarium and sell off Miguel's psychiatric practice. The single common denominator to this whole mystery is Alejandro, our sick, twisted, Dominican friar."

"What year was Ortega elevated to Cardinal?" Mikel asked.

"1980, I think," Maria said. "He didn't enter the priesthood until 1960, when he was 39."

270

"Priest to cardinal in 21 years?" Paskal said. "When have you ever seen that happen?"

"Remember, he was in church politics before entering seminary. You can imagine what secrets he took with him. Someone wanted him on the inside where he could be controlled."

"Who had that power?" Dietrich asked.

"Who is higher than a cardinal?" Maria said.

"No! It can't reach that high!" Rubio protested.

"There are many positions of power in Rome below the Pope," Alantso said. "The Curia, which reports directly to the Pope, has been known to reach down into the ranks when the church needed to touch someone. My great uncle once served as a secretary in the Congregation for the Bishops which is the *dicastery* of the Curia that deals with all things associated with the clergy. Not all movement within that body is always transparent."

"What are you saying?" Maria asked. "That Rome in some way is involved in this?"

"I'm not saying anything," Alantso said, "I'm just suggesting that stranger things have happened in the course of church history. Ask yourself, why has everything that has cropped up since Alejandro Diaz surfaced in Rubio's algorithm, involved him in some way; San Sebastian, Tolosa, Santiago, San Pedro, Miguel, Domingo, Vitorio, Cardinal Ortega. I believe in coincidence, but come on! Ten to one the hold-up on Maria's case is tied to him through one of these characters. I just don't know how to make the connection."

"Mikel, what do you think?" Dietrich asked.

"I believe Alantso may be on to something. I don't think the answer lies here. It may lie in Rome, and I don't have a passport to the Vatican. We need to get a look at the Curia records. Any ideas?"

"Yes." Maria said. "I know someone who may be able to get you in—Father Giuseppe at St. Francis. He has a long and well-established position in the church here in Bilbao. His record is impeccable. It shows him refusing advancement in order to serve his flock at St. Francis. He's recognized as a scholar in the archdiocese. If he petitions Rome to do research for a book about the church in Bilbao, I don't think they will refuse him."

"But he doesn't know what we're looking for and I doubt if he's ever owned a computer," Rubio said.

"Rubio, you and Mikel are about to become priests," Maria said. "Father Giuseppe can get you into the Vatican archives where you two can do your thing. I don't think it's illegal to wear a priest's collar, even if you're not ordained. I hope he will agree. I don't think he needs to know all the gory details behind the suspected machinations of the church."

The dubious look in Father Giuseppe's eye told Maria that she had not completely sold her story.

"Father I know you have a duty to uphold the church. You also have a duty to hold the leaders of the church accountable when they stray. Just look how long it took to uncover the widespread sexual abuse that went on for years. If some Father Giuseppe had spoken up sooner, then how many young children would have been spared their pain."

"Maria, Dietrich, you're sure there is a cover-up of some kind here?"

"Too many unexplained things have happened to be coincidental," Dietrich said. "Alejandro Diaz was at the center of a conspiracy of silence. We don't know what it was or why, and we don't have enough evidence to bring to the authorities. We believe the answer may lie in the archives in Rome. We don't have access to those records. We think you do. We want to see what ties all these events together and then we may be able to draw a conclusion. If there's nothing there, then no one will be the wiser, but at least we will know."

272

"Please Father, I need to know why my husband was involved in this and why he didn't tell me. It may have something to do with the hold-up of the tribunal's decision."

"Very well, my child, I will ask the bishop's permission to go. He will need to make the arrangements in Rome."

"If he agrees," Dietrich said, "I can fly you down. I'll call Zurich and have them send over a plane."

36

Fiumcino lies across from *Ostia*, at the mouth of the *Tiber River* where it flows into the *Tyrrhenian Sea*. *Ostia* was Rome's seaport for centuries, overshadowing tiny *Fiumicino*. Fast forward to 1960 and the advent of long range, jet air travel. *Fiumicino* no longer lived in *Ostia's* shadow, after it was chosen as the site for Rome's new *Leonardo da Vinci International Airport*.

Two gleaming cruise ships were discernible through the clouds below, moored at the *Civitavecchia* docks, 40 miles north of *da Vinci*. The Falcon 10 added flaps to slow its descent into runway 16R. It was the first ride on a private jet for Mikel Muñoz, Rubio Salazar and Giuseppe Calderon and all three were wired. The cabin attendant provided sandwiches, beer and wine for the two hours and 10 minute flight. All three were well oiled by the time they landed. The driver waiting for them at the customs exit held a sign reading Giuseppe Calderone. He had added an 'e' to the priest's name, the more common spelling in southern Italy. Father Giuseppe, the priest, was well aware of his notorious namesake, Don Giuseppe "Pippo" Calderone, former head of the Italian Mafia. The limo driver was relieved to see this Calderon dressed in a priest's habit.

The Mercedes limousine dropped the three 'priests' at the entrance to *Residenza Paolo VI* across the street from the Vatican. Dietrich had arranged rooms for them overlooking St. Peter's with views of the square and dome. Father Giuseppe was nearly overcome with emotion at finding himself so close to the heart of his faith.

The small hotel shares its premises with a *St. Augustine* monastery, having expropriated and converted one wing. The annex facing *Via Paulo VI* features a terrace atop its fourth-floor affording guests an unparalleled view of St. Peter's Square. Giuseppe sat at a desk under the window in his room, his arms folded, mesmerized by the spectacle of St. Peter's. He had dreamed his entire life of being here. It was not yet noon in Rome and he was anxious to tour the cathedral. He had asked Mikel and Rubio to meet him in front of the hotel at noon where he would take them inside.

It was drizzling rain as they left the hotel. The concierge handed each an umbrella.

"Are you going to St. Peters?" he asked.

"Yes, it's the first visit for all of us," Giuseppe answered, in flawless Italian.

"*Bene, bene*, with the rain the crowds will be less. Enjoy."

"*Grazie amico.*"

As promised, the wait was only ten minutes before they mounted the ancient steps of Michelangelo's architectural masterpiece. The front reception hall was lined with priceless sculptures and artwork. Upon entering the cathedral proper they came face to face with the most venerated of all religious sculptures, the *Pietà*. Michelangelo's masterwork took their breath away, but it was merely prelude to the magnificence and majesty of the entire basilica. The human mind struggles to comprehend the splendor of this shrine to St. Peter. The three pilgrims wandered from room to room, past the altar with its four carved, serpentine columns, each rising thirty meters in the air in support of Bernini's baroque canopy.

After three hours of oohing and aahing they made their way out past the Swiss guards that have served the Holy See for over 500 years. They walked to the far reach of the square and looked back at St. Peters. The awe they had previously felt for

275

this holy place had been amplified ten-fold during the tour. Giuseppe was near tears as they trudged back to their hotel.

"Dinner at eight on the terrace okay?" said Giuseppe. "I can't get enough of that view. I'm going to try to get in some more sights before dark."

"Fine by me," Mikel said.

"Me too," Rubio added.

The crowds at night in St. Peter's Square are generally hushed and reverent. Groups of various sizes wander about, their cell phones resembling the random flashes of giant fireflies in the darkened square, as they take photos and selfies.

"What a day," Giuseppe said as he savored his dessert and coffee. "After I left you I went to see the *Sistine Chapel* and the *San Sebastian* catacomb beneath St. Peter's. I've often heard the phrase, 'See Rome and die.' Now I understand it."

"Mikel and I wandered down toward the Forum and the Coliseum. Pretty impressive stuff those guys built 2000 years ago." Rubio said.

"Yes, it's amazing how much of it has withstood the ravages of time and war," the little friar said.

"Not to put a damper on such a glorious day Father, but what's our schedule for tomorrow?" Mikel asked.

"I have a letter of introduction from my bishop in Bilbao certifying that I am on a research mission for the diocese. It states that I am looking for documents pertinent to diocesan history as research for a book about the church in Basque country. God help me if the bishop ever finds out what I am really doing. You two will probably be excommunicated and I'll wind up spending my old age at a little chapel on a small Balearic island.

"I will present my credentials to the secretary of the "Congregation for the Bishops", the dicastery responsible for priestly personnel matters within the church, especially at the bishop level and above. I'll explain that you two are helping me

276

with my research. Keep quiet. Don't give him any reason to suspect you are not ordained priests.

"Assuming we get past that deception, we'll ask to see historical archives pertaining to the Bilbao area. Then it'll be up to you to find whatever it is you're looking for."

"Fair enough, Father," Rubio said. "Hopefully we can find it and get out of here fast. What time?"

"I'd say about nine. Give them time to have their coffees and settle in for the day, so let's meet at 7:30 for breakfast."

A Vatican civil servant was on the desk in the Congregation for the Bishops library, a small bit of luck for the "non-priest" priests. No awkward religious questions to answer. The clerk took Father Giuseppe's letter and copied it. He had the priest sign in with all three names and titles. Giuseppe prayed no one would check the records for Fathers Mikel Muñoz and Rubio Salazar from Bilbao. He asked the attendant for directions to the area housing records from the Bilbao area of Northern Spain.

"Down this main aisle and through the door at the end. Turn left as you enter the Spanish section. Northern Spain will be in the fourth aisle. Good luck. Call me if you need any help."

"Thank you, my son," Giuseppe said. "You're very kind."

Mikel and Rubio followed Giuseppe down the corridor. They finally felt free to exhale.

"So far so good, Father," Rubio said.

There were no other researchers or library personnel on the floor that early.

"Where will you begin?" Giuseppe asked.

"Angel Ortega became a priest in *Santiago de Compostela* around 1960 and was elevated to cardinal in Valencia in 1980. We'll need to comb through the years around those times for clues to any unusual activities.

"Alejandro entered seminary the same year Ortega rose to Cardinal, 1980. Alejandro died in 2011. Before that he was transferred and hidden away several times over a period of thirty

277

years. We need to know who allowed that to happen, since he was a known pedophile? The buying and selling of the *Sanitaria de San Pedro* occurred in 2008 so that's a key year as well. Alejandro went to *San Sebastian* around 2005 and started seeing Miguel in 2006 or so. Let's start with the volumes that cover San Sebastian, Bilbao and Santiago from 1955 to 1965.

"There are five for *Santiago*, three for *Bilbao*, and two for *San Sebastian*," Rubio said. "*Santiago* rates its own archbishop while Bilbao's bishop reports to Burgos and San Sebastian's to Pamplona. Mikel, you take Santiago, Father you take Bilbao and I'll take San Sebastian."

They carried the heavy, leather bound volumes to large tables with typical green-shade reading lamps.

"Well here we go," Rubio said. "Good luck."

"After an hour and a half Mikel looked up and rubbed his eyes.

"I've got to come up for air," he said. "I need some water."

"Let's all take a break," Rubio said, "my neck is getting stiff."

"I can tell you two have never spent much time studying the scriptures," Giuseppe said. "This is child's play. Go to a seminary sometime and you'll see what real study is. But, I will go with you for a drink."

They found vending machines near the reception desk and were told they could not take food or drink into the stacks. They downed their drinks and headed back to their labors.

Half an hour later Mikel sat up straight and let out a low whistle.

"What is it Mikel? Have you found something?" Rubio asked.

"Maybe, take a look at this. In late 1959 there was a big flap over some articles that began to appear in "*El Observador Galiciano*." They kept cropping up every few days and they hinted strongly at malfeasance by highly placed church leaders in Santiago."

278

"I remember that newspaper," Giuseppe said. "It was northern Spain's equivalent of *"L'Osservatore Romano,"* the official newspaper of the Vatican. However, there was nothing official about it, little more than a scandal rag to titillate the masses. It was always in hot water with the church hierarchy in Santiago. The interesting thing is that the editor was Angel Ortega Oria."

"The same Ortega we're looking for?" Mikel said.

"Exactly," Giuseppe said.

"Father you keep digging there and I'll take the volume that covers 1960. Look for anything about Ortega. I'll see if I can find anything around the time he went off to seminary. Rubio, fire up that lap top and look for internet entries about Ortega, his newspaper and the church in Santiago for 1959 and '60."

"This is interesting," Giuseppe said half-an-hour later. "In March 1960 there is an announcement that, *"El Observador Galiciano"* is closing and the editor Angel Ortega Oria has been accepted into the *Compostelan Major Seminary*. He is to begin his studies for the priesthood immediately. He was recommended to the rector of the seminary by none other than His Excellency Gaspar Carrillo Santos, Archbishop of Santiago de Compostela.'"

"Wow!" Mikel exclaimed, "Now there's a story. The very man who is bedeviling rhe church in Santiago suddenly decides to throw down his arms and join the enemy, all with the assistance of the opposing general. Rubio, have you got anything in the public domain about that time?"

"Couple of things. There were rumors that officials in the local church hierarchy were enriching themselves through a scheme that involved coercing gifts to the church from pilgrims coming into Santiago and who were staying in certain "preferred hotels" or church facilities. There were actual articles in Ortega's paper accusing certain high officials of pressuring the travelers to donate to certain bogus charities and then pocketing the money. If you are good at reading between the lines it hints that it went all the way to the top. This had been going on even before

279

Carrillo Santos came to Santiago. Some articles suggested that the extravagant lifestyle he was leading couldn't possibly be sustained on a bishop's salary."

"Within days after the last article was published in *"El Observador"* the announcement of Ortega's entry into seminary was released. That cannot be a coincidence," Mikel said.

"At about the same time," Rubio went on, "another local paper published an editorial questioning the strange timing of these two events. It strongly implied that there must be a *quid pro quo* between the church and Ortega. The church countered that the editor was merely seeking payback on Ortega after years of bitter competition, and they brushed it off."

"Rubio, look up Cardinal Ortega's family tree," Mikel said.

A few keystrokes later Rubio spun the laptop around to display Ortega's lineage.

"Let's see," Mikel said, "Ortega's second cousin on his father's side was the mother of Alejandro, Domingo and Lucrezia. Lucrezia told me the story of Alejandro and Domingo but never talked much about Angel Ortega. It shows Miguel Ortega as Angel's grandnephew by another brother. Was Angel married before he entered the priesthood?"

"No," Rubio said, "but there are newspaper articles suggesting that he was quite the man about town. His name appears in numerous society columns with photos of glamorous women on his arm, most of them quite a bit younger than he."

"Interesting! What conclusions can we draw from all of this? One, there most certainly was an impending church scandal in Santiago. Two, the scandal disappeared shortly after Ortega's newspaper closed. Three, Ortega suddenly got religion and joined the priesthood. Four, twenty-one years later he became a Cardinal. What happened to Carrillo Santos?"

Rubio worked his magic again.

"In 1960, just ten years after he was made Archbishop of Santiago, he was summoned to Rome. Pope John elevated him to Cardinal Deacon in charge of the *"Congregation for the Bishops."*

"The Curia consists of five Cardinal Deacons," Giuseppe explained. "They oversee the major *"Congregations"* of the church. I remember when Carrillo went to Rome as head of the *"Congregation for the Bishops."* There were a lot of spinning heads, not only here in Spain but in Rome as well. No one could figure out why the Pope moved Carrillo to that position, but it certainly wasn't based on his sterling service in Santiago. His reign was filled with controversy, and he was only 50 years old. No one has ever held that position at his age in modern times."

"The answer to that mystery is the key to unraveling this whole state of affairs," Mikel said, "and I think I know where to find the loose thread to start tugging on. Let's take notes on anything we can find in these books and then get out of here."

By mid-afternoon the trio began buttoning up and preparing to leave.

"Thank you, my son," Giuseppe said to the attendant as they left, "this has been very helpful."

"Good luck on the book. I look forward to reading it," the young clerk said.

"I'm afraid he'll have a long wait unless you two want to help me with it," Giuseppe said as they crossed the square to the hotel.

"Maybe after this whole affair is over we'll do that," Rubio said. "Right now, we have bigger fish to fry." He immediately recognized the offense to Giuseppe and added, "Not that a history of the church in Bilbao isn't a pretty big fish."

The Falcon 10 swooped in to *DaVinci* at dusk. They were loaded and ready for takeoff as the *Tyrrhenian Sea* began turning dark. Mikel had the pilots reroute the plane for its return. First stop, Santiago de Compostela.

"Father, I want you and Rubio to go back to the cathedral reading rooms and look for anything related to what we found in Rome and anything on Alejandro and Domingo in particular."

"Where are you going Mikel?" Rubio asked.

"I'm going to pay a return visit to *Señora Lucrezia Diaz Santos.*"

37

For the second time in a week Mikel parked alongside the white picket fence circling Lucrezia Diaz' house. She had been reluctant to see him again when he called. He told her he had uncovered some new information that would be of interest to her. She reluctantly agreed to his visit.

"Señora, it was kind of you to allow me to come again. I realize that these are some painful memories, but I felt you would want the full and true story to be told."

She looked unconvinced.

"You said you had new information?"

"Yes, my friend found references to Alejandro in the records at the Santago cathedral. He traced them back to the Santo Domingo convent in A Coruña. There he found records of the births of Alejandro and Domingo Oria Diaz to Lucrezia Diaz..."

Mikel stopped in mid-sentence. The frail little woman had turned pale. Her eyes bore a look of sheer terror. She clutched at her chest and sank to the sofa.

"No! You musn't!" she gasped.

"Señora, if we were able to find these records, others will too. Won't it be better that I tell your story, as you wish it told, rather than by others with different motivations?"

"What do you know?" she whispered, looking up at Mikel beseechingly.

"Your mother died in Louro by the Sea in 1949. Two months later your father went to his priest and asked him to find a convent where you could go to have your child in secrecy. The priest sent you to the *Santo Domingo* convent in *A Coruña* where six months later Alejandro and Domingo were born. The convent records list you as the mother and Angel Ortega Oria as the father."

Lucrezia buried her face in her hands and sobbed.

"When the twins were six months old," Mikel continued, "your father moved here to Villestro and brought you and the twins to be with him. He told the neighbors that his wife had died in childbirth. He said you were his oldest daughter and you were helping to raise the boys. He contacted Ortega and insisted that he take responsibility by marrying you. Ortega refused. Someone within the church hierarchy also saw the birth records and went to the archbishop with the whole story. Archbishop Carrillo took this as an opportunity to get Ortega off his back by threatening to expose him.

"In exchange for his silence he offered for Ortega to publicly disavow his charges of wrongdoing by the church and to repent of his sins. In so doing the archbishop said he would forgive him, but his penance was to renounce the secular world and embrace the church. Carrillo made a big occasion of Ortega's contrition by announcing that the penitent was enrolling in *Seminary Major* to study for the priesthood, and under the righteous patronage of the archbishop himself. Carrillo told Ortega that as long as he remained silent he would be protected. There was a tacit agreement between them that, as long as he did so, Ortega would receive favorable treatment within the church. When Carrillo was elevated to Cardinal and moved to Rome, Ortega's path to Cardinal was preordained.

"Your father was convinced to remain silent when the church deeded this former rectory behind Santa Maria's cemetery to him and gave him employment for life as the sexton. Everything worked exactly as Bishop Carrillo planned until

284

Alejandro became a problem, so Carrillo directed the newly minted Cardinal Ortega to take care of the escalating embarrassment of his priest son. Ortega's solution was to turn it over to Domingo who was now in Valencia with him. Am I right so far?"

"I never told my sons that I was their mother and not their sister. Angel told Domingo to help persuade him to go to Valencia with him. Domingo told Alejandro in the false belief that it would help to turn him around. He thought that knowing his father was a cardinal would change him. It didn't.

"When it became obvious that Alejandro was not going to change, Angel persuaded Domingo to come with him. He paid for Domingo's education and then took him to Valencia with him when he became Cardinal. He helped Domingo find a good job. When Domingo left his position, Angel arranged for him to go to Madrid as an official with the national health ministry.

"Did Ortega and Domingo arrange Alejandro's transfers to the monasteries for treatment?" Mikel asked.

"Yes. They kept hoping he would change. Alejandro worked so hard to overcome his compulsions, but he never could completely resist them. I never fully understood his sickness. I was torn between my love for my son and the realization that he was committing mortal sin against God. I prayed that the church could redeem him, but in the end, it could not."

"What happened then?"

"Domingo knew that his cousin Miguel was practicing psychiatry in Tolosa and discreetly treating many of the wealthy residents of San Sebastian there. He arranged to have Alejandro transferred to *Sagrada Familia* so that Miguel could treat him without raising any alarms."

"What happened to cause Miguel and Domingo to establish *Sanitaria de San Pedro?*"

"Alejandro became very ill. Miguel never told me exactly what it was. I put two-and-two together and assumed it was a venereal disease, probably untreated syphilis that had infected

285

his brain. Alejandro became violent. He went on rampages. He assaulted a worker at Miguel's clinic and one of the priests at *Sagrada Familia*."

"Why didn't they just institutionalize him in a Catholic mental institution?"

"Alejandro was out of his mind and ranting. Over the years he had become privy to all the secrets that Angel and Carrillo were trying to hide. Domingo was afraid that he would expose them all if he were sent to an institution they did not control. During his sessions in Tolosa, Alejandro had already told Miguel everything he had learned about his father, brother and Cardinal Carrillo.

"Domingo went to Miguel and asked him to find a suitable facility that could house Alejandro, away from the prying eyes of the public and the rest of the church. That's when they decided to buy the old abandoned lighthouse fortress and convert it. The purchase and renovation would take some time, so they had to find a place for Alejandro in the meantime. Domingo bought a villa near the lighthouse. It was secluded and had a cellar that could be used as a temporary asylum for Alejandro. He brought some trusted helpers from Valencia to care for Alejandro while renovations were going on. When they were complete he moved Alejandro to the sanitarium, along with some others Carrillo and Ortega wanted isolated and controlled."

"Why did Miguel sell his practice?" Mikel asked.

"He was weary of treating the rich, spoiled socialites of San Sebastian. He envied the lifestyles of Domingo and Angel. He coveted wealth like theirs for himself and he wanted to live in a large city where he could achieve social prominence. He had squandered his small inheritance on gambling and was deeply in debt. He pressured Domingo and Angel into appointing him to the Basque Health Ministry position where he could extract patronage for favors. He knew that Angel was being paid to look the other way at corruption in the Valencia labor unions and that

286

Domingo was taking money from people doing business with the national health system. He wanted his own piece of that pie."

"How did he know all this?"

"Despite his problems, Alejandro was still well connected to the church through all the institutions he had served. Information found its way to him and through him to Miguel."

"So, Miguel had no money? How did he invest in the sanitarium, and why?"

"I don't know. You'll have to ask him. Maybe Angel put up the money for his nephew since he couldn't have his own name on the deed. Maybe his friend Vitorio Elizondo loaned him the money"

"Why would Vitorio get involved with this?"

"Again, you'll have to ask him."

"Why have you told me all of this?"

"My conscience hurts for allowing myself, my father and my sons to be used by a man who has no basic morality, no sense of decency, and certainly no loyalty to the church he professes to serve. Angel Ortega used me, and he used my sons—his sons—in different ways to achieve his own selfish ends. Then he used the church for his personal gain. His whole life has been a lie. He's an old man now, surrounded by nurses and drooling in his soup, but he's still wearing that red biretta. I've waited too long. The world needs to know how corrupt he is and how he and Cardinal Carrillo stained the reputation of the church."

"That leads me to a final question. How did Archbishop Carrillo get promoted to Cardinal Deacon in Rome at such a young age?"

"Who was the Pope then?" she countered.

"John XXIII, I think."

"Yes, and what major announcement did John make soon after becoming Pope?"

"I don't remember."

"Who was Vatican Secretary of State?"

287

"I don't know."

"If you will study that period of church history, I think you will find your answers."

Mikel drove back to St. James cathedral in Santiago pondering the mysteries Lucrezia had left him with. Father Giuseppe and Rubio were still poring over the archives of the period in question. Rubio looked up as he entered the room.

"Mikel, welcome back, how did it go with Señora Diaz?"

"She confirmed everything you learned about the twins. She also verified that Miguel Ortega, Domingo Diaz and Cardinal Ortega were co-conspirators in a cover-up. She found out through Alejandro and others about the deal-with-the-devil made between Carrillo and Ortega. She also knew that the cardinal had taken Domingo to Valencia and used his position to penetrate the criminal hierarchy there. He used that information to extort contributions from the longshoreman unions and the farm cooperatives.

"Then when Domingo left his industry position, Ortega arranged for his appointment to the Spanish Health Ministry. Through Domingo he held sway over developments in the Spanish pharmaceutical industry. Between the Valencia unions and Domingo's control in the medical arena the two amassed a fortune. So, I believe that Cardinal Ortega and Domingo bankrolled the development of *Sanitaria San Pedro.* Alejandro was becoming a major liability and uncontrolled he could expose their crimes."

"Then why were Miguel and Vitorio listed as co-owners of the property?" Rubio asked.

"There must have been something beyond their criminal history that Cardinal Ortega and Domingo were hiding and couldn't allow to become public. Somehow Miguel and Vitorio became aware of those secrets and that threatened the cardinal and Domingo. Their ownership positions in the sanitarium were money-in-the-bank bribes for the two as long as they remained

288

silent. The cardinal also needed Miguel's professional credentials for legal control of the sanitarium and its inmates. When Alejandro died, the sanitarium was no longer needed as a cover. It was sold, and part of the proceeds went to Miguel and Vitorio.

"Miguel sold his practice, paid off his gambling debts, and moved to Bilbao as head of the Basque health system, thanks to Domingo. Earlier, Vitorio had racked up substantial losses in speculative bond trading. He covered them with the money from the sanitarium sale. Now both men were complicit in criminal acts and all four were locked in a conspiratorial embrace."

"Father Giuseppe, when I asked Lucrezia about Carrillo's elevation to Cardinal Deacon and Ortega's move up to Cardinal she replied with three questions: 'Who was Pope at the time? Who was Secretary of State? and What major initiative had the Pope announced?'"

Giuseppe sipped his wine, closed his eyes in deep thought, and plumbed his memory before speaking.

"Angelo Giuseppe Roncalli became pope in late '58. One of his earliest proclamations was to call for a Second Vatican Council. He announced it in January, '59, just three months into his papacy. It had been over a hundred years since the first Vatican Council concluded. John was calling for a major review of doctrinal issues within the church. It was his view that the Church had become sclerotic and was falling woefully behind in a rapidly changing world. He argued that without major change the Holy Roman Catholic Church could become irrelevant. His announcement set off a massive struggle amongst church leaders. Both liberals and conservatives began to stake out their positions.

"Chief among the opposition was then Vatican Secretary of State, Fabio Antonelli, a known conservative. However, Antonelli was very clever. He publicly supported and praised the Holy Father for his modern vision for the church while behind the scenes he was scheming to guide the deliberations and the agenda in directions of his own choosing.

289

"The circumstances of Roncalli's election were unusual. He was called the accidental pope by some. He was a very agreeable person, from humble roots, and not necessarily seen as a formidable religious scholar. He took Antonelli's public pronouncements of support at face value. However, Antonelli's major ally and front man was Cardinal Alfredo Ottaviano, a fellow member of the Curia. Ottaviano was old, ill and nearly blind but he gladly accepted the role of protector of the Church's conservative doctrines. Antonelli and the Curia had also heavily influenced the selection of cardinal candidates. That's what put Carrillo in line for a red hat; two members of the Curia pressing his case with John. Antonelli needed to control events behind the scenes. By the time the Council first met in 1963, John XXIII was gone and Carrillo was a member of the Curia. With three of five members the cabal had sufficient power to manipulate the Council's agenda."

"What were they after?" Mikel asked.

"There were those within the church who said that Antonelli and Ottaviano were scared to death of the Council's proposals to change the Vatican financial accounting systems. They believed that the two had diverted huge sums from the church treasury into their own private accounts and then to Carrillo's as well when he joined them. A rigorous audit would have discovered their misappropriations and led to serious consequences for all three. They couldn't allow that to happen. By the time the first session of the Council was convened in 1963, Giovanni Battista, Paul VI, was pope. Paul had been Archbishop of Milan prior to his selection. Guess where he served prior to that?"

"I don't know," Mikel said.

"In the Secretariat of State—for sixteen years. Antonelli, Ottaviano and Corrilla grudgingly acquiesced to the modernization of the mass and other doctrinal changes," Giuseppe said, "in exchange for control of the treasury and internal Vatican functions. They were able to suppress their

290

crimes. The intrigue and infighting were so intense that some even alleged Pope John's death was not from cancer but something more sinister."

"Was there an autopsy or inquest?" Rubio asked.

"No, if there was foul play, it was buried with the Pope."

"Okay, that explains everyone's motivation but Vitorio's. Why were the others afraid of him? What secrets did he and Miguel share that could intimidate Domingo, Ortega and Carrillo?"

"That's the $64 question," Mikel said.

-38-

The small Sagarin jet lifted off from the Santiago airport the next morning just as the sun was rising, to return the three priestly sleuths to Bilbao. Mikel stared absently out the window as the lush mountain valleys of northern Spain receded below. He closed his eyes in an attempt to visualize the Miguel/Vitorio relationship. He concentrated on what Lucrezia had told him. She had been open about how Angel Ortega had seduced her and then abandoned her after the twins were born. She also filled in the details about the Ortega/Corrilla dealings. She was less forthcoming about Miguel and Vitorio. Why? He needed help. Maybe the brain power back in Bilbao could figure this one out.

It was still early when Mikel dropped Father Giuseppe at St. Francis.

"Goodbye Father. Thanks for all the help. We couldn't have done it without you."

"You're welcome Mikel. I still feel a little sheepish about deceiving my bishop but otherwise I might never have seen Rome and St. Peter's. I guess for me it's a reasonable trade-off, a little good for a little bad. I'll tell myself that when I go to confession next."

Employees were still straggling into the clinic when Mikel pulled his new car into the garage. The cost to repair his old, bullet-riddled sedan was more than the clunker was worth. Dietrich chipped in for the down payment since the damage occurred in the line of duty.

"Good morning Maria," Mikel said as he and Rubio walked into her office. The four days they were gone seemed like a lifetime to the haggard pair.

"Good morning Mikel, Rubio. You two look like death warmed over. I thought that jet-setting around the Mediterranean for a few days would have invigorated you."

"If that's what the highlife is like they can have it. Aside from a tour of St. Peters we haven't had our heads up for more than an hour. If I have to pore through another dusty old record book I…" Rubio didn't finish the sentence. Dietrich had hurried in from the conference room.

"Hello boys, it's good to see you back. What did you learn?"

"A lot," Mikel said. "As a matter of fact, the only thing I can't figure out now is how Miguel Ortega and Vitorio Elizondo persuaded Domingo and Cardinal Ortega to include them in their criminal transgressions. What could they possibly have known that was incriminating enough to intimidate two of the most powerful people in Valencia. I'm going to need help with that one. Maria, I think we need to convene a session with the whole team for this."

Ten minutes later the conference room was abuzz again. Alontso was the last to arrive.

"Sorry, I was delayed by a call from SciGen," he explained as he got his coffee and torta. "Dr. Simpson had a question about one of our procedures. It sounds as if they are close to a gene splice solution for the Factor VIII andvon Willebrand 2n incompatibility problem."

293

"Yes, I talked to him yesterday," Dietrich said, "and he said he was going to call you. Were you able to answer his question?"

"Yes, he was on the right track. Just needed a little tweak on the protein splice."

"Good to hear," Maria said. "Now that Mikel and Rubio are back from their adventures they'd like to report their findings and seek your help. The floor is yours gentlemen."

"Good morning." Mikel began. "In Rome we found that Angel Ortega had been the publisher of "*El Observador Galiciano*" in Santiago when Cardinal Carrillo was the archbishop. It was little more than a scandal tabloid looking for dirt on the church, but it was causing huge problems for the archbishop. Ortega charged that Carrillo and others in the church were skimming vast sums from the charities that were supported by pilgrims to Santiago. That is, until someone discovered that Ortega had fathered twin bastard sons with Lucrezia Diaz. Turns out she is not the sister of Alejandro and Domingo Diaz—she is their mother."

There was stunned silence around the table as Mikel continued.

"Carrillo's spies uncovered Ortega's clandestine affair with Lucrezia Diaz and threatened to expose his hypocrisy. Ortega would have lost all credibility as a critic of the church. His publication would crumble.

"Carrillo offered Ortega a way out of his dilemma. He would have to retract all his allegations against the church and make a public confession of his sins and then shut-down "*El Observador Galiciano*." As penance Carrilllo insisted that Ortega publicly renounce his former persecution of the church and re-embrace it by becoming a candidate for the priesthood. In exchange for his silence Carrillo became Ortega's protector and benefactor. Carrillo and his cronies continued their pilfering of the charities unmolested. He also made sure that key members of the Curia in Rome were taken care of. Those allies in turn convinced a malleable Pope John to elevate Carrillo to the Curia

294

and anoint him a cardinal. That ultimately paved the way for Ortega's rise to the college himself.

"The twins were ten years old when Ortega became a priest and were unaware that Lucrezia was their mother. Later Ortega told Domingo as an inducement for him to come with him, which he later did. When Ortega became a cardinal, he took Domingo to Valencia with him and set him up in a cushy job. As Angel and Domingo's influence increased they, were able to infiltrate the unions in Valencia and extort money from them.

"Ortega then procured a position for Domingo at the Spanish Health Ministry in Madrid where he continued his larcenous ways. Their control over the pharmaceutical industry in Spain was akin to opening their own mint. So, there's no doubt the two subsidized the purchase and renovation of *Sanitaria de San Pedro.* The question is why they included Miguel and Vitorio on the deed, because once they did that it was like admitting the four of them were in some sort of criminal collusion. Their names on the deed assured them of a handsome payoff when the sanitarium was sold, as it was after Alejandro's death.

"We learned that Miguel had a gambling addiction and much of his share went to pay off his bookies. Vitorio had substantial bond trading losses that he had been kiting for months. He used his proceeds to get out from under them. Obviously, he didn't learn his lesson."

"No," Maria said, "since he turned around and got in over his head with the credit default swaps. It's odd that I was not aware he was under any stress then, as he was later."

"Whatever Miguel and Vitorio found out that threatened the cardinal must have occurred well before 2005 when Alejandro transferred to *Sagrada Familia* in San Sebastian," Dietrich added. "And, it must be something they discovered together or shared with each other. What do we know about their relationship Maria? You were with them in Valencia at university where you met both of them. When was that?"

"We were in Valencia from around 1980 until 1984," Maria said.

"That would have been the first four years of Ortega's reign as archbishop in Valencia," Mikel said. "Domingo would have been there too. Did you ever meet him?"

"No, I met Miguel late in our junior year. He introduced me to Vitorio a few months later, so we were together less than a year. Miguel never told me he was related to the cardinal. I don't know if Vitorio knew. He never mentioned it. In retrospect Miguel may not have known Domingo was a cousin, and the cardinal's son, but he must have known that he himself was related to the cardinal."

"When were you and Vitorio married?" Dietrich asked.

"Not until I finished medical training and came back to Bilbao for my residency. Vitorio and I went our separate ways until then. In the meantime, he had moved to Bilbao with Banco Santander. We renewed our relationship then and married in 1988. I had lost track of Miguel until he came to the wedding as best man. He and Vitorio had stayed in close contact. Then Miguel moved here several years later with the health ministry."

"So, something occurred during that period which jeopardized the cardinal's little criminal enterprise," Rubio said, "but what?"

Paulo Echeverria, who had been characteristically quiet, leaned forward to offer a suggestion.

"Whatever hold they held over them it had to be tangible. Nothing else could have intimidated the cardinal and his son. Whatever it is, it was obtained during a known period of time in the eighties. It is most likely a document or a photograph. I lean toward a photograph. I can't imagine the cardinal or Domingo committing any of their activities to paper. But a photo of what? My guess it's either of some criminal interaction with the unions or a compromising liaison. I think it's highly unlikely that two young college students would even be aware of their extortionate activities, so that leaves the liaison option.

296

"We know that Ortega got into trouble in the first place because he couldn't keep his pants zipped. According to Rubio's research he was a well-known womanizer even before he got his cousin Lucrezia pregnant. Do we think the leopard changed his spots just because he put on priest's robes? Probably not, in my opinion."

"That makes a lot of sense, Paulo," Mikel said. "If you ever want to give up your bio-med gig you can join my firm."

"Assuming Paulo's right," Diego said, "How will you ever get your hands on those photos?"

"We know that neither Miguel nor Vitorio would keep them at home," Mikel said. "They'd want them in a safe, secure location where Ortega and Domingo couldn't get to them. The most likely place would be where they work. I can't think of a more secure location than the top floor of the Basque Health Ministry building. It's guarded twenty-four hours a day and I'm sure Miguel has a safe at his disposal in his office."

"Suspecting that they are there and getting to them are two different things," Dietrich said.

"That's true my friend," Mikel responded, "but I've had tougher challenges."

The fire alarm sounded at three in the afternoon. Workers poured out of the glass tower in a panic. Miguel Ortega bolted down the stairs to join the throng of workers on the sidewalk across the street.

"Don't panic," he shouted, "I'm certain the firemen will quickly find the source of the smoke. Just stay calm until they sound the all-clear."

Smoke was pouring into the atrium from the third and fourth floors as two pumpers and a ladder truck pulled up to the curb.

"Is everyone out of the building?" the fire captain shouted at Miguel.

"As far as I know. We're taking a head-count to see. Hurry! There are a lot of records in danger in there."

One of the firemen following the captain into the building did not exit from any of the trucks. He stepped from behind a non-descript van parked near the ministry. He wore an oxygen pack which fed the mask covering his face. He carried an ax and a small tool box. A dozen more men filed in before him, dragging hoses up the stairs to the fire. They entered the two floors that were belching smoke. The man in the mask kept climbing. He entered the offices of Miguel Ortega where he began searching for a safe. He found one in a small alcove behind the minister's desk. He shucked off the mask and opened his tool box. He put on latex gloves and held a very sensitive microphone to the safe door. He twirled the dial, listening for tell-tale clicks through ear buds. Five minutes later he had recorded four numbers on his kneepad. Slowly, he rotated the safe's dial to the right until he heard a click, then left - click, right – click and left again - click. He pressed the handle down and breathed a sigh of relief as the door swung open. He reached past several stacks of money and glass vials to a manila envelope sitting on the back shelf. Slowly, he slid the contents out. Eureka! There were five color photographs which he quickly laid out on the floor. He grabbed the Minox camera from the toolbox and started shooting. When he was satisfied that he had the shots he needed he replaced the envelope and closed the safe door. He put the mask back on and headed down. He entered the floor where the other firemen were congregated around air conditioning vents.

"Must be an electrical fire," the captain said. "Get those vent covers off, so we can get in there. Aldo, take three men and go up to the roof. See if you can find the source of the smoke."

The air conditioning units were on the roof of the adjacent building with ducts running down the space in between. Aldo yanked the cover off a smoking unit.

Here's the problem," he shouted. "The motor's anchor bolts have come loose, and it has shifted so that the shaft is binding. Juan, pull that fuse!"

The motor screeched to a stop and the smoke began to dissipate. Once everything was secure Aldo turned to his junior man.

"Pedro, you stay to make sure it doesn't flare up again. I'm going down to help clear the smoke from the building."

Aldo didn't notice the fifth man in his group as he held back, concealed behind a large compressor. When Pedro turned his back, the man dropped over the parapet dividing the buildings and disappeared down the adjacent stairwell.

Mikel Muñoz slipped the tool box and duffel into the back of the van, got in, and drove away as the all-clear sounded and the ministry employees began re-entering the building.

Mikel Muñoz spread the five color photographs across the conference table in Maria's office. Only Maria and Dietrich were present.

"My God!" Dietrich exclaimed, "No wonder they were terrified. As a relative, they may have been able to control Miguel, but with Vitorio having copies of these pictures the entire enterprise was threatened. Reputations and careers would have been ruined. If these photos surfaced in Rome, Cardinal Ortega would be defrocked and excommunicated...then there are the civil authorities."

Maria glanced at the pictures and quickly turned away, visibly disturbed at the sight of them. The photographs had obviously been taken through a hole in the ceiling directly above a large bed. It was unclear what building the room was in, but there were crosses and icons on the walls creating the impression of a convent or a monastery. The room was large enough, and the ceiling high enough, to allow the lens to capture the entire space.

Sitting on the edge of the bed in the first picture is Cardinal Angel Ortega dressed in the ecclesiastical robes of his office. His right-hand rests on the thigh of a young girl, no older than eighteen. She appears to be asleep or drugged. She is nude and spread-eagled on the bed with her arms and legs tied to the bed posts. Her clothes were draped across a nearby chair. The black

300

and white garments and the simple headdress bespoke those of a novice.

The second photo shows a young priest assisting the cardinal in disrobing. The girl remains motionless, eyes closed.

In the third picture Ortega has straddled the girl and begun to penetrate her. Eyes still closed, her back is arched as if trying to resist him.

The fourth picture captures the moment of ecstasy for the cardinal as he collapses onto the limp form beneath him. Tears trickle down the girl's face.

In the fifth photo the young priest has returned and is assisting the cardinal with his robes. The girl is still trussed in the bed, eyes flaring, struggling against her bonds.

"How in the world did Miguel and Vitorio come into possession of these photographs?" Maria wondered aloud. "It's unlikely either took them. There's no rational explanation for them having access to the attic of a convent or monastery. Someone who knew Miguel and knew of his relationship to Angel must have taken them. But who? And why?"

"The girl was almost assuredly a novice at that facility," said Mikel. "The photographer may have known Miguel through the university or through the church."

"Or," Dietrich posed, "suppose it was a nun or priest who discovered what the cardinal was doing and was so repulsed by it could not remain silent. Approaching their superiors would be risky. They couldn't know who might be complicit in the matter."

"But why Miguel?" Maria added. "As Angel's nephew, wouldn't he be unlikely to report the cardinal?"

"What if they weren't trying to expose the cardinal *per se,*" Mikel said, "but just wanted to stop him and prevent further sexual assaults?" Mikel said. "Suppose whoever took those pictures needed a way to ensure that the rapes would not continue, so they gave copies to both Miguel and Vitorio. Whoever set this up must have known of the relationship between the two. They obviously counted on at least one of them

301

confronting the cardinal and apparently, they both did. Thus, began the blackmail, which means that Vitorio has a set of these pictures as well.

"With enough digging, I imagine I can find multiple financial transactions flowing between Valencia, Tolosa and Bilbao around the time Miguel started his clinic and Vitorio opened his investment firm. And, they would all bear Domingo's imprint. The cardinal could not be involved."

"You think this has been going on since the two finished university?" Dietrich asked.

"Yes. The photos were taken some time in the early eighties. Miguel and Vitorio may not have realized at the time how much power those pictures gave them. Angel and Domingo certainly did. When Domingo became aware of them is a question mark. Angel needed someone to interface with the two. He couldn't. Domingo was an obvious choice. How much Domingo knew about the content of the pictures is unknown, however, Angel surely painted a picture graphic enough to get Domingo's attention. The pressure must have built for a long time. I imagine the cardinal tried to coerce the two to sell the photos to put an end to the threat, but Miguel and Vitorio were clever enough to realize their continuing power over the cardinal. By the time they were ready to establish their own businesses, Angel had no choice but to finance them.

"Then, somehow, Alejandro became aware of the pictures. When his crazed behavior became a threat, something had to be done. That's when he was exiled to the sanitarium and held there incommunicado until his death. Then the two conspirators again approached the cardinal and Domingo; Miguel for an appointment to the Basque Health Ministry and Vitorio for money to cover his trading debts."

"Something doesn't add up," Maria said. "This cabal has been ongoing for over twenty years. One would think, with the cardinal's and Domingo's increasing power, they would have found a way to quash the threat. There must be something more

302

to the equation than just the photographs, as damning as they are."

"What are you thinking?" Dietrich asked.

"Subsequent to the pictures, something else must have transpired that bound the four conspirators together even more strongly. Something that carried as much danger to Miguel and Vitorio as it did to the cardinal and Domingo."

"But what?" Mikel mused.

"I don't know, but I think you need to spend a few days in Valencia to see if we can find out. You may need to persuade Father Giuseppe to play detective again."

Giuseppe balked at assisting Mikel in another caper. He was adamant that the church should not be used for such purposes. The detective pleaded and cajoled. He resisted showing the pictures to the little friar. He knew how great the shock would be, but he also realized they were now the only thing that could win his cooperation. Mikel slipped the packet from his bag and wordlessly handed them to the priest.

Giuseppe warily slid the photos from the envelope. His eyes bulged and his face flushed as he stared at the revolting images.

"Where did you get these?" he shouted.

"They were in the possession of Miguel Ortega. We think Vitorio Elizondo also has a set."

"How did you get them?"

"I'm not at liberty to say, but Miguel is unaware that I have them."

"When were the pictures taken?"

"We think sometime around 1984."

"Were these used to blackmail the cardinal?"

"We think so."

"Why not take these directly to the proper authorities for prosecution?"

"We think there is more to it than the cardinal's reprehensible behavior. We think something else occurred afterwards, something that later ensnared all four conspirators in their web of deceit. We think the answer lies in Valencia, and we think you can help us find it."

"When Maria called me I said no," Giuseppe said. "She asked me to hear you out. Nothing you have said convinced me until I saw those profane photographs. The acts depicted there are so hostile to everything I hold sacred about my church that I feel compelled to help expose them. I will go with you to Valencia."

"Here are all the church facilities that existed around Valencia in 1984," Giuseppe said as he handed a list to Mikel. The Falcon 10 had just lifted off from the Bilbao airport. "The icons and pictures on the walls are typical of those found in the rooms of a convent, particularly in the rooms of novices. The silver pendant on the young girl's habit appears to belong to the order of the *"Poor Sisters of Saint Clare."* I'm very familiar with the order since Ste. Clare was a devoted follower of St. Francis, my patron saint. The fact that the girl's hair is cut so short indicates she was a relatively new postulant. That is consistent with the rite of receiving the veil.

"The only *Santa Clara* convent in the Valencia diocese in 1984 was about thirty-five miles south, near Gandia. It makes sense. Ortega would not be so brazen and careless as to commit such sacrilege in Valencia proper. He needed the sworn allegiance of someone in Gandia who could arrange such a thing."

"Where should we start?" Mikel asked.

"I think we should go directly to Gandia and see what we can find. Starting in Valencia might arouse too many questions. If there are those still around who knew of these activities they're probably still in the area. Nuns seldom wander far from the area of their training."

"Do you know anyone in Gandia?"

"Yes, there is a monastery about five miles from town. The monks there are of the Hieronymite order. The abbot of *Sant Jerome* is Monsignor Gilberto Garafolo. He and I served together early in our ministries. He has been there for at least twenty-five years. He went there about the same time I came to Bilbao. We've kept in touch and we see each other occasionally at church conclaves."

"So, Ortega had been the cardinal for the Valencia diocese for ten years or so?"

"Yes."

"Do you think Garafolo knows anything of the cardinal's misadventures?"

"Not much goes on at the diocesan level that doesn't filter down to the parishes. The priests in the field don't often see the fire but they smell a lot of smoke. You can be sure that Gilberto heard rumors."

"How do you think he can help us?"

"*Sant Jerome* is the official repository for all church records in the Gandia parishes. The monks there are compensated for archiving the records. If there is any more damning evidence of Ortega's activities, we'll find them there."

The monastery of *Sant Jeron de Cotalba* sits on a rise between the large manicured orange groves surrounding Gandia and the hundreds of small, terraced properties inhabiting the hillsides above. From its bell tower, contemplative monks enjoy a panoramic view of the groves and the Mediterrean beyond. A young acolyte, dressed in the traditional white robe and brown *scapular* of the Hieronymites, answered the bell.

"Good morning, I am Father Giuseppe from Bilbao. I have an appointment with Monsignor Gilberto."

"Yes Father, please follow me. The abbot is expecting you."

305

They were led down a long, gothic-arched galleria. The sounds of water falling from the aqueduct feeding the cisterns and gardens provided a soothing and reverential backdrop for the cloistered complex. The monsignor was seated at a table in the Orange Tree patio, a 16th century gift from the Borgias. Rodrigo Borgia, Pope Alexander VI, was born thirty miles away in Xátiva.

"Giuseppe, how wonderful to see you. Pardon me for not rising. My gout makes it very uncomfortable."

"Think nothing of it my friend. Age has a way of humbling us all. This is my friend Mikel Muñoz. As I explained when I called, we are here on a most delicate matter. I trust we will not offend you."

"Do not worry. I know you well enough to know that your purpose is serious *and* discreet. Welcome Señor Muñoz. Won't you join me? I'm indulging in a glass of Ricardo's most delectable wine with lunch. May I offer you something to eat?"

"No, thank you. We had a bite on the drive down. The wine sounds good though. It'll help to wash away the dust from the road. Father Giuseppe says Ricardo bottles the best *Tempranillo* in this part of Spain."

"For once I must agree with my good friend—on other subjects, not so much," the abbot said with a chuckle. "We've had some really heated discussions on the interpretation of certain church doctrines. Felipe, two more glasses please.

"What is this tender subject you wish to discuss with me Giuseppe?" he said after Felipe had poured the wine and was out of earshot.

"Certain irregularities have arisen concerning some high-ranking members of the clergy in Valencia. If true, they have ramifications far beyond this diocese. They may affect several of my parishioners as well as others."

"These clergy, are they currently serving?"

"No, we are talking about events of twenty to thirty years ago."

306

"I see. I assume they occurred during the reign of Cardinal Ortega over the diocese of Valencia?"

"Yes. Certain evidence has been uncovered that implicates Ortega in criminal and sexual activities."

The abbot raised an eyebrow as a smirk played across his lips.

"Can you be more specific, my friend?"

"Ortega and his son Domingo are implicated in graft and corruption scandals that have been ongoing in Valencia for years if not decades. I'm sure that is not news to you. No charges for those crimes have ever been brought, that I know of. The more damning charge is that the cardinal used his office to sexually force himself upon young initiates in this parish, in particular at the *Convento Santa Clara* in Gandia."

"When I came here in the early nineties," the abbot said after a pause, "there were unsubstantiated rumors that the cardinal was acting in ways inconsistent with his office. There was never any concrete proof offered and the rumors soon died out. I delved into his history and concluded that based on his earlier behavior in Santiago the rumors might be well founded. But, as far as I know, no proof was ever offered. No one came forward to accuse him of anything. You surely understand that his power and his close association with Rome sheltered him."

"What if I showed you irrefutable proof that the rumors were well founded."

"Then I would say a case could be brought against Cardinal Ortega. However, in his rapidly declining condition I'm not sure what good would come of it."

"Where is he now?"

"The Catholic University of Valencia operates a nursing home for retired priests as an adjunct to its nursing school. The cardinal has been there for two or three years. He is in the early stages of Alzheimer's disease."

"Have you seen him lately?"

307

"I was in Valencia six months ago. I stopped by to visit and old friend. Ortega was there in the parlor. I spoke to him."

"How did he seem?"

"It was apparent that his short-term memory was diminished but he remembered with great clarity events in the past."

"If we show you the proof will you help us?"

"That depends."

"How so?"

"On what you intend to do with anything you may find here."

"Our concern is with current developments that may affect critical medical research ongoing in Bilbao. We have learned that before Ortega entered the priesthood he had fathered twins with a cousin. One of those twins, Alejandro Diaz, entered the priesthood. His life and his associations figure prominently into all this. Records indicate he is dead, however we are not certain. If he is alive, he has a blood profile that could be crucial to the research. "

"What could Ortega offer at this late date?"

"We're not sure, but we think he harbors other secrets that might be decisive in discovering the truth about Alejandro, secrets that could be critical to our search."

"Show me the pictures."

Mikel moved the wine glasses and spread the photos on the table.

Gilberto stared at the photos for a long time before raising tired eyes to Giuseppe, eyes that reflected the deep sorrow that came with knowing that the man who had ruled over the Catholic Church in Valencia for so many years was such a corrupt and degenerate libertine.

"Take them away! My soul cries out in anguish. Not since the debauchery of the Borgias has such transgression been visited on my people. How can I help you?"

"We want to know who took the pictures and what happened afterwards. We know who came into possession of them later, and we know they were used to blackmail Ortega and his other son, Domingo. Whoever took them knew the two people who received the pictures and knew or hoped they would confront Ortega with them to stop his abuse. If we can narrow down the dates, we may be able to identify the photographer and any collaborators. They may be able to shed light on what occurred after that."

Gilberto drained his wine and signaled for Felipe to join them.

"Felipe, my son, take these two gentlemen to the record vaults and help them find the documents they need."

"Yes Father, right away. Father Giuseppe, Señor Munoz, follow me."

The vaults were housed beneath the westernmost wing of the monastery. Felipe led them down a steep flight of stairs and along a passageway between two rows of supporting columns. The columns separated the vaults on one side from the catacombs on the other. He stopped in front of a wrought iron gate and selected a large key from a ring hanging on his sash. The door opened to the loud shriek of un-oiled hinges.

"Which records would you like to see?" he asked.

"Those associated with *Convento Santa Clara* between 1983 and 1986," Mikel responded.

"You know Mikel, for someone who doesn't enjoy digging through musty old books you sure do spend a lot of time doing just that," Giuseppe chided as he surveyed the five volumes spread on the reading table.

"You gotta go where the evidence takes you, Father. What can I say?"

"Where do you want to start?"

"You take the 1983 book and I'll take the two for 1984. That seems to have been a busy year."

"What should I look for?"

309

"The names of the sisters in charge, any celebrations or festivities, any visits by dignitaries from Valencia or other church locations, things like that. Jot down the items and pages you find interesting and I'll check them out."

"Very well," the little priest said.

Mikel began to flip through the first 1984 book.

"Mother Superior Angela was the abbess in 1984," Mikel said. "What about 1983?"

"Yes, the same. Apparently, she served here for many years."

The two detectives continued to thumb through their respective volumes. After a half-hour the priest stopped and tapped Mikel on the shoulder.

"Look at this. In August of 1983 Cardinal Ortega came to Gandia for a conclave with the priests and bishops in this area. It was advertised as a call for rededication to service among the poor. It was held at the *Basilica of Santa Maria* and lasted for three days. Here's the interesting part. After the others departed to their home parishes the cardinal stayed over for a special ceremony at *Santa Clara* in which several postulants were to undergo the veiling ceremony in the chapel. In a very unusual move, the cardinal asked that accommodations for him and his priest assistant be provided. A note from the Mother Superior said, '"His Eminence" wishes to spend some time in reflection and prayer in the peaceful confines of the abbey in order to renew his spirit following the conclave and the veiling ceremony, before returning to his duties in Valencia.'

"Anything more?" Mikel asked.

"No. He apparently stayed two nights and then drove back to Valencia."

"Does it identify his assistant?"

"Yes. Father Arturo Duarte."

Mikel fired up his computer to run a search but discovered the monastery had no wi-fi system.

310

"Damn!" he said. "I guess cloistered monks don't have much need for cell phones. Sorry Father. I'll check on him when we get to the hotel in Gandia. Let's keep digging."

After a few minutes Mikel slapped the table.

"Look at this. In March of 1984 Ortega convened an assembly of all the bishops in the diocese of Alicante. Why would he do that?"

"Alicante is a suffragan diocese to Valencia. The archbishop of Valencia, in addition to his duties at home, is also a Metropolitan. That means he has certain other administrative jurisdictions under his wing. Alicante was one of Ortega's."

"So, he had a plausible reason for doing that?"

"Yes, it was within his jurisdictional discretion."

"What about the stopovers he made at *Convento Santa Clara* going and coming?"

"Now that's unusual!"

"I wonder if he was aware that the convent kept such scrupulous records or that they would be preserved for posterity?" Mikel mused.

"Once you reach the level of power that Ortega did one sometimes assumes his own omnipotence. He either didn't know, or didn't care."

"Let's finish reviewing the records to see if he came back to the convent," Mikel said.

Two hours later, exhausted and red–of-eye the two sleuths closed the last of the journals. They returned to the Orange Tree patio to resume their conversation with Monsignor Gilberto.

"Well, did you find anything interesting?" he asked.

"Indeed." Giuseppe said, "Ortega visited this area on three occasions during the period of interest—once in late '83 and twice within a week in early '84. The act of visiting is not as consequential as what he did while here. He spent two nights following a conclave at the *Convento Santa Clara,* which seems extremely peculiar. Then in early 1984, as Metropolitan he

311

convened a bishop's assembly in Alicante, stopping at the convent for the night on the way down and then again on the way back. Both times he was accompanied by his priest assistant Arturo Duarte."

"I knew Duarte," the abbot said. "He seemed to be a fine young man. All reports confirmed his piety and rigid adherence to church doctrine. It's hard to imagine his complicity in such irredeemable behavior."

"Do you know where Duarte is now?" Mikel asked.

"No, but I heard in the mid '80s that he left the cardinal's service and reverted to his Franciscan roots. He transferred to the St. Francis Monastery on the island of Menorca, which is also under the aegis of the Valencia diocese. I remember because it seemed quite a departure from his former duties with the cardinal. Typically priests so honored go on to much larger things."

"Do you know if he's still there?"

"No, but that information is available in the diocesan directory. I'm sure you can find it on the internet. I'm sorry we don't have that modern convenience available here at *Sant Jeron.*"

"Thank you Monsignor Garafolo," Mikel said. "You've been a big help. I'm sorry we had to meet under such dismal circumstances. This is such a beautiful place. Maybe I can come back someday to visit."

"Thank you, Mikel, but our rules do not allow outsiders to enter on a normal basis. You can thank Giuseppe for this visit. I wish you well in your search, wherever it may lead you. Go with God."

-40-

Mikel asked Father Giuseppe to drive to the convent, so he could fire up his cell phone. He was anxious to trace Sister Angela and Father Arturo. He downloaded the diocesan directory and keyed in the names. Tragically, he found that Sister Angela had died of cancer in 1999. She was replaced at the convent by Sister Francesca who is still in residence. He had better luck with Father Arturo. The 62-year-old priest, now a monk, is still at his post on Menorca in the monastery of St. Francis.

"Father you are a Franciscan, are you not?""

"Yes, why do you ask?"

"Have you ever heard of a Franciscan monastery on the island of Menorca?"

"Yes, one of my fellow seminarians committed to the order there when we left school. I don't know if he's still there."

"What's his name?"

"It was Henrico when we were in seminary, but I understand he took the name Marco when he made his vows to St. Francis."

Mikel returned to his thumb-waggling. A few seconds later the screen refilled with the diocesan directory. He keyed in Brother Marco - St. Francis of Menorca and waited. Two names popped up."

"There are two Marcos at the monastery," he said.

"How old are they?"

"One is 73, the other is 57."

313

"The 57-year-old fits the time frame. That's probably my old friend."

"Great! So, we now have three people to track down— Sister Francesca, Brother Marco and hopefully his fellow monk, Arturo, although Arturo probably took another name at the monastery."

Convento Santa Clara is nestled among a warren of narrow, cobblestone streets southwest of Xàtiva. The drive from *Sant Jeron* took them higher into the lush green foothills above the sea. The small village surrounding the fifteenth century convent complex, another largesse from the Borgias, sprawls haphazardly across the undulating hillsides. It was necessary to park the car in a nearby plaza and proceed on foot. An acolyte dressed like the young woman in the pictures answered the bell.

"Good afternoon, may I help you?"

"Yes," said Father Giuseppe, "we have come from the *Sant Jeron* monastery. We are trying to find a sister who may have been a resident here. The records indicate that she was. Her family is trying to locate her. Her mother is very ill and wishes to see her before she passes."

"Oh, I'm so sorry. Come in. I'll summon the Mother Superior." She led them into a small sitting room off the entryway. "Have a seat. I'll be right back."

Mikel scanned the iconography in the room.

"These pictures and icons are very similar to those in the photographs. I think this is where the rapes took place."

"I believe you are right," Giuseppe said. "Now, how do we convince the abbess to cooperate without telling her the truth?"

"I took the liberty of photo-shopping the pictures to extract the wall hangings and a head shot of the novice. Maybe they keep class photos."

"Clever. We'll see."

Sister Francesca, all six feet and 250 pounds of her, burst into the room, dismissing the trailing postulant.

"I am Sister Francesca. I am abbess of *Convento Santa Clara,* I understand you are looking for one of our former novices."

"Yes Mother. I am Father Giuseppe from *St. Francis Cathedral* in Bilbao. This is Mikel Muñoz, one of my congregants who was kind enough to drive me here. Another member of our parish is very ill and wants to see her daughter before she passes away. They lost touch over the years. The last contact was from here around 1983 or '84. The mother gave me a picture of her daughter which was taken during her veiling ceremony, along with others of her class. I had it cropped from the picture and enlarged. We hoped that you might be able to help us."

"May I see her?"

Giuseppe handed the photo to the abbess.

"My, she looks frightened to death. I hope we don't appear so threatening as that."

"I'm sure the photographer caught her at a bad moment. Do you keep pictures of each class?"

"Yes. Just a minute."

Sister Francesca opened a file cabinet behind her desk and removed a wooden box. She thumbed through the folders inside and removed one stamped "1983." There were eight postulants in freshly starched habits with simple wimples, their veils removed for the photographer. There, third from the right, was a matching face.

"This looks like your picture," she said as she handed it to Giuseppe.

"Yes, it does. What name did she take?"

"Sister Maria Joseph," she said reading from the list on the back.

"Is she still here?"

"No, she left in 1984."

"Where did she go?"

"There is no indication," she said.

"Are any of the nuns in her class still here?"

315

"Yes, there are two, Sister Angelica and Sister Margarita."

"Would it be possible to talk to them."

"I'll send someone for them. I'll need to be present when you speak to them."

"Quite all right Sister."

The acolyte returned with the two nuns in tow. They both had quizzical looks. The Mother Superior introduced them.

"Sisters, Father Giuseppe is trying to trace the whereabouts of Sister Maria Joseph. I believe both of you were here when she left."

"Yes Mother, we were. Has something happened to her?"

"No, her mother in Bilbao is very ill and hasn't heard from her in years. Have you corresponded with her?"

"I received a letter from her a few months back," Sister Margarita said.

"Do you know where she is?"

"No, she doesn't say. The letters have no return address. The postmarks are illegible, as if purposefully smeared so I can't respond."

"Sister," the priest said, "do you remember what the circumstances were when Sister Maria transferred? It seems an unusual occurrence at that stage of her novitiate."

Sister Margarita gave a searching glance to the Mother Superior as if she were hesitant to discuss the matter.

"It's all right Sister, feel free to speak."

"I would feel better if Señor Muñoz were not present."

"That's fine Sister," Mikel said, "I'll just stroll around a bit. Father call me when you are ready."

"This is a delicate subject Father," Margarita said as the door closed behind Mikel. "You see, Sister Maria was with child. We aren't certain who the father was. We assumed it was one of the workers around the convent. Mother Superior Angela tried to get her to say who it was, but she refused. We didn't have facilities to care for her and it was embarrassing for Sister Maria to be seen in that condition. Mother Angela placed a discreet call

316

to Valencia and spoke to a Father Arturo. He had visited here with Cardinal Ortega. She asked for his guidance. He called back and said arrangements had been made to transfer her to another convent."

"So far as you know, is she still there?"

"Yes, I believe so."

"Thank you, Sister, you've been a great help. I hope we can reunite your unfortunate Sister with her mother while she is still with us."

"Is that all, Mother?"

"Yes, you both may return to your prayers."

"Father," the abbess said, "I pray that this information will be handled in a most discreet manner. The Sister has suffered enough for her indiscretion."

"Trust me Mother, her secret is safe with me."

"Thank you, Father Giuseppe, Sister Tomas will see you out."

Mikel was leaning against the convent wall having a cigarette when Giuseppe emerged. He ground out the butt.

"Well, tell me. What did you learn?"

"Sister Maria Joseph left here in 1984. She was with child. Arrangements were made by Father Arturo Duarte. Mother Superior Angela contacted him in Valencia when she realized the girl was pregnant. It was a few weeks after the cardinal's last visit. I don't believe she knew with certainty who the father was, but I think she suspected the cardinal. I also think she arranged for the photo session on Ortega's return visit from Alicante. She must have suspected his ulterior motives for so many visits. Especially, when there were several monasteries he could have stopped at. That still doesn't answer the question of who arranged the tryst, but it does explain why the scandal was contained. Sister Angela must have known, or knew of, Miguel and Vitorio in some way and had the pictures delivered to them. That seems to have put an end to the cardinal's penchant for

317

visiting *Santa Clara* and brought an end to Ortega's depraved perversion of this sacred place."

"Where did she go?"

"They don't know. Sister Margarita has heard from her but with no return address."

"Is Sister Maria still there?"

"Sister Margarita thinks she is. She had a letter from her a few months ago. What's your next move Mikel."

"I'm tempted to go back to Valencia and confront Ortega but that's probably not a good idea."

"No, I think not."

"So, let's spend a day or so at the beach in Menorca. Maybe we'll tour the Franciscan monastery on *Monte Toro.*"

"Sounds like a plan."

The ancient monastery resides on top of *Monte Toro,* a five-hundred-foot escarpment overlooking the island's capital, Mahon, and the nearby commercial airport which was enlarged and extended after the island became a major tourist destination. In the decades following WWII northern European families sought out its quieter beaches, away from the frenzied nightlife of neighboring Ibiza and Mallorca.

The Falcon 10 deposited Mikel and Giuseppe in the lush semi-tropical paradise near dusk. The drive to Hotel Mirador, overlooking the boat harbor, took only ten minutes. The bone-tired travelers checked in and agreed to meet for dinner at nine, after taking delayed siestas.

"Where can we find a good seafood restaurant nearby?" Mikel asked the hotel concierge.

"My favorite is *Ses Forquilles* and it's within walking distance. Their seafood was swimming in the sea this morning. I think you'll enjoy it."

"Thanks," Mikel said, handing the concierge five Euros.

"I'm feeling a bit extravagant," Mikel explained, "since we are spending Mr. von Hesse's money."

"Thank you, Mikel. I *am* getting hungry and fresh seafood sounds good."

True to the concierge's word the restaurant was only a short fifteen-minute walk away. It was immediately recognizable by the sign out front featuring six large, shiny forks.

"That was a magnificent meal my son," Giuseppe said as they walked back to the hotel. "much better than that served in the rectory at St. Francis. Not that I'm complaining."

"I agree Father that was outstanding. I wonder if we might extend our stay here a little," he mused jokingly. "I could dine there every night."

They stopped at the front desk to retrieve their keys. There was a note for Mikel to call Maria. Mikel looked at his watch. Almost midnight.

"There's a message to call Maria. Didn't sound urgent so I'll wait til morning. See you for breakfast at eight."

"Good night Mikel. Thanks for dinner," Giuseppe said with a wave.

"Maria, this is Mikel, you wanted to speak with me?"

"Yes. It's about the nullity situation. The presiding priest tried to reach Father Giuseppe but couldn't, so he called me."

"What's up."

"The nullity tribunal has asked me and the Father to appear, with Vitorio, to discuss his newest claims on my financial holdings. I'm having Rubio look into them to see if they hold water. I need you to get back before the meeting."

"Okay, we should be able to wrap this up today and be back in the office tomorrow."

"Great, pass this along to the Father and I'll see you tomorrow. By the way, how's it going?"

"You won't believe what we've uncovered. Turns out the cardinal

319

continued his wanton ways after he received his red cap. He impregnated a postulant at a convent south of Valencia and then had her shipped off to another facility. She gave birth there but we're not sure what happened to the child. We hope to find out today, at a monastery here on Menorca. We think the mother is still at the convent. We want to talk to the priest who made the arrangements. We should have a clearer picture for you when we get home."

"Wow, you continue to be full of surprises Mikel. Thanks. See you tomorrow."

On the drive up *Monte Toro* Mikel filled Giuseppe in on his conversation with Maria.

"Any idea what that's all about?" he asked the priest.

'I'm sure it's still a tactic on Vitorio's part to separate Maria from her fortune. I don't think he has a leg to stand on, but he's proved to be a very cunning and calculating character. Maybe Soares has come up with a new wrinkle. We'll find out soon enough."

The whitewashed, fortress-like, addition to the 15th century monastery gleamed in the early Mediterranean sun. Mikel pulled around to the parking area adjacent to the original structure. A statue of Christ, with arms outstretched, stood surrounded by three prominent cell towers. The sight of the towers, juxtaposed with the sacred statue, were upsetting to Father Giuseppe.

"What's becoming of this world?" he exclaimed in disgust. "Just look! There we see the transcending love of Christ reaching out to humanity only to be profaned by those modern towers of Baal. We're no better than the Canaanites with their golden calf."

"Some people would call it progress Father."

"Well, I'm not one of them," Giuseppe groused. "Come on; let's see if we can find Henrico. I mean Marco."

320

A brown-robed monk greeted them at the massive wooden door to the abbey. He wore the traditional robes with a white rope sash.

"I am Father Giuseppe from St, Francis in Bilbao. This is my friend Mikel Muñoz. Is the abbot available?"

"Yes, just a minute. I will summon him."

Minutes later the sound of sandaled feet reverberated in the vaulted entrance.

"Greetings, I am Brother Humberto, abbot here at St. Francis. I understand Father Giuseppe that you are a Franciscan friar as well."

"Yes, I serve a parish from St. Francis cathedral in Bilbao. This is my friend and driver Mikel Muñoz.

"Welcome both of you to our home. How may I be of service to you?"

"Firstly," Giuseppe said, "I am looking for my old fellow seminarian companion Father Henrico. I understand he may have taken the name Marco here."

"Yes, Brother Marco has been here longer than I. He is one of our most devoted and effective brothers. Just a minute and I will send for him."

Humberto sent the monk that had greeted them to find Brother Marco.

"I appreciate that you have come all the way from Bilbao to renew acquaintances with Brother Marco, but I assume there must be a deeper motivation."

"Very perceptive Father," Giuseppe said. "I have come at the behest of friends in Bilbao who are doing vital research in blood disorders. In a very convoluted way we think one of your Brothers here at St. Francis may be able to shed some light on the whereabouts of a person who may be able to help with that research."

"Who might that brother be?"

321

"When he came to St. Francis over thirty years ago he was called Father Arturo."

"Yes, Father Arturo is now known as Brother Tomas. He too preceded my appointment here. Shall I send for him?"

"No, please wait until we have a chance to greet Brother Marco."

"Very well, I hear him approaching now."

A stooped figure rounded the corner of the room, fingering the three ritual knots in his sash, representing his vows of poverty, chastity and obedience.

"Henrico," Giuseppe greeted the fragile looking monk.

"Giuseppe, is that really you. It's been so long. What brings you to Menorca?"

"Why, to see you of course."

"Still the comedian I see. It's wonderful to see you after all these years. How are you?"

"I'm doing well. You appear a little worse for wear though."

"I've been ill for a while, but with the help of God and the doctors, I'm on the mend."

"That's good to hear. I wish you well."

"Thank you, my friend, I assume there must be other reasons for your visit as well."

"There are. I have a congregant in Bilbao whose company is working on some critically important research into blood disorders. We are searching for a person who may hold a key to the problem they've encountered."

"And how does St. Francis fit into that situation?"

"It's a long and complicated tale, but we think your fellow monk, Brother Tomas, may know of this person's whereabouts. He came here as Arturo."

"Yes, Brother Tomas and I occupy adjoining cells here at St. Francis."

"Do you know him well?"

"If you mean 'has he shared his secrets with me?' then yes."

322

"Can you divulge them to us?"

"No, they were told to me in confidence. You'll have to talk to him. I can tell you that Arturo, Tomas, came to us from Valencia a very troubled young man. As you probably already know, he was an assistant to Cardinal Ortega. He has not disclosed all the details, but something occurred that led to his exile here on Menorca. He has spent the past thirty years praying daily to God for forgiveness. The transgression continues to weigh heavily on his soul."

"Do you think he will talk to us?"

"Yes, but I don't know if he can ever reveal his demons. I'm sure he has confessed them to Father Humberto over time, but those conversations are sacrosanct."

The abbot stared at the floor, his fingers pressed against his lips as if confirming his vow of silence.

"Brother Humberto, can we talk to Brother Tomas now?" Mikel asked.

"I will summon him."

A gaunt figure emerged from the shadows of the corridor. The shriveled man's eyes were rheumy and sunken. His shuffling gait spoke of knees hobbled by unending hours of penitent prayer.

"Brother Tomas this is Father Giuseppe and Señor Munoz. They have traveled here from Bilbao. The Father and Brother Marco attended seminary together and are renewing old acquaintances. However, there is another reason for their journey here. I'll let Father Giuseppe explain."

"Brother Tomas, we have traveled thousands of miles over the past few weeks in search of answers that may lead to life saving scientific discoveries. Sadly, our quest has led us to you. In 1984 a young novice was sent away from a convent near Xàtiva to bear her illegitimate child. We think you may be of help in our search. We are reasonably certain that the father is Cardinal Ortega."

323

Mikel watched the faces of Humberto and Marco for reactions. Both remained placid with only the rapid blinking of their eyes as a tell. The words had struck home.

"I realize how painful this must be for you Brother Tomas," Mikel interjected, "but what you can tell us may be crucial to the research. What you did, and what you may have been coerced to do, is between you and your God, but I can assure you, He has forgiven much worse in this sinful world. I stand in testament to that.

"What you may not know is that the cardinal, before he entered seminary, had fathered a set of twins in *Santiago de Compostela*. One became a priest and we have reason to believe he had the rare blood type we are seeking. The problem is, he is thought to be deceased. We are operating on the theory that the cardinal's child by the postulant may exhibit the same traits. That's why we came seeking your help. Will you tell us where she was sent?"

Tomas looked first at the abbot and then at Marco for guidance.

"Brother Humberto what should I do?"

"Everyone present here is now aware of the sins committed by Cardinal Ortega. What he did to that girl—and to you—borders on the unforgivable. He now sits in Valencia with a mind that has left him. He is beyond harm—or redemption. If, by revealing the location of his victim, you can contribute to saving other lives, then in some way it will be expiation for at least a portion of the iniquity he created."

"Thank you, Brother," Tomas said with an audible sigh. "The girl, Sister Maria Joseph, was sent to a small convent near Tolosa called *Santa Cruz*. That convent has been used for years as a repository for, shall we say, church embarrassments."

Mikel was dumbstruck. He could almost hear the pieces falling into place. He stifled an impulse to shout *Eureka*.

"Is she still there?"

"I believe so. I've had no contact for a long time."

324

"Do you know what happened to the child?"

"Actually, there were twin boys. I believe they were placed in an orphanage for troubled children nearby. There were hints that there were problems."

Mikel was dumbfounded. What were the chances?

"What kinds of problems?"

"I'm not sure. Developmental problems maybe. I understand it was a difficult birth, she being so young, and twins."

"Thank you, Brother Tomas," Giuseppe said. "You've been a tremendous help. May you accept God's forgiveness and continue to beseech his blessings upon us all."

"I know how painful the years have been for you," Mikel added. "I hope that what you have told us today will help us to find the answers we are seeking. God bless you. I will keep in touch to let you know what happens."

"Thank you. *Vaya con Dios.* Do his work."

-41-

Mikel stared out the window of the Falcon 10 as the plane sped them back to Bilbao. He contemplated the events of the past two days.

"You know Father, I'm almost afraid to go back to Tolosa. What if, after all this digging, we don't find what we are looking for? What if it's all a dead-end? What do we tell Dietrich and Maria? What happens to Rupert?"

"My son, you do everything that God gives you the power to do, then you must leave it up to Him. Que sara, sara."

Maria's BMW was parked in its regular space as Mikel pulled into the clinic's garage after dropping Father Giuseppe at St. Francis. He looked around for Dietrich's car. It was not there. Most of the workers had left for the day. He went directly to the fifth floor. He could see Maria on the phone and hesitated at the door. She looked up and motioned him in.

"Mikel, I've been on pins and needles waiting for your return. Fill me in."

"I noticed Dietrich's car is gone. He'll want to hear this."

"He had an urgent call from Stanford. He left shortly after noon."

"Is it serious?"

"Rupert had another seizure and the doctors placed him back into an induced coma. They're hoping to get permission to

326

try the new gene splicing protocol but have run into the usual bureaucratic road blocks."

"Poor kid. He's really been through the wringer."

"To say the least. Dietrich said he would call as soon as he got to the hospital. All we can do is wait, and pray. In the meantime, tell me about Menorca."

"Well, as we were told at the convent, Father Arturo knew where the nun was sent. As a matter of fact, he made the arrangements, under orders from Cardinal Ortega. She was sent to a small convent in, of all places, Tolosa."

"You've got to be kidding me! Tolosa? Is there a connection to Miguel Ortega?"

"I don't know yet. That's my next stop, *Convento Santa Cruz.*"

"This is unbelievable!" Maria said. "We've now come full circle. When will you go?"

"When is the nullity hearing?"

"Tomorrow. Father Giuseppe will go with me. No need for you to stay."

"Okay. I'll go to Tolosa tomorrow. I don't know if I'll need the Father to run interference for me. If I run into problems, I'll give you a call."

Therese's voice had cracked when she told Dietrich about Rupert's latest setback.

"What does Doctor Askew say?"

"He is surprised that there was another occurrence. He doesn't think it's life threatening at the moment, but he is evidently worried. He asked if you would be coming in soon. I told him you were on the way. He said something about news from a Dr. Le Clerc. Does that ring a bell?"

"Yes, he may be key to our ability to use what we've discovered to help Rupert. I'll fill you in when I get there. Did your folks get back home all right?"

"Yes, yesterday."

"How are you holding up?"

"Okay. It's the mental strain that's the hardest. I can handle the rest." She began to cry. "Dietrich. please tell me our son is going to be all right."

"I'm doing everything I can to see that he will. We're close, but it's always the last ten percent that takes forever. I'll be there in a few hours. Keep your chin up."

The now familiar bridges and colorful salt ponds of lower San Francisco Bay appeared out his right window. The reassuring sounds of sliding flaps and lowering wheels told him that he would be with his wife and son within the hour. His car was waiting in its usual space.

"Marcel, I don't know how long I'll be here. Check into a hotel and I'll call you when I know my schedule."

"Yes sir. I hope Rupert is okay."

"Thank you, Marcel."

Therese was dozing in her chair near Rupert's bed when Dietrich tiptoed into the room. The night nurse was reading. She arose as he entered the room. Dietrich put his finger to his lips.

"Don't wake her," he whispered. "How is he?"

"All his signs are stable. Dr. Askew was by about midnight. He seemed pleased with the progress."

Dietrich stood over his son's bed, overcome at the obvious deterioration in Rupert's robust physique and the pallor in his sunken cheeks.

"Oh God," he prayed silently, "please let me help my son. Give me the strength to see this through and to find the answers."

Therese stirred. She opened her eyes.

"Dietrich, oh I'm so glad you are here!"

He reached for her as she rose from the chair, embracing her lovingly.

"It's going to be all right darling. We're close. I can feel it. Just a bit longer."

"Oh, I so want to believe that, but when I see him as he was today, I become frightened that we're going to lose him."

"I know, I know. Don't despair; I'm not going to let him die."

"I want to believe that but it's so hard watching him slip away a little each day."

"Come, get some rest. He's in good hands. Wearing yourself out won't do him any favors. Come, let's go to bed."

The morning sun flooded their bedroom. It was past nine and they both had slept through. Therese lay cupped in Dietrich's embrace, sleeping as she had not for days. She woke to his movement.

329

"Good morning," he said. "You had a good night."

"Yes, I haven't slept like that in days."

"I'm going to slip out and see how Rupert is doing. Why don't you get a shower?"

"Okay, call me if he's changed."

"I will."

"How is he?" Dietrich asked the nurse.

"All his vitals are good, and he slept well. I think the crisis is over, but the doctor may want to keep him under for a couple of days more to let everything settle down."

"Were you present when he had the episode?"

"Yes."

"Was it diagnosed as a thalamic response like the other?"

"Yes. Dr. Askew said it was caused by a residual reaction to the earlier drugs. He doesn't believe anything your son is currently receiving caused it."

"Good. I'll be meeting with Sterling later today for a full run-down. Thanks."

Dietrich stroked Rupert's face. A tear slipped down his cheek and landed on his son's shoulder.

"Oh God," he prayed, "save my boy."

Sterling Askew was alone in his office when Dietrich arrived.

"Good morning, Mr. von Hesse. Sorry to drag you back here but I thought you'd want to catch up with Rupert's treatment. Also, I've heard from Dr. Le Clerc in Andorra."

"What did he say?"

"He was intrigued by the work we are doing. It parallels some of his own efforts in France. He will meet with us in Bilbao. He has next weekend open if that can be arranged."

"I'll make sure it happens. Are you available?"

"Yes, but I'll have to be back at Stanford by Monday for a seminar."

330

"Okay, I'll get Simpson ready and have Weiss flown in. We have a helicopter at the Zaragoza facility that can pick up Le Clerc. I think that covers everyone. Can you leave Wednesday evening?"

"I think so. I'll get someone to cover my lecture on Friday. By the way, have you spoken to Rob in the past couple of days?"

"No."

"He confirmed to me that the CRISPR gene splice to ameliorate the Factor VIII and von Willebrand problem has been replicated sufficiently to give him confidence in its efficacy."

"Fantastic! Now we believe we have solutions to two of the three problems—the excessive bleeding and the seizures—now we need to find that elusive candidate that can unlock the hereditary key to the hemophilia complex."

"Where does that stand?"

"Keep your fingers crossed but Maria Elizondo believes they have narrowed their search to a small village in the north of Spain. She said her investigator will be going there today. Pray that she's right."

The three priests for the nullity hearing were seated when Maria and Giuseppe entered the hearing room. Vitorio and his swarthy attorney Soares were waiting at the door.

"Good morning Maria," Vitorio said liltingly, "and to you Father Giuseppe."

"Good morning," she replied frostily.

"Come in and we'll get started," the presiding priest said.

"Señor Elizondo we have reviewed your amended petition and have a few questions for your attorney. Señora Elizondo, Father Giuseppe, have you received the new documents?"

"Yes, your Excellency," Giuseppe answered. "We received them a few days ago."

"Good, then you've had time to study them.

331

"Señor Soares, you state in the addendum that you have discovered new interpretations of the nullity doctrine that justify an equal distribution of all family assets, if nullity is proclaimed."

"Yes Father."

"Please proceed."

"One of the petitioner's claims is that my client never intended to have children, an *a priori* requirement of the church. I have in hand a document provided to my client before he married stating that he is impotent and therefore could never have procreated. A copy of that document was included in the papers submitted to the church before the ceremony. This is *prima facie* evidence that both parties were aware of this defect and chose to proceed anyway. Therefore, my client and the petitioner obviously were aware of his condition and so there could not have been deception. As for the claim of infidelity we continue to point to the obvious assignation the petitioner had with Señor von Hesse as proof of her ongoing infidelity. Therefore, we ask this tribunal to deny nullity and recognize my client's inherent property rights from the marriage. If Señora Elizondo insists upon a legal separation from my client, then he will pursue a court ordered division of all family assets."

Maria sat grim faced during Soare's testimony, staring fixedly at the man she had loved and married. She glanced at Father Giuseppe as he gathered his papers and walked to the lectern facing the priests.

"I ask the indulgence of this panel as I prepare to defend Maria Elizondo's right to a declaration of nullity from Vitorio Elizondo. I do not have the legal credentials of Señor Soares, but I do have two strong advocates on my side—God and the truth.

"The truth is, I have an affidavit from the archivist at St. Francis swearing that no such document on Vitorio's impotency was included in the original papers submitted to the church. It becomes apparent that the defendant induced someone to produce and plant that document after the fact. That being said, I have uncovered other evidence that will obviate any exhibits thus far presented by anyone in this tribunal."

"And what is that Father Giuseppe?" the priest said, leaning forward.

"That Vitorio Elizondo was, and continues to be, married to someone else."

A pin dropping in the room would have sounded like an earthquake.

"The timing of that first marriage was impeccable," the priest said while looking at Vitorio, his words dripping with sarcasm. "A few months later and the requirement for the public posting of marriage banns would have no longer been necessary. The Pope decreed the obsolescence of such a rule. Vitorio's wedding notice would not have shown up in the digital archives of the local paper. The internet is an amazing thing. It wasn't too difficult for our investigator to uncover it."

Giuseppe handed copies of the newspaper article to the three priests.

Vitorio's face turned a vivid red. He had assumed that the civil marriage documents, buried in the musty vaults of that small village north of Valencia, had died along with his short-lived civil marriage. His shotgun wedding to a pregnant classmate was over before it even began. He had fulfilled the demands of the girl's father. He left the girl there and returned to school.

"Are these claims accurate Señor Soares?" asked the presiding priest.

Soares looked futilely at Vitorio. It was clear by the stare on his face that he was as blind-sided as the tribunal by this new information.

"I am not aware of these new presentments Father. I will need time to research them for validity."

"Vitorio," the priest said sternly, "you can save us all a lot of time, effort and embarrassment if you will answer my question. This is not a court of law, but I advise you to think long and hard about your answer. Are these claims accurate?"

333

Vitorio squirmed and looked around for an escape that was not there.

"Yes Father, they are," he said while staring at the table in front of him.

"Señor Elizondo, you have broken every conceivable standard of civil society and you have brought disgrace upon yourself and shame on the church. You have sullied the reputation of the church and that of Señora Elizondo. I believe I speak for my two associates on this bench when I declare that your marriage to Maria Elizondo is both null and void. These findings will be reported to both the civil and church authorities— bigamy is still illegal in Spain. I suggest, Señor Soares, that you find criminal counsel for your client. And, Vitorio, if I were you, I wouldn't count on partaking of the Eucharist anytime soon. This tribunal, having fulfilled its obligations, stands adjourned."

Vitorio and Soares fled the building before being forced to confront Maria and Giuseppe.

"Father, do you think it's finally over?" Maria pleaded.

"Yes, Maria, I don't think you'll be hearing from Vitorio concerning your marriage any more. About his implications in the ongoing Alejandro Diaz investigation, I'm not so sure."

"Once again thank you for helping Mikel in Valencia. We would never have discovered those connections without your help."

"Think nothing of it. Thanks to you I've seen more of the world in the past few days than I ever dreamed of. By the way, you picked a prize when you hired Mikel Muñoz. His investigative skills are amazing."

"I agree, he is amazing. I promised him a grand dinner if he could find our man. It looks like he may collect soon."

"Has he gone to Tolosa yet?"

"He'll be there today. Keep your fingers crossed."

"I will."

"And Father, there'll be a large check in the collection plate on Sunday at St. Francis, made out to you. Do with it as you will."

"Thank you, Maria. I never run out of causes. I may buy a new robe for myself, though."

"Buy whatever you want *Padre,* you deserve it."

-43-

The return trip to Tolosa was less nerve-wracking. Mikel wasn't facing the grave possibility of arrest for breaking and entering However, the purpose of his mission remained the same; continue to unravel the Gordian knot created by the conspirators.

"Where is the *Convento Santa Cruz* located," Rubio asked Mikel as he prepared to leave the clinic.

"You remember that giant white cross above the town. The convent's almost in its shadow. It was established there after the cross was erected and took its name from it."

"What do you know about it?"

"The convent has been used for decades to conceal many disturbing secrets of the church."

"Do you think the pregnant postulant who was sent there is still around?"

"The monk who sent her there, at Cardinal Ortega's order, thinks she may be. Hopefully, I'll find out today."

The convent was situated on a side road halfway up the mountain. It was not visible from the roadway. A wrought iron gate barred the way. The sign attached said entry was by previous appointment only. Once again Giuseppe had paved the way. Mikel pressed the button fastened to the gatepost. Within seconds a feminine voice answered.

"Yes, may I help you?"

336

"My name is Mikel Muñoz. I believe Father Giuseppe Calderon of St. Francis in Bilbao made arrangements for my visit."

"Yes, he did. I'll open the gates for you."

The massive gate creaked open allowing him to drive through. As he rounded a rocky bend he could see two large buildings. One was in the standard architecture of most Spanish convents. The second however, set off to one side, looked more like a white fortress. Bars covered the windows on all three floors. A nun in a white habit greeted him at the top of the steps to the convent building.

"Welcome to *Santa Cruz*," she said. "I am Mother Superior Agnes. Please come in."

She led Mikel to a sitting room off the vestibule.

"May I offer you some tea?" she asked.

"No thank you Mother. I stopped for lunch on the way over."

"Father Giuseppe said you were looking for information on one of our community here at *Santa Cruz*. He asked that we cooperate fully with you. He said it was for a humanitarian cause. Normally, we don't discuss our resident's histories. Can I be assured that you will protect this information from public exposure?'

"Yes, Mother, you have my word," Mikel said. "She would have come here in early 1984 from Valencia province. She was a novice at *Convento Santa Clara* in the village of Xàtiva. Under circumstances which haven't been divulged, the young woman became pregnant."

"That would not be unusual. *Santa Cruz* has played host to many in the church who may have strayed. What was her name?"

"Sister Maria Joseph."

"Wait while I check the records. We did have a nun here by that name."

The abbess entered a small room off her office that was lined with filing cabinets. She was heard sliding several drawers in and out. When she returned she held a thick manila folder.

"Sister Maria Joseph arrived here in April of 1984. She was delivered of twin boys in October. It was a difficult birth and the twins suffered from oxygen deprivation in the process. They were kept in the infirmary for three months. When they were released they were sent to one of our orphanages for continuing care."

"And what about the mother?"

"I'm sad to say that she passed away a few months ago, of cancer."

"Where was the orphanage?"

"It is near Pamplona. They were there for quite a while, until a problem developed with one of the twins. Then they were returned here to *Santa Cruz* and placed in psychiatric care."

"What happened?"

"Both boys were diagnosed with autism, presumably due to the oxygen deprivation. Pablo's situation was more severe than Gabriel's. He became very difficult to manage in an orphanage environment. He was scheduled to come back here alone but he became extremely violent and upset when he was separated from Gabriel, so they elected to send them back together.

"Gabriel was diagnosed with Asperger's Syndrome, a neurological disorder now included on the autism spectrum. Prior to 2013 Asperger's was a disorder unto itself. The lead psychiatrist in Pamplona also diagnosed Gabriel as a musical savant. His mastery of the piano and of musical composition is uncanny. His talents have been compared to those of the youthful Mozart, who, by the way, was retroactively diagnosed as an Asperger."

"Amazing! Are the twins still here?"

"No, Pablo became increasingly difficult to control, even here. Finally, he became more than our staff could cope with."

"Where are they now?"

"They were sent to a highly secure psychiatric sanitarium near San Sebastian."

"When was that?"

"Let me see. I believe in 2009 or '10."

Mikel held his breath. His hands shook. His mouth became dry.

"Do you have the name of the facility?"

Mother Agnes thumbed through the dossier.

"Here it is. They were sent to *Sanitaria San Pedro.*"

Mikel could hardly contain himself.

"Are they still there?"

"I don't think so. I believe that facility was later closed, and I don't have a record of their whereabouts after that."

"Did you have any contact with them while they were there?"

"Yes, a Doctor Hernandez was on the staff. He had consulted here before. He was intrigued with Gabriel's extraordinary abilities. I asked if he would keep me updated on his progress and he agreed."

"Are you still in touch?"

"No, I had one letter from him following the closure of *Santa Cruz* but nothing after that."

"Do you still have the letter?"

"I believe so. I kept all the correspondence in the twin's folder. Yes, here it is."

"May I see it?" Mikel asked hopefully.

"I don't see how it can hurt now, after all this time."

Mikel took the yellowing letter with a trembling hand. He scanned the contents while memorizing the return address:

Dr. Antonio Hernandez
Calle de Castro, 289
San Sebastian de España

"He doesn't mention where the twins might have gone. He alludes to some tragedy at the sanitarium before it was closed

339

but doesn't elaborate on it. Do you have any idea what happened?"

"No, that was his last correspondence. I tried to contact him at that address but got no response," Mother Agnes said.

"Thank you for talking to me. You've been very helpful."

"Señor Munoz. If you find out what happened to the boys will you let me know. Gabriel was such a dear boy. We would sit and talk for hours. Mostly about music, but he had a brilliant mind and was very well versed in other subjects as well. He read all the time. Occasionally, he would become obsessed with one of the subjects and he'd need medication to calm him down. I can close my eyes and still hear the beautiful music rising from the chapel organ as he played Mendelssohn or Rachmaninoff. He knew all the classics by heart. God indeed blessed us with Gabriel. I pray that he is all right."

Calle Castro in San Sebastian is a small side street located near the Donestia hospital. 289 was half-way down the block. Mikel rang the bell. He could see a secretary inside. The door buzzer responded to her press of a button. Mikel stepped inside.

"May I help you?"

"Yes, I phoned your office from my car but didn't get through. I wonder if I could have a word with the doctor."

"What is this concerning?"

"It's about a patient of his from several years ago. He was at the *Sanitaria San Pedro.*"

"That was before my time. What was the patient's name?"

"Gabriel."

"Just Gabriel, no family name?"

"Just say Gabriel the savant. He will understand."

"Very well, I'll ask if he can see you."

Mikel sat across from a wall covered in framed degrees and honoraria. The secretary returned after a few minutes and asked Mikel to wait.

340

"The doctor will see you after the last patient leaves."

Mikel was on his third magazine when a young woman walked out of the doctor's office.

"Dr. Hernandez will see you now," the receptionist said, "please follow me."

"Doctor, this is Señor Muñoz," she said as she closed the door behind her.

"Come in Senor Muñoz. I was wondering how long it would be before someone knocked on my door and asked about Gabriel."

Mikel was taken aback. It was not the response he expected. He strained to control his curiosity.

"And, why is that Doctor?"

"As a medical professional I have certain ethics and laws to uphold. As a devout Catholic there are also certain vows I have taken. Sometimes these two duties conflict with each other. The past few years I have lived in fear of this moment. But now I am actually relieved that you are here. Now maybe we can get this sordid mess behind us and I can get a good night's sleep."

"What mess is that doctor?"

"You don't need to be coy Senor Muñoz. I'm sure the authorities now have it all figured out."

"Why don't you tell me what happened, and I'll see if it is consistent with what we know."

"Where to begin? I was called in to the sanitarium soon after it opened. One of its first patients was a Father Alejandro Diaz. I didn't know anything about him or his background, I was just asked to diagnose and treat him. He was suffering from the latter stages of dementia, apparently brought on by untreated syphilis. He was manageable as long as he took his medicines."

"Go on."

"Then, around 2010, twin brothers were transferred to the sanitarium from Tolosa. One of the twins, Pablo, was violently autistic. His brother Gabriel had Asperger's. Are you familiar with that disorder?"

341

"Yes, go on."

"Gabriel was a delight. He was a musical savant. Most days he was as normal as you or me. His talents were such that he should have been playing the piano on world concert stages; except that he occasionally lost it when he felt Pablo was being mistreated. As different as their conditions were, the two were devoted to each other, and almost inseparable. Okay so far?"

"Yes, that conforms to what we know," Mikel said without having a clue.

"Well, one day several of the patients were out on the quadrangle taking the air when Father Alejandro walked up behind Pablo and violently garroted him with his rope sash. Pablo screamed. Gabriel ran from the far side of the yard. He grabbed a large stone from the path as he ran and crushed Alejandro's skull. The man was dead before he hit the ground, but not before he had collapsed Pablo's larynx and broken his hyoid bone. Pablo lived for two days after that but finally succumbed to the trauma."

"Then what happened?"

"The church authorities and the management of the sanitarium were frantic that this incident not get beyond the gates of *Sanitaria San Pedro.* They said they couldn't allow the events to become public knowledge. They called all the staff together and swore them to silence. Doctor Ortega seemed especially anxious. The dead priest, Alejandro, was cremated and his ashes buried in a San Sebastian church yard. They had Pablo cremated also and strew his ashes into the sea."

"What about Gabriel? What happened to him?"

"He was disconsolate. He attempted suicide and had to be physically restrained. Several weeks later, when they got him calmed down, and medicated, he was transferred to a small church-ordained psychiatric facility near Gorliz, out beyond the lighthouse. The church seems to have an affinity for such isolated locations."

Mikel almost choked. Could it be that his search all over Europe had now led him back to Gorliz, his new home? God certainly does work in mysterious ways, he thought.

"I go there to see Gabriel on occasion," Hernandez continued. "Curiously, he is the only patient there. The small building was once a part of the coastal defenses. There is even an old cannon mounted on the walls. He is well cared for and seems to thrive in his solitary confinement, as long as he has his music. The authority's major concession to Gabriel was a piano. One can hear his music floating out to sea as you approach the building."

"Were there other patients at the *San Pedro* sanitarium?"

"Yes, a few. They were scattered to other facilities in Spain when it closed. I haven't heard anything from them."

"Have you been in contact with the church or civilian authorities that you reported to there."

"Only the ones in Gorliz. Of course, as you know, Senor Ortega is in a ministerial position in Bilbao."

"Why do you think the sanitarium was built in the first place?"

"There were always hints that the impetus for the whole development started in Valencia. On one occasion I overheard a conversation between Dr. Ortega and a Señor Domingo Diaz. There seemed to be a connection between Domingo and Alejandro that went back a long way. I knew that Dr. Ortega had treated Alejandro before he came to the sanitarium. They talked about the finances of the sanitarium and mentioned the bishop in *San Sebastian* several times. There was a third man there on occasion who seemed to have an interest in the finances of *Santa Cruz* as well. He kept asking questions about its value. I never caught his name.

"The entire development never made sense to me. There were numerous facilities that could have housed these people. Why build one from scratch? It all seems to go back to Valencia. I assumed that something went on there that had to be covered up

343

and this isolated light house was about as far as you could get from Valencia and still be in Spain.

"Am I close?" Hernandez asked, "What can you add to my story?"

"You are very close," Mikel admitted. "I can't go into the details but there was a conspiracy to cover up crimes and abuses in Valencia and several other locations around Spain. And, yes, Domingo and Alejandro were brothers, the illegitimate sons of a highly placed church figure."

The psychiatrist complexion had turned ashen.

"My God! What will happen to me?"

"I am not a policeman and I can't answer that. Ultimately, charges will be brought against everyone involved, both civil and religious. If you are called to testify just tell the truth. If you do, I think the courts will go easier on you."

"If you're not a policeman, then who are you?"

"I'm a private investigator. I'm looking for Gabriel. He too is the bastard son of the same cleric. We believe he may carry the rare blood condition that we have been searching for. If so, he may be able to help our medical researchers find a cure for a devastating disease."

"When will you know?"

"As soon as we can get Gabriel to Bilbao and run some tests."

"Can I help?"

"Yes, does Gabriel ever leave the facility?"

"Every few days he is allowed to walk down to the cliffs above the sea. He usually has two orderlies accompanying him. Getting out in the sea air seems to calm him."

"Can you find out when his next walk will occur and let me know?

"Yes, I usually go out on Thursdays. I will recommend they take Gabriel outside for therapeutic reasons."

"Is the facility gated?"

"Yes, there's a keypad at the gate. They change the code each day. I call them from the gate and they give me the code."

"Good, write the code down and leave it on the ground near the pad. I will follow you in and wait for Gabriel's walk."

"You should be aware that some of the orderlies are armed. Be careful."

"Thanks for the heads-up. I'll see myself out. You've been a great help. Hopefully, this whole mess will be over soon."

-44-

Mikel left San Sebastian and headed back to Bilbao. Again, he violated his own rule and dialed Maria's number as he got into his car.

"Hello, Mikel I've been waiting for your call. What did you find out?"

"Are you sitting down?"

"Why, yes, why?"

"Not only did I find where the mother went, I found out where the twins went."

"Where! Tell me!"

"The mother was at *Santa Cruz* as we thought. She passed away a while back. The boys were born there, both with autism; one severely affected the other with something called Asperger's Syndrome. They were shipped off to an orphanage in Pamplona for a few years until the severely autistic twin became unmanageably violent. They were brought back to Tolosa, but ultimately he was too much even for them to handle."

"Go on, what happened then?"

"Grab onto something! Are you ready? They were sent to *Sanitaria San Pedro.*"

"You're kidding me!"

"No, it's true! You think that's something, listen to this! Alejandro strangled the severely disabled twin in a rage and the

346

other twin bashed Alejandro's brains out. So, those *are* his ashes buried in the *Sagrada Familia* cemetery."

Maria paused to catch her breath.

"That accounts for two of the three who disappeared when they closed the sanitarium. What about the other one?"

"That would be the other twin, Gabriel, who just happens to be a musical savant."

"Mikel, this can't all be true?"

"You think not! There's more! Where do you think they took Gabriel after they hurriedly closed the sanitarium?"

"I can't even hazard a guess. I'm in a state of shock."

"Gorliz!"

"No!"

"Yes! They converted another small fortress building out near the light house. He's the only patient there."

"Who controls the facility?"

"The church, with a small staff."

"What next?"

"We have to talk about that. I'll be back within an hour. Can you stick around?"

"I wouldn't leave for all the tea in China. See you then."

The streets were emptying as Mikel pulled into the clinic garage. There were only a few cars still there. One was Maria's BMW. He caught the elevator and went right up.

"Mikel, I still can't believe this is all true," Maria said, meeting him at the elevator. "That's amazing work on your part."

"Well, I've had a lot of help."

"What next?"

"When will Dietrich be back?"

"He called this morning. He'll be in tomorrow, together with two doctors from California. And, he's bringing in someone from Zurich and a Dr. Le Clerc from Andorra of all places."

"Andorra? Where's that?"

347

"It's a small principality in the Pyrenees. Kinda like Monaco."

"What's that all about?"

"I'm not totally sure, but he said he would explain everything when they all get here."

"Maria, I'm going to need your help to get Gabriel out of that prison."

"What kind of help?"

"I want to borrow Rubio. I plan to snatch Gabriel from that place. I need Rubio plus one of my men. I need Rubio to drive. They will take Gabriel for a walk along the cliffs tomorrow afternoon. I can get us in and Josè and I can snatch Gabriel, but I need Rubio to drive us out of there. We'll have our hands full and the attendants may be armed."

"Shouldn't you get the police involved?"

"There's nothing to charge them with until we get all this evidence to the authorities. We don't have time for that. Rupert von Hesse could die at any time. We need to get Gabriel's blood tested, *now!* We'll ask for permission later.

"I'd like you to be prepared for the testing as soon as we get back here. Then we need to hide Gabriel away somewhere until we can go to the authorities. Can you take care of that?"

"Yes, I'll make arrangements for him. We can have blood drawn and most of the analysis done when the team arrives. I just pray that we have found the right candidate. The fact that Alejandro had the golden blood leads me to think Gabriel will also. Isn't it strange that Cardinal Ortega fathered two sets of twins? It'll be an ironic twist of fate if his licentiousness turns out to be of service to mankind—silver lining, ill wind, and all those other clichés.

"What time do you need Rubio?

"Noon, here. I'll pick him up. We should be back by three, if all goes well.

"It's been a long day. I could use a drink. Want to join me?"

348

"Why not? I can use one myself."

Maria watched Mikel as she followed him down to the street and out onto the sidewalk. For the first time she took notice of his casual bearing and virile manner. She noted his self-assured swagger. She began to see him in a new light. They crossed to the Redondo bar where they had first met with von Hesse. Maria ordered a white wine. Mikel had his usual, a *patxaran*.

"Have there been any more black vans through your neighborhood since Navarre ran off that cliff?"

"No, things have been blessedly quiet."

"Good. Based on the nullity ruling I see no reason for Vitorio to harass you anymore. He's got more serious problems to worry about."

Maria stared into her wine, hesitating to broach the subject of Mikel's private life. She decided to forge ahead.

"Mikel, when you divorced your wife, Clarice I believe? was it recognized by the church."

"It must have been. The guy she married is a catholic. They married in the church in Boise."

"Then you could get married again too, as a catholic?"

"Yeah, I guess. I haven't really thought about it much since I got here. Been too busy."

"Changing subjects," Maria said. "how did you get all that information on Gabriel?"

"The Mother Superior in Tolosa had corresponded with one of the shrinks at *Sanitaria San Pedro* after the transfer. She still had his name and address in her files. It surprised me how open he was. He'd been living in mortal fear since the sanitarium closed and just wanted to get it off his chest."

"Lucky for us."

"Yeah, I don't know how we would have found Gabriel if Dr. Hernandez hadn't cooperated. We'll need to remember that when the trials start happening."

Maria reached over, gently touched Mikel's arm, and smiled.

"Thank you for all you've done."

"My pleasure, see you tomorrow morning."

After two drinks, three tapas plates, and a dozen arbitrary subjects, Maria and Mikel headed for their respective homes. Tomorrow was certain to be a climactic day. They both needed to be fresh and alert.

The Falcon 50 lifted off from SFO with Dietrich, Rob Simpson and Sterling Askew aboard. Also aboard were several boxes of specialized medical equipment, to be used should a promising candidate become available. The trio settled in for the long flight. The twinkling lights of the city played hide-and-seek as the fog bank rolled in.

"Sterling, will Rupert be all right until we can get back here?" Dietrich asked.

"I believe so. I have left him in the capable hands of two of my most trusted associates. They have been instructed to be at the hospital or on call 24/7. If Rupert continues to respond well they will bring him out of the coma on Friday."

"Have you spoken to Le Clerc?"

"Yes. He said he has made preliminary contacts with the Andorran officials, the French health authorities and the Archbishop of Urgell. He prepared a white paper explaining his ideas and rationale for the experimental treatments, asking all three bodies to review them and to respond as soon as possible, stressing that time was of the essence. He is optimistic that Andorra and the archbishop will agree. He is more concerned about the French bureaucracy."

"Are the French aware of the extensive presence of Sagarin in their country and its contributions to the French economy?" Dietrich said with pique.

"They are, but Le Clerc also understands the French psyche and how sensitive they can be to perceived pressure. He's treading lightly."

"Do you have any clout with them?"

"A little. I've worked with the minister on a couple of international medical conventions. I think it best that I not intervene unless it becomes necessary."

"Okay, but we may need to move Rupert to Andorra soon."

"I understand, and so does Le Clerc. If they can be convinced, he is the one to do it."

"I certainly hope so."

Everyone deplaned in St. Johns to stretch their legs. Dietrich called Zurich to check on David Weiss. His assistant, Marlene, answered.

"Yes, Herr von Hesse?"

"Marlene, we are in St. John's for refueling. What's the status of Weiss and Le Clerc?"

"Herr Weiss left for the airport about ten minutes ago. The helicopter from Zaragoza is scheduled to pick up Mr. Le Clerc at two p.m."

"Splendid! Does Weiss have all the materials I asked for?"

"Yes sir."

"Good. I'll be in Bilbao later. Call me if anything comes up."

"Yes sir, I will."

Sterling Askew sat down across from Dietrich when they re-boarded. He looked concerned.

"I checked in with Stanford. Rupert is not responding as well as I had hoped. His white cell count is rising, and his respiration is more labored. He'll be kept under until those metrics correct."

"What can they do?" Dietrich asked.

"He'll probably need more blood, and the supply is dwindling. We're not sure they will give us more."

"Is there anything else to do?"

"We're getting more AB Rh-negative plasma that he can tolerate, but we're not sure it will be enough to rebuild his red count."

"What else?" Dietrich pleaded.

"Pray and hope for a breakthrough in Bilbao."

Dietrich held his head in his hands. He began to lose his composure.

"After all this, are we going to lose him?" he asked.

"Not if we can help it. Don't lose hope. We'd all better get some rest. There's much to be done when we hit the ground in Bilbao."

The Falcon 10 and a blue and yellow helicopter were parked on the tarmac as the 50 taxied into place alongside.

45

Mikel picked up the small scrap of paper that was partially hidden under a rock. He read off the numbers as Josè punched them into the keypad. The gate opened slowly inward. They hopped back into Rubio's Fiat SUV and pulled through. The gate clanged shut behind them.

"What now?" Rubio asked.

"Just drive slowly toward that high wall in front of the building. Google Map shows a small stand of trees to the left. Pull in behind them so that we are hidden from view. The path to the cliff passes close by. José and I are going to hide behind those large oaks bordering the path and wait. When they pass us, we're going to grab them from behind. Maria gave us two plastic bags with chloroform soaked cloths inside. Hopefully we can subdue the guards before they know what hit them, and then grab Gabriel. By the way did you bring the tape for your license plates? We don't want to provide them any more help than necessary in finding us."

"Yeah. I covered the plates while you were opening the gate. I noticed a camera on the inside pointed down to record incoming plate numbers. I don't think it had a view outside the gate."

"Good. Josè and I are going to move into position now. As soon as you see us jump those guys, come running. We need to get out of here in a hurry. My contact said they'll be leaving the

353

building for Rupert's walk about two. It's one-fifty now. Let's go Josè."

Two burly guards in white uniforms exited the hospital doors, one on either side of Gabriel. Both wore sidearms. Mikel began to sweat. He'd encountered armed men in Boise but that was a long time ago when he was on the right side of the law. If these palookas take a shot at me, and I shoot them, I'm not sure how the police will view it. Better not let that happen.

"Josè, take off your shoes. We gotta be as quiet as possible. Go ahead and pull the rag out of the bag. When I tap you on the arm jump out and clamp that rag on the nose of the closest guard. I'll take the other one. When they go down, grab Gabriel so that he can't run. He'll be scared. We need to get him to the car and calm him down."

"Right!"

"Here they come! Be quiet!"

The men were less than ten feet away, bantering with each other about yesterday's football games as they walked down the path past the trees. Mikel tapped Jose on the arm. Both men burst out of the copse from behind, surprising the guards as they clamped the drugged rags across their faces. The guards were so totally surprised that they took a moment to react. By that time, it was too late. After a brief struggle they both crumpled to the ground.

"Leave the rag across his nose. We don't want them to wake up for a while."

Gabriel reacted with shock and turned to run. Jose tackled him and got him in a hammer lock. The sound of a gunning engine and flying gravel filled the air as Rubio screamed around the corner.

"Get in you guys. I saw some men running from the house and I think they're armed."

Mikel threw Gabriel into the back seat and climbed in behind him. Jose jumped in the other door. Rubio floored the accelerator and spun off toward the gate as shots rang out. The

354

sound of glass shattering and lead hitting steel prompted Mikel and Josè to duck and drag Gabriel down with them. Rubio sped through the gate before it could fully open, tearing both panels from their hinges.

"Looks like Dietrich might be on the hook for another car," Mikel laughed nervously. "Get us back to the clinic; pronto. I don't know if any of those guys ID'ed us, but we can't take any chances."

Mikel looked down at Gabriel, cowering on the floor, his eyes wide with fear.

"Don't worry Gabriel, we're not going to hurt you."

"Who are you? How do you know my name?"

"We're friends who are going to give you back your life. We know about that man who killed Pablo and about the prisons you were held in. We're going to help you."

That seemed to calm Gabriel. He stopped shaking.

"Did you kill the guards?"

"No, they were just drugged to sleep. They'll be fine. Do you know who the other men were who shot at us?"

"No, but I heard one of them called Domingo. He was talking to Dr. Ortega. Dr. Ortega comes to see me quite often."

"Well, you don't have to worry about them anymore. You're safe now."

Rubio dropped Mikel, Jose and Gabriel at the elevator and drove his bullet-riddled car to the farthest reach of the garage. He grabbed a large tarp from the trunk and draped it over the bullet holes and the mangled grill then ran upstairs.

"…and someone ran out shooting when we took off," Mikel was saying, "and I don't know if anyone knew who we were. Rubio's SUV has a few ventilation holes in it and the front-end is all smashed up, otherwise we're all fine. From what Gabriel told us both Domingo Diaz and Manuel Ortega were there. I don't know if they made us or not, but I'm sure they know who kidnapped Gabriel."

355

Maria was sitting on a sofa next to Gabriel, trying to reassure him that they were all friends and wanting to help him. He was contentedly sipping a soda and munching on a candy bar.

"Why do you want to help me?" he asked.

"Because the people who have imprisoned you for the past few years didn't want anyone to know who you are."

"Who am I?" he asked.

"It's a long and complicated story. We'll get into that later. In the meantime, I have a huge favor to ask of you."

"What?"

"When the doctors examined you in the past, did they ever take some of your blood?"

"Yes."

"And, did they ever tell you anything about your blood after they took it?"

"No."

"We think you may have a very special and rare type of blood. We think it may help us to find a cure for a rare disease that will save many lives. Would you agree for us to test your blood?"

"I guess so. Will it hurt?"

"No. We'll be very careful."

"Okay, but can I have another Coke? They wouldn't let us have those in the home."

"You can have all the Cokes you want, Gabriel. Now come with me and we'll take that blood for our tests."

Maria handed Gabriel another Coke and walked him back to her lab, where she took a syringeful of his blood. She handed the sample to Dr. Alantso Zubiri.

"Alantso, do your thing. This vial of blood may look red, but if it is what we think it is, it's *golden*."

Doctors Le Clerc and Weiss were waiting in the first-class lounge of the Bilbao airport when Dietrich and his two companions came in.

"Dietrich, this is Dr. René Le Clerc, and I assume this is Dr. David Weiss?" Sterling Askew said.

"Yes, how are you David? Good to meet you Dr. Le Clerc," Dietrich said, extending his hand. "This other gentleman is Dr. Rob Simpson. He heads up our SciGen unit in Los Altos, California. Looks like we all made it in okay. Shall we go? I'm anxious to find out what Mikel Muñoz has turned up."

The five men piled into the limousine awaiting them at curbside. Even in the afternoon rush they were at the clinic in fifteen minutes. The four distinguished doctors followed Dietrich von Hesse up to Maria Elizondo's offices.

"Maria, how good to see you," he said bussing her cheek.

Dietrich proceeded to introduce the four men to Maria.

"Welcome to Bilbao gentlemen and to our clinic. If you will follow me into the conference room, we have a presentation for you."

Mikel Muñoz and Alantso Zubiri were standing at the far end of the table. Dietrich made the introductions and turned the floor over to Maria.

"Since we last talked, Mikel has tracked down the candidate we were looking for. I'll reserve all the details of that adventure until later. Right now, I want Alantso to show you what he has found. Alantso?"

"Gentlemen, the slide I am going to project on the screen is a blood sample from Rupert von Hesse."

The screen flashed as several helical strands of Rupert's DNA filled the screen.

"This next slide is a similar sample from the blood of Gabriel Diaz."

More strands filled the right half of the screen.

"Now I will superimpose the two samples."

357

Alantso maneuvered the samples together on the screen. As they merged, the helixes blended into an almost perfect copy of each other.

"All the other samples we tried from the various Rh-null donors were missing one or more of the key antigens we need or one of the von Willebrand traits.

"Gentlemen, Maria, we have our candidate. Now the real work begins. My colleagues are already hard at work deciphering the genetic codes of Gabriel and matching them to those of Rupert's. Once we are satisfied that we understand the anomalies between the two we hope that Dr. Simpsons CRISPR protocols can help us decide where to snip and replace Rupert's mutant genes with Gabriel's healthy ones. If we can do that and replicate it in sufficient quantities, we may be able to purge and replace Rupert's blood with the modified blood so that his natural cell development processes will take over, without the mutations."

There was a stunned silence around the table. Dietrich dropped his head into his hands as the tears began to flow. He couldn't believe this wild odyssey might actually culminate in a cure for Rupert.

"We musn't succumb to euphoria," Rob Simpson declared brusquely. "This is excellent news and it seems to promise an answer for Rupert but, we still have to complete all the tests, processes and protocols to prove their compatibility. Then, we must get permission to use them experimentally on a human being. There are a lot of hurdles in that process, but I must say it certainly looks promising."

"René, where do you stand with the authorities?" Sterling Askew asked.

"Andorra and Urquill are on board. It required a little arm twisting but Mr. von Hesse gave me a few bargaining chips to use. The French are being a bit more intractable. There is one doctor in the approval chain who is proving difficult. I've asked him to come to our clinic in Andorra when we are ready and to see firsthand what we are planning. I believe when he sees the work on the ground he will come around."

"Let me know if there's anything I can do," Dietrich said.

Maria stood and walked to the head of the table.

"I believe it will be useful if each of the teams working on this will bring the group up to date on their findings and progress to date," Maria said, "as well as what needs to be done here to integrate the individual work. While you do that, I have a date with a young man who needs to experience a normal environment. Mr. Gabriel Diaz and I are leaving you for now while I introduce him to the real world.

"Before I go Dietrich may I have a private word?"

He followed her into her office.

"What's up?"

"I wanted you to know I was granted nullity by the church."

"That's great news Maria, congratulations!"

"Thank you. There's more to the story. I'll fill you in later. I'm off to see to the safe keeping of Gabriel Diaz. I'll see you tonight at the hotel."

The empty vagabond was still parked across the street when Maria and Gabriel arrived at her casa. There was no way to predict how the conspirators would react to the kidnapping. She had to assume the worst. Maria hurriedly packed some of her clothes and some that Vitorio had left behind. Gabriel was near the same size. While she was busy doing that, Gabriel spied the piano in the parlor. A calm came across him as he sat down to play. Maria stood at the bottom of the stairs marveling at such artistry. She walked over and placed her hand on Gabriel's shoulder.

"Gabriel, when this gets all sorted out, I promise you I will buy you the finest concert grand piano available."

"That will be nice," he said.

"Come now, we have to get you somewhere that you will be safe."

359

Maria had booked the entire upper floor of the Gran Hotel Domine; four luxury penthouse suites and two smaller suites. She was going to stay there with Gabriel until any threat blew over. She and Gabriel would occupy one suite, Dietrich and his retinue the other three. Mikel would staff the smaller suites with trusted security guards to be stationed outside Maria's suite 24/7. Others would watch the elevator and vet anyone coming to that floor.

Maria made one other arrangement for her suite; she had a grand piano moved in.

"Well here we are Gabriel. This will be your home for a while. I will be staying in the other bedroom. Food will be brought in for us and you can play the piano anytime. If you want anything else, just ask."

"Can I have pizza?"

"As much as you want."

46

"Well gentlemen," Dietrich said, "your presentations here today give me great confidence that we can produce the treatments needed to save my son's life. SciGen's work on maintaining the Factor VIII and von Willebrand bond and Zurich's work on a drug to suppress thalamic seizures, may solve two of his three conditions. Now we must use the unique structure of Gabriel Diaz's blood to supplant the mutant genes that caused Rupert's hemophilia in the first place. It sounds like Alantso and his team, together with Rob's CRISPR protocols may be able to do just that. It's getting late and we've all had a long and hectic day. I suggest we retire to the hotel for drinks and dinner. Maria is already there with Gabriel. Mikel, why don't you and Alantso join us?"

"Thank you, Señor von Hesse," Alantso said, "but I think I'll stay here to work with my lab team."

"Me too, boss," Rob chimed in, "I'm fascinated by what they're doing, and I may be able to help tweak the protocol if needed."

"Very well, how about you Mikel?"

"I have nothing to offer in the laboratory, so I'll be happy to join you. It'll give me a chance to check up on my security team at the hotel."

Dietrich and Mikel rode the elevator to the top floor of the Domine, leaving Le Clerc, Askew and Weiss at the bar. The door opened onto a small vestibule. The guard posted there stood leaning against the wall to one side, his weapon at the ready.

"Jordi, good to see you so alert," Mikel said. "Everything okay?"

"Yeah, boss. Couple of room attendants. I checked their badges. All legit."

"Good! Stay alert."

"Yes, sir."

They moved down the corridor to the right. The second guard was seated outside the door to Maria's suite. He got up to greet Mikel.

"Hola José. Cómo van las cosas?"

"Muy bien, Señor."

"Good. Did you get Rubio's car taken care of?"

"Si,Senor. It's in the shop now. It'll be ready in two days."

"Did you see anyone suspicious hanging around the garage?"

"No, sir."

Mikel saw the puzzled look on Dietrich's face.

"Oh, I didn't have time to go over the day's activities with you. We were ushered out of the compound where Gabriel was being held by a fusillade of gunshots and Rubio took the entry gates off on the way out."

"Sounds exciting. Give me the details later."

"Will do."

Maria opened the door to the sound of the familiar voices. The expansive sweep of Suite P710 behind her revealed a stunning vista of the Guggenheim in the gathering dusk. Small rectangles of light began to appear in a hop-scotch pattern as each museum space lost its sun. The strains of a Mozart composition drifting in from the adjacent sitting room added to the surreal setting.

"Gabriel?" Dietrich asked.

"Yes," Maria said. "Between eating pizza and staring out the windows, it's all he's done."

362

"What an amazing talent. What's your take?"

"He's definitely on the Asperger portion of the autism spectrum. I think his developmental capabilities have been inhibited by his confinement. What Mikel told me about his conversations with the nuns at *Convento Santa Cruz* leads me to believe Gabriel is capable of living a near normal life, given the educational and cultural advantages now available to him. His major challenges will be in the social, inter-relational areas. Over time, I believe he can overcome those. It will be exciting to find out."

"Are you concerned that what we're doing with Gabriel will cause problems with the authorities and social welfare?"

"Maybe, initially, but I think when the whole story is made available to them they will see it was appropriate to free him from his confinement. As for the experiment, who's to say. Hopefully it'll blow over."

Dietrich crossed the room to watch Gabriel play. He was totally enraptured with the music and took no notice of the visitors.

"It's amazing what the human mind is capable of. Here nature has taken away certain basic skills from Gabriel while compensating by giving him this incredible talent. Mysterious."

"Shall we join the others for dinner?" Maria asked.

"Yes, let's. I'm starving."

It was approaching midnight when the dinner party disbanded. The celebratory mood had overcome the earlier tension and the jet lag. Finally, even the *bonhomie* of the evening could no longer hold back nature's demands.

"I'll see all of you in the morning," Dietrich said as they exited on the seventh floor. "I'm going to call the hospital to see how Rupert is doing."

The day nurse answered Dietrich's call.

"Good afternoon Mr. von Hesse," she said.

"Good afternoon Ms. Robbins. I just wanted to check on Rupert before heading to bed. Any change?"

"Dr. Aldridge was just here. He had some tests run earlier and your son's white cell count is still elevated. His respiration is still higher than normal, and his temperature is up."

"Is Aldridge still there?"

"He went for coffee. He said he'd be back in a few minutes."

"Have him call me at this number the minute he returns."

"Yes, sir, I will."

"Is my wife there?"

"Yes. Sir. She was up late last night, and she went in to rest for a while."

"Fine, don't bother her. Be sure that Aldridge calls."

"I will Mr. von Hesse."

Dietrich hung up and called Sterling Askew's room.

"Sterling, glad I caught you. I just talked to the nurse at Stanford. Her report on Rupert doesn't show any improvement. I asked her to have Dr. Aldridge call me as soon as he gets back from his coffee break. I don't like the sound of this. Can you come over and talk to him?"

"Certainly. Let me put a robe on and I'll be right in."

The phone was ringing when Dr. Askew came through the door.

"Hello. Yes, this is von Hesse. Hang on. I'm going to put you on speaker-phone. Dr. Askew is here."

"Hi Eric, I understand the meds didn't correct the problem."

"That's correct. I was sure they would control the infection but there appears to be a more deep-seated problem."

"What's his temperature now?"

"101.5.

"What's the white cell count?"

"It spiked to 25,000 about an hour ago. I ordered a stronger anti-biotic, but it hasn't taken effect yet."

"Have you used cooling blankets?"

"Yes. They seem to have checked the rise for now."

"It's midnight here. Stay with him tonight. Call me immediately if his temperature goes above 102."

"Yes sir, I will."

"You look worried Sterling," Dietrich said as the phone settled in the cradle.

"With all the anti-biotics and other therapies, he's had," Askew said, "his infection should be under control. The spike in his white cell count is worrisome. It means his body is trying to fight the infection but can't gain control. Let's see what the morning brings. It should come down."

"You don't sound convinced," Dietrich said.

"We're in uncharted waters here. We've never encountered this combination of blood disorders in a single patient before. We've administered all the standard procedures." He paused. "They may not be enough."

"What do you suggest?"

"We need to accelerate the work here in Maria's lab. If he continues to weaken we'll need to transport him right away and take our chances that we will be ready when he gets to Andorra. My worry is that if his temperature spikes dramatically before that, it could kill him."

"Is there anything to be done?"

"There's a company out of Atlanta that's doing cutting edge research for NASA. They've been working on cryo-systems that will enable extended space travel by inducing suspended animation that lowers the body temperature sufficiently for humans to essentially hibernate for several months. They recruited me to consult on their project at the Palo Alto NASA Ames Research Center. While they haven't achieved their long term suspended animation goals, they have succeeded in placing primates into *torpor* which is a similar technique used by some animals, such as bears, to survive the winter. They've had good success with trials of up to two weeks with no post resuscitation damage; all cognitive functions remained intact.

365

This all takes place in the lab environment at Ames. If it comes to it, we would need to be able to transport Rupert, in suspension."

"What do you need for that, for say a forty-eight-hour period?"

"A controlled environment with external access for monitoring and adjusting the patient's internal parameters."

"Hang on."

Dietrich picked up the phone and punched in a French area code.

"Allo," a groggy voice answered, "who is this?"

"Sergei, it's Dietrich."

The groggy voice became suddenly alert.

"Yes, Monsieur von Hesse, what is it?"

"Sergei, you know that project you've been working on for the cryo-genic transport of humans?"

"Ye...ss," he said, quizzically.

"How far along are you?"

"We've transported two primates."

How long were they in suspension?"

"One for two days, the other for five."

"How long will it take to get a unit ready for a human?"

Dietrich could hear Sergei's labored breathing as he considered the question.

"About a week."

"How about a day. We have to transport Rupert from California to Andorra."

"Andorra?"

"It's a long story. Can you do it?"

"I won't know until I talk to the engineers tomorrow."

"Don't wait until tomorrow. Get them to the plant tonight and begin work. We need that container ASAP."

"Yes sir, I'm on it."

"Call me in the morning and let me know what the engineers think."

"Yes sir, I will."

366

"Okay Sterling, we may have that cryo-pod you need."

"Amazing! I didn't know Sagarin was in the cryogenics business. NASA could use you."

"I'll worry about that when this is over. First things first. Rupert is priority one."

"Understood."

The team had regrouped in Maria's conference room. The bleary-eyed scientists swilled coffee to keep themselves awake. Alantso Zubiri was again at the video screen.

"As you can see we were able to snip out the defective genes in Rupert's mutant chromosomes and insert the concomitant genes from Gabriel's in their place. The guys are still in the lab trying to ramp up the replication of the altered genes to produce sufficient quantities for Rupert. We expect to be ready with that by tonight.

"Dr. Simpson helped us to fine-tune the CRISPR tool to avoid damage to the telomeres and adjacent chromosomes. Assuming sufficient ramp-up of the modified blood quantities we will be ready to go."

"That's fantastic news," Maria said.

"It's more than that, it's miraculous," Dietrich added. His cell phone rang.

"Yes. Good morning Sergei. What news?"

"Wonderful. Tomorrow morning? My plane will be in Biarritz tonight. Dr. Askew and I will meet you there. I want you and your best engineers to take the cryogenic unit to Stanford. You can instruct Dr. Askew on its operation during the flight. He and Dr. Eric Aldridge at Stanford University Hospital will assist you in hooking Rupert up for transport. They will accompany us to Zaragoza, Spain where a helicopter will meet us at the airport and take us to the Meritxell Hospital in Andorra. The team here will meet us there.

"Maria, gentlemen," Dietrich said after ending the call. "Dr. Askew spoke to his associates at Stanford just before we left the

367

hotel. Rupert's temperature continues to rise. He is in danger of cardiac arrest. Dr. Askew instructed them to begin placing Rupert into a state of suspended animation in preparation for transport to Andorra. We're now operating way out on the bleeding edge of medicine—and technology, but it's the only hope we have for saving my son. Rob, David, Maria, can you get everything you need to Meritxell in the next 24 hours? If we push it, we should have Rupert in Andorra shortly after that. Dr. Le Clerc, can you go ahead and make sure your cohorts are prepared to receive us, and can you get the French official there who's being so obstinate? The helicopter is at your disposal."

"I will leave right away and with your permission, I will send the helicopter to Paris for Monsieur Clement. It will play to his ego."

"By all means. We can bring in another craft from Barcelona to take the others to Andorra."

"Good!" Maria said. "It looks like we are ready to ride. Good luck everyone. Dietrich can I speak to you privately?"

"Certainly."

"Come into my office."

Dietrich picked up his coffee and followed Maria. Mikel Muñoz was already there.

"Good morning Señor von Hesse. I hear things are going well on the medical research front, but not as well for your son."

"Thank you, Mikel. No. Rupert's condition continues to decline. We're getting ready to take him to Andorra, where we hope to treat him with the procedures we've developed in the last few days. It'll be touch and go that we can bring it all together in time."

"I hope you can, I will pray for you."

"Thank you."

"Maria, what did you want to discuss? I assume it involves Mikel."

"Yes, Mikel wants our permission to go to the authorities concerning Miguel, Vitorio and Domingo. He also wants to go with Father Giuseppe to Zaragoza to see Archbishop Alvarez there. Alvarez is the senior archbishop in the Spanish Catholic Church and widely recognized for his decency and integrity.

"We think he is the safest bet for getting the ball rolling in the church," Mikel said. "Giuseppe will be able to lend credence to the information I will bring to His Excellency, Archbishop Alvarez. The wheels may grind slowly in the justice mills of the Catholic Church, but they will grind exceedingly fine. I would not want to be a church official in Santiago, Valencia or on the Curia in Rome, tainted by any of this, when it all comes down. I understand Pope Francis is not one to take such corrupt and sinful behavior lightly. Don't expect huge public headlines, but the tectonic plates along the Tiber River in Rome will definitely begin to slip."

"Before you open this Pandora's box, Mikel," Dietrich said, "I'd like you to run it past my legal team. They may be able to strengthen your case, especially for the criminal activities. You don't want this to get bogged down in legal challenges over technicalities. They will not go down without a fight and they have many connections. Let's do it right and nail these guys."

"Okay, where do I start?"

"I'll have my lead attorney in Zurich contact you and set up a meeting. Expect a call today. He'll probably retain some local legal talent here to bridge the gaps in his knowledge of Spanish law."

"Right. I'll be standing by."

"Meantime, Maria and I, and all those guys next door, have got a lot of work to do in the next few days. We'll check in with you when Rupert is out of danger," Dietrich said—more out of bravado than self-assurance.

He shook Mikel's hand.

"Thank you, Mikel. None of this would have happened without you. Go get 'em tiger!"

369

"Yes sir, I will. In the meantime, Maria, what about Gabriel?"

"Mikel, will you stay here and look after him until we can get back?

"Certainly, I'm getting used to this high life."

"Maybe it doesn't have to end when this is all over," Maria said.

47

"Sorry for screwing up your schedule at Stanford, Sterling," Dietrich said as he pulled into the rental lot at the Biarritz airport in the early morning darkness.

"Don't worry about it. Someone will cover. This is much more important."

A scissors lift loaded a large coffin-like container onto the Falcon 50 as the two men approached. The forward seats had been removed to accommodate the cryo-pod.

"Sergei, I see you made it. Great work. I'd like you to meet Dr. Sterling Askew. You'll need to bring him up to speed on your cryogenic container as we head to California."

"Yes sir, I will. After I get a few hours' sleep. I haven't been to bed since you called. None of us have."

"I understand, and I truly appreciate it. Sterling and I have a lot to talk about anyway. I'll wake you in Newfoundland."

Marcel pointed the jet's blue nose skyward and set the auto-pilot for St. John's. He turned off the seatbelt light as he cleared the clouds at 20,000 feet.

"Sorry, we had to leave Jacques in Zurich, Herr von Hesse," he said over the intercom. "Not enough room with the missing seats. He stocked the bar and pantry if you need anything. There's coffee and Danish. We should have you in St. John's in seven hours, California in fifteen. Headwinds aren't too fierce at 42,000 feet. If we can get your son aboard within a

371

couple of hours after landing, the relief crew will be standing by to fly you back to Zaragoza. You should be back in the air before dark."

"Thank you, Marcel. I apologize for all the frenzied activity lately. I fervently hope this will be the last emergency flight for a while."

"If Rupert lives, it will have been worth it sir. May God be with him—and you and Madame."

The stop in Canada went without a hitch and the Falcon 50 was back in the air within an hour. Sergei and Sterling hovered over the cryogenic chamber pointing and gesturing like new fathers in a hospital nursery.

"You understand we weren't able to give this box the full shake-down we normally would," Sergei said, "however, all the critical systems were put through every test we could devise. I think it will achieve its purpose."

"As a doctor, I must defer to you on the technology. It appears to have all the connections and controls needed to maintain Rupert's cardiovascular system intact and functioning at the lowered temperatures. I spoke to Dr. Aldridge from St. John's, and he confirmed that his temperature had stabilized and that the procedure to lower it was well under way. If we can maintain a reduced heart rate and slowed blood circulation in the cryo-chamber, we should be able to get him to Andorra in reasonable condition."

"I spoke to Le Clerc," Dietrich said. "He's on the way back from Paris with Clement. He says the personal helicopter ride seems to have melted some of the man's reserve. Maybe he'll come around completely when he sees the array of doctors and scientists who are putting their own reputations on the line. Besides, if Rupert pulls through, it'll be a feather in Clement's hat. If he doesn't, God forbid, what happens in Andorra will stay in Andorra.

"I also spoke to Maria. The chopper from Barcelona was due any minute. She said they were all packed and ready to go. Keep your fingers crossed Sterling. We're about to make history."

Therese stood at the head of the gurney. Rupert lay in a cushion of ice with several tubes attached. His lips were blue, and his skin was mottled from the cold. The temperature monitor read 78 degrees and the heart rate monitor pinged between 48 and 50. Her phone rang. The caller ID displayed Dietrich's number.

"Hello, where are you?"

"We just landed and are on the way to the hospital. Is Dr. Aldridge there?"

"Yes, he's right here. I'll put him on."

Dietrich handed his phone to Dr. Askew.

"This is Aldridge."

"Eric, this is Sterling Askew. Are you ready?"

"Yes sir."

"Then get Rupert down to the emergency dock, we'll be there in twenty minutes. Have a second car available. There won't be enough room in the ambulance for everyone plus all the equipment."

"Will do. See you there."

"Mrs. Von Hesse we're taking Rupert down to the ambulance loading area. If you'll have your bags taken down they'll be here shortly."

"I'm ready Dr. Aldridge. May I go down with you?"

"Of course."

The wail of sirens assailed Therese's ears long before the flashing lights appeared and the ambulance roared into the ER bay. Dietrich, Sergei and Sterling piled out onto the platform, clearing space for Rupert's transport. Aldridge and two attendants wheeled the gurney aboard and locked it in place. Askew joined them while the others piled into the waiting car.

Both vehicles roared out the gate with sirens blaring and lights flashing.

Dietrich sat beside a trembling Therese, holding her as her pent-up emotions came pouring out. Torturous sobs convulsed her. She burrowed her head into Dietrich's chest, seeking refuge and relief from the constant anguish she had endured at Rupert's bedside. He could only stroke her hair and try to reassure her. The ambulance screamed through the gate at SFO. She was finally able to compose herself. She sat up, dried her eyes, and straightened her clothes. She looked at her husband with a wan smile which said she was okay—for now.

The area around the plane erupted in a beehive of activity. The ground crew quickly transferred Rupert onto the hoist and lifted him to the jet door. He disappeared into the maw of the jet where Sergei and Sterling took command.

"Okay men. Get the equipment into place and secured before we move him," Askew ordered. "Sergei and his technician will show you how to hook up all the external wires and tubes. Then we will gently lift him in and make all the internal connections. We'll give it a minute to see if he remains stable then we'll attach the cover. Everybody on board?"

Nods all around acknowledged readiness. The external connections were swiftly completed. Askew nodded and six sets of hands lifted the inert body of Rupert von Hesse into what looked for all the world like a coffin—only this one designed to preserve life; not bury it.

Dietrich placed his hand on his son's shoulder while Therese kissed his cold cheek. Sergei fitted the cover and fastened it. The only sound was the muffled rumble of the fans and motors that now held the boy's life in suspension. The clear plastic plate above Rupert's face fogged over momentarily until the internal controls took over and cleared the air. The plane's engines came to life as the co-pilot dogged the hatch shut. Ten minutes later they were airborne. As soon as the seat belt light went out, Therese and Dietrich resumed their vigil on either side

374

of Rupert's bier. One or the other would remain there for the remainder of the journey.

Lengthening shadows stretched across the tarmac of the Zaragoza airport as the plane carrying Rupert von Hesse's weakening body taxied to the terminal. Two helicopters, painted the same vivid blue and yellow waited there, their rotors spinning in anticipation of an immediate departure. The jet rolled to a stop a few meters away. Ground crews were at the ready. They lowered the cryogenic chamber to a waiting baggage cart for towing to the larger copter. Within minutes it was safely aboard and secured.

"Therese there's not room for all of us with Rupert. Sterling, Eric and Sergei need to be with him. There's room for you. I'll follow with the others."

The brave smile she returned expressed all the love she held for this man.

"Thank you, Dietrich. I'll see you at the hospital."

The larger copter clattered into the air, followed immediately by the smaller one, for the 150-mile dash to Andorra. Scudding clouds promised snow at the higher elevations of the Pyrenees. Forecasts indicated a possible blizzard before nightfall.

"Henri," Dietrich said, "how long will it take to the hospital?"

"A little less than an hour sir."

"Can we beat the storm?"

"I think so. It depends on the wind coming off the mountains above."

"You know why we're going there, don't you?"

"Yes sir, Marcel told me."

"Then you know how important this flight is. Get us there!"

"I'll do my best sir. I flew a rescue helicopter at Chamonix. I've seen a few blizzards. So has Philippe in the forward copter. We'll get you there if it's humanly possible."

The moisture laden winds flowing up from the south stoked the heavy gray cloud front straddling the border. The choppers bounced around like beach balls riding the incoming waves. Sergei unstrapped his harness to check on Rupert. The needle on one indicator gauge had slipped into the red zone. He tightened a connection and watched it return to the green area before grabbing a strap to prevent falling.

"We're crossing the border now," Henri announced. "Only a few kilometers to go. I'll have you at the hospital in ten minutes."

Therese breathed a sigh of relief. Her stomach was in her throat. This flight couldn't be over too soon for her. She looked across at Sergei Romanoff. He was green and appeared on the verge of vomiting. The copter landed without mishap. The emergency access to the hospital proper was only 25 meters away. A crew was waiting with a cart to take the cryogenic container into the hospital. Maria and David came out to meet them.

"You must be Dietrich's wife, Therese," she said taking Therese's hand. "I'm Maria Elizondo."

"Maria, he's told me so much about what you're doing to help us. Thank you."

"Right now, we need to get Rupert inside and begin prepping him. The facilities are ready."

"Thank God."

"Where's Dietrich?"

"He's in the second helicopter. They're coming in now."

The smaller chopper slipped from side to side as it approached the pad. The pilot pulled back on the yoke for a second pass before negotiating the gusty winds. Henri brought the craft in at a steep angle. He was hit by a sharp downdraft that dropped the last meter, severely jolting the passengers. The door burst open as the occupants hurriedly scrambled out, thankful to have survived.

376

Rupert was passing through the emergency room door as Dietrich caught up with the two women.

"I take it you two have been introduced?" he joked. "Maria, did René get back?"

"Yes, they're waiting by the OR."

"Did you get Clement's temperature?"

Maria hesitated while translating the idiom.

"Oh, you mean his attitude? He was friendly enough, but when I spoke to René alone he said he doesn't yet have his commitment."

"Son-of-a-bitch! Sorry ladies, excuse the language. Is René still with him?"

"Yes, as far as I know."

"Do you think you can distract him long enough for me to get Clement aside?"

"I think so."

"Good. I've got to convince that preening bastard to sign that paper. If I can't I may have to just..." he let the thought trail off.

Sergei Romanoff caught up with them in the corridor. He saw Dietrich's reddened face and clinched jaw.

"Herr von Hesse, what is it?"

"That little Parisian peacock Clement hasn't signed off on the procedure yet. I'm going to get him aside and apply a little pressure."

"Sir, may I suggest a different approach. He's French, I'm French. Let me have a crack at him first."

Dietrich looked at Sergei.

"You think you can persuade him."

"It's worth a try."

"Okay, you have fifteen minutes. If he doesn't agree, I'm coming in. There's a small coffee bar near the OR. I'll introduce you and you can offer to buy him a coffee."

A thin man in a tailored suit stood next to René Le Clerc. His pencil-thin mustache, dead gray eyes and angular face screamed bureaucrat. Sergei had confronted dozens of his ilk in the process of getting his factory in Bayonne built and then getting his drugs approved.

"René, I see you were able to get Monsieur Clement here in one piece."

"Yes. Monsieur Clement, this is Sergei Romanoff, he manages Sagarin's operation in Bayonne. It was his team that built the cryogenic box used to transport our patient here."

"I'm very pleased to meet you Monsieur Clement. I understand you are with the French Health Ministry in Paris."

"Yes."

Sergei eyed his adversary, quickly drawing conclusions.

"You and I must be about the same age. I attended the *Ecole Militaire* before getting my doctorate at the Sorbonne. You look familiar. Were you there in the seventies?"

Clement's haughty exterior seemed to sag a little. Here was a man of substance. He needed to tread carefully until he could take his measure.

"Yes, but I was attending law school at Paris University Navarre."

"No kidding? We probably have some friends in common then. I have several friends who went there.

Sergei took Clement by the arm and guided him toward the coffee shop.

"Let's continue this over a café," he said.

"*Certainment*, I could use some caffeine after that helicopter ride."

Sergei paid for their order and guided Clement to the table furthest from the door.

"It's really sad about the von Hesse kid," he said.

"Yes, very unfortunate. I don't think I've ever run across his set of disorders in one person before."

"It is extremely unusual. A few years ago, we had a case in Biarritz that was almost as complicated. We needed to use an experimental drug to clear an infection of the pancreas. The kid was near death and we couldn't reach all the people in the approval chain."

"What did you do?"

"We called an old friend of mine who was able to cut through the red tape. Five hours after we administered the drug the boy rallied. He made a complete recovery. It was really gratifying to see."

"Wonderful," Clement said cautiously, "who did you call?"

"Nicolas."

Clement did a double take.

"As in Sarkozy?"

"Yeah, he and I go way back. We had a reputation for closing all the bars on Place Pigalle in our, shall we say, more immature years. Do you know him?"

"I've met him a couple of times at government functions."

"He was quite the lady's man. I couldn't keep up with him."

"Yes, so I understand."

Clement was politically astute enough to know what had just happened. He had been trapped, and now had no choice but to agree to the procedure. He dared not risk another call to Paris and he didn't relish having to explain his refusal to the politically powerful. Besides, the signatures of the head-of-government in Andorra and the archbishop of Urgell gave him plenty of cover.

"Monsieur Le Clerc, Herr von Hesse," Clement said as he rejoined the group clustered around the OR waiting room, "I have reviewed your proposed procedure and find it in compliance with French regulations for experimental compassionate use, therefore, it is with great pleasure and deep personal satisfaction that I give my consent to the procedure. Monsieur Romanoff convinced me that the young man will die without it and that this is his only hope. If the treatment is successful, it may also give hope to others suffering from the same condition."

"Monsieur Clement, thank you," Dietrich said, "I shall always be in your debt."

He motioned Sergei to the side.

"What the hell did you say to him?"

"I made him an offer he couldn't refuse," Sergei grinned. "one Frenchman to another. Like all bureaucrats, he understands influence and power."

"Whatever you said, thanks. You're still sure you don't want to move to HQ in Zurich?'"

"I'm sure. I prefer the beach to the snow."

"Dr. Askew, Dr. Aldridge, shall we begin," Le Clerc said as he pushed open the doors to the OR.

Rupert had been disconnected from the Cryovac container's tubes and wires and lay once again in a temperature controlled bed. Hospital perfusionists were finishing the painstaking task of attaching him to a heart-lung bypass machine. Once the machine was prepped and functioning properly, arterial and venous canulae were inserted to begin circulating and re-warming Rupert's blood. The digital temperature readout slowly crept up from 78 degrees, reaching 98 after a few minutes. Now the tricky part began. Dr. Askew infused the six liters of CRISPR modified blood from Maria's clinic, the anti-seizure drugs from Zurich, and the clotting factor drugs from SciGen. In a delicately coordinated procedure, the new blood had to be introduced into the arterial cannula while an equal amount of Rupert's blood was being withdrawn through the venous cannula. At Eric's signal Askew opened the valve into the arterial cannula. Seventy-five seconds later, the dye used to mark the initiation of the exchange appeared at the machine's input valve. The exchange was complete. The heart/lung valves were closed, trapping Rupert's blood in the machine. His cardiovascular system was pulsing with the new, genetically modified blood.

"Well gentlemen," Askew said to the team, "now we wait."

The pallor began to recede from Rupert's face as the transfused blood surged through his body. After thirty minutes, Askew stepped back and removed his surgical mask.

"I think we can move the lad to the cardiac care unit now. Eric, if you'll see to that René and I will report to the parents."

"Where are the von Hesse's?" Dr. Askew asked as he entered the waiting room.

"They went to the chapel," Maria said. "How is Rupert?"

"He's not out of the woods entirely, but the procedure went well, and he seems to be tolerating the new blood. Eric is taking him to the CCU."

"I'll get the von Hesses," Maria said, "Thank God their prayers have been heard."

Twenty-four hours after the blood exchange, Rupert was transferred to the intensive care unit where the doctors began the process of removing Rupert from the coma. In the early morning hours Therese and Dietrich were dozing in their chairs on either side of their son's bed.

"Mama."

Therese had prayed to hear those words again from the lips of her firstborn. At first, she thought she was dreaming, then they came again.

"Mama."

"Yes, my darling, I am here."

"Where am I? This is a different room."

"You are in a hospital in Andorra."

"Andorra? Where is that?"

"It's this marvelous place that allowed the doctors to save your life. We'll tell you all about it later, when you're better, and we can take you home."

Dietrich roused to the sound of their voices.

"Rupert! Thank God! You're awake!"

"Hi Dad, what's going on?"

"It's a very long and complicated story. I'll tell you all about it when we get back to Zurich. You just rest for now."

381

The End

Epilogue

Dietrich von Hesse adjusted his goggles. The morning sun reflecting off the packed snow was blinding. He picked up his ski poles and turned to the skiers standing beside him.

"Are you ready?"

"Sure," his son Rupert said, "lead off."

Dietrich gazed across the valley at the Matterhorn and marveled that he was standing here, one year later, on the slope where his son had almost died. He dug his ski poles into the snow and pushed off, Rupert and Therese following him down the Petrullarve toward Blauherd. The tears escaping from beneath his goggles froze on his cheek. Halfway down Rupert came roaring past to lead them into the Trockner Steg way station.

"Come on inside," Therese said, "I'm freezing. Besides, there's someone waiting for us."

The restaurant on the rear of the building, facing the Matterhorn, was practically deserted this early in the morning. Three people sat at one table located beside the panoramic windows. The skiers removed their paraphernalia, leaving it to dry on racks near the door, and joined them.

"Good morning Rupert, and congratulations," the raven-haired woman at the table said. "How does it feel to re-visit the scene of the crime?"

"It's an eerie feeling to think I almost died here a year ago. It makes me realize how precious life is and how important family and friends are."

Maria was sitting next to Mikel Muñoz, her husband of six months. In the weeks following the mad dash to Andorra the two had become close as they aided the authorities in the prosecution of Manuel Ortega, Domingo Diaz and Vitorio Elizondo, all three of whom now languished in a prison near Valencia, adding a final ironic touch to their criminal activities, which began there.

The third person at the table was Gabriel Diaz, now a member of the von Hesse family, courtesy of a Swiss adoption court. In the loving environment provided by the family, the young man had blossomed into an accomplished pianist and was in great demand for performances around Zurich. He was rumored to be in line for a concert tour of Switzerland with his companion and manager, Alex Eisner. Dietrich chose the brother of his housekeeper, Maxim, to be a guide and live-in companion for Gabriel.

"Mikel what's happening on the ecclesiastical side of the scandal?"

"Most of the culprits in Valencia and Santiago have moved on or passed away, including Cardinal Ortega. Others have mysteriously disappeared from the church rolls. Several labor leaders in Valencia have been indicted and are awaiting trial."

"What about Rome?"

"There's been a major purge of the Curia. Pope Francis replaced three of the cardinal bishops and there's been a wholesale change in the administrative ranks. It's fair to say that the revelations in Spain reverberated all the way to the Vatican."

"And you, Maria? Is life settling down for you after all the excitement?"

"No. The year has been a whirlwind. First the trials, then the wedding, plus all the extra work generated by our genetic discoveries. But, it's all good. Especially finding this guy," she said, poking Mikel.

"And the charitable institute we established, how's that doing?"

"Marvelously! The Father Giuseppe Calderon Charitable Institute for the Treatment of Blood Disorders is up and running and Dr. Zubiri is reveling in his assignment as its first president. Father Giuseppe is quietly relishing the acclaim. Inez Figueroa has joined the team as head of their computer group. The mayor of Bilbao will dedicate their new building on the first of March with Father Giuseppe as his honored guest. I hope you can be there."

"I wouldn't miss it. We will all be there."

FINIS

Made in the USA
Middletown, DE
18 February 2018